TILLMAN'S BOUNTY

TILLMAN'S BOUNTY

SCOTT GASTINEAU

WHEELER PUBLISHING
A part of Gale, a Cengage Company

Wheeler Publishing, a part of Gale, a Cengage Company.

Wheeler Publishing Large Print Western.
The text of this Large Print edition is unabridged.
Other aspects of the book may vary from the original edition.
Set in 16 pt. Plantin.

LIBRARY OF CONGRESS CIP DATA ON FILE.
CATALOGUING IN PUBLICATION FOR THIS BOOK
IS AVAILABLE FROM THE LIBRARY OF CONGRESS

ISBN-13: 978-1-4328-5216-0 (softcover alk. paper)

Published in 2020 by arrangement with Scott Gastineau

Printed in Mexico
Print Number: 01   Print Year: 2020

ACKNOWLEDGMENTS

I would like to thank those who have taken it upon themselves to preserve the history of our frontier. The reality I discovered while stumbling along through real history made the Old West even more fascinating to me. My imagination came alive as I read the works of writers of real history such as Thomas Edwin Farish, Marshall Trimble, Robert K. DeArment, and Nancy Burgess.

I would also like to thank the people at the Trinidad History Museum, Santa Fe Trail Association, Santa Fe History Museum, Fort Union in New Mexico, and the Sharlot Hall Museum in Prescott, Arizona. These organizations and their staffs do an amazing job of preserving, displaying, and teaching the real history of places many of us only know from legend. Their resources brought me back in time as I conducted the research for this book.

Kami, my love, thank you for your encouragement and for traveling with me into the past.

CHAPTER 1

Max Tillman and Wayne Townsend pushed the cart of rocks from the mouth of the mine toward the large stack down by the foreman's big tent. The rocks showed some sign of copper, but lately they'd been bringing up only very small deposits coming from this mine. They'd been working the claim for four months now and had only found one solid deposit. It was a long day's work for little reward. The Newton Mineral Company had sent them here, outside of Trinidad, Colorado, from a site in west Texas when that mine had yielded little pull.

The foreman's wife, Evelyn, and little boy, Clayton Jr., came out of a tent with a basket of clothes, heading toward the stream down the hill. Clayton Stephens was in town at the moment to see if they had received supplies and payroll. It was two weeks late, and that had the men worried. A processing expert should have arrived as well to oversee the extraction of the copper. The bank in town should have sent a message to the camp when the payroll arrived, but, even after several visits to town, they had no news. Clayton was going to send a telegram to the home office.

"Hi, Max, Wayne," Evelyn called out.

"Morning, Evelyn, Little Clay."

The eight year old waved back, then went skipping ahead. Max had spent quite a bit of time with Clayton's family. From the time Max joined the crew at age fifteen, Clayton had taken him under his wing like a little brother. He still sent him into the dangerous narrows because he was scrawny, and that was the job he'd been hired to do. They lost one of every three men who climbed into the narrow spots looking to see if the tunnels ended or if there was any sign of a mineral deposit. The majority of those sent were the Asians, but the language barrier made that frustrating.

After a year of eating the two meals a day he received for his work, Max grew another two inches and gained forty pounds. He could no longer squeeze into the narrows, but Clayton kept him on as another helper, and he worked hard, hauling out rocks, picking the walls where they looked promising.

The pay was little more than their food and a spot to sleep in a crew tent. A job with a bigger outfit would likely pay more, but still it was more than he had when his mother had been trying to feed him, his little brother, and herself. There had been days both he and his mother had gone with little more than a small chunk of bread so the toddler would not starve.

His mother did odd work, cleaning and sewing for men who lived alone, but it was not steady and paid little. It had been a shame that there had not been an opportunity for her to teach. She had gone all the way through school as a girl, the daughter of a successful store owner back East. Max often wondered how she was doing. He had written letters, but mail could be unpredictable, and they moved every so often, so she may have sent a letter that went to nowhere.

They began unloading the rocks into the large stack. Once they got them down so far, wiry Wayne put his hands on the cart and hopped into it. Wayne had started a couple of years earlier and had just gotten big enough last fall that climbing through the narrows was difficult. Stripped to the waist, Max could see that with the dwindling portions of food, Wayne was back down to a size where he could go down the narrow tunnels again. While Max stood almost average height and was lanky, Wayne was still short and even thinner. With more food, Max may have been closer to stout like his father, but portions in the camp had been even more meager than usual this last couple of months.

With the rocks scraping in the cart and hitting among the others in the stack, they were surprised when a voice spoke from behind them. "You boys seen this man?"

Max lurched around to see the big man sitting atop his horse looking down at them. His blond beard had more than a few white hairs in it. His eyes were keen, and there was something about them that seemed more dangerous than the guns on his waist. He had a pistol on his right side and another on his left turned around backwards.

Max stepped closer to take a good look at the drawing. It was of a dark-haired man with full beard. His thick eyebrows and slightly crooked nose stood out to Max, but he'd never seen him. The name printed underneath said *Carl Bradshaw*. Max was shaking his head when Ricky walked up from the mine opening.

"How can we help you, Mister?" Ricky was second in charge and did most of the hunting for the camp when they were short on meat, which meant he had been going out a lot lately, but with little success. He stared not at the guns at the man's waist but at the rifle strapped to his saddle.

The man, seeing he was a few years older than Max, turned to Ricky as more of an authority. "You seen this man?"

Ricky studied the picture. "No. Is he supposed to be around here?"

"Maybe," the man said, eyeing the questioner. "He's a dangerous one; killed at least one man to steal his horse, suspected of dry-gulching another to take his horse and gear." That was all he said, and then he turned to head the other way.

"I think that was Jack Sutter," Ricky said when the man had ridden a distance from them.

"Who's Jack Sutter?" Wayne asked.

Ricky looked at him like he was stupid. Ricky could be a bit condescending and sometimes even a bully. He and Max had actually gotten into a fight two months before, with Max getting much the worse of it, but he had landed a couple of good shots before one solid punch to the jaw had dropped him.

Ricky sighed. "He's a bounty hunter, a full-time bounty hunter. He supposedly

11

brought in the bodies of the Murphy brothers after they slaughtered that posse." Ricky looked after the man again. "That rifle is one of the best long-shot guns made."

"What about yours?"

Ricky rolled his eyes at Wayne's comment, but Max knew he really looked forward to talking about these things. He liked to think of himself as the tough one of the camp, which was probably the truth. He and Clayton were the only two who owned rifles, although Max and Yin Su had practiced a couple of times with them in case of bandit or Indian attack, when one of the two was deep in a mine. But Ricky said, "That Chinaman will never touch my rifle," so they only shot with Clayton's.

Now the proud man pointed to his tent where the rifle was. "That's a '73 Winchester Repeater, the most common rifle sold, same as Clayton's. Now, granted, I've taken great care of mine, and it operates as good as it did the day it was made; it's made for common use." He pointed to the distant trees where the man had disappeared. "That man had a bolt action German model, I believe, made for distance and power." Ricky sighed. "I'd love to have that rifle, and those pistols may be the ones I'll choose also." He nodded at Max. "You'd have a horse and a gun now if you didn't spend so much on books and candles."

Max nodded. "You're right, but the books help fight the boredom at night."

That brought another roll of the man's eyes, then he looked at the two of them. "Get back to work." Ricky walked toward his tent.

Max and Wayne shoveled the rubble out of the bottom of the cart and then rolled it back toward the mine. It was extremely hot down in the mine, and he was looking forward to the day being over. At the beginning of the previous summer they had hauled five men out of a mine due to heat, two already dead, and one who died later. The two who had survived were not the same for a couple of weeks. Max headed back into the mine, thinking about washing off in the stream later.

The clank of picks against rock echoed through as they made their way down the shaft. They heard the sound of drills grinding into the rock below them. Max looked at the wooden beams wedged against the ceiling and felt his stomach clench a bit. Probably tomorrow they would need to put up more, but it seemed that rocks always started to fall just before they did. He and Wayne shoveled the rock and pebbles that had been chiseled away into the cart and then started back out.

Late afternoon sun beat down on them as they exited the mine. Pushing the cart up the shaft had taken a lot of effort, and the sun hitting him now drained nearly the last bit of energy out of Max. Wayne was wheezing as well.

When they got the cart next to the pile, Max stumbled away into the nearby tent and grabbed his canteen. He came out and offered it to Wayne, who was leaning on the cart as if it were all that was holding him up. Wayne straightened. "Thanks. I think we need that mule to help pull this thing out."

"The mule hasn't had enough to eat to pull two days in a row, and Clayton's got the fresher one."

"I haven't had enough to eat either."

"I hear that. Let's finish unloading and ask Ricky if we can go try to catch some fish."

Wayne took a deep breath and nodded. He downed the last of the water and dropped the canteen next to the shovels, and they went back to unloading rocks. Fatigue had them moving slowly, and, when Max heard the sound of hooves within feet of them, he jumped.

He turned to see Clayton riding in on the mule, both looking exhausted. Sweat dripped from the boss's head down into his light-brown beard. Max could see in his face that there was something wrong.

"What's the word?" Ricky called out as he walked up, his rifle in hand.

Clayton looked at his second and paused for a moment. "Go get the men out of the mine; I'll tell everyone at the same time."

"Clay, why don't you tell us before the Chinamen and the redskins. They . . ."

"Ricky, get the men!"

"All right. You're the boss." Ricky shook his head as he stalked toward the mouth of the mine.

Clay sighed and called out. "Eve?"

"I think she's down at the creek washing clothes."

"Wayne, run down to the creek and tell her to come back. Help her bring the clothes."

"Yes, sir!" Wayne started off at a trot.

"What is it, Clay?"

"Bad news, Max. Go into my tent and get the rifle." He paused and looked Max sharp in the eyes. "For just in case, you hear? Only if they get out of control." Clayton pulled the pistol out of the pocket hanging on the mule's saddle and put it through his belt.

"Shit!" Max made for the tent at a staggering run. Obviously, the payroll was not coming.

"And try to stay calm," Clay called quietly after him.

The rifle was hanging on a couple of wires between two support beams in the tent, out of the reach of little Clay. Max grabbed it and pulled the lever, loading the chamber. It was a much more beat-up rifle then Ricky's, but it shot all the same.

Max stopped and took a deep breath. Clayton had pulled the saddle off the mule and was watering the animal. He looked up. "Don't hold it ready. Matter of fact, sit on that stump and lean it against the stump like it just happens to be there."

Max did it and was glad to be sitting, to keep him from pacing.

Ricky came walking back, followed by the miners, stripped to the waist. First was Raymond, half-Sioux, half-Mexican. Then came Yin Su, Xou Ling, Kim Yon, Leaping Fox — a full Cherokee — and Kyle Dalton, a 15-year-old orphan. They were a mix of excited hope and concern. Ricky looked like he had figured it out. He was not a humble man, but not a totally stupid man either.

Clayton spoke up. "Men, I got some food when I went into town, and we're going to

16

have a good meal tonight." That brought some smiles to their faces, all but Ricky's. Max started to worry. What would happen if Ricky, holding his rifle, got angry?

"I also heard some disappointing news. Newton's gone under."

Faces dropped. Ricky nodded his head like he thought it had been coming; Kyle looked confused; Raymond closed his eyes, looking crushed. Xou Ling and Kim Yon started to snarl. "What, no pay?" That triggered Leaping Fox and Kyle. "We've been working for free?" Yin Su turned and kicked the cart with the flat of his foot.

"We can split up the supplies here and take them," Clayton yelled out, "or I'll sign over the claim to you if you want to run it. I'm out money, too. I'm going to have to go to my father-in-law's until I find something."

"You kept us working when they weren't paying us!" Yin Su yelled, pointing at Clayton.

Xou Ling's hand balled into a fist. "We are just like slaves to you."

Ricky turned on the others. "Easy!" He kept the rifle at his side, but he still held it, and the men noticed. "Clayton Stephens has been a great boss to all of us. He was not told either! He is in the same spot as you!"

"His name's on the deed!" Yin Su yelled.

"Just to cover the law that the owner has to work the mines himself," Ricky said, shaking his head. "You know that, Yin!"

"Listen," Clayton started again. "If I could do anything I would. You know that, Yin." Yin looked at him blankly.

Raymond raised his head and spoke up. "It's not Clayton's fault. He has been better to us than any white person I've ever met."

Raymond stepped forward and offered his hand to Clay, who took it and shook it. Ricky followed Raymond with his eyes like he was hiding a dagger. Leaping Fox hung his head for a moment before stepping forward. "I was wrong to anger so much."

"It's all right." Clay offered his hand.

Kim Yon nodded. "Not your fault, boss." He turned and went to his tent. Xou Ling just looked at Clay before following.

Kyle also looked ashamed. "Sorry, boss."

Yin Su looked around, then to Ricky with the rifle. "I'm sorry, Mr. Stephens, I just get angry when this guy's around." With that he walked back to his tent. Ricky looked like he was going to go after him.

"Ricky," Clayton called to him and stepped up next to him. "Thanks. You really

18

helped to put that fire out."

Ricky shrugged. "You made me your second for a reason." He clapped Clay on the shoulder. "I guess we'll be packing up."

"What are you going to do?"

"My father had a small ranch back East for a couple of years. I suppose I can look at ranches around here." He nodded towards Max. "If that don't pan out, I read some of those papers he has you pick up. The rail's going into Arizona soon. Maybe they could use someone with supervisory and blasting experience. And, there's always other mines. We'll see."

"You'll do all right, Ricky. You're a good man."

Ricky nodded to him and walked toward the tents.

"How about you, Max?"

"I'm not sure."

"Well . . ." Just then Clayton saw Eve, Clay, and Wayne coming up from the river. "We'll talk later, Max."

"Uh-huh." Max turned and walked away. He figured it was not going to be an easy thing for Clayton to tell his wife they were going to need to ask her father for help. It was not an easy thing for a man's pride to take, being out of work. He knew Clayton had some money stored up, but he had used some of it to get the last batch of food and supplies from town, not counting today's. He heard Clayton sigh as he walked toward his wife.

Wayne looked at Clayton's face and how he was focused on Eve and hurried to catch up to Max. "No money from Newton?"

"No, Newton doesn't exist anymore."

"Aw, shit!"

"Clay said we could split the supplies and go, or we could take over the mine ourselves."

"It hasn't yielded much."

"No. There's other mines around and, like Rick said, railroads, cattle. There's jobs out there."

"What you gonna do?"

"I don't know yet. I suppose I can go into town and see if I hear of anything or can sign on with somebody." Max sighed.

"It ain't right," Wayne said weakly.

"It happens."

"I know, but sometimes I wish I had more to look forward to than mining, or that type of work. You know I thought of leaving when we heard of the cave-in the other side of town, but I don't know what else I'd do. I've not done anything else, and, until you and Clay started teaching me, I couldn't read a single word . . . still can't much."

"I know what you mean. I think that one day I'd like to have my own farm or have my own claim I could make a good bit of money on. But that only happens for a few people. The good land's already been granted, and now few people can make it on the land they get. They end up working for the wealthy who bought the foreclosed land 'cause they couldn't improve it the way the government said or needed a loan to get supplies. A lot of them end up doing our work for the railroad. Once the rail work's done, I don't know what everyone will do."

"So you're content?"

"Not content, but reconciled to who and what I am." Max shrugged. "I'm eating better than what I did before leaving home, I work with a lot of good men, and I am out among this." He eyed the trees and mountains around him. "Why wish for what you can't get, when you can enjoy what you have?"

Wayne leaned back and squinted into the low sun as he looked around. "I see what you're sayin'. I'm just not sure if I can get there."

Max smacked him in the arm. "Go wash up. We're getting decent food tonight."

It was a couple of hours before supper was ready. Eve cooked, and Max thought that

Clay had joined in once he washed the road dust off. The slices of ham were salty, but a welcome change from rice, even if there was not much for each of them. They each had a couple of cooked potatoes, and a chunk of bread the size of their fist. There were also a couple of cups of boiled green beans for each of them.

Clayton told them that he bought some jerky for each of them to take in the morning.

It was a feast. Ricky lamented that the only thing missing was a big mug of beer. Raymond agreed with him, and the two of them talked about wanting to go into town to down the foamy beverage. The mood was near jovial after the tension of earlier. The three Chinamen had changed to a voice of optimism. They had heard of how well some of the men were being paid for the railroad and were going to head down south toward Arizona first thing the next morning. Leadville, west of Pueblo, had been an option, but Clay told them that there were supposedly too many miners there already.

Raymond intended to go with the Chinamen, then further south into Mexico. His cousin supposedly had a ranch down there. "I can ride some, and life will be different for me down there." Max nodded. He knew

22

that people looked at Ray and thought he should be on a reservation, or across the border to the south.

Leaping Fox planned on going back to the reservation. "I think of the women there often," he said.

"I think of women everywhere often," Ricky joked.

Wayne leaned back and sighed heavily. "I suppose I'll just head into town and ask around."

"That's my plan, too." Max shrugged. "We'll walk in together."

"We may all go together," Clay said. The talk of the supplies and the mine claim came up then. There were the picks, hammers, drills, the cart, and a dozen lanterns, and they had a very small supply of explosives. The explosives were the most valuable, but they had nearly run out, and nobody relished traveling with them after they had been sitting in this heat.

"What about the mine claim itself?" Wayne looked back at the tunnel they had spent over a month working.

"It's yielded little. We'll be lucky to get eight dollars for it. If we'd found some coal, instead of copper, we'd still be doing all right, but those prospectors who chose this spot for Newton sure weren't worth much.

Guess that's why Newton's gone." Clay shook his head. "We should all meet in town at the supply store and sell the stuff and split the profits."

"There would be a better price directly to one of the other mines," Ricky said.

"I know, but the only ones being worked right now are the coal mines the other side of town, and we're all wanting to head out. It makes sense that we sell them in town, split what we make, and head out after supplying up."

Ricky nodded. "What about what we mined?"

"It's going to cost nearly as much to process the rocks as you can get from them." Clay shook his head again. "Bad prospectors."

"If we only knew a place with a good pull, we have the supplies to start our own company," Wayne said aloud.

Clay looked at him and then to Ricky, who shrugged in response before looking back at Wayne. "You're right of course. We'd keep all the profits instead of passing the lion's share upstream, and we'd do well if we got a good start. The question is . . ."

"Where?" Yin Su finished for him. They all nodded. Finding a good strike was not easy, or nobody in the mining business could become wealthy, because there would be too much supply and too little demand, driving prices down. The men seemed to arrive at a decision together.

"So, how do we get the stuff into town?" Yin Su asked.

"Manpower," Clay said. "We'll load up the cart and push it in."

Max did not cherish the thought of pushing that cart all the way into town. "Maybe we can rig up a harness for Hardy."

"My horse is not for pulling carts." Ricky was frustrated to be having this conversation again. "It takes away their speed, and they are more likely to get injured when they aren't used to it."

"All right, but if we push it in then we should get more of the money."

"As second to the foreman and hunter I was supposed to be paid more, so Clay and I have been cheated more than any of you."

"We split what we get equally." Clay looked around. "I'll take a turn at pushing the cart. Eve can drive our wagon part of the way."

Nobody argued, but it was obvious some did not agree completely with the decision. Yin Su glared at Ricky out of the corner of his eye, and Kim Yon's jaw seemed clenched. Everyone's mood was made lighter by a full

25

stomach though, and all retired to the tents to prepare to leave for good the next morning.

Max thought he was all right with everything, but his stomach clenched as he tried to sleep, not knowing what would become of him if he did not find work. If he did work for the railroad, what after that? He realized for the first time that he had not worried about having food and shelter for years. Now, he was thinking past the next job.

CHAPTER 2

Max awoke at first light tired, with little sleep, but rushed to pull his pack together so as not to hold up the others, who were almost ready to pack up the tents. Clay was folding up his tent to put it in the wagon when Max stepped out into the light. Breakfast consisted of a cup of coffee and chunks of bread with some honey smeared on. It was delicious and just what Max needed. Kyle ran the coffee pot down to the river for a quick cleaning while the rest of them packed up the other goods.

As much tension as there was usually between Yin Su and Ricky, they were completely different when it came to packing the nitro. The twelve remaining tubes were cushioned with leather in the box nestled between the cloth of the two tents so that nothing hard could strike them. They debated whether someone should carry it separately, but nobody wanted that task. It had made the wagon ride in, and Clay figured it was plenty stable enough to make the cart ride out.

They started out with only a full hour of sunlight in the sky. Clay figured they would make it into town around early to mid-afternoon. Between the eight workers under the foreman and his assistant they could guide the cart steadily along the trail while resting two at a time. Kyle and Wayne took the first rest, and Max drew duty at the rear of the cart, pushing along with Raymond while the others guided it around rough areas and slowed it when going downhill.

Max had been on the trail three times before this day — once when they arrived, driving wagons down the road and then off along a small trail that ran near the mine. The two other times were when he and some of the other workers went into town. It was going to be quite a long walk moving the cart along with them.

Before mid-morning they picked up the road following the Purgatoire River that ran into town. The river was the reason the area had become a stopping place along the trail. There were even thicker trees along the river, but the road was well used.

Those moving the cart had worked up a sweat, just as if they'd been moving rocks up to the surface. Ricky rode along next to Clay's wagon on his saddle horse for a while before trotting off ahead of the rest of the group.

"Where's he going?" Yin Su called back to Clay.

Max looked back to see Clay sigh before answering. "He said he's going to talk to a couple of nearby ranchers to ask about work." There were grumbles from everyone, including a growl from Max. "He said if they needed other workers, he would put in a good word for any of you." Clay tried to use a calming voice, but, although Ricky did have a good side to him, he also could be very selfish at times, and they all knew it. Eve looked like she was biting back words of her own.

They took a break toward late morning before moving on. The metal of the cart was becoming hot. Max had a break at the moment and walked back next to Clay's wagon.

Clay looked to the others all around the cart and talking, moving fairly easily over the flat ground. He kept his voice low as he began to talk. "Max, I'd ask you along if I could, but we're worried that even just the three of us will be too much of a burden to her father."

"That's all right, Clay." Max did feel a

little better. He had thought that he and Clay had built a closer relationship than the others.

"If you do have trouble, make your way to Wichita, and I'll help however much I can."

Max nodded to him. Clay was selfless, perhaps to a fault. Max wondered if Ricky would end up much better off than the foreman because he took care of himself first.

It was a hard day. By the time town came into sight in the distance it seemed like they had worked nearly two full days in the mine. The sun beating down on them was probably a large part of it. The mine could get hot, but the sun definitely added a different type of heat. Then the town seemed like it took twice as long to reach from the time they saw it as Max thought it would, a trick played upon seeing your destination from the distance. Ricky had not caught back up to them like he'd promised. When they finally did make their way into town, all the men who had pushed the cart were drenched in sweat.

They passed the large adobe residence of Filipe Bacca, one of the town's founders. He had passed on, but his wife and children still lived there in the house with a Victorian flair. There were some other houses of similar style being built or just completed further up the hill behind the large house. Just a few paces down the road was the U.S. Hotel, one of the two-story structures on the street at the time, but there were buildings in progress further down the street. Trinidad was booming from the rail and the coal.

Many walking past them in the street looked at them like they were dumb dogs annoying them. Others tried to glance in the cart or wagon, wondering if any valuable metals had been found. Clay had his rifle resting between his body and Eve's to discourage any aggressive curiosity. The store they were going to was at the other end of town, and they made their way through without having to slow, except when a dog chased tumbleweed past them, with his boy owner running behind. They passed two stores on the way down Main Street, Thatcher & Co. and Jaffa Brothers, but they were less likely to buy the used items. Before reaching the Grand Union Hotel, an enormous luxury hotel — easily the largest building in town — they turned off Main. Most people were still working somewhere around the town, and that left the streets fairly empty, except for those constructing new buildings and houses.

Max, pulling at the front of the wagon

now, saw the store owner's little boy, Will, run into the store as they approached. Calvin Sorenson came walking out as they reached his storefront. "What have we got here, gentlemen?" His voice was nearly jolly. He was a large man, supposedly a former blacksmith until a few months before. He was not a city type merchant by any means. It was said an outlaw tried to rob him a few years ago and received a beating that was talked about to this day. He always had a pistol in his belt but truly seemed to be among the friendliest men in the town. He was well respected and well liked.

"We have some supplies you could turn some profit on," Clay told him, hopping down from the wagon after tossing the reins into Eve's hands.

"Hmm. I heard about your investor drying up." The man's lips tightened within his thick, dark facial hair as he moved to look inside the cart.

"Hold on," Yin Su said, motioning for Max to help him. They tossed the men's bedrolls off the cart and then moved the tent on top. They carefully separated the material from the tent underneath it and lifted it up to expose the box that sat cushioned underneath.

"You boys are either brave or stupid to

have pushed that cart here with that in there."

After they had put the tent on the ground Yin Su carefully opened the top of the box to show the twelve vials of nitro.

"It's not a lot," Clay said, "but I thought I heard Anderson may be out of blasting supplies at his mine."

"I don't know about that." Calvin stroked his dark beard thoughtfully. "What else you got?"

"The two large tents, six shovels, five picks, five large hammers, the two drills, the cart, and the mine claim itself."

Calvin laughed. "If that was worth something you wouldn't be selling it." He looked at the stuff thoughtfully. "I'll give you fifty-five."

Young Kyle began to sputter, but Clay held his hand to the side to quiet the youth. "Come on, Calvin. I could sell the nitro by itself directly to Anderson for well more than twice that. Give me one-fifty."

Calvin shook his head. "Anderson will get supplies shipped in at some point, but I don't want to stand here haggling all day, so I will make a good offer of one hundred dollars."

"Make that one-ten and you have a deal."

Calvin looked at the items a moment and

nodded. "All right. Come on in and sign the deed to the mine over to me. Chinaman, you be real careful carrying that stuff in. My family's in there. The rest of you unload the cart. Put it, the tents, and the tools at the back of the store."

Max sighed. "Eleven dollars each."

"Better than nothing," Raymond said, grabbing the tent out of the cart after Yin had picked up the box.

Max picked up the tent off the ground and followed along behind them. Calvin called out as he walked into the store, "Luke!"

"Yeah, Pa?" a boy's voice came from where he was stacking cans.

"Run find the marshal or mayor to be a witness to a deed signing."

The red-headed boy put the can in his hand down and scrambled past them out the door.

Max walked through the narrow aisle, having to turn the tent roll to fit past the hanging dresses, stacks of shirts and britches, and bolts of cloth and blankets. He smelled cooking chicken coming from upstairs, then looked at the shelves: cans of beans and tomatoes, jars of honey, and sacks of grain stacked underneath next to bins of corn, and potatoes. He was feeling hungry again.

On the other side of the store there were a couple of small hammers, a bin of nails, rope, chain, brooms, and buckets.

There was very little room in back. There was only a small tent there, but there were a couple of shovels and a sledgehammer leaning against the wall. He set the tents down next to the smaller one and then moved aside for the other guys to get past to lay the tools alongside the others.

Calvin was gently placing the nitroglycerin behind the counter. As Max walked by, he called out. "When you bring the cart in put it against the wall and the shovels and other stuff inside it."

Max nodded. Kyle behind him grumbled about him not being their boss. "It's not going to hurt anything to help," Max told him quietly. "Then we'll get paid, and you don't have to take orders until you find a new boss."

Kyle sighed but helped Max, Raymond, and Yin Su hoist the empty cart up the steps so they could roll it to the back. After setting everything inside, they went back up to the counter where the marshal had just entered. John Kreugar was a lean man who was starting to show gray in his black beard. He witnessed the signing of the deed and stayed around while they completed the transaction. Trinidad's marshal was hard nosed when it came to not allowing any disputes to erupt in the town. It seemed to work and kept crime from happening. Calvin looked up nervously at the large group of men as he pulled out the lock box and counted out the money. He knew most of them, though, and went ahead with the counting.

Max walked up to the marshal nervously. "Marshal Kreugar, sir?"

"What is it?"

"I was just wondering if you've heard of anyone hiring around here."

Kreugar looked him over before answering. "Anderson may be hiring, out at the mine west of town." He rubbed his hand through his beard. "If you can ride, Clarkson's ranch to the north may be able to use one of ya. Of course, there's the coal mines around here and in Morley. I don't know what other skills you have besides mining, but for what you have, I heard there's a lot of jobs over in Arizona right now."

Max ducked his head. "Thank you, sir." He thought he wanted to do something different than mining. He had been mining since he left East Texas. Maybe it would be good to be working out in the open, seeing the sky.

Clay turned from the counter with the money and began to pass out everyone's share. Max waited for all others before he took his and put it in his pocket. The other men were looking at the shelves for supplies for their journey.

Max sighed and extended his hand to Clay. "I'm going to try to make it out to that ranch before dark."

Clay took his hand. "Take care. You'll do well. And if you see Ricky, tell him we're staying here in town to rest the animals before starting the trip early in the morning."

"Will do. He's probably got the job I was wanting."

Max pulled a handful of jerky from next to the register, and Calvin wrapped it and charged him fifty cents. He laid the money down and put the jerky in his pocket.

Max stopped to see what Wayne was doing. Wayne looked at him and shrugged. "I'm going to Anderson's mine in the morning."

"All right. If I hear of a good spot for you, I'll try to get word to you. Take care, men," he called to the others and waved before striding out the door.

He grabbed his bedroll on the way off the porch, calling goodbye to Eve and little

Clay. He pulled his canteen from his bedroll and pumped water from the town well. By the time he was ready to leave town, he saw the sun descending on the horizon. His legs were tired from the journey today, but he forced his steps to quicken over the rolling hills. He took a big gulp of water, then pulled one strip of jerky from the package and chewed. It was amazing how good simple jerky was when you were really hungry.

The road forked ahead, one path heading out to where their mining camp had been, the other more directly north. Max started up that road. It was little more than a wide trail through areas where the trees became thick. The thicker the trees became, the dimmer the light. As he headed deeper into the forest, Max started to feel that nauseous feeling in his stomach.

One of the things his father had done to feed the family was hunt, not just for food for them, but to sell extra meat, as well as the skins and antlers. They had lived in a shack of a house near the edge of a small town in Texas. He would take their small horse out and come walking back a couple of days later with rabbits, squirrel, deer, or wolf slung over the horse. One time he was dragging a black bear's carcass behind the horse.

He did not return from his last time out. Some had whispered that he had run off from his responsibilities. His mother did not believe that. Others said that he came across a black bear or cougar. There had been several livestock killings around that time along with the signs of a mauling at a campsite. A bounty had been offered on bears and lions, and his father had been hoping to collect on it.

Max was wary of being in the forest ever since, especially at night. The sounds coming from amongst the trees seemed to be louder at the moment, and he was constantly looking to both sides and behind him as he walked.

He was relieved to see a rider in the distance coming toward him on the road. Men could be even more dangerous than wild animals, but it still eased his nerves. The rider was moving very slow, and he thought the horse must be very tired. He realized that it was Ricky and his horse after a while. Ricky had tired his horse riding so far to check things out.

"Ricky!" he called out, and the man's head raised. The movement looked awkward, and Max realized Ricky was not well.

He ran forward. The horse started dancing back at his approach. Max slowed to a walk. "Easy, Hardy, it's me." The horse recognized the familiar voice and came forward for Max to brush his hand over his muzzle.

Max looked up to the rider. "What happened, Rick . . ." Then Max noticed that the dark-brown shirt Ricky wore seemed wet down the side.

"I . . ." Ricky could not talk, and then he coughed, and blood trickled down the corner of his mouth.

"You've been shot?" Max moved around to the side of the horse, looking at where the wound was nearly in the armpit. Max exhaled. "We'll get you to town." He took Hardy's reins and started at a near trot down the road. The horse let him lead them and walked alongside him easily.

"Wait!" Ricky's rasping call came, and Max saw that he was sliding off the horse. Max stopped and caught him as he slid down. "I . . . I . . . sorry," Ricky said. Then his eyes closed.

"Ricky! Ricky!" Max swallowed hard, gasping, as a tear started to roll down his cheek, and he sat down with a thud.

Max realized he'd been there for a few minutes. He looked at Ricky. He heard a faint rasp. He was still alive. He pulled the blanket roll from behind Ricky's saddle and set to tying it around the injured man. Ricky mumbled at first but called out in pain the second time Max lifted him, but he did not regain consciousness. Max tied the blanket firmly around his chest where the wound was, and then he shot a look up the road the way Ricky had come. He stood and pulled the rifle from Ricky's saddle. He could not see anything up the road that way, but it was getting darker.

Max pulled Hardy over to the closest tree and tied the reins to a branch. He looked back down the road. Seeing nothing, he laid the rifle down and hoisted Ricky onto Hardy, bringing forth a stream of obscenities from the injured man. He pulled loose some of the saddle ties and lashed them quickly to Ricky's arm and leg. He almost forgot about his bedroll. He fastened it onto the saddle and grabbed the rifle. Looking back down the road one more time, he grabbed Hardy's reins and started towards town at a very quick walk.

Darkness descended quickly on them, and Max found himself thinking of how he would not have made it to the ranch before dark. Then, he wondered if Ricky had been at the ranch, or if he had been shot before making it that far. That was all guesswork.

Ricky was slung over the saddle, mumbling in a high-pitched tone about his father's chickens the last Max could make out. He was not going to tell him what had happened anytime soon.

Max did stop after thinking a moment about that. He felt Ricky's head, and it was very warm and sweat covered. Max pulled the canteen that hung from Hardy's saddle and poured some water over Ricky's head. He then tried to hoist up the man to take a drink. Most all went in and then back out of his mouth, but Max thought that a small amount had made it down the man's throat. He poured the rest over his head and moved on quickly.

The lights of the town suddenly came into view as he came over a hill, and he brought Hardy to a trot. It was still several minutes before he entered town. He came in gasping for air. On his first attempt to call out he only managed a string of coughs. Finally, his voice came out loud and clear. "Doctor! We need the doctor!"

The next thing he knew Marshal Kreugar was at his side. "What's wrong with him?"

"Shot." Max said without hesitation, seeming somewhat surprised at how calm that sounded compared to how he felt. He had seen men injured, even die, in the

42

mines, but for some person to have done this made him feel somehow like all his beliefs were being questioned. Was anything safe?

"The doc's office is up the road, across from the Grand Union." They moved the horse along Main Street and turned down the street where the Grand Union stood. As they neared a house Kreugar called out. "Thomas! Hurry, it's bad."

It was bad. Max's hand brushed against the part of the blanket covering the wound, and it was moist. Max still thought he heard labored breathing, though the breaths were farther apart. Max hurried his tired legs as they carried Ricky to the door. It opened after only a couple of seconds to show Thomas Owen, a man near middle age, though his dark hair and heavy mustache had not started to show signs of graying. He motioned them to carry the body to the table, where a candle was being lit by a woman. Max and Kreugar laid Ricky down. The doctor called for supplies, and the woman moved with quick experience to grab the antiseptic, scalpel, and tweezers.

"Go!" the doctor yelled at them. "I'll come find you."

Kreugar put a hand on Max's shoulder and guided him out. "Owen's not the normal doctor, but Dr. Beshoar's out of town. Thomas Owen's actually likely to be our mayor, but he was a physician and patched soldiers up during the war, so he's a good man to handle this. Go find Clay and . . ." He stopped talking when Hardy met them at the door, standing with his nose in the air.

Max sighed and took the horse's reins, lightly rubbing his neck. "It's all right, boy." He turned to Kreugar. "Ricky took care of Hardy almost like he was a child."

Kreugar nodded. "Hardy?"

"He named him that because he never acts tired. He just wants to keep going. The horse lived to please him." Max realized he had used the past tense, and, before he started to tear up, he led the horse back to Main Street and started back toward the stables and the hotel where Clay had said he was staying. He stayed long enough to see Hardy into the stall and fed and watered. He paid two dollars for the horse's care, but it was worth it. He did not mind throwing in the extra to see he was well taken care of.

He reached the top of the stairs as Clay was coming out of one of the rooms. "Max. Change your mind on heading out . . . what's wrong?"

"Ricky," Max told him. "He got . . ." His tears could not be stopped now. He finished the sentence in tears. "He's shot through the side, up high."

Clay looked at him a moment, eyes blank. "Is he dead?"

"No. He's over at the doctor's just across from the Grand Union."

Clay clapped Max on the shoulder as he walked past. "He's strong. He can make it."

Max followed him at a near run back to the doctor's office. Clay opened the door, and Max was close behind as they entered. The doctor was washing his hands in a basin, and a blanket covered Ricky's face.

"Uh-h," Clay grunted, and he turned with his eyes welling up. Max burst out sobbing.

Chapter 3

Max had slept only in patches of minutes by the time he pushed himself off the floor of Clay's hotel room the next morning. The marshal had asked him questions the night before for which Max wished he had known the answers. He had simply found Ricky on the road; that was it. Clay had insisted on Max receiving Ricky's pay, his horse and rifle, and other belongings. "You did your best to save him," Clay told him. "Ricky liked and admired you a lot." That had just brought more sobs.

Max woke feeling almost numb. He and Ricky had not been close, really. Ricky acted as Ricky did, and Max resented him for it. Ricky did have his moments, though, when you would see the person he could be, and working close like they did in the dark, depending on each other, a bond did develop, even if a strained one.

Max rode Hardy alongside Clay's wagon,

which held Ricky's body. Ricky had liked hunting, so Clay said they should bury him in the woods. Max had only ridden a few times, so he did not feel that comfortable in the saddle, and, despite Hardy's easy gait, he was sore by the time they stopped. The part of the crew that had not started out the afternoon before had camped just outside of town. Max had found a recently abandoned camp when he had gone to look for them, earlier that morning, so it was just him and the Stephens family that gathered a little after noon when they covered the grave and Clay bowed his head. Eve and little Clay imitated him. Max stared ahead in a daze as Clay spoke. "Lord, please accept our friend Ricky into your bosom. He was on his way to being a great man. His heart was beginning to open, and his shine beginning to show. He was taken early, maybe before he could find his way. Have mercy on him, Lord, and care for him. Amen."

Clay left from there for Kansas after he and Max shook hands again. "Have a safe journey."

"You as well, Max."

Clay started the horses down the road and looked back. "Find your way, Max."

Max only nodded to him. He was not sure

what he meant. He had just buried a friend. He felt exhausted, and the last thing he could think of was heading toward that ranch to ask for a job. He patted Hardy's neck and leaned down and whispered in the horse's ear. "One more night of rest, eh?" Then he brought the horse to a trot back to town.

On the way back to town he thought about Ricky riding away to find a job he may have liked better than mining. He thought about how he had stood up for Clay the afternoon before. It all seemed so unfair. Ricky would not have mouthed off to anyone he did not know, much less attacked them unless he felt threatened. Hardy tossed his head and bared his teeth, and Max wondered if the horse was thinking the same thing, or picking up on its rider's mood like some of his books said.

Regardless, by the time he got to town in the late afternoon he had decided to get drunk. He had only been slightly drunk once when he, Wayne, and Ricky shared a full bottle of whiskey. But he was tired of thinking and wanted to get things off his mind. After seeing to Hardy, he entered the hotel common room, his belongings in hand, and, after purchasing a room for the night, he started up the stairs to stow them.

"You pissants can't afford to gamble with me." The rough man's voice was coming from a table where three men were playing cards. Max glanced down toward the noise. The man who had spoken in a condescending voice was large with a full, dark beard, thick eyebrows, and a crooked nose. He also wore a holstered pistol. Max felt his muscles tighten as recognition hit him.

Max dropped his saddlebags and raised the Winchester repeater, cocking it. The room froze for a moment. Eyes turned to Max.

On seeing him the loud man smiled.

"Carl Bradshaw?" Max called out.

The man moved fast, pistol in hand before Max could think. Max pulled the trigger, and Bradshaw stumbled back. Others in the room scattered away, to the corners or out the door. Bradshaw raised his pistol, and the noise seemed to echo. Max felt as much as heard the bullet hit the wall behind him. He re-cocked and aimed at the center of the large man's chest as the man cocked his pistol again. Max pulled the trigger and saw Bradshaw's head snap back. The large man fell back, the pistol shooting up into the ceiling, sending down splinters of wood.

Max stood there eyeing the body a second, then cocked the rifle again and aimed it.

The man did not move. Max then saw the spot in the man's forehead where he had hit him. He exhaled, lowering his rifle. One of the men in the corner, who had been playing cards with Bradshaw, ran out the door.

Kreugar came in almost simultaneously as the man left, his pistol in hand. He saw Max with the rifle in hand and then the dead body on the floor. He pointed the pistol in Max's general direction as he looked around. For a moment, Max thought he was going to be shot. Somewhere in his mind a voice told him to shoot the marshal before the marshal shot him, but instead he dropped the rifle.

"What's going on here, George?" Kreugar called out to the innkeeper in the other corner of the room.

"He just shot him."

"Max?" Kreugar took better aim now, narrowing his eyes.

"He pulled his gun. That's Carl Bradshaw, a wanted man," Max said.

Kreugar looked again at the body on the floor and nodded, lowering his gun to his side. "I remember getting the poster a couple of days ago when the mail came in." He looked around more. "Anyone else hurt?"

"No." The other card player was standing

directly under the staircase, putting his pistol back through his belt. "I think he was cheating, too. Can I get my money back?"

Kreugar looked at him, and his eyes narrowed again. "No."

"All right." The man looked up at Max. Seeing no gun in his hands, he hurried past him toward one of the rooms. "Nice shooting."

Max could not say anything, but his eyes widened at the thought of him shooting anyone. He had aimed at the man's chest, yet hit him in the head. He let out a long sigh.

Kreugar saw the look on Max's face and shook his head a little. "George, go get Ken, will ya?" George nodded and left at a limping stride. "Come help me carry the body then," Kreugar called up to Max.

Max took a step down, then looked back to his belongings. "Just a second." He grabbed the bags and the still-warm rifle and set them in his room before locking the door and hurrying back down the stairs.

The marshal was looking through the man's saddlebags and then checked his pockets. "You just made yourself seventy-five dollars." The marshal put the man's gun belt in the saddlebag and the bag on the man's stomach and grabbed his feet, leaving the shoulders for Max to grab. "You'll have to wait for it. I'll need to telegraph to Missouri in the morning to get the authorization to give to the bank here. You should have it by late afternoon tomorrow."

"OK." Max followed the marshal out the door in a daze. In the dying light of the evening, he saw that the man's right side was wet with blood from his first shot. He had shot and killed a man. He had thought maybe this man, a wanted man, had killed Ricky, plus knew there was a reward. He had not really thought about what was going to happen. He looked up at Kreugar. "Wanted for horse theft, right?"

"Assault and horse theft," Kreugar said. "He pulled a man from his horse, beat him, and took the horse. There was another witness aside from the man, and the man had some spare money to put up for the reward, so Bradshaw here must've only been lucky at cards. Says he's suspected of ambushing another man for his horse and gear also."

Max nodded. They carried the man down to the outer corner of town, where there was a cemetery. Ken, the undertaker, lived just a hundred yards away from the resting place. There was a shed by the cemetery, and that's where they dropped the body.

The marshal grabbed the bag, and he and

Max started back. Kreugar waved to the chubby, gray-haired undertaker as they passed him. "It's a simple, cheap one, Ken."

"That's what I figured."

"Follow me real quick, Max." They walked to the stables near the other end of town, and the marshal opened the door and looked over the near dozen horses in the stable. He turned and walked back toward the jail in the center of town, Max still following along. Once in the jail, Kreugar sat down at the desk and opened the drawer. He pulled out a stack of papers and shuffled through, pulling out two Wanted posters. He put one of them back in the drawer with the other papers. He read the print at the bottom of the poster, then looked up at Max. "Yep, seventy-five dollars. There was the dark-brown horse they'd seen in the stable, with white on the feet and nose. Would have been fifty if the horse hadn't been there, but you knew that, right?"

Max looked at him blankly. "Yeah, sure."

Kreugar grinned and pulled out a pen. "Spell your name for me, Max."

Max did, and Kreugar wrote it across a blank space on the poster as Max spelled it, then slid the poster in his drawer. "OK, Max. Go get some sleep. I'll wire this in the morning."

"Thanks, Marshal." Max walked out into full darkness and crossed over to the hotel.

When he walked in George was back behind the bar talking to three men. "I didn't know why he'd pulled it at first, but he calmly brought it up and took aim." He looked to the door when Max entered. The three men turned. Two looked like local ranchers, but the third Max had talked with recently.

The bounty hunter Jack Sutter glared at him. "I wouldn't make it a habit of going after my prey, miner boy."

Max was too tired to think of how he should react. "I wasn't planning on it, sir." He made his way up the steps, opened his door, and locked it behind him. He lay down in his bed and closed his eyes. So much for making an early morning ride out to the ranch. Of course, he had just made over two months worth of wages. He opened his eyes and sat up. He had made that much money in just a couple of minutes. He realized he was hungry and grabbed the saddlebag and pulled out the jerky. Obviously, Sutter had to take time to track the men, and Max was lucky that he had stumbled across Bradshaw. Max was also lucky Bradshaw had missed with his shot. He had also been lucky that he had hit Bradshaw at all. The last two days replayed in his mind a couple more times, and, after two sticks of jerky, Max lay back down and closed his eyes.

The light coming into his room woke Max. He had slept well. He rolled out of the bed and went to the wash basin, pouring water before splashing it onto his face. That felt so good he thought of the bathhouse downstairs. Smiling, he pulled his spare clothes out from the bag and went downstairs. The water kettle was next to the tub. Max just had to light the fire underneath. A small amount of water was already in the bottom. He undressed and climbed in, beginning to shiver as the cool water covered his feet. He grabbed the brush and began to scrub. After a few minutes, he picked up the large ladle and dipped out the warm water and poured it over his head. The water relaxed him, and he poured two more ladles over himself before grabbing the soap.

After cleaning up he was hungry, and he smelled the food cooking in the kitchens. He gave his dirty clothes to George, who said one of the laundry women could have them ready by afternoon. George acted differently to Max. He told him he had been told why Bradshaw was wanted, and that

Max had handled himself well. Max made for the common room. There were eggs and biscuits. It tasted great. Max didn't mind spending a little extra money. He had come into extra, with Ricky's share, and then he would get a large sum from the bounty. He thought it should feel odd eating in a room where he'd shot a man, but surprisingly it did not seem to be the same room. He felt like that had been several days ago, not the previous night.

Max walked over to the marshal's office, where Kreugar was just arriving. "I just sent the telegram. It will be a while, like I told ya last night."

"I know. I was wanting to take a look at that other poster."

Kreugar sighed. "Are you sure you want to do that, boy?"

Max looked at him a moment. Being addressed as "boy" angered him, but he forced himself to stay calm. "Yes, sir."

Kreugar pulled the drawer open and gave him the poster. "Got a few copies. You can have one."

Max took the poster and held it up so the light from the window shone on it.

Ben Kennedy, wanted for two counts of rape in Santa Fe, $220, plus $50 if alive.

*Last seen riding north of Santa Fe with
another man. Fee paid by the territory of
New Mexico.*

The drawing showed a middle-aged man
with a slim, pitted face and a hard look to
him. He looked like so many other men you
would see in towns around the territories,
probably with sun-darkened skin and lanky
strength.

Max nodded to the marshal. "Thank you."

Leaving the jail, Max walked back to the
stables to make sure Hardy was fed and had
water available. He had a good-sized stall,
where he had lain down, but he stood and
came to the gate when Max's footsteps
woke him. Max stroked the horse's muzzle
and patted his neck for a while before heading back to the hotel. Having this much free
time was a tough thing for him. Even when
they took Sundays off at the camp, he would
wash his clothes, gather firewood, help clean
the fish, or skin whatever Ricky might bring
back from hunting.

He nodded to George and told him he
planned on checking out later in the afternoon. Once in his room he lifted the rifle
and looked at it. He had cleaned Clay's rifle
for him once, over two years ago, with Clay
directing him while he cleaned his pistol.

He unloaded the rifle, then pulled out the cleaning kit Ricky had carried in his bags. Max began to clean the rifle, carefully committing to memory how he disassembled the parts in order to put them back together. Working with the oil and brush from the kit, he polished all the moving parts and then reassembled it. It seemed nerve wracking, but, as he finished, he knew he had put it back as it had been. He reloaded and then counted the bullets he had remaining — fifteen in the rifle and another six in a small canvas pouch. He closed the pouch and sighed. Then he left his room and headed down to the general store. People on the street looked at him oddly, warily. Max did not like being looked at differently but had to admit it was nice to feel respected in any way.

Calvin looked up and arched an eyebrow as Max came in the door. "What can I do for you?"

"Hi, Calvin. I need some bullets for a '73 Winchester."

"The forty-four, right?"

"Yeah, that's it."

Calvin reached back onto the shelf behind him pulling out a box. "Thirty enough?"

"That should be enough."

"I heard how you spent a couple of them."

Max looked up at the man. He looked like he had asked a question. Max did not know what to say at first. "I saw him, and things just happened."

The store owner's mouth tightened, and he nodded. "I suppose so." He set the box on the counter. "Three dollars." He continued as Max pulled his money out. "I just never figured you the type, but I guess with what happened to your friend, well . . ."

Max put the money down. "He was a horse thief and a low life."

"You're right, and it sounds like he had it coming, but then again we all have our bad points."

Max grabbed the box of ammunition. "Thanks, Calvin." He walked quickly out.

Luke was standing outside by the porch. "So, why don't you wear a pistol?"

"I don't own one; they're expensive."

"You're a bounty hunter now, aren't you?"

"I am for the time being."

"Then you need a pistol, or two like Mr. Sutter."

"I only know how to shoot with my right hand."

Luke looked at him for a second. "I don't think you will make a very good bounty hunter."

Max shook his head, walking away. "I

hope you're wrong." He walked down the street thinking about riding south, this afternoon if the wire for Bradshaw's reward came in early enough.

"Hold up, Max."

Max turned quickly. Calvin was trotting up behind him. "I want to talk to ya."

"What is it, Calvin?"

"Let's walk this way." Calvin turned down the small cross street that was really more like an alley that went between a residence and a café. "I want to give you some advice, please."

Max looked at him, then nodded, following.

"Now, you may know this already. You have a good head on your shoulders from what I can see, and you saw firsthand what a gunfight is like. You know trading bullets is not like how it's described in the little booklets that you purchase." Max was nodding. It was not anything like that, and, of course, he knew it. "Very few men have faced each other in the streets and had quick-draw competitions. Only fools who have copied those books over the last couple of years really do that. There's only been a few men in the last hundred years who can shoot with both hands. Most are lucky to be a good shot with one."

"What about Sutter?"

Calvin chuckled, then stopped, glancing over to Max. "The extra guns are for when one runs out of bullets. Listen: you go after bounties, you will usually not find the men. Plus, you don't have a badge. The badge at least means people may think twice about shooting you. You may run into other killers looking for the bounty, and if you are 'lucky' enough to run into the bounty before he is taken by another chasing him, you may have rode a hundred-plus miles, spent your money and your horse just to get a bullet put in you. That's the plain and true of it, kid. I would know." Calvin stopped walking.

Max looked at him. The man was speaking from experience, and everything he said made sense. "I appreciate the advice, Calvin, I really do."

Calvin smiled at him. "But there's some things you have to learn the hard way."

"I suppose."

"Before you think you are close, don't start a camp fire." With that he turned and started back down the alley.

Max sighed. The fact was, he realized he had felt more alive since he had recognized Carl Bradshaw. There had definitely been a fear, but the fear had not been as much during the shooting; he hadn't time to be afraid then. It came after, when the marshal came into the hotel. Now there was a fear about chasing Ben Kennedy, but a bit of excitement as well.

Truth was he would be one of several men after Kennedy. Sutter would probably be going after him. And most would have a much better idea of how to chase him, experience and all. Max sighed. Hopefully Clay was not just trying to build him up, telling him he was smart enough to do anything. He smiled, though. He was excited about his life now, and he could not say that before all this happened.

Back at the hotel he packed his bags and put the bedroll on top. He was ready to go, just waiting on the wire to release the money. Sitting there in his room he started to think about what Calvin had said. He thought about how now, with a horse and a little bit of money, he might have other options. Maybe he could become a ranch hand. Maybe there was something else. Maybe . . . He shook his head. He wouldn't live out of fear. He was at least going to give this a run.

Santa Fe should be easy enough. It was the oldest and most major hub up in north New Mexico. He could make it in a few days, he suspected, if he got to leave before nightfall.

A knock on the door shook those thoughts. "Max, it's Kreugar." Max stood and opened the door. "Let's go to the bank and get you your money."

Max nodded and went to grab his gear.

"Leave it," Kreugar told him. "They don't allow guns in the bank, unless you're the law."

Max nodded. That made sense. He locked the door and followed. He had heard of a few robberies of late, Jesse James imitators. Few remained uncaptured as long as James had managed. Hmm . . . That was probably the largest bounty of them all. He caught himself shaking his head a little. That was in Missouri. There was in over your head, and then in *way* over your head.

Kreugar was quiet on the walk, and Max didn't mind. They got to the bank, and the marshal pushed the wire to the banker. He took it and read, looking up at Max, then back to the wire. "Just a moment," he said. He pulled out a paper with writing already on it and filled in a couple of empty places, then pushed the paper across the counter. "Please sign on the right, Mr. Tillman, and, Marshal, you on the left." Max signed on the line and passed it to the marshal. Then the banker pulled out several bills and passed them across the counter to Max. He counted it back and put it deep in his pocket. It was a lot of money. "Thank you."

The marshal nodded to the banker and left, Max following on his heels. Kreugar looked at Max outside the bank door. "Good luck to ya, Max."

"Thanks, Marshal."

With that Kreugar walked the other way down the street. Max sighed and walked briskly toward the hotel. In only a few minutes he'd gathered his items, paid George and the stableman, and was riding out of town alongside the rail forking off to the south up into the mountains.

After an hour, he realized he had never spent much time alone. There was a whole lot of alone time in front of him. He had gone from his mother's house to the mining camps. The longest trips he'd ever taken on his own were a few miles to the nearest towns from camps. He reached into his pocket, checking for the flint. Then he looked around into the brush. A storm had passed through a couple of days back, but he should be able to find some tinder dry enough to start a fire. He knew he would not sleep well without a fire. He probably would not sleep well anyway, fire or not.

He smiled, laughing at himself inside. He was going to be a bounty hunter but was afraid to sleep outside on his own. That was at least a couple of hours away, though. A couple more hours in the saddle. How did men do it? He was already feeling a little tender. If he ended up riding to Santa Fe, that meant another six to seven days in the saddle. They had come up through Santa Fe to Trinidad when Newton had sent the crew there. It was a well-traveled trail and right around two hundred miles. Max had alternated between walking and being in the wagon on that trip.

Max rode through the afternoon, heading uphill to the mountains. As the sun began nearing the horizon Max found a clearing off the trail. After unsaddling Hardy, he quickly went into the trees, picking up dead branches and dried twigs for tinder. The dirt in the center of the clearing had ash so was obviously a prime place for travelers to set up camp. He worked the flint for several minutes before the tinder caught. Then he moved that onto the dried branches, holding a couple over the smoldering tinder until they ignited. Sighing, he rolled out his blanket and pulled out the jerky along with an apple. He had given Hardy a carrot and a small feed of oats. The horse could graze what grass there was tonight. He would get a larger portion of oats in the morning for energy. It was going to be a long day.

Max lay on his side, eating, feeling relaxation come over him. Then in the distance he heard the howl of wolves. Great! He pulled the rifle onto his lap. He looked around as he heard the wolves' howls again, only closer. Hardy was uneasy, probably picking it up from Max. He thought he heard movement in the brush to his left, by Hardy. He sprang to his feet, pointing the rifle that direction. Gazing into the dark he did not see anything. He thought about shooting to scare them away but then wondered if the sound would attract something else.

He turned to see two glowing sets of eyes at the edge of the clearing looking at him. He yelled and shot in that direction. Both sets of eyes vanished, and the sound of movement relayed their hasty retreat. Max tossed more wood on the fire and sat back down. The night stretched out, him lying there looking around as he heard brush move. Most likely it was small animals scurrying through, but his mind made more of the sounds. He would hear the wolves in the distance occasionally, but they did not come closer.

CHAPTER 4

Max's eyes popped open to see light was easing into the sky. He had fallen asleep sitting up and had made it through the night. He looked over to where Hardy was standing and sighed. With the sun just rising, the air was still chilly, and he hated to stand out of the blankets, but he had to make water.

He stood and walked to the edge of the camp to relieve himself. While he did he looked at the mountains to the northwest. He felt a draw to change directions. He wanted to know what was there . . . perhaps one day. Then, after packing and putting the saddle back on Hardy, he walked to the edge of the clearing with his rifle focused on the branch of a tree twenty yards away. He brought the stock to his right shoulder, took aim, and fired. He saw leaves above the branch move, so he cocked the rifle, aimed a bit lower, and fired. This time he saw pieces of bark fly off the branch. The third time he missed completely and wasn't sure where the bullet went. The fourth time was a direct hit on the branch, sending bark into the air and shaking the branch. The fifth shot saw the branch break.

He took aim at a branch about ten yards further away. After another six shots he saw two hits. He sighed, reloaded his rifle, and walked back to mount Hardy. He was only a few minutes on the trail when a rider came speeding by, a remount in tow, likely a messenger of some sort from Trinidad heading to one of the towns in northern New Mexico, or maybe to the mine above.

He thought about the fact that the poster had reached Kreugar three days ago, making it probably six days since the poster had been out. How many men closer to the area would be looking for Kennedy? How far had Kennedy gotten? For all he knew, Kennedy was back in Trinidad right now.

Max sighed. He would be in Raton shortly, as he saw several tents and a building that must represent Morley up ahead. There was a church as well. He rode up to the closest of the three men in the camp. The muscle on the balding man spoke of someone who had labored in lifting and pounding for some time, much like some miners Max had seen in his day. The man stopped packing a wagon as Max rode up. "Curious, any jobs in the coal mine?"

The man glared at him and shook his head. "Hired two men yesterday. Probably overmanned as it is."

Max just stared at the man for a moment. The man moved his hips forward, emphasizing the pistol stuffed through his belt. Max tried to give him a friendly smile. "You seen a man named Kennedy? I got his portrait here." He reached into his bag, took out the poster, and unrolled it. The man glanced at it, then back at Max.

"No. You a bounty hunter, boy?"

"Until I find another job, seeing as your group isn't hiring."

The man shook his head. "Good luck to ya. Guy sounds like an asshole who needs putting in the ground."

Max nodded to him and rode on, following a couple of riders who had passed him. He didn't like how the narrow trail was right up against the rail. He heard the sound the same time Hardy started dancing. A train crested the hill above and was coming back down the rail heading to Trinidad. Max brought Hardy to the far side of the trail like the other riders, but in this narrow part of the pass he was only about eight feet away from the rail. He patted the horse's

69

neck and was as calming as he could be as the train sped by, with two cars in tow. One was a passenger car, and he noted a few heads in the windows. He wondered how much that short trip cost those passengers as he started Hardy back up the remaining part of the incline.

The trees thinned not long after he crested the top of the pass. When he started back down the ridge, he saw the several tents surrounding the wood and adobe buildings in the distance that made up Willow Springs, the old town, with Raton's newer buildings and ongoing construction a short distance to the west. When he and the other Nelson men came through on their way to Trinidad, there had been fewer of the Raton buildings up. The railway had bypassed the old town, creating the new one.

He rode past the tents, where a few men were guiding mules or carrying packs themselves alongside the rail. Past the tents, he entered the old town, and the stables were just past the outer three houses. He slowed as an older man came out waving to him. "I bet a lot of people mistake your horse for a common mustang." Max nodded. Many had called Ricky's horse a mustang over the years. "You wouldn't be interested in selling, would ya?"

Max shook his head. "He's my horse 'til one of us dies."

The man nodded. "Choctaw's a really good horse. I wouldn't sell it either, if I wasn't a horse trader."

Max nodded. Ricky had claimed his horse was somewhat rare and known as a good cow horse, but Max had never known if that had just been his fondness for Hardy. Max guided Hardy over to the man, leaning down and extending his hand. "Hi, I'm Max Tillman."

The man took his hand, showing more strength then Max had given the smaller guy credit for. "Ron Stark. Stable and trade horses."

"Good to meet ya, Ron. You mind me asking if you've ever seen this man, Ben Kennedy?" He went to give the man the rolled-up poster, but Ron shook his head.

"Big blond-haired man with two pistols asked me that same thing yesterday afternoon. I don't know the man on the poster."

"Jack Sutter?"

"He didn't give his name."

Max sighed. Sutter had warned him away from chasing his prey. "He staying here in town?"

"He stayed in Raton last night. I was there early this morning talking to the stableman there. I saw him ride out this morning." Stark paused, looking Max over. "You don't seem like the same type of man."

"I'm not really, but I'm trying a different type of work. Thanks for the information, Mr. Stark." Max started thinking about how far it was to the next town. He had plenty of oats, so he started Hardy off.

"He must've found something out," the man called after him, bringing Max to halt Hardy. "He asked how far it was to Taos."

"And how far?"

"Near a hundred miles west. You'd be going through Cimarron, an outpost, about forty miles from here."

"River there, right?"

"Yep."

Max sighed and climbed off his horse. Walking back to Stark, he flipped a quarter to the man. "Thanks."

He went to the town well and filled up on water and let his horse drink before starting out west. He didn't think he would make it to Cimarron today. The trail brought him through rolling hills of prairie, dotted with patches of trees that thickened further to the west as you approached the mountains. It was not a place to ride in the dark, as there were gullies that lined the land. He had seen crops being grown not too far west of Raton, and cattle. The land was not nearly as fertile as the land in western Louisiana and east Texas where he grew up, but men made it work here.

Hours would pass before he would see another traveler. The first travelers he saw just after leaving Raton. A family in an open wagon, leading a cow behind, was heading into town. Around noon there were two men riding with a pack mule towards Raton. Late in the afternoon he saw a lone horseman coming from the opposite direction. He was short, wearing a cap. Max realized as they approached each other that the man had a rifle cradled across his saddle. Max looked to where his rifle was sheathed. He tensed as they met but nodded to the man, who nodded at him. The man eyed his waist and hands, then picked up the pace and rode quickly past. Max shook his head. The man had been scared of him.

Max veered off the trail to find a place to camp as the sun was about to touch the horizon. He'd heard of the dangers of camping close to the trail. There were men who would sneak in and steal your horse and all your belongings, and, if you were lucky, you'd only receive a good beating.

He was weary from the road, so, after taking care of Hardy, making a small fire, and eating a little, he went to sleep.

Max jumped to his feet, managing to grab the rifle next to him, at the sound of Hardy's whinny. The fire had nearly burned out, but having had his eyes closed he was able to see in the dark better than usual. He peered around the horse out into the dark. He thought he heard something moving through the brush, but it was moving away, and all he caught was a bit of movement of tall grass.

He sighed and spun around, looking out from his campsite. He thought he had heard there were Indians wandering this area, plus cougar, bear, and wild boar, not to mention the road agents. He told himself that being afraid did him no good. Fear could keep him from living the life he should be living. His dad had died young out in the woods. Perhaps he would also, but if he let fear stop him, then what kind of life would that be? He went and lay back down, and, surprisingly, the next thing he knew he was waking up to the beginnings of light. He woke up feeling good and rested. He was still sore from so much time in the saddle, but it actually didn't seem as bad as the day before.

He rolled his blankets and set them next

to the saddle, then walked a few steps to relieve himself. While going, he glanced down and saw tracks. He was not an expert but was sure he knew what mountain lion tracks looked like, and these could be fresh. It had likely been a mountain lion the night before. He swallowed and, after fastening his pants back up, saddled Hardy with haste. Once back on the road he began to think, and his fear began to fade. A mountain lion had been close, and he had survived. It hadn't attacked. He patted Hardy's neck. "We're gonna be all right."

The first half of the day passed like the day before, riding the trail that narrowed where brush grew heavy and the pale grass tried to claim the trail. He had to move off the trail a couple of times as wagons and a stagecoach moved past. After he had taken a midday rest he noticed more homesteads and knew he must be nearing Cimarron. Cimarron was supposedly the Indian name for the mustang, wild and untamed. It was nearing mid-afternoon when he rode into the town. It was a bit smaller than Trinidad, and there were other differences. The enormous structure as he neared the center of town had the look of a hotel, or possibly a large mansion. Next to it was a Lambert's, a large hotel with a saloon and restaurant attached. He saw the mill rising from behind the store across the street. He had heard that mill had supplied the local Indian reservation before skirmishes broke out years ago.

He saw tents at the edge of town. Gold had been discovered nearby a few years back, and, as always, that led to a growth of the town. Of course, the growth of Trinidad and Raton was surpassing Cimarron due to the rail passing through. Max considered looking for work in one of the camps nearby. He knew he had no idea what he was doing chasing wanted men, but he wanted to do something different. He circled around Lambert's to where stables stood next to a hardware store.

He had read that there were names associated with this town. Davey Crockett, the nephew and namesake of the famous explorer who'd lost his life at The Alamo, and Clay Allison, the gunfighter and rancher, were two of the biggest. Cimarron had only a few years ago been a town of chaos and mob lynchings. The anarchy heated up during the beginning of the Colfax County war and had been one of the most popular subjects of newspapers at the time. Clay Allison had since moved to Kansas and made the news there. Crockett died in a skirmish with a sheriff and his deputies. Although Max had not read of a resolution of the dispute between the Maxwell Land Grant Company and the settlers, Cimarron had recently become calmer, or at least the newspapers had found other towns and characters to write about.

All the same Max did not feel comfortable when the olive-skinned stable boy nodded to his rifle when he made to carry it out of the stable with his bags. "Not supposed to carry arms in the city."

"I saw the sign at the edge of town, but I see plenty of men with pistols in their belts."

"Not quite the same as carrying a rifle. Sheriff Rinehart may take a dislike to ya."

Max nodded, set his belongings down, and pulled the folded poster out of his pocket. "You seen a man that looks like this, named Ben Kennedy?"

The teen looked at the poster and shook his head, but there was recognition in his eyes.

"You not tellin' me something. What is it?"

"I've not seen this man except in the same poster earlier today."

Max nodded. "Big blond-haired man, two pistols, Jack Sutter."

"Yes, sir."

Max looked down the stalls. He was not sure he would recognize Sutter's horse if he saw it, but there were a dozen stalls in this barn. Max sighed and gave the stable boy two bits and asked about the big building in the middle of town.

"The Maxwell House." The boy waited. Max had heard the name before but couldn't place exactly what it was. The boy shrugged. "About twenty years ago Lucien Maxwell had it built; you know, the man that ran the Aztec Mill." It was starting to come back to Max now. "Well, he sold everything and moved, but the Maxwell House now has offices of the Maxwell Land Grant Company. That and hotel, saloon, gambling rooms, and brothel."

Max nodded. He must've been tired not to remember reading about that. The Maxwell Land Grant Company was one side of the war that took place in this town.

He asked about the hotels. Then he wrapped the ties on his bag around the rifle and left carrying it backwards, to show he had no plans for using it between the stables and the hotel in case he ran across the sheriff.

He walked into the hardware store next door to take a glance. Max noted the number of shovels, shifts, pans, and picks.

Behind that was everything else a working man could need in the world. Grain and feed, rope, twine, canned goods, lanterns, even the tack and gear for horses. The last had probably been taken in trade, but it was in good shape. He nodded to the owner, presumably the stable boy's father, and left.

He chose a smaller boarding house down the street from the Maxwell House and Lambert's. He stored his stuff in a room upstairs, including his rifle. He did pull his knife from his pack and slid it through his belt, although that would do him little good against a sidearm. He was beginning to think his decision not to buy a pistol was not a good idea. He was going into the infamous Lambert's. It was said that the common question in the mornings in Cimarron's wild days was, "Who was killed at Lambert's last night?" But that was a couple years ago, and it was supposed to have really good food. The main reason he was going, though, was that it would be a good place to hear news.

Max noted that it held only a few customers, there still being more than a couple of hours of daylight left. He went to the bar and nodded his head to the pudgy, dark-haired man working behind the counter. "Too early to get some food?"

"Got some stew that's been simmering since lunch. Won't be cookin' steaks for a while yet."

"Sounds good."

"Drink?"

"Beer?"

"Yep." The man pulled down on the tap and filled a glass. The beer was not cold but not warm either, probably just brought up from the cellar earlier that day.

"Been away from towns for a while," Max lied. "What's the news?"

"Another man shot on his small ranch a couple days back," the barkeep said, turning to spoon some stew into a bowl. "His family's moving out."

"Any idea who did it?"

The man turned around and gave him a blank stare. "Do you know nothing about the goings on around here, boy?" He didn't give him time to answer. "It would be stupid for me to tell ya what I think happened, and it's not that smart for you to ask." He set the bowl in front of Max and put a spoon in it and a chunk of bread next to it. "Fifty cents."

"I hear ya. Just tired and haven't talked to anyone for a while." Max pulled out the money and laid it on the counter. "Except this guy I rode alongside for a while. He said he was in Santa Fe a week ago. Said he was riding out and some men stopped him and nearly shot him, saying he looked like some guy wanted for rape. Said he pissed himself the way the men came at him."

The barkeep nodded. "Heard about that. Guy's got a big price on him now, that's why they stopped your buddy." He waved to another customer who came in. "Hi, Frank."

"Hey, Pete, need some whiskey."

Max shook his head. "Bet he won't last long."

"Probably not," Pete said, pouring and sliding the glass down the bar. The man laid down a coin and took the glass. "But ya never know. If he has half a brain, he'll go into hiding for a while 'til things die down."

"Maybe with some distant family or something."

"Nah, too easy to find. I'm talking the woods. It's not too cold right now, just gotta be able to handle the wildlife and catch your own food."

Max nodded. "Wonder if the guy knows about any of that."

"Who knows?"

Max ate a couple of bites of the stew. It was good. It was made with chunks of beef, potatoes, carrots, and corn. After a swig of beer, he nodded. "Good stew."

"Yep."

"Know of any work around here at a ranch or a mine even?"

"No damn idea. Ask around here later, when more people come in."

"All right. Thanks."

Pete went down the bar to refill another customer's drink. Max finished his stew and wiped the bread around the sides to get all the gravy. He downed the last drops of beer, then left for the store across the street to buy a few supplies.

He considered buying a pistol there if they sold them, but he had not shot a pistol more than twice in his life. It would not do him any good now. On the street, a man with a white collar stepped in front of him. "Young sir, do you feel like you are missing something in your life?"

"Possibly." Max stepped around him.

The man called in a soft voice behind him, "Please consider what that may be."

Max focused on what he needed for the trail. To get to Taos he had to go through higher mountains. That meant colder temperatures. Spring had long arrived in the lower areas, but cold would be hanging on in the tallest mountains, especially at night. Max thought it through. He had gone through last winter without a heavier coat, so he decided that he could make it through the mountains in late spring without one also. He would buy another box of ammo so he could practice more, more oats for Hardy, and perhaps more jerky, but that was it. He had to watch his spending until he found his next payroll. He really did mean what he said when he asked about the work at a ranch, mine, or another place. He had come to realize that he was more out of his element than he had previously thought. He did not know the first thing about tracking a man, and he did not fit in at places where he figured he would gather information, like the saloon. He sighed. The truth was he was doubting that he should move on to Taos.

The store was nearly directly across the street from the enormous building he'd seen earlier. Max remembered that the former leader of Cimarron had built a mansion, saloon, hotel, gambling house, and brothel all in one large building. He remembered what he had overheard about the Maxwell House. The former owner of the Aztec mill — and likely much of Cimarron — had built it before gold was discovered and things started getting out of hand in the town. That explained why the general store had mining gear also. He picked up the supplies he had needed and paid the older woman behind the counter.

When Max left the shop he was daydreaming of finding his own bonanza somewhere and striking it rich. He had read that the area around Independence, Colorado, had many rich claims. Perhaps he was chasing the wrong type of bounty, riding in the wrong direction. It was something to sleep on, but before he went to his room he walked down the street a little, passing the jail, which was just a block south. It looked solid, built of big gray brick, with metal plates pierced with holes rather than bars on the windows. He thought about talking to the sheriff or asking a passerby on the street but decided against it. Would likely do no good. His next stop would be Taos. He went up to his room and lay on the bed as the light began to fade. He was so tired. He did not know what he was actually chasing. Likely Sutter would get Kennedy, or Kennedy was not even going to be found by anyone. He drifted off to sleep.

He woke a few hours later when it was pitch dark outside. He heard some voices still traveling up from downstairs, so he expected it was not too late. He sat up and looked out his small window. There were windows lit down the street at Lambert's and the brewery across from it. A couple of men walked down the street toward the saloon. He lay back down and thought. He could go down the street and try to find information. He sighed.

A gunshot broke the night silence, making him jump. It had not been very far away. He looked out the window and saw a man running down the street. Two others ran after him, soon accompanied by the flash and the loud pop of gunfire, and the man fell to his knees, then forward.

Max watched as a couple more men came to join them and look over the body. Others came out of doors but turned back and went inside after seeing the men. The men turned and ran themselves, in between two buildings as three other men came from the south carrying rifles. They looked around and inspected the body before they started wandering down toward Lambert's.

Max lay back down, reaching over the bed to feel the rifle on the floor. He decided he would stay in the rest of the night. It was a couple of hours before he fell back asleep. He woke as the grayness from the first hints of dawn showed in his window. He sat up and decided right away that he had come this far, and he would ride on to Taos. He grabbed his bag and his rifle and made his way out of the hotel and down the street to the stables.

He pushed open the door and stepped through. He was struck in the side of the head from his right and stumbled sideways into the dark until the boards of what must have been the first stall caught him. The horse in the stall began to whinny. He nearly dropped his belongings and did consciously let his bags drop. He had just begun to wrap his fingers solidly around his rifle when another blow struck his mouth, and his knees buckled. The rifle was kicked from his loose hands, and another punch hit his cheek, sending him down to the ground. He closed his eyes, expecting to be kicked, but it didn't come. He felt the blood dripping down his lip that was fattening, and he opened his eyes. He saw his rifle kicked further away from him by the boots he was at eye level with.

The man knelt down, and Max looked up and stared Jack Sutter in the face. The man wore a mean sneer. "I told you to stay away from my bounties. If I see you again, you pissant, it might not be just a beating." Max saw his legs walk away, and in the light of the open door he saw Sutter's legs and a horse's legs walking out the stable. He heard a horse trotting outside, then the sound of footsteps nearby.

The stable boy pulled at Max, and he struggled to find balance to sit up. After a couple of tries he pushed up to his feet and stumbled across the barn to sit on a bale of hay. "You all right, mister?"

"Not really. I just got the shit beat out of me." Max could feel his cheek under his left eye swelling, and his lip was already fat.

"I've seen worse."

Max thought about what he had seen out of his hotel window. "I suppose so."

"You need the doctor?"

Max felt his cheek, but there was nothing to be done about that. He felt the side of his head, and there was a small lump. He could feel the bleeding from his lip had already begun to slow. "I don't think so. You mind saddling my horse for me?"

"You're going after him?"

"No, I'm riding the other way."

The boy walked down the stalls, but Max heard him. "Good idea."

CHAPTER 5

Max poured cool water that the boy had pulled from the well over his cheek and thanked the kid by giving him a dollar. He put the bag of coins back in his pocket. He tested his steadiness as he stood and found that his balance, while not normal, was good enough to take a couple of steps toward his horse. He concentrated and pulled himself onto Hardy. "Kid, you hear of any work at the mines or ranches?"

"No. There's a few men looking for work around here. Some say the gold is drying up."

"Thanks." With that Max trotted out of the stables and northeast back the way he had come. He would make it to Raton tonight, and hopefully they had a room, because he thought he needed a good bed to rest in for tonight. The people in the streets looked at him as he rode out of town. He could imagine how he looked.

The buildings and houses of Cimarron faded away behind him. The jouncing in the saddle made his head and cheek hurt worse. Every now and then he would pour a bit of the water over his eye again. When he pulled out the apple he had for breakfast he realized how hard it was to eat with a swollen lip.

He missed Clay. Perhaps he would search him out. Being alone was harder than he thought. Riding along, he began to plan out his trip to Kansas. He would have to backtrack through Trinidad, then take the trail into Kansas. He would stay clear of Dodge City. Cimarron had been all he could take of "wild towns."

As midday approached, the heat was picking up, and the water in his canteens was no longer cool. So he stopped pouring it over his eye. It had not swelled completely shut, so there was that. He was thinking about hunting on his way to find Clay, because he was not sure how far his money would last.

He heard a noise in the brush and turned, looking around for its source. He had camped near this area last night. He was topping a rise on the hill so he looked back, seeing for miles, and noted no activity on the trail behind or within sight in front. He peered into the trees and saw only a squirrel. That would have made a fine meal if he wanted to take time to cook. He looked ahead to the small valley below and the next rise nearly a mile away.

At the bottom of the hill he was wondering how much of an inconvenience he would be to Clay's in-laws when he saw the rider coming from the top of the next rise. Had he come out of the gulley to the side of the trail, or had Max not noticed him coming over the hill? He was riding at a good pace also. From the distance, he seemed like too big a man to be a delivery rider. Max started to tense but dismissed it as being paranoid from the beating he took earlier that day. There were likely plenty of homesteads or trapper shacks in the woods to the west. He glanced around and saw a rider descending the hill behind him as well. There had been nobody within miles behind him at that last rise.

He reached for his rifle. The man about two hundred yards in front of him must have figured he had made them as road agents, because he had pulled his rifle and was galloping down on him.

Max cocked the rifle and shot at the man in front of him, then cocked again and turned, shooting back at the other. Max then turned Hardy back into the trees beside the trail. He was struggling to weave through just off the road when a searing pain in his upper left arm jolted him back. He'd been hit. He lost his balance and fell out of his saddle. He almost managed to get his feet underneath him but fell against another tree, hitting his head. He grunted but pushed himself up. Hardy wove through the trees away from the gunshots, and Max gave chase. He had dropped his rifle while falling and had no idea where it was.

He heard hooves behind him and ducked behind a tree. The shot seemed to be far wide. He looked to his right and saw the man from the east was entering the brush but would soon be upon him. Max's mind raced. There would be no help. The men probably watched the other directions from those hilltops to be sure nobody else would come upon them while they robbed and killed people in that valley.

Max felt his pocket and found where he had several coins. He pulled the bag out. Would they leave him be if he just gave them the coins? He peeked around the other side, and the man was weaving his horse through trees almost ten yards away. There was another shot, hitting the tree somewhere as bark flew. The man cocked and went to shoot again but had to move his arm around a tree he was passing.

Max hurled the leather bag of coins, pelting the man right in the nose. He fell backwards, his gun going off into the air above him. Max lunged for the man's horse but then turned, getting to the man just after he'd hit the ground and was reaching for his dropped pistol. Max dove for the gun, gripping the handle as the man grabbed at the barrel. He pulled back the hammer as the man pulled, and his finger hit the trigger. The man's head snapped back.

Max rolled over, and a shot hit the ground where he had been. He recocked and shot in the direction of the horsed man, hitting the tree next to the ducking man. The man turned his horse and bolted as Max got off another shot but missed. Max stood and ran a couple of steps to get around the trees. The rider slowed, looking back as he was nearing the edge of the tree line. It hurt when Max raised his left arm to help steady the gun, but he took careful aim and hit the rider square in the back. The rider toppled as his horse continued out of the brush. Approaching, Max recocked the pistol and took aim at the man lying on his back who was weakly flailing his arms, trying to get to the rifle. But when Max pulled the trigger, there was only a click. Empty.

The man was groaning in pain but stopped trying to reach the rifle and pulled his pistol from his holster and arched his neck to take aim at Max. Max started to duck behind a tree when he saw the pistol fly out of the man's flopping arm. He had little control of his arms. Max walked over and took the pistol as he looked down at the man, who was spitting blood with every wheeze.

Max shook his head. "Better than you deserve." He cocked the pistol and aimed at the top of the robber's head from three feet away and put him out of his misery.

Max sighed. He leaned back against a tree and pushed the gun through his belt. He looked at his arm. The bullet had just grazed him. He dusted off his hands and tore his sleeve from around the wound and pulled it off. Then he pulled the sleeve inside out and wrapped it around the wound, tying it off by holding one end in his mouth.

He pushed himself up and looked around. Hardy was about fifty feet away milling around; the horse of the first man to go down had stopped near him. He called Hardy and whistled, and the horse trotted back to him. The other was hesitant. It followed Hardy but stopped a bit away from

Max. Max got his canteen and took a drink before taking Hardy's reins and giving the horse a chunk of apple he had carved off from breakfast. He had another and approached the other horse, feeding it and tying its reins to a sturdy branch. He collected his coin pouch, along with his own rifle and the other man's rifle. He then checked the two men. One of them wore a holster, and Max put it around his waist and holstered one pistol, putting the other in a saddlebag. Between the two of them, they had only eighteen dollars on their bodies.

Max considered taking their boots but didn't like the idea. He climbed onto Hardy's saddle, took the reins of the other horse, and made his way to the road. He kept an eye on the brush as he rode. As he climbed the hill two riders and a wagon crested the top riding toward him. He thought about pulling his pistol but realized he would then look threatening, and they probably had business of some sort in Cimarron. The men trotted slowly like anyone would, but they looked suspiciously at him as they neared. He led another horse, had a wounded arm and a beaten face, and felt every bit of pain from the day so far. He understood why they would be suspicious.

"We thought we heard gunshots," a solid

looking gray-haired man said, his hand resting on his leg near his pistol.

"Yeah. Road agents tried to rob me. They're both lying in the group of trees back there."

The man looked him over again, considering. "Good for you, but it looks like it was a hell of a fight."

"Yeah, the face comes from getting jumped this morning. It's been a bad day."

"You might want to travel in company from now on."

"I was thinking that."

The lead man looked at the horse and nodded, smiling. "Got something out of it anyway. Take care."

They rode in opposite directions. Toward the top of the hill, Max nearly missed seeing the black horse standing in a gulley that started alongside the road, where he likely was used to waiting for victims with his owner. Max tied up the other two horses and slowly approached, taking the reins of the third horse. After tying the reins of all the horses together, he checked the saddlebags of both robbers' horses. He found jerky, rope, bedrolls, a load of ammo, and another one hundred and sixty dollars, almost worth getting shot at.

The sky was just starting to darken for the

evening when Max rode into Willow Springs leading the two horses. He rode up to the stables, and a man walked out to meet him. "I'm back, Ron. You got room for three horses?"

The older man looked at Max's face, then his arm. "Did you end up finding that Kennedy fellow?"

"No, that Sutter fellow, the one who showed you the poster before me."

Ron looked back at the horses and then sighed. "Neither one of them's his horse, so I'm guessing it was a one-way conversation."

"Yes, I'm afraid it was." Max loosened the lead rope to the horses and handed it to Ron, who started for the stables. "These belonged to a couple of road agents who were out to take my horse and whatever else was of value."

"Sounds like you can handle yourself, son, even with one eye nearly swollen shut."

"It wasn't my right eye. You want to buy these horses, Ron?"

The man glanced over the two horses, measuring their soundness as he tied their reins to the hitching post outside the barn. "I assume these road agents won't be coming to lay claim to the horses."

"No chance of it." Saying that brought

home to Max that he had ended two lives. But it had been him or them, and they had probably killed others and would have killed more.

"It's hard to give them a good look over in this light, but they look like they're in good shape. "Twenty each?"

Max sighed and then put a smile on his face that he didn't really feel. It was Ron's business, and horse traders would haggle. Max had just never had to deal with one. He imagined there were far worse than Ron. "Come on, Ron, twenty?"

Ron shrugged and looked at the horses again. "Twenty-three apiece."

Max shook his head. "Ron, should I ride into Raton and see what someone will give me for them? That may be what you're gonna do anyway."

Ron shrugged. "Thirty for the black and twenty-five for the other. There's still a chance someone may claim them, since those men may have stole them."

Max sighed again. He did not want to go haggle with any buyers himself, and the two had not been easy to guide during parts of his journey. He wanted to be done with them. "Seventy-five for both and the saddles and bags."

Ron shook his head. "Seventy, and I'll

look them over in good morning light before it's final."

"OK, seventy, but you throw in a night's stabling of Hardy and take care of him tonight."

Ron extended his hand. "Done. I'll groom them and look at them again in the morning."

"Agreed." Max shook Ron's hand. He was fairly sure Ron would sell the black with the saddle for around sixty, and the other for almost fifty, but he did need to make a profit. "Got two more questions for ya," Max said, climbing down from Hardy and tying the reins on the post. "Where's a decent place to stay, and is the gunsmith here as hard to bargain with as you?"

Minutes later Max walked into the store to see a large-bellied, balding man walking toward the door with a key in his hand.

The man looked at Max's face and at the bags slung over his shoulder and the rifles and bedrolls in his hand. "What's all this?"

Max looked over to the tan Lab sitting by the counter. It was so still he had thought it stuffed at first. "I came here before the hotel to catch you before you closed."

Max set the bags down next to a shelf of canned goods, and the man walked back toward the counter. There wasn't a gunsmith, but Ron said the general store sold guns and knew them pretty well. There was another store in Raton also, but Ron said that this man would treat him well. There were two rifles and two shotguns standing on a shelf behind the counter with a chain running through the trigger guards and a lock through the chain at the end.

Max took two of the bedrolls, the Springfield, and a bag to the counter. After setting those down, he looked at the man. "What do you have for pistols?"

The man looked at Max's belt, a holstered pistol on his side and another through the belt. "I got a brand new Colt 45, and a 44. I also got a used Colt and used Schofield and SW Model 3."

"What do you suggest?"

"Can I see your pistols?" Max pulled them out and laid them on the counter. "These are 45-caliber Colts, decent shape. Why new pistols?"

"These belonged to a couple of road thieves who were looking to kill me and take my horse. I just want to trade this stuff for new." He took off the belt and placed it on the counter also.

The man looked at his eye and looked at the pistol gripped in his hand. "How do I know that story's not turned around?"

"You can talk to Ron at the livery. He said to tell ya not to worry about that dollar you owe him from poker if ya deal with me right."

The man nodded, smiling. "I'm Gary, and I don't owe him a dollar."

"I'm Max." He offered his hand, and they shook. "And now, that argument can be laid to rest."

Gary looked back to where Max's Winchester leaned against a cabinet. "I'd go with a 44 caliber for ease in matching the bullets." He took one of the keys and turned around, opening up the footlocker behind him. He pulled out the five pistols and laid them on the counter. "The used Colt is 44 also and in good shape." He pointed to it. It didn't have quite the shine that the other Colts had. Max picked it up and looked down the barrel.

"You don't know pistols that well, do ya, son?"

"No, sir, to be honest I don't. But after my experience earlier today I thought I should get to know something about them."

"You shot one?"

"Yeah, my old boss had a Model 3 like that one right there." Max picked it up. It felt more familiar when he held it. "I took a few shots with it a couple of times." The dog was by Max's hand now, and Max patted the top of its head.

"Although it's a 44 caliber, the bullets don't fit the Winchester. It's a good gun, though. All of them are. I've taken shots with all the used ones, and they work pretty much as good as new. You know it's smarter not to carry it with the resting chamber loaded, so in case you fall or something it won't go off?"

Max nodded. "I know that much." He set the Model 3 down and picked up the updated Schofield model.

"Now a lot of people like the Schofield top breaking action." Gary took the Schofield and popped to where it hinged to leave the barrels open for ease of loading. "I myself don't mind the swing gate loading of the Colts, though." He switched guns to one that Max had brought in and half cocked the gun back, then swung open the small lever behind the cylinder. He spun the cylinder and shook his head. "Empty." Putting the gun down he continued. "Now the longer barrel of the Model 3 and the Colt 44s will give you a slightly more accurate shot at a distance according to some. The 45 has a five and a half-inch barrel, where these Colts have the longer." He reached behind the counter and pulled out another

Colt. "This is a four and three quarters; serves my purpose here fine, but I'd prefer the five and a half out on the road, or the longer."

Max looked at the guns. "How much does each run?"

Gary pointed to the two new Colts. "Seventeen and sixteen dollars." Then he tapped the used Colt. "Twelve dollars." Then in turn the Schofield and Model 3. "Fourteen and ten dollars."

"How much will you trade for all this stuff?" Max nodded towards the bag. "There's bullets for the guns in there."

Gary opened the bag and moved his hand around in it, then looked at the gear. "Twenty-eight dollars for it all."

Max nodded. "Trade you then for the two Colt 44s, plus I'd like a couple boxes of ammo and that holster." Max nodded to the holster on the wall by the gun shelf. It looked used but not in bad condition, made to slide onto a normal belt.

"Both huh?"

"Yep."

"Done."

Max reached out and shook the man's hand. "Will you show me how to take it apart and clean it?"

"Sure. There's a diagram comes with the

new one also."

It was full dark by the time Max checked into the small six-room hotel just across the street. Raton had more to offer, but the rooms would have been more expensive also. He stowed his items and went to the bath house to quickly wash up. Ron had asked if he wanted company for supper, and he did. He liked Ron, and the last couple days alone had been tough. He had always liked sitting around the campfire hearing the discussions and stories of the guys from the mine. He looked forward to eating with someone again.

The hotel had been there a while. Ron had told him that the rooms to the left of the entrance door were purely guest rooms. The other side of the stairs was used by the three "hostesses" at the hotel. People were rarely disturbed though. There was a small bar and a few tables where Ron said they served food, but he said Pete's Café was much better.

Feeling clean helped wash a bit of the exhaustion off Max, and he left the hotel in good spirits, considering his wounds. The weight of his new purchases was unfamiliar on his waist. He felt an odd mix of pride and self-consciousness about wearing them. He walked three doors down to Pete's. The place was busy. Those not eating were drinking, and there was a smell of roasting meat drifting from a door in the back. Max saw Ron sitting at a table near the wall away from the bar. He sat down in the other chair.

Ron nodded to his belt holding the two guns. "He treat you well?"

"He did, so supper and drinks are on me."

"Hope you don't mind I ordered for you. They were gonna stop cooking soon, so I ordered an elk steak for you."

Max nodded. "That's good with me."

Ron nodded to the bottle on the table, then started to pour into the two glasses. "This is good stuff — not that rot gut. Thought it might help some of the pain that comes with that eye and arm."

Max nodded and took the glass. "The eye's been causing me a dull headache all damn day, but the arm's just starting to itch like hell." He knocked back his shot and poured each of them another.

"Where you from originally, Max?"

"East Texas, near the Louisiana border, but the last six years was spent in different mining camps from Texas to Kansas to outside of Trinidad most recently."

"So you were a miner . . . in Trinidad?"

"Yep, until Newton went under."

"That man that was shot by a young

miner who had suspected his friend was killed by the other?"

"That was me."

"That's why you were trying a new job. I see." Ron stopped as the middle-aged woman brought out the plates. The elk steaks took nearly half the plate; the other half was sliced potatoes and green beans. Max thanked the woman and started carving his meat.

"Well," Ron began after sticking a fork load of potatoes in his mouth, "that means you've done some hard labor. Turns out . . ."

Ron stopped and looked up at the man who now stood over their table. Max looked up to see that it was very large, red-haired man, grinning down at him through his thick beard. "You got your ass kicked, didn't you?"

"I suppose so." Max looked to Ron, who looked up at the man.

"It was a misunderstanding with a big bounty hunter."

"Really? Was he bigger than me?"

Max refrained from commenting that Sutter was smaller but smarter and leaned away from the man, who was obviously drunk and looking for trouble. "Not quite."

Ron held up his hand. "Come on, Jim, we're just wanting to eat."

Jim held out his hand. "Why don't you buy me a drink and I'll go away?"

Max sat there, not saying anything, but his blood was beginning to boil.

"Jim!" someone called from the back, and a stocky, blond-haired man came out from behind a door. The serving woman watched from that door.

Jim looked back at the man. "Stay out of this, Pete. It's between me and my new friend."

Jim turned back as Max pulled the hammer back on the new Colt. Jim froze, staring down the barrel of the gun.

"Now, Jim, you're probably not this much of an asshole when you're not drunk, so I won't put a bullet between your eyes, unless you want to continue this conversation."

Max's voice had shaken when he spoke, and Jim looked at him and started to sneer.

"He already killed two men who tried to rob him today, Jim," Ron told the man. "Not to mention a murdering horse thief a few days ago in Trinidad. He will pull the trigger."

Jim stepped back and shook his head. "Without that gun, you'd get another beating."

"So, you are wanting to continue this conversation?" Max asked.

106

"Eat your food." Jim walked back to the bar, and Max uncocked his gun and put it back into the belt on his side. Max glanced back and saw Pete giving him a disapproving look before he headed back into the kitchen.

"You were going to shoot him, weren't you?"

Max looked back across the table. "I don't know. I didn't want to get beat up again."

Ron looked over to the bar. "Jim is different when he's not drinking, but he is drinking most of the time now. He was a part of the Santa Fe Rail's security team until their war ended with the Denver Rail. He worked on the rail as they passed through here until they fired him for being drunk in the mornings when they started working."

Max shrugged but glanced over to make sure Jim was staying put. "What were you saying before?" He put a big chunk of meat into his mouth and chewed. It tasted so good. He realized how hungry he had been.

"Oh, turns out I may have some work for ya." Ron looked back towards the bar. "If you can keep from killing someone. I don't want to be involved in that."

"I don't really want to be involved in that either, but I didn't think I was gonna have a choice." He sighed. "Ron, I was scared."

The two men stared at each other a moment, and Ron nodded his head. "Some of the cattlemen want to bring their cattle to the train for shipping. The men from around Cimarron don't like bringing them to Springerville — old bad blood still there. We'll need a large pen to keep them in to wait for the train, and a smaller one for extra horses that come with them, and I have space next to the livery. There's a lot by the rail in Raton, but they carry a hefty charge. We'll have at least a couple of weeks to build it before the first small herd from Cimarron is brought. You in?"

"How much?"

"Room and board for you and Hardy, plus fifty dollars when it's done. Then if you help watch the cattle and deal with the ranchers when they bring them in, I'll pay ya a couple dollars a day of work. It will probably run until the cold really sets in."

Max thought about it a moment, then nodded agreement.

"Take a couple of days to recover first, and I'll need to clear a spot for ya in my little house, but then you can start getting the wood. There's some left from some of the original building in Raton, and I've made a deal with the man to buy it."

Max wiped his mouth. "It's been a long

time since I had elk. It's good." He remembered his father bringing home deer. Elk was lean and tasty. That combined with the potatoes, green beans, and bread was a feast for Max. He and Ron talked about food that they had lived on in the past. In his early years in Willow Springs Ron lived mainly off of potatoes. They were inexpensive and filling.

Ron pointed to the corner table, stating that when it was not prime dining hours, they were allowed to play poker at that table. That was where supposedly Gary had lost several times to Ron, including a bet for eleven dollars that Gary conveniently remembered as ten.

After finishing their food, and a good portion of the bottle, Max paid the four-dollar bill, and they parted ways. Max was exhausted, and, upon locking the door to his room, he fell into bed and was asleep almost instantly.

CHAPTER 6

The next morning, Max's head was fuzzy, and his black eye itched, but the swelling was much less. He rolled over and fell back to sleep for nearly another hour. When he woke the next time, he pulled an apple out of his bag and laid there thinking about his job through the end of summer. That was not for today though. Max took the water skin from the top of his bag and took a long drink. He sat up and took his Colts, unloading them and taking them apart as he would to clean them, then putting them back together. He did not load them. He put on the belt and practiced pulling them out, cocking and aiming. He was far from fast, but he had read in a book that did not over-romanticize everything that fast was over-rated in comparison to accuracy. It made sense. Despite a sore head and jaw he felt pretty good. He had not slept so long since he was a small boy with pneumonia.

It was nearly noon when Max pulled on his boots and grabbed his bags to head to the stables. Ron was talking to a guy about Max's age, who was looking at the dappled horse Max had sold Ron the night before. Max waved and went into the stable to saddle Hardy.

He was among some brush about twenty minutes from town when he found the spot he wanted. Using pieces of the shirt he'd torn the day before, he hung three thick strips weighted with sticks from a long branch woven through the bottom.

He pulled out one of his new Colts, loaded the six chambers, and emptied it at one of the targets from thirty feet away. Only two hits. He pulled the other and shot at the second target. Three hits.

He reloaded both and did the same thing, managing four hits with the first gun, but only three with the second. Sighing, he put both into the belt and practiced pulling, cocking, and aiming before reloading.

He managed only three hits between both guns on his first attempt, but after reloading again he managed five. He stopped there, feeling good about his improvement and not wanting to use more ammunition. It was a start. If he could do this a couple of times a week he could be decent. He might even try bounty hunting again after his job with Ron ended. He sure would feel better traveling the roads. He reloaded each chamber again before heading back to town.

After brushing down and feeding Hardy, he went to a store and bought a new shirt before going to Ron's to take him up on his supper invitation. The stew was good, and Max was glad when they drank water as opposed to whiskey. Ron filled him in more on what they would be doing for the cattle corral and told Max to enjoy his Sunday rest the next day because he would be working hard after that.

Max did enjoy his rest on Sunday. He stayed in the hotel room and read, cleaned his guns, and took a nap. He met Ron at Pete's for a late afternoon supper of roasted lamb and then moved his belongings to the pallet in a corner of Ron's main room.

Ron had talked to the town council and received approval to cut down a few of the trees near the northern edge of town. The man in Raton that had the extra wood was going to give a try at producing lumber. He had some saw experience and a teenage son who would help him. In order for them to receive the wood for the fencing, Max would have to replace it with raw wood.

That was where Max spent Monday, axe

in hand. He'd brought down many trees in his time for support beams for the mines when shaped lumber was not handy. By afternoon, the sun brought the temperature up to the hottest of the year, and he was not used to the sun. It was a trade-off, the sun for fresh air. He'd just decided that he would take the fresh air and the heat and leave the cover and stuffiness of the mines for others when people started coming to where he was working, asking what he was doing. Three trees were down, and people were curious.

"I am cutting the trees down for wood for the corral to hold livestock."

"Yes, we received permission to do this. It was from the town council. No, I don't know who will be keeping their livestock there. Yes, I am new in town. Yes, I do work for Ron. Watch out, I'm bringing down this tree."

When he worked underground, people didn't happen by and ask questions. He answered most of them to each person who stopped by. He set to the trees with a saw in the afternoon. Ron came and helped for a time before going back to tend to things at the stable.

It was a hard day's work, but Max felt good using his muscles all day again. He devoured the ham and beans that Ron made that night on his stove. The next couple days were similar. He made quicker work of the trees the second and third day, partly due to fewer questions, but mostly due to falling into the rhythm of what he was doing. On Thursday and Friday he used a couple of mules to haul the wood he'd cut to the man who owned a building not far from the stables. On Saturday morning he hauled the first load of shaped lumber back to where the corral would be built. He had begun putting the posts into the ground. Ron was happy with their progress, and he and Max went to Pete's Café for supper that night.

They had beef steak, tomatoes, and corn bread, along with a couple of glasses of beer. Ron told him his father's stories of trapping in the area when he was younger than Max and there was little else around aside from Santa Fe. His father had supposedly run across Hugh Glass on his way out west.

Max had heard the story of Hugh Glass before but listened to Ron tell it. Hugh Glass was famous for his trek across nearly a hundred miles after being mauled by a mother grizzly while out trapping nearly sixty years earlier. Although badly slashed by the bear's claws he managed to kill the bear. Different versions of the story credited

Glass for killing the bear with his hunting knife, or with his rifle, while some said his hunting partners came to the rescue. Regardless, he put up one hell of a fight. He was left for dead by two of his fellow hunters while he lay unconscious. When he woke, his back was so badly ripped open that his ribs showed. He set his own broken leg. He also lay on a rotting tree so the maggots would eat the dead flesh to prevent gangrene. He mostly crawled back to civilization. He was aided by friendly Indians, who sewed a bear hide to his back to cover the wounds.

"That story again, Ron." Pete's wife, Maggie, put two more beers on the table. "You could at least tell your own stories and not those of a man your father met."

"I don't have many of my own. I live a safe life and like it that way." Ron continued the story as Maggie walked off shaking her head. He told Max that Hugh Glass finally reached Fort Kiowa on the Missouri and, after a long recovery, set out for revenge against those who left him for dead. He ended up sparing them, one because he was very young and the other because he had joined the army, and killing him would have put a death mark on Glass. The man had been tougher than the grizzly he wrestled with.

Max thought about his father again.

"You all right, Max? Your face just sagged like ya heard bad news."

"Yeah, that story just reminded me of someone. They were obviously no Hugh Glass."

Ron almost asked but stopped and held up his beer mug. "To those who made it in the wilderness and those who didn't. They braved it all the same."

Max bumped his mug against Ron's, and they both took a long drink. Ron was right. Brave all the same to go out into it. Max reflected at the moment that he was truly happy.

Max was sitting facing the door and saw Jim walk in. He was wearing his gun on his hip now, and he gave Max a grin and a nod of his head as he walked to the bar. Max closed his eyes. Nothing lasts. He casually reached down and eased his gun so that it was loose in his holster.

Ron's gaze followed Jim, so he did not notice Max's motion. He looked back at Max and shrugged, before digging into his food again. Max ate also but did not find the food as enjoyable. He glanced over his shoulder and saw Jim laughing with a

116

cowboy up at the bar. When he turned back he saw a woman walk through the door. She stood nearly as tall as Max, with wavy, dark hair, stunning green eyes, and full lips. Her blue dress with white dots was just tight enough to show her slim waist, accented by the curves of her hips and chest. Max then realized the young woman was with a well-dressed, tall, graying man who had entered with her, and his ice-blue eyes glared at Max.

Max averted his eyes as Ron turned to see what had caught his attention. Ron turned back and smiled. He leaned in and lowered his voice. "She's very easy on the eyes, huh? They came and stabled their horses with us earlier. Fine animals; brought them in via the train they rode in on. They are making their way to Cimarron tomorrow. He was through a few years back I think. Must be why he stayed here instead of Raton — more familiar."

Max nodded and saw them take a table near the door. He didn't need to turn around to know that they — or more precisely she — had drawn the attention of everyone. Maggie may have been the only other attractive woman Max had seen in Pete's the three times he had eaten here. She had aged well and drew the eye of many of the men who spent too much time with his fellow workers. But she was middle-aged, married, and likely had never brought a room full of men to a buzz like this.

Max took another two bites of his steak, suddenly feeling hungrier. Maggie went to the couple's table to let them know that their choice was steak or ribs. The man greeted her, asking her name, and then he introduced himself as Jeff McNulty, and his daughter, Sara. He asked if they had wine and ordered the red table wine that was available along with two steaks.

He seemed like a good man, protective of his daughter as was understandable, and pleasant with those he dealt with. Max liked him. He stabbed his fork into the stewed tomatoes and enjoyed the juice as the flavor wet his mouth.

He and Ron finished their meal and turned down a third beer. Ron did tell him a story of his father's. He had been dressing an elk and was down on one knee. He had grabbed his rifle to push himself up when he heard several taps behind him. He spun around just in time to see that the taps were the approaching footfalls of a mountain lion, and he grabbed for the trigger of the rifle and squeezed it. The mountain lion knocked him down, scratching his shoulder and chest, but he found out the big cat was dead after he fearfully scrambled, hitting it and pushing it off him. It was as much luck as anything that saved him.

After that Ron's father brought the elk and cougar pelts and meat back east to Lawrence, Kansas, sold them, cleaned up, and went to call on Jennifer Kacey, as he felt like he should ride that luck and go after what was important to him. Less than a year later, Russell and Jennifer Stark had a son they named Ron, and here he sat nearly forty years later.

Ron looked up, and Max followed his gaze. Jim was walking, a little unsteadily, from the bar towards the McNulty table. Max and Ron looked at each other. They both were guessing what was coming.

Jim stopped, and Sara glanced up but put her head back down, dabbing her mouth with her napkin. Jeff McNulty looked up and nodded to the large man. "Hello, what can I do for you?"

Jim patted McNulty on the shoulder. "Nothing. Pardon my interruption, but I just wanted to get a better look at this beauty that has come into Willow Springs."

Sara glanced up and then looked down. "Thank you for the compliment, sir."

"Yes, thank you," her father said, then

looked back down, cutting into his steak. "Have a good evening." When Jim stayed there, McNulty looked up, and those icy blue eyes glared at Jim. "Was there something else?"

Jim looked confused for a second that he was not being placated. He then leaned down a bit. "Do you think because you wear those fancy clothes we are all servants to be dismissed so easily?"

Ron stood up. "Jim, easy now."

Jim stuck his hand out, pointing. "Ron, you are going to piss me off one too many times! I'm not talking to you, but to this man and his daughter, with the sugar down under her dress."

McNulty's face changed to rage, and he stood, head butting Jim as he did so. He moved quicker than Max would have thought. He threw a left cross, followed by a right uppercut that sent Jim staggering back. He stepped forward to throw another right, but Jim barely dodged it and grabbed the man, spinning and throwing him. McNulty caught his foot on the floor enough to take a couple of steps but stumbled forward into Max and Ron's table, knocking it over. Jim stepped forward, but the cowboy he had been talking to grabbed one arm, and Ron stepped forward grabbing the other. Max stepped up to help as did Pete, running from the back.

Between the four of them they shoved Jim out the front door. Pete yelled after him, "You cannot come in here anymore if you're going to drink!"

When Max turned around, McNulty was pushing himself to his feet. Sara was helping, a tear streaming down her cheek. "I'm all right, dear," her father told her. He nodded to the four. "Thank you."

"Don't mention it," the cowboy told him and tipped his hat to Sara before walking back to his drink.

McNulty straightened his coat and looked no worse for wear when he sat back down. When Sara sat back down across from him he smiled and patted her hand. Then he went back to his food as if nothing had happened. He did stop and call to Maggie as she crossed the room. After, she came to Max and Ron's table, which they had put back upright, to let them know that Mr. McNulty insisted that it would be his honor to pay for their bill as well as the cowboy's. Ron made to argue, but Maggie said that the man made her promise that she'd let him pay. Ron looked to the man and nodded, mouthing "thank you," and the man lowered his head and raised his glass to him.

Something in that moment touched Max to the point that tears almost formed in his eyes. These two men had gained his admiration, which was rare. Aside from Clay, there were few men he could truly say as much of.

As they left Pete's the voice of a yelling man drew their stares down the street. It was dark, but they saw the silhouettes of three men pulling another towards Raton. Obscenities and threats were being yelled, and Max was sure it was the voice of the large man, who must be Jim.

Ron sighed. "That's a shame. Looks like the sheriff was called for. Jim's got some good qualities when he's not heavy in the drink."

Max shrugged. "I've never seen them."

"Maybe you will. You're like a lot of men. You've seen a lot more bad in people than good."

"I've seen good, but some people are just bad."

Ron clapped him on the shoulder. "You wanna go to church in the morning? We won't be working on Sundays around Willow Springs."

"I think I'll pass, rest and relax."

"If you change your mind, you should come. There's a lot of cute girls from out on the homesteads. Plus, I'd bet that Mr. McNulty and Sara will attend before riding out."

Max looked at him. "Is that the reason I should be going to church?"

"One of many."

"I'll think about it."

Max slept in the next day. He heard Ron leaving but stayed in bed a bit longer, before rising and saddling Hardy and riding out to his clearing for target practice. He was reloading for one more round of practice when he heard horses and turned quickly. Three men rode into the clearing.

The older man in front waved. "We were just riding in to see what the shooting was about. Didn't expect anyone to be out shooting right after church."

Max holstered his pistol and waved, walking up. "I'm Max Tillman, temporarily working in Willow Springs."

"Ron Stark's man. Heard you were a good worker."

"And dangerous with iron," one of the ranch hands offered from behind him.

Max shrugged. "Maybe I'm just lucky." He knew that was the real case.

The older man bent down, offering his hand. "Charlie Alden." After shaking his hand the man threw his head back to the road. "We have to get back to the women, but it was good to meet ya."

"You, too, sir."

Max waited until they were out of sight before he pulled his first pistol and cock and pull, cock and pull, six times. He hit the target five. He holstered and pulled the other pistol, scoring four hits with that one.

He was getting better. Smiling, he reloaded the pistols and mounted Hardy, pulling his rifle from his saddle. He would now look for his and Ron's supper.

He rode through the brush with the barrel of his rifle resting on his shoulder. He scanned the ground for movement. It was a good ten minutes before he saw his first squirrel. He was too slow, and while moving to aim the squirrel ran into a hole. Max sighed, and, as he turned Hardy he saw movement. Twenty yards away a large rabbit moved along the ground. Max aimed and the rabbit went behind a tree. Max aimed at the spot just the other side of the tree. As soon as he saw movement, he squeezed off a round and hit the rabbit in the side of the head. Max patted the side of Hardy's neck. He was used to being a mounted hunter from years of riding out with Ricky.

Max led the horse over to retrieve the rabbit. He held it up and let most of the blood run from the wound. He stuffed it in a sack he pulled from his saddle and rode for town. He and Ron ate rabbit and beans that night. Neither seemed talkative. That was odd for Ron, but Max assumed the man had his quiet times as well, and he retired early.

Early the next morning Max took two buckets to the well at the center of the old town. He would need to make two more trips to have enough for the horses in the stables, then another for his and Ron's water.

A woman was making her way to the well at the same time. She was a couple of years younger than Max, with dark-red hair and a charming smile. "Ladies first." Max pumped the water into the bucket she laid at the spout.

"Thank you, Mr. . . ."

"Tillman, Max Tillman. You can call me Max."

She giggled. "I'm Kayla." She held her hand out.

Max took it gently. "Pleased to make your acquaintance. May I carry this back for you?" He stood with the bucket, but she shook her head and took it.

"No thank you, Max. I appreciate the

chivalry, but I will leave you to your work for the stables."

Max could not think of what to say before the attractive woman walked off. "So, you know where I work." He began when she was out of earshot. "Have you been watching me? Why would you do that?"

A man laughed behind him, and he turned to see Ron there with two more buckets. "Kayla is a fair girl, lad, but she is the daughter of the freight man, who's been here a while; almost has his big house in Raton finished. He's done well for himself and is hard on his daughter's suitors."

Max turned and looked toward the house that Kayla entered. "I hear ya."

Ron clapped him on the shoulder. "Thanks for bringing in the rabbit yesterday."

Max nodded. "Sorry it wasn't more."

"It was plenty with the beans. No need for you to be sorry. I'm sorry I was so quiet." Ron sighed. "Watch out, Max. I think Big Jim is pissed at both of us, and I'm not sure what he'll do."

Max looked at him, and Ron shrugged. "I didn't want to tell ya last night. Thought you might get pissed and do something stupid, but then last night I realized you may be in danger, too. Jim strode by yesterday while you were out. He threw a rock and nearly hit me. Then yelled that I wouldn't know when it was coming, but it would come."

"Over the other night?"

"I guess so. Between that and his getting arrested, his temper has been set afire."

Max nodded and realized he did not have his holster around his waist. "Let's get this water back."

After taking care of the horses and eating some corn bread for breakfast Max went back to work on the corral. Clouds were rolling in, and Max fought the urge to work quickly. Speed was not going to exactly space the posts for the crossbeams.

It was not long after he started working that he heard the rumble of the train coming in from the pass. He looked up and watched it come downhill as he had several mornings. The engine pulled one passenger car and four cargo cars. Three of the cargo loads were flat, stacked with rail ties and steel rail. It slowed as it made its way into Raton, passing behind the buildings in the distance.

Max wondered about conductor work on the rail as he heard the locomotive idle down. There would be a postman at the station ready to gather the bag of mail. Max thought about what opportunities there might be for him aside from mining, or hunting down wanted men. He had never considered anything but mining all those years with Clay.

Max continued to bore the holes in the fence posts to build the gate. They had thick leather straps to put in place to hinge the gate. He became lost in the work, and when darkness came upon him, he was putting up the gate. He fastened it and looked at the corral with one gate and half the posts not up. Those would go quick though. He turned for Ron's house. Kayla was sitting on a sawhorse that he had been using earlier.

"So, you've been watching me. Why would you do that?" The words came out without him thinking.

Kayla giggled. "Because you are new and interesting, and not crude like some of the men who are around."

Max nodded. "I hope I'm not. I have spent a fair amount of time around rough men, though."

"Explains the black eye when you came into town," she chided and went on without missing a beat. "So, Max, what will you do when this corral is finished?"

"I'll work with Ron a while longer while I figure out my next move."

"No idea what your next move is? You are one of those wandering adventurers."

Max smiled, and he stopped just short of laughing.

"What?" Kayla's voice was sharp now.

"No, I'm just a guy looking for work and taking what's available." Her frown deepened. "What did I say?"

She shrugged. "You just don't paint a very promising picture to a girl you want to court."

"Court? Well I . . ." She raised an eyebrow at him, and he closed his mouth. "I am thinking of maybe trying to get a job for the railroad, conducting or keeping track of the freight."

A smirk crossed her lips. "Oh, so now you're using me to have my father put in a good word."

"No, that's not it at all. I didn't think of that."

"Hmm. I'm going to have to go home and rethink this. Good night, Max Tillman."

"Good night, Kayla. I hope you enjoyed busting my chops."

She turned smiling at him. "It was amusing."

Max smiled. He was fairly sure she was flirting with him and not making fun of him. Well, at least not to be mean. He walked towards the barn, thinking of Kayla.

Ron was there brushing down a white horse that was new to the stables. "Wanna go to Pete's tonight?"

"Sure. Is there a reason aside from not wanting to cook?"

"Food's ready inside. We'll go after. Don Holbrook's in town. Man is like a performer to watch when gamblin'. Pete, he isn't that big on gamblin', but Don's got a charm that Pete gives into. It's gonna be crowded, so let's go eat."

"His horse?"

"Yep."

"Good horse."

"He said the same about Hardy when he looked around the stables. When he's not gambling, he trades some in horses. He's got a good eye."

They washed their hands quickly and ate the meal, potatoes with a few chunks of beef. It was good, and Max felt his weariness from the day's work disappearing.

Max had a big chunk of potato in his mouth when Ron spoke. "So, looks like you will be courting Kayla after all."

Max started coughing, and, after several seconds of chewing fast to swallow, he said, "What are you talking about?"

"I warned you that it might not be a good

idea to pursue her, but it looks like it's the other way around. I don't know how much her father could have to say about that. Although from what I understand he had John Alden picked out for her."

"Charlie Alden's son?"

"Yeah. You know Charlie?"

"Met him Sunday while I was out hunting."

"Good man. Got a good ranch."

Max nodded. "I really don't know what my plans are, Ron."

Ron laughed. "Sometimes it doesn't matter what your plans are. The world has a way of making them for you. I'd say if it isn't bad, then why not go along?"

Max looked to the side, thinking a bit. "I wouldn't put Kayla on the list of bad things."

"I never thought you were dumb."

"Aww, thanks, Ron, but save your sweet talk for the women."

Ron smiled. "It takes you a bit of time to loosen up and show yourself, doesn't it? You may be more sarcastic than me, ya smart-mouthed son of a bitch."

Max smirked. "I doubt it, Ron. Anyway, how do you know it's not you rubbing off on me? So this Don Holbrook ever beat ya bad in cards?"

131

Ron sighed. "Sure did. Lost a good horse to him once. Of course, it was his to start with. Sold it to me, then somehow I got goaded into playing against him."

"Think he cheats?"

"Only if you consider verbally confusing and frustrating the hell out of his opponents cheating. You'll see. He does make a lot of people sitting opposite him angry."

"Where's he from?"

"Back East. I think Virginia or Tennessee maybe. You can ask him when you meet him." Ron stood and put his empty plate in the dishwater. Max stuffed the bite of beef he'd saved for last in his mouth and brought the plates over and washed them both quickly while Ron scrubbed the cooking pan. Ron seemed to step a little more lively. Max was interested in seeing this gambler.

CHAPTER 7

When Ron and Max walked into Pete's, the tables were arranged differently. One of the bigger tables was back toward the kitchen by itself, where people at the small bar could easily watch. There were people eating, but already seven people stood near the table watching. Five sat at the table with only a sixth seat left. The lanky man in the white shirt with the dark-brown vest must have been Holbrook. He had a neatly trimmed salt and pepper beard that matched his full head of hair. His eyes seemed to smile, although his mouth did not. He bent his head slightly to the man next to him, and the man's mouth was tightened in frustration. Pete came out carrying two plates, pausing to glance at the table before squeezing past to a table at the front of the café where a father and son sat.

"Max?"

Max turned around to the calling of his

name, and the man who had just had his food delivered looked him over. He was dressed like a merchant, nice but not like a politician or judge. He was middle aged and a bit thick around the waist. "May I have a quick word?"

It did not seem like a request, but Max looked to Ron and was nodded on so he went.

"I'm Thomas Fleshman, and this is Dean, my son." The son looked Max over as if considering whether he was a thief or not.

Max reached out his hand and shook each of theirs. "Max Tillman. Good to meet you."

"I'm glad you think so. This may be a bit awkward, but I've heard mixed things about you, and I was wanting to judge for myself."

"You . . . Why?"

Fleshman chuckled. "I'm Kayla's father."

A heavy sinking feeling hit Max's stomach. "Oh, very nice to meet you! Your daughter's very beautiful, and quick, I mean smart . . . sharp with her mind."

Fleshman sighed. "Yes, she is. Very strong willed, too. She actually helps a lot with the detailed work of my business. She speaks very well of you. Says you are a hard worker and that your reputation is not fully your responsibility."

"I don't believe it is, sir, and I've worked

134

hard since I was able. No other way to be sure you have a job."

Fleshman nodded. "I like that. If I'm going to consider hiring you to work with me and the train, I hope you mean it."

"Sir, I appreciate that, but I really was not trying to get a job by talking with your daughter. Don't get me wrong; once my work with Mr. Stark is done, I'd love to work for you, but I don't want it to be for the wrong reasons."

Fleshman leaned back. "What reason do you think I'm hiring you?"

"Because . . ." Max tried to think of the best way to put it. "Well, it should be purely because you need a man, and you think I will work out better than any other."

"Are you saying that there will not be any other connection between you and us?"

It was Max's turn to sigh. "No, I'm not sure of that yet. I'm sort of confused about what all this means, but I just wouldn't want any special treatment."

Fleshman smiled. "I admire that, and I like you, and now that we've spoken, I think you would be a good candidate. We should need somebody real soon." Fleshman looked to Dean, and then outside for a moment. "I've been trying to convince Kayla that I knew who the best choice for her future was, and she has humored me at best with that but has been fairly uninterested in him. As a matter of fact, she has shown little interest in anyone. But she's always gone after what she really wants, and she's decided she really wants to get to know you." He looked back at Max. "I can see you are interested by how you stumble over yourself about it, not to mention, I know she's a grown woman now and attracts most men's interest. I'm willing to see what you're really like and see how this goes."

"Plus, he likes the fact that you're shy around her," Dean added smugly.

Fleshman gave his son a glare. "Yes, there is that as well." He looked back to Max. "Will you and Mr. Stark consider joining us on a walk to church on Sunday, and then to dinner at our place after?"

Max nodded nervously. "That sounds great, sir."

"Good. I'll tell my wife to plan on guests. We'll see you then."

Max turned around and walked over to the bar. Ron turned sideways so Max could squeeze into a place and handed Max a beer he ordered.

Each man had their two cards face down in front of him. And they had just laid down the three in the middle of the table. Holbrook chuckled and raised the pot three dollars.

The young cowboy next to him peeked at his two cards again, as if he did not know what was underneath. He sighed and pushed his two cards away. "Fold."

The man next to him — a local rancher, Max thought — looked at the younger man with raised eyebrows and then turned back and threw in three dollars. Mike, the blond-haired local gambler, tossed three bucks out without even looking up. Gary, the shop owner, looked at each man in turn, then folded. He reached out and flipped the next card out of the deck face up with the other three in the middle of the table. That jack of clubs went right next to the jack of diamonds. The other two cards were the four and six of hearts. Holbrook looked at the cards, tapping his lip. Max thought it a show of trying to decide, although Max figured he already knew. Holbrook checked, not raising. The rancher smiled and threw another couple of dollars onto the pot. Mike shook his head and threw in a couple of dollars. Holbrook's check hit right after.

The next card was an ace of hearts. Holbrook steepled his fingers for a moment, his right pointer finger tapping the other. He let out a small breath. "Check."

The rancher pulled five more dollars and tossed them into the pot. Mike looked at Holbrook a moment and then reached into his stack and threw out five.

Holbrook leaned back and looked relaxed as he tossed out five and then five more. The rancher nodded and checked. Mike looked like he was waiting for the rancher to raise, but when he did not, he let out a sigh but put his five in the same. Then he flipped over his cards as if he already knew he had not won. He had a four of spades and a six of clubs. His hand was two pairs . . . jacks and sixes.

The rancher smiled and turned his cards over, a jack of hearts and king of spades. Three jacks was usually a winning hand, but Max looked to Holbrook, who said the same out loud, then turned over his cards, a king and two of hearts. He had an ace high heart flush. The rancher looked nearly sick, and Mike just shook his head again.

With the original half-dollar blind put in by each man, there was forty-seven and a half dollars in the pot Holbrook pulled into his stack, a thirty-two dollar gain in one hand. The next three hands he won twenty-three dollars when everyone folded, lost nineteen dollars when his pair of threes lost to the young cowboy's two pair, and won sixty-seven dollars when Mike's three aces were beat by his full house, tens over aces.

Max looked at Ron. "He's won more in a few hands than most men make in a month."

Ron nodded. "He has more good nights than bad, but the bad can be pretty bad."

Holbrook looked toward them. "Don't jinx me, Ron. Buy me a whiskey instead."

"You should buy me one with your winnings."

Ron nodded to the bartender and then took the drink over to him. "Remember, beer after this. I've seen what too much whiskey does to your game."

Holbrook held up his glass to Ron in salute and then downed it.

"I know when I'm outmatched." Gary stood.

The cowboy nodded. "I'm stopping while I'm ahead."

"Good thinking, Joey," the rancher said but stayed in his seat.

"Gentlemen," Holbrook said pleadingly. "I will drink more whiskey if you like."

"Thanks for the game," Gary told him.

Ron looked around and then whispered to Max. "Looks like nobody else wants to risk it. Most who live around here have heard about Don, if not seen him play themselves.

There's a couple of strangers here, though. Must not have the money to gamble."

Holbrook shrugged. "There are a couple of extra seats . . . Ron?"

Ron shook his head, and Holbrook motioned to a clean-shaven man dressed nearly as well as Holbrook in a light-blue shirt and dark-brown pants. "How about you, sir? You look like you know a deck of cards."

"Not tonight. Maybe another time."

"A game of cards, sir?" Holbrook called toward the door.

It was Jim approaching the bar. He eyed the table. "You cheated me out of money last time you were here. Not going for it again."

"That is a heinous thing to say because you did not win."

Jim glared at him for a moment before ordering a whiskey. The bartender held up his hands. "Sorry, Jim, but I was told not to serve you any spirits."

Jim looked at him and then glared down the bar at Ron and Max like it was their doing. He glanced back toward the door, and Max saw that the middle-aged sheriff was eating at the table Kayla's father and brother had occupied earlier. The sturdy lawman was watching Jim wearily. Jim growled and turned, his arm thumping a seated patron's head as he stormed back out.

"That is one sore loser," Holbrook commented, passing the cards to the rancher to deal.

Ron sighed and leaned back. Mike and the rancher quit after three more hands, and Holbrook's winnings grew by nearly twenty dollars. The cards were put away, and Ron, Pete, and Max joined the other three men at the table. Holbrook did buy a round for the table, and he began telling the table of his trip to Tip Top, a mining town in Arizona. He played out how he had gone from losing nearly all his money to leaving the table five hundred dollars richer, and in that week he'd left with nearly thirteen hundred dollars. He had lost a bet on a horse race, in which he was the rider. He admitted that it was his lack of skill as a rider, and not the fault of his top-line horse. That led to him giving Ron a hard time about the horse that he had sold him and then won back from him.

Then the talk turned to horses, which Keith the rancher joined enthusiastically. He wanted to breed horses but had not sunk the money into the initial breeders he wanted. He wanted to cross a strong quarter horse with a good pure Spanish or Hungarian breed to produce a hardy horse to handle the back country.

Don offered to stud out his Hungarian half-breed for a fee if Keith had the mare. They started talking about the possibilities and the places where they could get good horses to breed in the region. Gary said that he knew a man that claimed he would put his mustang against any other horse in a race and did not see Don roll his eyes but then talked about a "Kinsky" horse he'd seen; thought perhaps it was Russian. "It was a big, strong, fast, horse. Maybe one of the best all-around horses I'd ever seen," he told them.

"Why didn't you buy it?" Pete asked.

"Or win it," Ron added.

"Wasn't for sale, and the man was not a gambler. He was a wealthy immigrant I met in San Francisco, my one time out there."

Max sat back, enjoying the conversation, but he left the others for bed after the fourth round, leaving Don, Ron, and Keith to their plans that had grown into a grand horse ranch in Colorado by this point. Walking toward the house by the stables he looked back and saw a large shadowed silhouette, with his arms crossed, looking at him intensely, he thought. Max stopped, turning around to face the man. The man did not move. Max sighed and turned back and walked to the house. He fought the urge to look back, but he listened intently, expecting to hear footfalls behind him. He rounded the corner of the Boones' house and turned, looking back when he reached Ron's door. Nobody. He sighed and laughed at himself before unlocking the door and heading straight to his pallet.

He thought about Kayla, and meeting her family on Sunday. She was beautiful, and he liked her sarcastic humor. He could make a life here. He thought about making a good impression with her family, her father especially, but told himself he had until Sunday to worry about that and rolled over, closing his eyes.

Max woke up to the sound of a horse outside. Another late arrival. The big stable doors were chained and locked when either Ron or he were not readily available. There were a few small holding pens outside and a couple of grooming brushes so that customers could leave their horses if they wanted, and Ron would put them in the stables later and collect when the owners came back.

Max did not hear Ron stirring so he started to stand. Something just did not feel right. Then the sound of a horse galloping down the street caused Max to rush to put on his boots. He grabbed his holstered gun, ran out of the house, and saw the stable doors wide open. "Ron!" he called into the house and ran to the front of the stable, looking down the street. He thought he could make out the horse and rider in the distance, but they faded into the night or rounded a corner. There was a man toward the end of the street watching the rider. Max ran into the stable and looked in the stalls. Right away he noticed Don's horse was missing.

He stepped back out and looked to the house. Where was Ron? He must have drunk a bit more after Max had left. Strapping on his belt and holster he looked quickly around the stables, making sure that there wasn't anyone else hiding inside. Then he shut the doors before he went in to wake Ron.

He stopped as he pulled the left door toward himself. The inside handle had the chain through it, and a bundle of keys hung from the lock. Max stared at them. It was a minute before he came out of his daze. He pulled the door shut and locked the chain through the two handles, then turned and ran out the side door only big enough for a man, just throwing it shut.

He ran in the house and checked Ron's room. The bed was empty. "No!" He was out the door and around the neighbor's fence when he saw a man kneeling down by the side of the hotel. As he got closer to the alley, Keith glanced back. "Joey went to get the doctor."

The rancher was putting pressure on Ron's gut. Ron looked barely conscious. Max knelt down beside him. "Ron, what happened?"

Ron looked up at him, and his voice came out weak and raspy. "Man robbed Don and . . . augh." He weakly reached toward his stomach. Max noticed that his shirt was wet with red. The blood smelled heavy in the air.

"Looks like a stab wound," Keith told him. He nodded his head down the alley.

Max's gaze followed, and he saw another man lying there. As his eyes focused he recognized Don's clothes. Max stepped towards him.

"He's dead," Keith said. "Throat's cut."

Footsteps sounded, and Joey was running back. "Doc says that there's nothing he can do in the street. Get him to his place, and he'll tend him, there."

"Damn it! We can wrap the wound at least, stop the bleeding."

Max pulled his shirt off and extended it to Keith.

"No, I'll lift him. You wrap." Keeping one hand on the wound, Keith put his other underneath Ron and lifted. Ron grunted, and Max saw that he was unconscious now. He pulled the shirt underneath Ron, and they tied it to the side, the wide part covering the wound. "All right, let's get him there." Keith grabbed him at the shoulders, and Max bent down, hoisting him at the legs and hips from the side. They hurriedly walked across the stretch of open ground that led to the house that sat a quarter mile from the main buildings of Willow Springs. Joey hurried in front of them until Keith told him to go get the sheriff.

The doctor was a soft-looking man nearing his forties with only a few white hairs touching his dark mop of hair and beard. He looked like he knew what he was doing from how he took charge, though. He looked at Ron and shook his head. "Shirt cloth was rammed inside when he was stabbed; I need to get that out, but, worse, looks like something inside was nicked. Internal bleeding's bad. Martha!"

"Right here." The plain-looking redhead came in and grabbed a small net-like contraption that she stuffed with clean cloth.

"Good," the doctor said. "We need to stitch that bleeder quick. Get started."

146

She put the net-like contraption over Ron's face and began to lightly pour from the bottle in her other hand over the top.

The doctor looked at Max. "Get that window open to keep the ether from making me groggy."

Max pushed it open. He waited intently, watching, but the doctor just stood there. The doctor noticed his impatience and spoke while watching Ron. "I can't get in there until the ether's taken the full effect. If he wakes and thrashes from the pain, then I could tear him all up inside." He glanced at Max and Keith. "You two wash up your hands and arms over there in the corner. If you're gonna stay you can hold him down just in case."

There was a lot of blood, and, when the doctor started, opening up Ron more to find the bleeding veins, the smell of blood was as strong as the ether. Max was putting light pressure on Ron's left shoulder with Keith on the right. It seemed like forever before the doctor grabbed the needle and began to sew on something inside. He finished quickly though, then sewed up the wound on Ron's flesh. Max was relieved as the doctor finished the stitching, but then he felt the rise and fall of Ron's chest stop.

"No." He looked to the doctor.

Instantly the man stepped forward, then began to breathe into Ron's mouth and pump on his chest. Max just watched helplessly, trying to think of something he could do to help. This went on for a couple of minutes before the doctor stopped and stepped back, falling into the chair behind him exhausted.

"I'm sorry; I did my best."

"We know you did, Doc," Keith told him and put his hand on Max's shoulder. Max sat down on the floor. He did not feel like standing anymore. He buried his face in his arms over his knees. "Why?"

"To steal Holbrook's winnings and his horse." The sheriff was at the door when Max looked up. He was a tall, stocky man, with a thick, brown mustache, but clean-shaven otherwise.

"Who?"

"I saw him ride out of town heading southwest," Joey said. "Was the thin man with long, blond hair that had been standing at the end of the bar watching the game."

Sheriff nodded. "Must've been waiting for Holbrook by the hotel. Keep his face in your mind, Joey. Maggie can draw good. We'll get a picture drawn tomorrow."

"The horse, too," Max said numbly. "Hungarian half-breed, white with dark mane, looks like a racing horse."

"Hopefully the ownership certificate's in Holbrook's room." The sheriff looked at Max. "Proof for the town constable wherever he ends up."

Max stood. "Let's get after him!"

"Just a couple hours till it starts to get light. Once Maggie draws those pictures, then we can go after him. You can come, but get one thing straight: I'm in charge, and we're going to bring him back alive if possible."

"I'm coming, too," Keith told him. "How about Joey? He knows what the man looks like."

"So do I," Max said, looking to Joey. "Gray shirt with a small tear at the end of one sleeve?"

The young cowboy nodded. "Yeah, that's it."

Sheriff looked at Max. "All right. From what I hear you've hunted men before. Should make sure Ron's stable has got someone to run it, though. It'd be a shame if his life's work falls apart now."

Max sighed. He had not even thought about that.

CHAPTER 8

Max was leaning against the sheriff's office waiting to ride out of town less than an hour after sunrise. The sheriff was getting the pictures from Maggie. Gary and Pete together were going to see to the stables.

Gary had suggested that Max stay and do it himself. He said, "Ron liked you so well he would have left them to you, Max, had he known this would happen." Max had just shaken his head. He would go after blondie and see that he was captured and hung. Then he would decide about that.

"So, the little man got his, did he?"

Max looked over to see Jim standing at the end of the walk. In two quick bounds, he barreled into Jim, knocking him off the walkway. The big man fell back, landing on the dirt street. Max's boot clipped Jim's temple when he tried to rise, sending him onto his back again. Max was on top of him, fists pounding the man again and again, until he was hoisted back. The sheriff and Keith had hold of his arms. Jim lay bloodied and unconscious with his nose broken.

"Why'd you do that?"

"He mouthed off about Ron."

"You can't jump a man and try to beat him to death for words." The sheriff's fist clenched and unclenched, and he shook his head. "You'll sit in jail till we get back."

"No!" Max roared, pulling his arms and causing the men to tighten their grip.

"You're stronger than you look," Keith said. They hoisted him up and carried him into the office before sitting him in the jail and taking his guns.

"Max. I understand your being mad, and Jim is an asshole, but I can't let this go." With that the sheriff called to the deputy sitting at the desk. "He's here until we get back. If Jim's all right it'll be time served for battery. He was egged into it and extenuating circumstances and all. See that Jim gets to the doctor and Max pays for it."

"Come on, Sheriff, let me out." The door shut behind the man, and Max slumped down, back against the wall. "He had it coming!"

Max sighed and sat there, stewing. He threw his head back, hitting it on the wall, and the sensation through his head brought some release. He let out a long breath and thought about trying to find a way out. Have the deputy come close and grab him and the keys. That was stupid. He knew it. He would just have to wait it out. He likely had a full day or two in jail.

He pushed himself up and lay down on the thin mattress. He could feel the boards underneath, but it was no worse than lying on the ground with bumps and small rocks. He thought about Ron, trying to remember if he'd ever said anything about any cousins or such that should be contacted. He fell asleep at some point and awoke near noon. The deputy asked him if he wanted any lunch, and he shook his head and rolled over, closing his eyes again. The skies outside the window were darkening when he opened his eyes at the sound of his name.

He rolled over to see Thomas Fleshman standing there. "I'm sorry about Ron. I heard the two of you had become good friends."

"Thank you, sir."

"He was a good man, hard-working and honest. I hear they're thinking that you may inherit his business and house."

Max stood and walked to the bars. "I don't know about that. He's got other good friends here, like Pete and Gary. And I don't know about other family. I only knew him about a week."

"Yeah, but it doesn't take much time sometimes."

"I don't really know what my plans are now."

Fleshman nodded and stepped back, looking toward the window. "That's why I came to see you, boy. I think it best we put off you coming to our house."

"Oh. I . . . understand."

"Listen, from what I've heard that Jim has pushed you and Ron for a fight since you got here and probably deserved a beating. But the brutality of it . . ." Fleshman shook his head.

"How is he?"

"He's all right. Black and blue and breathing through his mouth right now, but he's awake and lucid."

Max sighed. "That's good."

"I find myself liking you, Max, but you need to understand: I don't feel comfortable with you courting Kayla. With your past, and that temper, and the brutality . . . It's . . ."

Max turned and walked back to the bed and lay down facing the wall. "I don't think I'll be staying anyway."

He heard Fleshman walk away, and then

153

the front door shut.

"You want some food?" the deputy called.

"No."

"You haven't eaten all day."

Max fell asleep again.

He woke while it was still dark out. He was hungry, but there was nobody in the office. He lay there staring at the ceiling, no longer able to sleep. Things had seemed to be going so good for him, until this man killed Ron and Don, taking their lives, and his life now suffered. He hoped the sheriff would return with the man in the morning, and that he would see him hang before he left Willow Springs and Raton.

The cell window faced east, and Max watched the slow progression of light enter his cell. The deputy came in shortly after with some oatmeal and handed it to Max through the bars.

"Thank you." Max took it and ate hungrily, and when it was gone he used his finger to wipe the sides of the bowl to get every last bit.

"Looks like you got your appetite back."

"Yeah. Carl. It's Carl, right?"

"Yeah."

"When's Ron's funeral?"

"This afternoon."

Max sighed. "Do you think I could go?"

"Sheriff said . . ."

"I know. I promise I'll come back right afterwards. Come on; I haven't met many people that I like or trust like I did Ron. He was like an uncle or cousin I never had."

Carl looked down at the floor a moment. "All right. You pay the fifteen dollars to the doctor for Jim, and you'll stay in my sight. That's how it'll work."

"All right, Carl. I'm much obliged. The money's in the bag you confiscated."

Carl pulled the bag out and counted out the money. "I'll go pay the doctor and come get ya just before the funeral."

"Thanks."

He spent the next few hours alternating between pacing the three steps from wall to wall in his cell and falling onto the bed frustrated. He was going stir crazy and was miserable.

He was lying down, about to fall asleep again, when the deputy came back in and walked to the cell door. "You promise to keep in sight and cause no trouble."

"Yes, sir."

The lock clicked, and Max felt relief pass through him. He had never been locked in anywhere. He realized how much worse it must have been for those men who had died in cave-ins. Many were not killed by the falling rocks and debris. It was the closing off of the tunnel, the loss of air. They were trapped and just waited it out until the air was gone. He had been there when it happened twice, fortunate enough to be on the other side of the fallen rock and dirt. They had tried to dig out one of the trapped men but had been too late. The other had been such a large collapse that it left the entire shaft too unstable to make any rescue attempts.

He followed Carl out into the air. The momentary relief he had from being outside was dampened by the upcoming funeral. He had been to funerals, the ones for the miners who had died. There had been none for his father, on account that there was no body. He and his mother had mourned, but, when nobody knew they were near, they overheard people say he had run off on them.

He had not. His father would not have done that. He had been a good man, just like Ron. Apparently, good men did not stand much of a chance in this world. Look at Clay. He had done the best he could for the mining company, for his men, for his family, but he had little to show for it. That was the way of life.

Max followed Carl to Willow Springs, joining the large crowd of people who walked east to the edge of town, past the small church where a small cemetery stood. It seemed nearly the entire town was there. Pete and Maggie had shut down the restaurant. Gary was there. Charlie Alden and a couple of his men, the doctor, and so many that he did not know. Max stood near the foot of one of the coffins. Carl walked around and stood on the other side.

The Fleshmans were there, including the ones he did not know, an obviously younger brother and the mother. The mother was an older version of Kayla, appearing to have just a bit more size and a bit more age on her. She could pass for an older sister.

Kayla looked up at him, and her lips tightened, and the corners of her eyes drew down. Max looked away. He did not want her pity. He looked at the elderly minister, who was flipping through his Bible. He stopped on a page, squinted, and scanned down before he looked up, clearing his throat.

"Rest in the Lord, and wait patiently for him; fret not thyself because of him who prospereth in his way, because of the man who bringeth wicked devices to pass." He shut his Bible and looked up. "The days of the blameless are known to the Lord, and their inheritance will endure forever." He looked at one of the boxes. "Most of us here knew Ron Stark well. We know he was a man of principle, a man who would help those in need. He did have his small faults as do we all, but we know that he knew the Lord, and he is home now with our Father."

The minister looked at the other box. "Few of us knew Don Holbrook beyond his legacy as a gambler. Many will have opinions on that, but let us not concentrate about that speck of dust in his eye. His Creator and he know the truth about his heart. He appeared to be a kind man, who cared about all whom he talked with. I will tell you that I did see him in our church one Sunday morning last year. He sang the hymn, and a joyous smile was on his face. I love to see that in all who worship the Lord. That I will remember about him.

"These two men were taken too soon from our company, but let us not ponder on that, but on what they gave us when they were here.

"Lord, we ask for comfort in this time of our loss. We don't understand all Your ways, for You are much greater than us. Amen."

Max did not know the man standing next to the minister, but he began to belt out *Amazing Grace*. The rest joined in. Max sighed and turned to walk back to the jail. Carl followed him but not hurriedly. Max was in his cell with the door closed by the time Carl entered.

"Ron Stark was a good man, Max." He stared in at Max while Max kicked off his boots and lay down. "You could take over his stables. The people here like ya. What happened with Jim will blow over by next week. I bet after a month even Fleshman will forget."

"No, I don't think so. I did think of staying before, but now, I just don't think so."

"I'd think on it. It's not a decision you have to make right away."

"Carl, I think it's best if I leave. I'm starting to see that things just don't go well for people I know."

"Max, that's just foolish. That superstitious talk shows what you don't know. When was the last time you were in church?"

Max chuckled. "Was gonna go this weekend, but I've been uninvited. Anyway, if there is a God, he don't like me much, so I think I'll pass."

Carl started to say something, then closed his mouth and shook his head, walking back to his chair. "Just think on it."

Max lay back in his bunk, wondering where he would go from here.

■ ■ ■ ■

Max had been stir crazy for the last two days. He mourned Ron, but he had been sitting in jail for four days. The last two he had only been out to use the outhouse. He paced the three steps from wall to wall. Joey had come in to tell him everything was going well at Ron's stables. He had been asked to run it while Max was not available. He said that Hardy was restless. He had let the stallion into the small corral for a while, but the horse wanted to run. Max wanted to ride out now. He had his mind set on heading south after all this was over. Arizona supposedly had mines and railways with work. He could look down there. There was the Tip Top mine that Don had mentioned, the Vulture mine in Wickenburg was still being worked, Globe had mines, and there was some mention of mining outside of Prescott. Then railways were being laid across the north and through the middle of the territory.

He could find work there. He would go back to doing what he knew, good hard labor, and forget the thought of owning a business, or chasing wanted men. That was not him. He asked Carl to tell Pete and

Gary that he'd like to see them.

He sat down, waiting, and time stretched. They were working, and it was nearly mid-afternoon when they made it to the jail. Pete brought a basket of food. "Sorry, Max, but we had a good afternoon crowd, men in from one of the ranches."

"That's all right, Pete. I wasn't going any-where."

"Guess not. Carl, can you open the door long enough to pass the food through."

"Thanks." Max nodded to the basket. When Carl passed it through, Max looked in and saw sliced ham, bread, and a bowl with stewed tomatoes in it. He set it aside and looked at the two. "The two of you were Ron's closest friends, and as far as I know there is no close next of kin, so I wanted to put an end to the talk of me taking over the stables and put in my opinion that the two of you partner up with it."

Gary shook his head. "Max, you quickly became Ron's best friend, and we don't have the time to —"

Max held up his hands. "Once I'm out of here, I'm riding south. If you two don't have the time, I suggest you have Joey manage it for you, give him most of the profits, and take what's left. It sounds like he's doing well at it."

Pete shook his head. "He is, but we just thought you would want to stay."

"I just don't feel like I can. Maybe I've moved from place to place too much as a miner, or maybe the killings and my being in jail put me off too much. I don't know exactly, but I'm just not staying."

Gary sighed. "All right, Max, but Ron would've wanted you to have it, so I'm going to give you something. I don't have a lot, but —"

"No. I don't want to make any money off of Ron's death. He gave me as much as any person ever has in friendship, so I'll just make do with what I have until I get a job."

Both men nodded. "Good idea about Joey," Pete told him. "Maybe we'll set him up on a four- or five-year plan to own it himself."

Max nodded. "Thank you, both. You're good men."

"You are also." Pete offered him his hand.

Max took it but said, "If I were, I probably wouldn't be in here."

"We all make mistakes."

Max just shrugged.

"I have to go get ready for the supper crowd, but, Max, please stop and say goodbye to me and Maggie before you head out. Have one more meal on us. Promise?"

Max sighed. "I'll think about it, but that's all I'll promise."

Gary shook his head but offered his hand, and the two left.

Max did not feel as hungry as usual, being cooped up in the small space not doing anything, but the food was very good, and he ate it all. He paced a little while after eating. He thought about stories of men that struck it rich on a claim, being able to sit out on the porch of their new big house with their feet up the rest of their life. Max was not sure that any of them actually did that, and, even if he ever did make it big, he did not think he could take sitting on a porch with his feet up. After several minutes he lay down, eventually falling asleep.

The next day he woke early and watched the sun slowly creep into the building through the windows in the front.

Carl eventually came in and walked to the cell. "How're you holding up?"

"I'm bored out of my mind."

"Not smelling too good either."

"I imagine not."

"We'll go out in a little while. You can stretch your legs and, if you want, buy a bath at the inn."

"Thanks, Carl." Max sighed. He had been

thinking on something all morning. "They've been gone quite some time. I thought they'd catch him and have him back in just a couple of days."

"He must have kept riding, knowing someone would be after him. They'll get him."

"You're not worried?"

"No. There were three of them and one of him, and Sheriff knows what he's doing."

Max sighed again, watching Carl make coffee. "I suppose you're right. Guess I still want to get out there; not like I did at first, ya know, but the important thing is he's brought to justice."

"Sounds like the few days in jail did you good. Tell you what, if the sheriff is not back by tomorrow night, I'll let you out."

Max nodded. "Thanks. Don't think I could take much more."

"Understandable. Want some coffee?"

"Yeah. Thanks, Carl."

Max brought the clothes he had packed for the ride, and it felt good to be clean, and, although the walk was short, just to the outhouse and the well to get a couple of buckets of water, it felt good, aside from the stares. Some looked at him sympathetically, and others as if he were a criminal, which was not surprising considering his boarding arrangements.

After coming back to the cell, he asked for clean bedding and changed it out. He lay down then and rested. In a couple of days, he and Hardy would be traveling, and he might as well get rest while he could.

Max had not had any breakfast, and as midday approached he was thinking about food. The front door opened, and the sheriff came in and tossed his hat onto the desk. "How'd it go here?"

"No problems. Everything's squared away with Max. Even seems to feel bad for what he did." The sheriff looked at the bars.

"You catch up to him?"

"No, lost the trail." He held up his hand to keep Max from saying anything. "We went as far as Fort Union and Watrous. None of the men on post or at the station could remember seeing him or the horse, but we left a picture and a description of the horse with them, and they were going to distribute it via the rail. They promised that if they found him, they'd take him into custody and contact us."

Max dropped his head, letting it bang against the bars. "You did what you could."

The sheriff nodded. "We did. You are free to go, long as you don't plan on fighting any more here."

"I don't."

The door clicked open, and Max collected his stuff and told Carl goodbye. Joey was brushing down the horses along with Keith when Max got to the stables. He waved to them but went straight to Hardy's stall and began to saddle him.

"I doubt you'll find him, Max." Keith sounded tired.

"I know, Keith, but I'm riding south anyway. Thanks for everything." Max fastened the belly strap and loaded his gear. "Take good care of the place, Joey. Please tell Pete, Maggie, and Gary I said thanks, and goodbye. Tell Kayla . . . never mind."

"Good luck," Keith called after him. Max waved back, and he was off at a trot down the street.

The area around Raton had few trees, but only a few miles southwest they appeared in clusters. The clusters were denser in the distance along the mountains.

It seemed like much further back than a few weeks since he had ridden this road. Max felt quite a bit older. It was odd how things could change so much in such a short time.

Max was not even sure which way he should ride from Cimarron. It was possible that the man rode for Springer, and then to Clayton and then who knows where. Well, he did not have to decide which way to go until he got to Cimarron. Perhaps the stable boy, whatever his name was, had seen the man. Max doubted he would have stayed in the next town over, knowing he was being chased, but maybe he had been seen. A person who works with horses would remember Don's stallion.

The next day, upon reaching Cimarron, Max found out he was right. The stable boy had seen the horse and described the rider as a match for Ron's killer. Unfortunately, he had not seen what fork the man had taken, and a few dollars did not help his memory. He had not seen the man or horse for several days now, so that, along with a glance through the stable, assured Max that the man had not stayed in Cimarron.

He dismissed Springer. The killer would likely stay clear of a town just down the rail. He could have gone to Taos, holed up in the mountains, or even doubled back around and gone north. Max did not know for sure, but he was riding south anyway. He would look for the scum along the way.

Max rode out of Cimarron at midday, following the trail. Oak brush spotted the prairie with occasional groupings of trees.

Mountains loomed in the distance ahead and to the west. He spotted the occasional ranch from the trail.

He rode through the settlement of Rayado with its red adobe buildings, the most prominent one a house with a railed covered porch. The trading post was close to the road, and next to it was the stage stop. He checked the adjacent stables, but the man told him that he'd already told the sheriff of Raton that the man they were looking for did not sound familiar. Max looked around, but the man clearly wanted to be left to his work. Max rode out quickly, not wanting to stay in town for the night. He lost sight of the town behind him before the sunlight began to fade and made camp a distance off the trail. He was settling in for sleep when the sound of hooves approaching brought him back to full alert. His hand went to his gun, and he spotted the large, moving shadow in the dark.

"Hello?" a voice called out.

"What do ya want?"

"Didn't mean to startle you. Just wondering if you knew how far to Cimarron?"

"It's still probably at least three hours' ride, over four in the dark." The horse kept approaching, slower now. Max pulled the pistol from the holster and glanced around.

The rider could be a distraction for someone else to sneak up. He was at a disadvantage being close to the fire; they could see his movements easier. Staying low, he crept back from the light, watching the way he was going. "You'll pass through Rayado first."

"I thought I was really close; that's why I kept riding in the dark. I'm a little hesitant to keep riding." The rider reached the edge of the camp. He was just a couple of years older than Max, slender and a little tattered looking. He paused, glancing around trying to look to the other side of Hardy. "Hello?"

Max, now twenty paces into the dark, glanced around one more time, then stood, cocking his pistol but keeping it held to his side. "Sorry, but that's what you should do. Keep riding. I don't know you, you don't know me, and sharing a camp with a stranger isn't a good idea."

The man was silent for a few seconds, and that made Max nervous, but finally he spoke. "You can take my gun for the night if that will make you feel better. I'll sleep on the other edge of the camp."

"What makes you think you could trust me?"

"If not, you'd likely have put a bullet through me before now."

Max thought about it. "Fair enough." He took a few steps closer. "Swing off that horse this side, move slowly, and put your hands up the second your feet are on the ground."

The man did as he said, and Max glanced around again . . . nobody.

He walked over and patted the man's pockets and saw he had no pistols.

"Only carry the rifle. A real good shot with it, though."

"Mind if I check your things to make sure you're not lying."

The man rolled his eyes. "Go ahead."

Max found only a big knife, which he took with the rifle back to where his bedroll was. He reached into his bag and pulled out some jerky and got up and handed it to the man. "I only saw oats for the horse."

The man nodded. "Thanks. Name's Martin."

"I'm Max."

"Hope you don't mind me sayin', you're awful jumpy."

"Maybe. I've had some things happen recently to make me jumpy."

"I see. I don't want any problems. Just in an unfamiliar area for the first time in my life. Spent all my life down around Gallup — a hunter, and cattleman when they really needed extra hands."

"Don't know the area. Desert or woods?"

"Kind of a mix of both. Where my cabin is there's elk run through those trees."

There was a bit of a silence as he unsaddled his horse.

"Max, mind if I ask what made you so jumpy?"

Max sighed. "A couple months ago someone killed one of my mining buddies. I found him riding into town, nearly dead as night was falling, and he didn't make it through the night. Then a few days later I was riding along the road, and a couple of men tried to ambush me. Then less than a week ago, a good friend of mine was killed in an alley walking home."

"I'm sorry, Max," Martin said quietly. Max thought he saw his eyes wetting by the reflection of the firelight in them. "That's a lot to happen to somebody in a few months. I sure see why you are skittish with strangers."

"Yeah, well, it's never wise to trust a man you don't know very well."

"You're probably right." Martin bit into the jerky and chewed. "Do they know who killed your friend?"

"Yeah. Someone caught sight of him riding a stolen horse out of town."

Martin nodded. Then he looked up quickly. "You going after him?"

"Yep."

"What happened to those two that tried to rob you?"

"I saw it coming and, after their initial attack, made it into the woods. When they chased me, I was able to get the upper hand on them, and I left the woods with their horses and gear instead of the other way around."

Martin sighed. "That's quite a story; should be posted to scare other road agents from trying the same thing."

"Wouldn't make a difference."

"Probably not." He chewed on the jerky some more. "And did they ever find the man who killed your mining buddy?"

"The next night in the hotel lobby, I ran across a man whose face looked like one that was on a Wanted poster. I called his name, and he drew and shot. I got off a lucky shot and put him down. Most people think it was probably him that killed my friend Ricky."

Martin sighed again. "I'd hate to be this man you're chasing after. Seems like you have a talent for dealing with men like that. You're just a different type of hunter than I am."

Max thought about that. Maybe Martin was right. Max had thought that he was not cut out to be a bounty hunter, but he did seem to be able to handle himself. Jack Sutter had got the drop on him, but he was an experienced bounty hunter. He would think about reconsidering his future.

"What brings you this way, Martin?"

"Brother moved to Cimarron not too long ago with his new wife, to help with her uncle's ranch. Going to visit, and help some with the roundup."

Max looked at Martin. "You never been there before, huh? Well, I'd advise you to watch yourself, especially if you're out at night."

"I'd heard things have calmed down."

"Perhaps they have by Cimarron standards, but, in my brief time there, I'd say a man who's used to a small, quiet, honest town may look like an injured bird for those wolves."

"First, you were afraid I was a road agent; now I'm some naïve country bumpkin," Martin countered.

Max took a deep breath. "Just trying to prepare ya. Suppose we should catch some sleep."

Martin lay down, pulling his blanket over him.

Max thought about saying something but instead lay down himself, pulling his blanket around him and easing his pistol out of his holster. He kept it under the blanket, his fingers touching the handle.

He had trouble sleeping. He kept opening his eyes to glance at the lump that was Martin. He finally drifted off. He popped awake a while later and instantly looked over to where Martin was sleeping. Max sighed and closed his eyes again, and, after tossing to find a comfortable position, he fell back asleep.

The next time he woke the sky was dim with coming light, and Martin was tying his bag onto his saddle. "Morning," Max said.

"Morning. Thought I'd get an early start."

Max pushed himself to his feet. "Martin, sorry if I was rude last night."

"It's all right, Max. I understand. Can I have my rifle and knife now?"

Max swept them from the ground and walked over and handed them to Martin, then offered his hand. "Good luck at the ranch."

Martin shook it. "Good luck on your journey, Max." He put his rifle in its place and swung onto his horse. "And, Max, remember, there are as many good men in the world as there are bad." With that he was off riding toward the road.

Max watched him ride off, then sighed and began packing his bedroll. The trail ahead beckoned him. He started out, feeling like he had not even rested. It was not long before the trees became thicker. The saddle began to wear on Max, and by noon he was walking Hardy back onto the prairie, the trees thinning and the sight of rougher land ahead. About two miles out of the trees Max descended into a small canyon and entered Ocate Creek. He followed it west until the sheer walls of the other side gave way to a place he could ride up onto the mesa. After making sure Hardy had drunk enough and filling his own canteen, he followed the ruts made by the many wagons that had come through over the years. He passed a wagon moving up the trail. The driver told him it was several miles yet to Fort Union, but he could make it by nightfall. Max pushed Hardy to a trot, over the hills. He crested a hill and looked down upon Fort Union. Tired as he was, he must have made good time, because the light had not yet begun to fade.

CHAPTER 9

The fort was the size of a small town. The palisades surrounded more than two dozen buildings. The far western rows consisted of smaller adobe buildings with chimneys rising out of them. Their adobe walls extended out, making protected yards behind them. Across the grounds from those quarters were larger buildings that appeared to be storehouses and large bunkhouses. In between there was a rectangular structure where steam was rising out of the yard in the middle, presumably the mechanics' corral where the wheelwright and blacksmith would work. Across a narrow path in the far eastern quadrant of the fort were sheds and corrals with additional quarters mixed in. Another large structure stood alone just past the southern tip of the most distant corrals.

Max rode down the slope and in minutes was riding alongside the corrals on the eastern edge until he saw what looked like a main pathway running down the middle of the fort.

As Max turned into the path, a bluecoat soldier stepped forward and held up a hand, stopping Max. "Hello, mister, what's your business here?"

"I was wanting to check and see if there was any news of a murderer being caught. Also, I could stand to buy some supplies."

"You'll need to go to the clerk's office to inquire about the fugitive. It's also the post office, northwest corner of the fort, all the way down this path and take a right all the way to the tip. There's a store and a saloon about two hundred yards off the western side of the fort. You'll see them if you look out from the other side of this path. You can buy some items there. The shops on base are temporarily only serving military personnel or their families. Water in the trough right over there for your horse."

Max watered Hardy and used the pump next to the trough to put water in his canteen before following the man's directions to the clerk's office. Riding along the other side of the fort he saw the adobe buildings in the distance that he would visit next.

He rounded the building at the northwest corner of the fort, dismounted, and tied his horse to the post. There was a wagon being unloaded across the yard. There were bags of flour or grain and crates of some sort being carried through one of the gates that blocked the paths between the storehouses. Max entered the clerk's office, and there was a soldier at the desk paying postage to another soldier, a corporal, Max thought.

The man behind the counter looked up as he took the coins and the letters. "Can I help you?"

"Yes, sir, I was told you were the man to see about whether a fugitive was apprehended."

"What fugitive?" The corporal motioned Max forward but called out to the soldier about to walk out the door. "Hold on a minute, private."

Max held out the poster, and the corporal took it. "What's he to you?"

"Killed a good friend of mine."

The corporal glanced at Max's two pistols before turning around and shuffling through some papers. "Vigilantism is not welcome around here."

"I was heading this way anyway and would just feel better knowing he was caught."

"We got this poster on him a few days ago."

"I know, I was just following up. He's on

a fine horse — Hungarian half-breed."

"Don't know about all the horses in the territory. Tell you what: leave your guns here, and private Walsh will take you over to the prison. I think we had a couple of men brought in, but I don't know anything about them."

Max unfastened his belt and handed it over to the corporal.

"Name?"

"Don't know his name."

"No . . . your name?"

"Max Tillman."

"You get these back when the private returns with you."

"Thank you."

"Yeah."

The private sighed after the door to the clerk's office closed. "Come along. I want to hurry up so I have some time to eat before my watch tonight." He then started off at a fast walk across the yard and around the outermost storehouse. Max hurried to keep up. They circled around and walked down a path that led between the store-houses and a line of sheds. Through a missing plank, Max could see a wagon and the corral of horses on the other side. As they passed the storehouses and the mechanics' corral, they heard the sound of hammers, and the smell of fire on metal and a vague whiff of leather. They left that smell as the odors of baking bread and roasting meats reached them. That indicated the catty-cornered building was the kitchen that fed the troops, many of whom were entering at the moment. Running alongside and across were several doors indicating quarters. Two women were wringing out clothes in front of the building attached to the kitchen. One looked up and waved to Private Walsh. He nodded. Max looked back at her . . . she was an attractive woman.

Walsh saw him looking back. "She's my wife."

"Oh, congratulations." Max was puzzled. "I'm sorry, I thought only officers' wives were allowed at the forts."

"Not if they agree to be a laundress."

Just ahead they reached the building that was obviously the prison. It was concrete, bar doors indicating the cells. Private Walsh told the guard that the corporal said that Max could look inside. There were only a few cells along the front, and Max looked in the fading light to see a couple of Indians, and a fat white man. The guard took Max around the east side and grabbed a lantern to hold up to the two cells there. There was a short soldier in one, and in the other occupied cell was a man with snow-white whiskers, decades older than the one he sought.

Max shook his head.

"Come on then." Walsh was off at a quick pace, and Max kept up. The women weren't outside anymore, but there were quite a few men crossing to the kitchen. Max and Walsh weaved through them and retraced their steps. Max collected his guns, thanking Walsh and the corporal, and was told that he could camp to the west near the suttler's store and restaurant.

Max gathered Hardy and walked him toward the lights in the distance. He stepped into the store to see a tall, lanky man with a dark mustache that dominated his face coming around the counter.

"I was just about to close."

"I'll be quick; oats if you have them, pound of jerky, three cans of beans."

"All right, easy enough." He took the bag Max passed across. "Want any of that cornbread there? Wife makes it every three days; travelers love it."

"Sure. Two biscuits."

"All right." His hands deftly pulled items off shelves and wrapped and tied the jerky and cornbread in a thin paper. "Two dollars and twenty cents."

181

Max shook his head but paid. An outpost like this could charge what they wanted, because even if it wasn't that far to the next store, you had no way of knowing when their supplies would run low.

Max curried Hardy and tied him in an empty section of the long picket line that was strung across to the sides of the building. There were two big wagons parked along the line, with men camping next to them. There was a team of four mules on one end of the picket line, and on the other end, thirty yards away, four large draft horses were picketed. A big paint was picketed toward the middle, and Max put Hardy a short distance from that horse.

Max walked inside. It was a mixture of activity. There were men and women quietly eating, while there were other soldiers clearly drunk, loud, and playing cards two tables away. The man and woman inside were serving venison stew, or beef roast with potatoes. Max had the venison stew, which had potatoes in it along with some tomato. It was seasoned with a little onion and peppers. It was good, as was the thick slice of bread that each person was given with their meal. It was some of the best bread he had ever eaten.

Max sat at an end of a long bench. There

were a few tables. One of them sat two officers and a pair of ladies, and another traveler, with some Mexican-Indian blood, sat by himself also. Max ate hurriedly and went back out. He checked on Hardy and then unfolded his blankets in the middle of where the two wagons were parked. The long day of travel wore on him. He quickly fell asleep.

"You married, mister?"

Max woke up and looked up at the man with thick, gray hair standing at a distance. He sat looking around in the fresh light. Although there was activity at the wagon to the west, the man was the only one close. "No, I'm not. Why do you ask?"

"You seem to be a healthy young man." The man paused and then knelt down. "I have not had any sons, but three daughters, and none of them are close to marrying. I was hoping during a visit with our family in Santa Fe they might have met somebody, but that did not happen." He leaned in. "Perhaps they are not as pretty as some men may like, but they are nice girls, and any man who marries one will get a share of the family farm outside of Rayado when my end comes."

"Hold on." Max looked over now and saw the two women pouring cups of coffee. The

183

man was right, although it seemed a terrible thing for a father to say. The girls' faces were wide and a bit masculine looking. Max looked back at the father. "Are you really trying to get me to choose one of your daughters to marry?"

The man nodded, and Max searched for the right words. "I'm sure they are lovely girls, but I'm not good for any woman, and I'm riding the other direction. I . . . um . . . appreciate the offer, but sorry. Good luck."

The man sighed and stood and walked back to his wagon. One of the dark-haired women peeked around their father to get a look at Max. He stood, putting his back to the wagon, and rolled his bedding.

He had the urge to leave now but smelled what could be ham cooking. He was not sure exactly what lay ahead, so he did not know the next time he would eat a decent meal. He entered the restaurant.

After a good meal of eggs, ham, and biscuits, Max was ready to move. Hardy seemed well rested also and set a good pace over the rolling plains. The trees and brush thickened around mid-morning, and Max saw the reason as they crossed the Mora River. Just after that, he saw the trading post that also served as a stage station. There was a man working with a horse on the other side of the trail. Max let Hardy drink from the trough, then was about to step inside when a man stepped out.

"Hello, there," the brown-bearded man called out as if Max was not right in front of him.

"Hi. This your place?"

"Yes, it is." He moved to open the door.

"I'm not in need of anything right now, perhaps on the way back through."

"What can I do for ya then?"

"I was wondering if you saw a man that looks like this." Max showed the picture to the man. "He may have been riding a fine white horse, with a dark mane."

The man looked at the picture for a few seconds then nodded. "No, sir. He a wanted man?"

Max nodded. "Killed my friend."

The man sighed. "Sorry to hear that. Hope you catch him."

"Me, too. Thanks." Max turned and slung back up onto Hardy and headed down the trail.

He rode on through the warm day, stopping in the prairie to let Hardy graze and rest. After several minutes, they were on the road again. The traffic on the road picked up about the same time that he noticed more groups of trees dotting the land, as well as farmhouses. He also saw a train heading south in the distance. He saw groups of houses up ahead and knew he had reached Las Vegas. He rode into the center of town past the large church and soon was in the square. A large hotel dominated the corner of the square, with a courthouse across and stores and a café filling in the rest of the square.

Max guided Hardy back down the street a ways to the stable and dismounted. He stepped into the barn to see a young blond-haired man working on a horse's hoof. The man looked up just for a second before returning his eyes to his work. "What can I do for you, mister?"

"Seen any fine horse come through with a slender rider, man in his mid-twenties with long, blond hair? Horse was a Hungarian breed, white with dark mane."

"No, sir. Horse stolen?"

"Yes. Man's wanted for murder also."

"Figured the horse was stolen, way you described it. Well, I've not seen a horse like that, but I don't see all the horses. Some don't stable their mounts with me. They can pay a couple of people at the edge of town to turn them loose in their corral while they're staying in town, then there's the stables at East Las Vegas."

186

"East Las Vegas?"

"Yeah, where the train runs, a mile east of the plaza. That's the more likely place for a horse thief and murderer."

"Why's that?"

"It's been building up that way since the rail was built there, a hell-on-wheels town. Gambling, drinking, and whores, that's what's there. Oh, there's some other places, but it's been the source of trouble. Got so bad them and us joined together to chase out some of the corrupt officials and lawmen over there."

Max nodded. He had seen the large corral not even half a mile out. "Mind if I leave my horse tied right out here a little while?"

"No, long as it isn't left there all day."

"Thanks."

Max sighed and walked toward the square and the courthouse. The courthouse held a jail underneath. Max went into the building, thinking that Las Vegas was even more built up than Trinidad, considering the fine courthouse. There was a constable office near the entrance, and he entered, holding the drawing of the killer in his hand. A large man with a mustache that matched his bulk stood behind a desk talking to another man. The badge identified him. He stopped and looked at Max. "What is it?"

"I was wondering if you've seen this man, maybe have him in jail."

The lawman looked at the picture, then handed it back shaking his head. "No, I got that poster a couple days ago. I'll arrest him if I see him, but we have our own issues here. Rudabaugh's still out there somewhere. Brown may be also. We aren't going to let them get away with what they did. They may even try to rob another stage."

"OK." Max had no concern about what the man was talking about. He collected Hardy. He stopped by the one house to the south with the big corral and couldn't find anybody to question. They must have been doing errands. Max glanced over the horses and did not see Holbrook's horse.

East Las Vegas was as lively as it had been described. Music came out from one dance hall, and there were several saloons and gambling houses. Max stopped by the stable first, having to pay a full two dollars for the stable owner to watch after Hardy and feed him. After checking the stalls and corral, he made his way around all the gambling houses, figuring if the man was there, he may be doing the same thing he did in Willow Springs.

Max received a dirty look and no answers after showing the poster in the first two places, so he just walked in and scanned the next three before turning around and walking out. Men still looked up at him, measuring him, seeing that he was looking for somebody.

After searching the gambling houses, he tried the saloons and eateries and finally showed the picture to the two hotel clerks. There was no indication that he had been seen. Max wondered if the man may have boarded the train at some point. He began to realize he might not ever find the man. He also thought that East Las Vegas could be as dangerous as Cimarron. He tried the marshal's office in East Las Vegas, but the door was locked. His final attempt was to show the picture to the stable man, telling him he would split the reward with him, if his information helped him catch him. After that statement, the man paid more attention, but still he finally had to admit he had seen neither the man in the poster nor the horse.

Max headed south down the trail.

Several miles out of Las Vegas, Max rode through a gap in between two rock formations. He remembered hearing about this gap, and its importance. An army general or colonel had staged an invasion and taken Santa Fe during the Mexican-American

War. Kearney, Max thought.

The day passed, growing warmer, but he rode on, only stopping for water as the sun touched the western horizon at the station near Starvation Peak. Max remembered hearing the story of the landmark. Supposedly Indians had cornered soldiers atop the hill. The men had the high ground and could hold off any attack, but eventually they starved to death because they were unable to come down.

Max camped a short distance from the building and slept well, waking up at the first sign of light and starting out after feeding and saddling Hardy. The trees were fairly thick now, and the Pecos River came into view. Max remembered hearing that the Pecos to Santa Fe was a day's ride, and he felt relieved that he would finally arrive at Santa Fe.

Across the Pecos was the Mission village of San Jose Del Vado. Max passed through, asking questions there. After letting Hardy drink, he hurried on, the thought of reaching Santa Fe before dark driving him.

It was approaching noon when he reached Kozlowski's station. There was a spring there where he refilled his canteen and let Hardy drink his fill. Max let Hardy rest, and he paid for oats for the horse. He himself had some bread and potatoes. The station man told Max that the place had seen better days, before the rail. Now most freight was being shipped through on the train, with fewer and fewer travelers passing through on the trail. He said that the traffic was already less than half of what it had been and worried that it was time to move on from his once-prosperous enterprise. Max thought about the decades of travelers coming over the trail, going back to when it used to be trade between two countries. He wondered what it had been like.

After the short rest, Max rode on. Only a few miles away from the station he spotted a monastery that was collapsing. As he got closer, he saw that the mission had been built among the ruins of old Indian structures, though they likely were not ruins before the mission. There were primitive stone walls all around the hill where the ruins were. Max fought off the urge to go examine the ruins. Santa Fe may be where the killer went, and, if Max slowed, perhaps he would miss the man before he moved on to another town.

Max rode on through the afternoon, past Pigeons Ranch, through Apache Canyon and Glorieta Pass. He dismounted and walked, leading Hardy by the reins for a couple of miles to rest him. The horse was tiring. It had been a long trip, and this day was one of the more demanding of the journey.

Finally, with the sun nearing the horizon, Max rode into Santa Fe. This was the busiest town Max had ever seen. He had passed two wagons on the road just before the city came into sight, and two entered just ahead of him. The buildings on the outskirts were a mix, some made of wood like the one Max had grown up in back in Texas, while others were stucco or a mix of stucco and rock. Some were small with little land between them and their neighbors, and others were larger with an acre or so around them.

As he neared the plaza, the buildings became bigger adobe structures. He passed a very old church building that was collapsing. Next to it was a large adobe structure, with a couple of boys leaving it with books. Max thought it may be a school. There was a very old mud building that looked to be washing away. You could see the wall surface had run during rains and then dried as it began to slide toward the ground.

Max reached what he thought was the plaza, because there were more people about. In the center was a grassy courtyard with trees surrounded by a white picket fence. There were a few men in suits talking near one gate, and two sitting on the benches. Max looked to the east, past the Exchange Hotel, and saw a large cathedral. To the west down San Francisco Street were lines of buildings, and men moving about carrying loads of goods.

The buildings were nearly all built in the usual old Mexican style. A Victorian balustrade did run along the top of the long porch of the building across the plaza that was supposed to be the Palace of the Governors. The balustrade aside, it did not look like much compared to some government buildings Max had seen. He noticed another building in mid-construction with its own balustrade to match. All the buildings in the plaza appeared to share walls, except where they needed openings at the street corners.

Max slowly rode a circle around the plaza, looking down the other streets to get an idea of the city, but it was difficult to make out very much, as full dark was settling. There were some buildings down the streets that looked to be separate houses on the second floor instead of on the first, the same with the businesses. They were all jumbled. There were still people, horses, and wagons weaving through each other toward and away from the center. It was so different from what Max was used to that he had a momentary urge to ride out.

He found the sheriff's office down San Francisco Street to the west of the plaza, nearly directly across from Burro Alley. Max had heard miners talk about Burro Alley being the heart of fun in Santa Fe, with saloons, gambling houses, and other entertainment you would not tell your mother about.

The jailhouse was a two-story adobe structure with a balcony at the top. It appeared to have a basement, where the cells likely were. Perhaps the knife man had already been apprehended. After tying Hardy to a nearby post, Max paused. He had spent days in jail, and he just hated the idea of walking into a sheriff's office, but he entered anyway.

There were a few men sitting around. But one man, who was stocky, average height, with a red beard, was sitting at the desk and looked to be in charge. "Good evening."

"Evening, sir. I was curious if you have heard anything further on that killer on the run from Raton?"

"Oh, that. No, I showed my deputy the picture, but neither of us have seen the man." He paused and looked at Max's holstered sidearm. "What's your interest in it?"

"One of the men he killed was my friend, and my boss."

"Thought maybe they'd put a bounty on it. Don't know which is worse though. Listen, leave it to us if he is here; we don't want any shootings, or other problems. Plus, he hasn't even been proven guilty."

"He was seen riding out on a stolen horse at two past midnight, riding out of a stable that had been locked before a key was taken off of my friend. There's no doubt it was him."

"I do remember them saying something like that, but . . ."

"The horse — you may have noticed that — a Hungarian half-bred, white with a black mane. Beautiful horse."

"There's lots of horses through here. Santa Fe's the main trading center for hundreds of miles."

Max sighed. "All right. Sorry to take your time."

"No reason to apologize. Just stay out of trouble." Max turned to leave but turned around when the man spoke again. "Wait. Really, I'm sorry about your friend. I've lost a couple of friends myself, and I know how it gnaws at a man."

"Thank you, Sheriff."

Max gathered Hardy and walked down

towards the stables. He was met by a short man with white hair and beard. "Fine looking horse." The man looked Hardy over.

"Thank you. He needs to be well fed. We've been doing some heavy traveling."

"Sure, most through here have."

"You seen another fine horse, tall, white with a black mane?"

"Hungarian half-bred?"

"That's the one."

"Sure, got it in my stable now."

"Really? The rider a thin man with long, blond hair?"

"No, Joe's more stout than thin, and he keeps his dark hair short."

"Can I see the horse? Hard to imagine there's two like it around here."

"Not without the owner's permission. But Joe did say he bought it just a couple of days ago, so the prior owner might be your friend."

"Where can I find Joe?"

"I'm not comfortable with this, mister."

"Well, could you tell Joe I'd like to talk to him, and I'll be at the hotel this side of the plaza? They serve food there, don't they?"

"Yeah, and it's pretty good, too."

"All right. I'm checking in and eating supper there. Name's Max."

"All right, Max. I'll let him know you're

at the Capitol Hotel. Can't promise he'll want to talk to ya, though."

Max sighed. "Please tell him I'd really appreciate it."

"All right. I'll take care of your horse first."

at the Capitol Hotel. Can't promise he'll want to talk to you, though."

Max sighed. "Make sure he hits the trail, and practice it."

"All right. I'll take care of your horse."

CHAPTER 10

Max sat in the café in the hotel. He ate steak. It wasn't bad, but he was tired of it. He found the taste blander than chicken, ham, or game, but he knew he was in the minority. It was the only thing being served at the café that night. The bread was warm, just out of the oven, and there were sliced tomatoes. He was hungry, so he finished most everything and washed it down with a beer. He was just thinking that Joe was not going to show up when a rugged-looking man with black and gray hair over his lip as well as his head approached.

"Max?"

"Yes, Joe?"

"That's my name."

"Have a seat. Would you like something to eat or drink?"

"No, thanks." He did sit down, though.

"Joe, that horse was stolen from a stable in Willow Springs seven days ago."

"You have proof?"

"The Santa Fe constable has been notified by the Raton constable. I imagine the man that sold it was slim, average height, long, blond hair."

Joe was quiet.

"Joe, I'm not wanting to lay claim to the horse. The man killed two other men, and I'm after him. When did he sell you the horse?"

Joe sighed. "Two days ago at my ranch, a few miles out of town. Said he was in need of cash, and the horse was all he had. I gave him an older horse and fifty dollars. He said he lost the bill of sale, left it the last place he stayed."

Max nodded. "Any idea where he moved on to?"

"Here." At that Max's eyes widened. "I saw him earlier today over at the Caliber Saloon, watching people play cards."

Max pushed his chair back and stood up. "Thank you, Joe. You got yourself a fine horse."

"Thanks, Max. Good luck."

Max left the hotel and looked down toward Burro Alley, where he had seen the Caliber Saloon when he rode past to the stables. It had looked busy, with a group of four men entering and a couple more following. He reached down, putting his hand on the Colt on his right hip. He was going to load the sixth chamber but dropped his hand. Five shots should be enough, and loading his gun in the middle of the street was likely to bring too much attention. He started walking down the street, moving out of the way of a wagon coming up behind him.

He was nervous. This was what he came all the way here for, and now he felt unsure. He thought about going into the saloon on his right and taking a shot of whiskey, but he steeled himself. He was here for his friend's killer. This man had killed two men he liked, stolen, and could get away if Max did not act now.

Max quickened his step, hearing the laughing and talking pouring out from the saloon as he rounded the corner and approached the doors. It was well lit inside, with several lanterns hanging from the support beams around the place. There were close to twenty tables. All had men sitting at them. A few saloon girls had joined the men at the tables. The bar to the right had men standing nearly all the way across. Two tables toward the back were full of men holding cards. A few men stood nearby, watching, and among them, acting only half interested, was a slim man with long, blond hair.

Max stood just inside now, observing as the blond man watched the men exchange money out of the corner of his eye. This was his scam, the way he made a living. He took money other men earned, whether by the sweat of their brow or the risk they took at the tables. The biggest winner would very likely be the biggest loser with him around.

The knife man turned his eyes back to his drink. Something had changed. Max started picking a path through the tables. Maybe the man had noticed him watching. The man bolted two steps, then vaulted over the edge of the counter and through the door behind the bar. Max pushed off the chair he was next to with his hand, hearing the man seated there call behind him. He vaulted up in a space between two men, causing one to drop his drink by hitting his arm. The bartender turned from the back room where the knife man had gone.

"Hold on!"

"He's a murdering thief!" Max pulled his Colt from his right hip and moved around the bartender. "Wanted for murder up north."

The bartender moved aside. The storeroom was lit by a lantern in the middle, but the edges of the room were dark. Max peeked in, looking around.

"He went out the back door to the alley," the barman said from behind him.

Max saw the open door at the wall to the left and ran through it. He stopped in the narrow, dark alley, swiveling, trying to make out anything from the walls. He saw movement in the shadows down the alley as the man was pulling himself up onto a low roof. Max aimed, but the man rolled on top before he could shoot.

He ran to where the roof was lower, hearing boots scrambling away across the top. He holstered his pistol and jumped up, grabbing the top with his fingertips, pushing off the wall with his boots. He saw movement above him and dropped just as a blade slashed air inches from his eyes. His feet hit the ground, and his gun came out, firing a shot just above the top of the roof. He heard boots scrambling away again. He ran down a ways. He saw a crate and pushed off of that to reach the roof, grabbing with one arm, and his gun arm leveraged as he looked. He saw a shadow climbing stairs to a second-story room across the way, and no other movement. Pushing himself up, he followed the shadow. Then movement out of the corner of his eye swung him around to see a man jumping across buildings. The other man must have been scrambling up to his home. Max ran leaping across the narrow alley. The man was another building over.

Max raised his gun to take aim but could not make out the man for sure. Sighing, he took up the chase. Could be another scared man. The roofs of some buildings were second-story walkways. Who knows whom he had scared with his shot?

He just made it jumping across the narrow alley, clipping his boot on the edge. He hit the rooftop and rolled. The man was at the other corner of the building and dropped down. Max ran to the closest edge and peered over. The man moved his aim from the corner, and Max dropped to the roof as the shot sailed over his head. Hearing running steps, Max rose up. The man was out of sight. Max dropped down and looked around. Nobody. He jerked around at movement, but it was just an elderly man looking out his window. Max walked toward the street, holstering his gun. Men were looking around in the street, talking. There had been shots, but most did not know the exact direction. Max saw the sheriff running towards the Caliber. Someone had run to get him before the shots.

But Max was just a couple of doors down from the stables, and he figured the blond man was ready to run. He kept his hand close to his gun as he reached the alley by the stables and peered around the corner. The man was walking toward him with his arms crossed. He uncrossed his arms, the gun in his right hand, and Max pulled his head back. No shot. Max's gun was in his hand, and he peeked around again to see the man running away. Max stepped into the alley, taking careful aim. Just as the man neared the edge of the building, Max fired.

The man fell forward, his gun flying out of his hand. Max ran down the alley, and the man was pushing himself up. He made it to his knees and looked around at Max. Max was close enough to see the blood on the man's left shoulder.

"No, please!" The killer now looked pathetic and weak. "I . . ."

Max squeezed the trigger, and the shot to the head sent the man to the ground, pieces of his skull flying out the other way.

"Drop that gun!" That yell from behind him jolted Max, but he instantly did what he was told. He had nearly turned around; he probably would have died then.

Max's legs were shaking. He slowly raised both hands and moved back to lean against the wall to keep from falling down.

The sheriff approached. Holding his gun steadily at the center of Max's chest, he reached over and took his second pistol out of his belt. Then he stepped back and looked at Max. "I saw you gun down that man on his knees in cold blood."

A tear rolled down Max's cheek. "Sheriff, he's a killer. Kills men with knives. He twitched, going for his knife. I shot him 'cause I didn't want to get gutted like my friends in Willow Springs. Or he could have had a second gun for all I knew."

There was a crowd at the other end of the alley, but another man holding a gun emerged, a deputy.

The sheriff waved his pistol at Max. "Keep your gun on him," he said to the deputy. Then he bent down next to the knife man. Out of his pocket he pulled a sheathed knife, blade about four inches long. He looked at the man's face.

"Well, he's the man in the picture, and he does have a knife." He stood up, looked at Max, and yelled, "Why didn't you come to me?"

Max looked at the sheriff, then the crowd. "He knew I saw him and ran. Ask the men at the Caliber. I caught up with him here, figuring he was going for the stables to get away." Max looked at the ground for a moment and then up into the sheriff's eyes. "If anyone had been in the stables he would've killed him. And at the Caliber he was watching the tables, same as he did in Willow Springs, looking for a new victim."

The sheriff looked at him with narrow eyes and took a deep breath. "Tomorrow we'll let the judge decide if you'll be charged or not. You stay in jail until that's decided. And if a stray shot hit anyone, you will stand trial!"

The street was lined with people as the sheriff marched him to jail. Max kept his eyes down on the ground in front of him. He was fairly sure he would be released. He'd told the truth, all except for the part about the man reaching for the knife before he shot him in the head. He had tried to kill Max. He had killed at least two men. Max really did the world a favor. It was ridiculous that he was going to jail for even a night.

In the basement of the jail there were four cells, and two were already taken. After the constable closed the main door to the stairs, the prisoner across the way stood up and called across. "What are you in for?"

Max ignored him and lay down on his bed. The man continued. "I was disturbing the peace, and Ted over there . . . well, he was just too drunk to stand, so they threw him in here. Yeah, this little fool of a man looked at me wrong when I said hello to his lady friend, and I got in his face and scared him something awful. A few of the men grabbed me and pulled me away, and the deputy happened along. They threw me in here for a day for that. Stupid, isn't it? Hey, I'm talking to you!"

Max turned his head to look through the bars at the man. "Yeah, you're right it was stupid. I would've beat the crap out of ya, or better yet just shot ya, and rid the world of your sorry ass." Max stared back at the ceiling.

"You're pretty tough through these bars. What if I see you out on the street?"

Ted spoke up in a half-sober voice. "Corey, there were shots, then they brought him in here. I'm thinking maybe he shot someone, so I think he might just shoot you as well if he got the chance. He probably won't get out of here, but best not to push him."

"He doesn't scare me."

Max sighed and closed his eyes. The rest of the night the only sound was the occasional loud voice from outside, and those stopped after a couple of hours. It was not until then that Max was able to fall asleep.

Breakfast came an hour after daylight had awakened Max. The deputy released the other two prisoners but brought him a muffin and a hardboiled egg. Max ate and then dropped back down onto the bed, waiting to see what news the sheriff brought. Maybe he would be set free, or maybe he would be hung. Did it matter? He did not know what he would do if he were set free.

The sheriff came in and unlocked the cell door. "You're free. Judge said he couldn't see a trial based on the facts. You would be best served to move on through, mister." The sheriff gave Max his guns and then several bills. "The man had several hundred dollars on him. Most of it supposedly came from one of the men up in Raton. We're keeping enough to bury him and a fee for our involvement in this, and sending half up to Raton to pay for those funerals and the posse's expenses. This is what's left, plus his horse, so I suppose you get something for tracking him. Caliber bartender did say he was watching the tables kinda sly like, so take this and please leave."

Max counted out the fifty dollars. "Sheriff, I'd like to rest a day here. I won't cause any trouble."

"Fine. Nothing I can do about that, and that man did kill your friend. It's over now."

Max nodded. He left and stepped outside, taking in Santa Fe for the first time in the daylight. He noted the mountains to the northeast, the direction he had come from, and mountains to the west. He went into his hotel and stopped by the desk, and the clerk looked at him, then down at his pistols. "I'm staying at least one more night." He laid down another two dollars.

The clerk nodded, not making eye contact. "All right, sir."

Max went upstairs and back to sleep.

He woke, and by the light in the window it appeared to be late afternoon. Standing up, he grabbed his guns and fastened on his belt before heading toward the door. He stopped at the door and pulled his Colt from his hip. He swung open the loading gate and replaced the three bullets he had shot last night.

He received a disapproving look from the clerk as he reached the bottom of the stairs and returned the stare until the clerk looked away. He walked down the street and gave the livery man another dollar for Hardy's care. Then he went down the street and into a saloon.

He stood at the bar and drank three whiskeys before a short little redhead in a strapped dress came over and asked him if he wanted to buy her a drink.

"Sure." The bartender poured the saloon girl a whiskey and put it down in front of her.

"My name's Katrina."

"Max."

"You're the one brought to jail last night for shooting that thief."

"Yah."

"That the first man you shot?"

"No."

"Really?"

"Don't care to talk about that, Katrina."

"What do you want to talk about, Max, aside from buying me another drink?"

Max nodded to the barkeep, and he put two more whiskies down. "I don't really feel like talking."

Katrina downed her whiskey. "Do you feel like doing something more exciting than talking? I have a place just through the alley." She nodded to the door at the back of the saloon.

Max looked at the back door, and then at her gray eyes and red lips, her pushed-up breasts, and her cinched waist.

"Ten dollars and I'm yours for half the evening."

"Sure, why not?" Max put down three

dollars for the drinks and followed Katrina
out the door.

CHAPTER 11

Max woke up with a headache and the terrible taste of stale alcohol in his mouth. It was late morning from the angle of the sun in the window. He rolled his legs off the bed and pulled on his boots. He stood up on unsteady legs and buckled on his belt. Slinging his bags over his shoulder he went downstairs.

He put the key on the manager's desk, ignoring the look on the man's face, and walked out into the sun. After a stop at the supply store, he gathered Hardy from the stable and was on his way out of town. He headed south, down the El Camino Real. He wanted out of this part of New Mexico. He had thought about going back to Texas, but he wanted someplace completely new. There were mines in Arizona, and soon the railroad, and who knew what else. He even thought about staying on the trail all the way down into Mexico. That would be completely new, but he knew very little Spanish. Max had time to decide.

His stomach felt queasy at the motion of riding, but he kept going until near dark. He went off trail into a clearing and quickly gathered sticks and logs to build a sizable fire. He imagined the land around Santa Fe was hunted out for nearly a day's ride each direction, but he didn't want to risk it. The region had bears, wolves, and cougars roaming about, not to mention the simple pesky animals like raccoons and foxes.

The queasiness had faded from his stomach, and he was a bit hungry, so he ate a little jerky and then collapsed into his blankets.

Max dreamed. He was mining, then he was hunting an elk, and then at some point the hunt changed, and he was being hunted, running from five men with rifles. He looked back and knew who they were: Carl Bradshaw, Sutter, the two highwaymen, and the knife man. Max ran down a trail and crossed the stream, running up the hill on the other side. He stopped. There at the top was Jim, aiming down the hill at Max with his pistol. Max reached to his hip, but there was no gun there. Jim didn't know that, though, so he squeezed the trigger. Max fell backwards, lying on the ground unable to move. Jim approached to stand over him, now holding a shotgun. No, it wasn't Jim; it was a smaller man cocking the shotgun barrel. No, it was Ron, his friend.

Max sat straight up and looked into the dimness of the dark around him. His fire had burned out. He reached over, grabbing his pistol, thumb on the hammer, looking around. "Damn nightmare."

A faint line of light was showing on the horizon to the east, so Max walked to the edge of the clearing and relieved himself. His jumpiness was not gone, so he continued to stare around. He thought he saw a pair of eyes in the distance, close to the ground, but then they were gone. Max fastened on his belt and holster before feeding Hardy and breaking camp.

The day grew cold as a chilling wind swept across the trail. Max passed farms as the morning wore away. Many farmers had already completed planting. Their fields were plowed and seeded. Several were still busy with men and boys at work, mules pulling plows, men dropping seed and pushing dirt over it with their feet as they walked.

As the clouds covered the sun directly above, wooden buildings at the edge of Albuquerque came into view. A large mountain to the east was the prominent landmark.

Max rode down the street toward the center of town. It was similar to Santa Fe. The central plaza was there with the courthouse next to it, a church, and then houses. It was much smaller than Santa Fe, but still a beautiful town. More building had begun toward the other end of town, Max assumed where the rail would come through. After a short trip through the town, looking around at the shops, hotels, and noisy saloons, Max went to the stable and put Hardy up before walking to an inn and saloon.

The place was not as noisy as a couple of places down the street, and they were serving food as well as drinks. Max leaned over an open part of the counter and motioned to the man behind the bar. The man was balding with white scattered through his dark, thick beard, and, although chubby, he glided quickly over to Max.

"Hi, I need a room."

"What's your name?"

"Max Tillman."

The man pulled out a book and wrote in it and passed it plus the pen across the bar. "Sign or put your mark next to the last line. It's three dollars. The rooms are out the back door, third room from the left end."

Max signed and put the three dollars down. "Is there a key?"

"No. It locks from the inside."

Max sighed. He sat down in the empty seat, set his bags down on the floor, and leaned his rifle up against the bar. "What's for supper?"

"Beef, corn, and bean stew, or a cut of steak if you want to pay more."

"I'll take the stew, and a beer."

"All right, a buck twenty."

Max dug into his wallet again and put the money down.

"You probably could've left your stuff in your room," the man next to him said, pushing his empty bowl aside.

"I'd just rather be safe."

"Good policy. I agree with it wholeheartedly, and not long ago Albuquerque was worse than most places, but Marshal Yarberry has cleaned it up a bit. Of course, the good folks of the town are turning on him now."

"Give it a rest, Nick." The bartender set the bowl of stew and the beer down in front of Max.

"I'm entitled to my opinion," Nick told the bartender. "You want to hear it, mister?"

Max sighed. "Sure, why not?" Max was not sure he did want to hear the man's opinion, but he had nothing better to do while he ate.

"Well, things were getting out of control around here, so we needed a marshal. Yarberry was supported by the sheriff, his friend, but he's a good man, so Yarberry got the job. There was talk about him being good with a gun, so that helped. His reputation improved when he went out after a pair accused of robbery and brought them in over their saddles. The town soon became more civil."

"So, that's why he was hired. Sounds like he did his job." Max took a swig of beer.

"Exactly, young man, that's what I say. He's good for Albuquerque." The man leaned a bit closer and lowered his voice. "But certain rumors that possibly have some truth started to spread. He came into town with a woman and young girl. The woman has a different last name, Preston. Well, the formalities of marriage in the West . . . eh, but then word was that Sadie Preston was actually the wife of his former partner in Cannon City, Colorado. He supposedly met them again in San Marciel, and rumors are that Yarberry and Sadie started back up what they did behind Tony's back while he recovered from a gunshot."

Max was interested now. While using a

217

chunk of bread to wipe the stew from the bottom of the bowl he asked quietly, "People claim Yarberry shot him?"

The man shook his head. "Actually, another man shot Preston, and Yarberry avenged him. Yarberry does not like people messing with his friends and him. It's said that in his youth he left someplace in Arkansas, I think, because he killed a man and then later killed a prominent rancher. A bounty hunter came after him in Texarkana, and that man was found dead, and Yarberry was on his way deeper into Texas. He joined the rangers there and was highly regarded. But then another bounty hunter showed up in the town where he was staying. Yarberry left the town, and a couple of days later that bounty hunter was found dead a couple miles outside of town."

"So Yarberry told all this to someone?"

"No, I haven't got to that yet. None of that stuff probably would've gotten out but for Dirty Dave Rudabaugh."

"Name sounds familiar."

"He was part of the Dodge City gang up in Las Vegas, outside of Santa Fe. Well, he came into the territory and eventually heard about Yarberry becoming marshal and supposedly told somebody that he was part of the Missouri Trio with Yarberry, robbing and cattle rustling in Missouri, Arkansas, and Kansas. Supposedly during that time, he killed that rancher."

"I see, but people aren't taken out of the territory very often."

"Well, not as often. Anyway, with Dave Rudabaugh on the run now, and having killed that deputy . . . well, any association Yarberry had with him makes the finer people of this region concerned."

"Oh, I remember now. Hoodoo Brown, Rudabaugh, and the other deputies were thought to be robbing stages themselves around New Mexico. One of them was caught, and they thought that it was Rudabaugh who tried to break him out."

"Yes, I see you read the paper."

"Yes, I did a couple of weeks ago anyway."

"So, you know Rudabaugh's story? Thought to rob stage coaches all the way to the Black Hills of South Dakota."

"But he was caught trying to rob a train years ago, right?"

"Yeah, but he cut a deal on his gang members to get free. Ha! Then Bat Masterson took him on with Atchison Topeka in the railroad war. The guy always seems to get away and have the better of it. After the rail war, he became a deputy with Hoodoo Brown. You can't tell the lawmen from the bandits sometime, but that's not Yarberry. Whatever his past was I think he's put it behind him."

Max rubbed his chin. "So, what's the price on Rudabaugh and Brown?"

"Don't know that there is one on Brown, but he's been chased out of the territory to Texas is what they say. Rudabaugh's a pretty healthy sum; I think three hundred." The man looked at the gun on Max's hip. "You a bounty hunter?"

"I've collected on a couple."

The man sighed. "Where are you from, mister?"

"Texas originally."

The man nodded. "Well, I sure wouldn't want to go after Rudabaugh. Might as well go after Billy the Kid."

"Nah, that's one I don't want to chase."

"Why not?"

"Got my reasons. Good night. Thanks for the talk." Max picked up his rifle and bags and headed for the back door.

The next morning Max woke and walked into the eatery and bought a quarter loaf of bread and walked down the street eating it, looking at Albuquerque in the daylight. It was busy with people moving about, mostly men carrying tools to the east side of town, where the sound of hammers carried as he walked the distance between. The train station was being completed and other businesses being added around the site. It was nearly two miles between the established town and the train, but the railway knew it would bring business and people.

It seemed a bit of luck him hearing about Rudabaugh while he was trying to decide his next move. He had been thinking about Arizona, but that would wait. He was sure there would be plenty of men looking for Rudabaugh, probably even Jack Sutter. Well, if he and Sutter crossed paths again, Max thought he might just pay him back for the beating, with interest.

He needed to find out about Rudabaugh, though, so he found the local newspaper office and went inside. The bearded man looked up from where he was working with a metal plaque of some sort. "Hold on just a second, young man." The man sounded older than he looked. His short, wavy hair was still a dark brown in every spot, and there was no balding or receding hairline. He looked fit, like he could have been a miner Max had worked with. He slid the plaque into a larger machine and then began pulling the crank in circles.

"What can I do for you, sir?"

"I wanted to buy a paper. I see that today's is being printed, so can I buy yesterday's?"

"Sure, but you can have a copy of today's when it dries in about twenty minutes; this is the last page."

"Fine. How much?"

"Ten cents."

Max pulled out twenty cents and laid it on the counter between them. "Anything on Dave Rudabaugh in there?"

"Only a couple of lines about his whereabouts currently being unknown."

"I've been in the wilderness for a while. What can you tell me about the story? Any hints on what direction he was traveling or anything?"

"If I told everybody the news, nobody would buy my paper."

Max put ten cents more down.

The newsman sighed but took a deep breath as he cleared the page off the press and put another one in. "Well, we actually thought it possible he would pass through our area a few days ago, but if he did he stayed out of sight. My guess is he probably knows that Yarberry would gladly put him down for the trouble Rudabaugh caused him, plus the reward. He obviously wouldn't head toward Santa Fe, as there's too much law and military around there. I would bet he goes east to Texas to join back up with Brown, or possibly south toward the border, but it's hard to say. He's a wild one."

"Thanks. I'll be back to get that paper."

"You going after him, aren't you?"

"I'm thinking about it."

"What's your name?"

Max started to tell him, then stopped. "Don't want a name, mister."

"I can probably find out."

Max looked at him a moment, then shrugged. "Yeah, but nobody would recognize it. You might as well use Joe Smith for all they would care."

The man chuckled. "No, Joe Smith won't do. Come back for that paper in a few minutes. I'll have it ready."

"Thank you, sir."

Max headed out and looked down the street. In the distance to his left was one supply store, and a few doors down to the right was another. He decided to go to the one that looked as if it might fall down. They needed the business and probably would charge less.

The thin man at the shop suggested what Max bought as much as asked him. He knew what men needed on the trail and did not try to sell him extra. He stopped by the newspaper office and picked up the paper and ignored the man's questions. Max felt something like excitement. He was chasing Dirty Dave Rudabaugh.

Max was riding out of town and had to nudge Hardy to the side quickly as four men came riding in hell-bent, laughing. Max wanted to say something or pull his gun but settled for spitting on the ground and continuing out of town.

He figured to sweep east a bit, asking people he ran across if they had seen Rudabaugh. Max camped as dusk was showing its first signs. He went off the trail a ways, but there was little brush in the area, so his campfire could be plainly seen from a couple of miles away. Maybe it would keep the animals away more than make them curious, but any bandits or renegade Indians out there could take advantage of it. But there was nowhere else to camp. He tossed and turned, opening his eyes at any sound in the distance. Sleep would not come.

Finally, he took a deep breath and broke camp. He did not feel like sleeping anyway. After kicking dirt over the fire, he took Hardy's reins, led him back to the trail, and began walking. His eyes adjusted to the dim light the half moon gave within a few minutes.

A movement low to the ground up the path made him jump, and he pulled his Colt. The shape stopped for a split second and then trotted into the darkness. Max realized it was a javelina and holstered his weapon. Only a few paces later the yips of coyotes broke the silence of the night. It was a large pack, but they would likely keep their distance.

Max could see well enough to see any holes in the trail, and Hardy's eyes were even better. The horse neatly straddled or stepped front and back hooves over the holes and strewn rocks.

The night walk became peaceful despite the yips and howls of the coyotes that were apparently heading in the same direction as him. The sky was clear, and it seemed the stars were brighter than usual. The stick next to his foot curled up and rattled. Max jumped back and Hardy reared up, nearly pulling him off the ground with his left hand caught in the reins. He fumbled his pistol out while trying to regain his balance and fell to the ground as he freed his hand. The rattler struck at his boot while he kicked the ground to scoot away from it, and he cocked his pistol and shot, hitting the coiled part of the snake, knocking it back. He cocked a second time and took aim, hitting the snake square in the head.

Max pushed to one knee while looking at the still reptile, now twisted on the ground. It had seemed like a straight stick when he nearly stepped on it. Max stood, looking for Hardy, who had bolted. The coyotes had stopped. The gunshots had made the night silent again. Max walked in the direction he had thought Hardy had gone, and, in the distance, he saw the horse trotting. Max whistled and called, "Hardy!" The horse stopped but did not return. Max strode toward the horse, stumbling over some brush. He heard a faint rattle somewhere nearby, not near enough to worry about, but he did worry, looking nervously around his feet. He tried to keep his distance from any brush a rattler could be coiled under. He reached Hardy and took the reins again, stroking his neck. He reached into his saddlebag, pulled out an apple and took a bite, then gave it to the horse. After Hardy finished eating, Max swung into the saddle and started back for the trail. The distant cry of a mountain lion broke the quiet of the night. Hardy's muscles tensed at the sound, and Max sighed, patting the horse's neck. "It's all right. It's far away."

The eastern sky was brightening when Max spotted a couple of adobe buildings on the top of the hill ahead. He continued to walk Hardy until he reached the yard and the trough, letting the horse take a good long drink. The house looked small compared to the animal shelter twenty paces from it. It was nearly as big as Ron's stables had been.

The door to the building opened, and a stout man walked out. "Water's a dime." Max noted that the graying man had a pistol tucked in his belt.

Max dug into his pocket and pulled out a dime. He walked over to hand it to him. "How much would a stall and oats for the horse and a place for me to nap cost?"

The man looked at Max's guns, then to Hardy, considering.

"My horse needs a few hours rest, mister."

The man nodded. "I see that. Two dollars and I throw in breakfast for you?"

"Two dollars!"

"Yes, two dollars, and that includes a bunk."

"Fine; better be good food."

"Come on. Let's get your horse taken care of." He turned toward the door. "Mary, we got another mouth to feed!"

"Thought so!" the call came back.

"What's your name, traveler?"

"Max."

"People call me Cal. You travel all night?"

"Yeah, trouble sleeping, a rattler, a bright moon, so I just decided to walk."

"Rattler'll make you jumpy for days, it gets close enough."

"Yeah, I guess I got careless. Used to watch for them closely when entering the shaft first thing in the mornings."

"Yeah, I did some prospecting years ago. Never any deep shaft mining, but some panning in California. Had to watch for snakes first thing in the morning doing that, too."

They brushed Hardy down, put him in a stall, and fed him.

"Fine horse."

"Thanks. Looks like you have quite a few."

"Yeah, a few of them are the stage line's that runs through. They'll switch them out on their ride through; they push them hard."

Max washed his hands before heading inside to eat. The man had a Mexican wife around his age, and a son and daughter in their early teens. And there were another two travelers at the table as well. The bearded man extended his hand and in a deep rough voice introduced himself as Tom Reese, and the youth in his mid-teens was Danny.

The eggs and bread hit the spot, and Max leaned back in between bites. "I was in

Albuquerque a couple of nights ago and heard that a fugitive, Dave Rudabaugh, might be coming through this way."

Tom glanced up at hearing the name. "You looking for Rudabaugh?"

"Just making conversation. Thought it was interesting, wondered what type of man he was and if he'd passed through here."

"He didn't stop here, thank God," Cal said.

Tom just eyed Max a moment. "Maybe, Max. Let me tell you what I heard. I heard that Rudabaugh has been hanging out with William Bonney."

"Billy the Kid?" Danny looked at his father.

His father looked at Danny and rolled his eyes. "If you did happen to be more than curious, I wouldn't go looking for him. It's a whole lot of trouble for one young man, no matter how good you are with those pistols at your side, no offense." Tom ducked his head. The man was big and had a pistol through his belt as well but eyed Max's guns worriedly.

"Mr. Reese, no offense taken, none at all. I appreciate the information." He looked from Tom to Danny. "It would never be in my slightest interest to come up against Billy the Kid. From what I heard and read,

229

he was no more in the wrong than those he was up against that brought the price on his head."

Reese nodded. "There's that, too."

"But, Mr. Reese, I would like to know whether you know it to be rumor, or fact, that you saw with your own eyes that Rudabaugh was with Bonney. There's lots of rumors that aren't true and wouldn't dissuade me if I was chasing Rudabaugh, but if a man such as yourself that I would trust not to lie to me said he saw it with his own eyes, then I am off in the other direction when I wake up."

Reese looked at Max for several seconds, and then at everyone else in the room before replying. "I saw them together yesterday at Fort Sumner. We own some property near there we were looking to graze out or sell to somebody, and I saw them pass through the eating house. I'd seen Rudabaugh's poster, and I've met Billy before."

"You know Billy the Kid?" Danny looked at his father as if he'd been holding out on him.

"I want to tell everyone in this room, especially you, Danny, that nothing but trouble can come from mentioning this to anyone. Innocent people at Fort Sumner might get hurt, plus if it got back to certain members of that gang that someone in this group gave their whereabouts, they may take it out on any name mentioned." He looked at Danny. "So promise me, son, this does not leave your mouth." Danny sighed and nodded, but Tom continued, "And remember, if you don't keep this secret, how can you expect anyone you tell to keep it?" That brought another sigh again.

Cal looked at his own family. "He's right." Then he looked at Reese. "Matter of fact I wish he hadn't said anything about it. So let's none of us say anything to anyone."

Both fathers looked at Max.

"Don't worry about me. I don't really like talking to people anyway." He took two more bites of his food and took his rifle and bags into the room he'd rented and closed the door.

He leaned a chair against the door so that it would fall over if somebody opened it and put his pistol down by his hand. As jumpy as he was, sleep came surprisingly easily. He momentarily woke to the ping of a horse being shoed in the barn but went right back to sleep. Noise finally brought him upright, several horse hooves and the creak of wheels. He stood up and looked outside to see the stage outside and two couples climbing down from the stage door. The driver and shotgun man were already walking inside. Cal and his son were unhooking the horses, six of them, their chests heaving.

Max smelled bread and chicken coming from the other side of the door. The direction of light coming through the window showed it was early afternoon. Max gathered his bags and made his way out of the room and saw Cal's wife cooking.

"Thank you, Mary, the meal and the rest were great."

"I made enough food for you as well, Max." She looked up as she was putting plates on the table. Even with her accent he could hear the motherly concern. "Storm's brewing in the distance. Perhaps stay the night and start fresh in the morning."

"No thanks, ma'am, I have to be moving on." He really didn't want to climb back into the saddle again, but he did not want to spend any more money either. The stage man standing on the porch still held his shotgun, and he eyed Max as he left.

Max glanced to the west and saw the dark clouds. That was the way he was riding. He nearly changed his mind, but, in the end, he went to the barn and saddled Hardy. Cal invited him to stay as well, but Max just thanked him, waving as he rode out. Then he stopped, thinking about going the southern route instead, but he decided that Albuquerque was likely to be the better way water-wise, plus he was more likely to hear rumors, and he thought he could find enough shelter in the town if the storm lasted. He brought Hardy to a quick trot, thinking to make good time before the storm was upon them.

It was less than an hour after starting out that the day turned dark, as if evening fell upon him in less than a minute. Lightning up ahead made him sigh, and the thunder after seemed to stretch for several seconds. It was only a few minutes later that the rain started to fall, big drops that turned from a few to a downpour over the next quarter mile. The lightning struck closer now, lighting up the sky that had turned nearly to night at mid-afternoon.

Max rode on but soon had to admit he was miserable. He was soaked and tired of being in the saddle. Hardy seemed to twitch a little with each lightning strike, and that made Max nervous. "Easy, boy." There was no place to shelter anywhere close. No thick cluster of trees. It would have to be a thick cluster, too, what with the heavy rain and the wind that had picked up, sending the rain sideways.

The only thing they could do was keep

going. The road became muddy, making Hardy's steps slower and more labored, and after a time, as evening neared, the sky was truly becoming fully dark. Max spotted a thicker cluster of trees than most he'd seen and made for them. He and Hardy found some raised ground that was only getting hit by a bit of the rain, and puddles weren't forming there. It was all he could hope for. He tied Hardy up and sat on the ground up against the tree, shivering. He longed for the sun and its heat again.

If he was lucky that would be tomorrow. It was nighttime now, and it was getting colder. Max began shivering, and took his coat out of the saddlebag. He put it on and huddled back up against the tree.

It could be worse. His boots had kept his feet dry, and for that he was grateful. He missed his tent from the mines. He wanted something to warm his insides; he should have bought some whiskey to bring with him in Albuquerque.

The lightning flashed, and he thought he saw something to the side. There was only brush, and falling water. He sighed, shaking a little. He had been warm in Albuquerque and at Cal and Mary's place. They really did not want him staying around anyway, but he could see they'd been worried about him. Nobody should have to worry about him. He was a man now and could take care of himself. He sat there under the tree riding out the storm.

It rained until mid-morning the next day. Max had trouble staying comfortable and had to get up and walk in small circles. He did manage to fall into a light sleep for a couple of hours somewhere in the night.

When Max lifted the saddle to put on Hardy, the horse danced sideways. "Hardy!" Max grabbed the horse's mane with one free hand. He put the saddle on forcefully and bent over to strap the saddle. He loaded the other gear and then began walking the horse back toward the trail, each step a slosh. He swung up into his saddle before reaching the road, and Hardy snorted, the horse equivalent of a sigh. They traveled at a slow pace through the muck.

A couple of miles down the trail it began to mist. It was not long before the mist turned to rain. Max let out a string of curses. He worried about the washes filling up to where they would be hard to cross.

After a while the rain stopped, and moments later the sun pierced the clouds. That lasted only long enough for Max to get his hopes up before the clouds shrouded the sun, and the mist fell again. The cycle continued all the way to Albuquerque. The rain was falling steady when he rode Hardy into the stable. The sky had been dim all day, but it was not completely dark, so Max guessed it was late afternoon.

He had not eaten since the night before, and he was cold and wet. He took the time, though, to brush Hardy himself and give him oats, plenty of them. He patted the horse on the neck before leaving. He had been hard on the horse the last few days. A couple of nights in town would be expensive, but they needed it. Hardy should not have to suffer for Max's stupidity. The rain would hopefully let up and give the ground a chance to dry some, give Hardy an easier step.

Max made his way to the hotel and saloon where he had stayed last time through. He walked through the door, and the pudgy man behind the bar held up his hand.

"We can squeeze you in a place to eat or drink" — the man waved to the room that had just a couple empty chairs at the table and a couple of places to stand at the bar — "but we don't have any rooms tonight. Booked up due to the rain."

Max sighed and walked back out into the rain.

He tried another small place before going

into the hotel, the nice one. One room was left, and he took it, having to put down twenty dollars for the two nights and a warm bath. But he could be warm and dry. He was not sure it was worth it, but he was done going out into the rain.

The warm bath felt nice, especially after getting out and drying off. He put on the best clothes he had before going downstairs into the café. He had already been extravagant with the room, so why not eat in the restaurant downstairs? He did not want to go back out into the rain, or mud or damp air. His best was a light-blue shirt, a not-yet-ragged pair of denim pants, and hurriedly cleaned boots.

He sat at a small table alone and drank a whiskey to help warm up his insides. They brought out a tenderized steak, potatoes, steamed carrots, and crusty bread. Max ate hungrily. It was not long before the white of his plate showed.

He leaned back, looking around and taking notice for the first time. There were rancher types at the other tables with their women, but also men in suits. Max glanced around, puzzled.

He gave it little thought before paying for his meal and going upstairs to sleep. And he slept well.

CHAPTER 12

Max stayed in his room dozing on and off until midday the next day, when hunger drove him out of bed.

After pulling on his boots, he made his way down the street toward the bakery he had stopped by last time he was in town.

A tall, lanky man with a badge waved to him from the walk. "Hold up a moment." The man rested his hand on his pistol. Max took a deep breath and slowly folded his arms to keep his hands away from his guns. "I'm the town marshal, and I see a rig like yours, makes me worry about you getting into trouble where you need two guns."

Max sighed. "Actually, I've found that two guns come in handy at times. I was jumped by two highwaymen not long ago, and extra shots can make the difference. This can be rough country."

Yarberry's stoic gray eyes looked him over. "Yes, yes it can, but men that travel alone tend to have more trouble. Plus, why are they traveling alone? Could it be because they make bad company?" He waited for a reaction from Max, but Max did not give him one. "Just best not to use those guns around my town, or I'll have to make an example of you."

"I wasn't gonna do anything. Just wanting to rest a day and move on."

"See that you do, son." The marshal nodded to him and then took a step back and leaned against the wall. Max started down the street, feeling the watching eyes on his back. A man fell in beside him who Max realized had been standing nearby during his discussion with Yarberry.

The man was sturdy looking, with kind eyes. He reminded Max of Ron Stark. "Don't take it personal. He's just wanting to make sure there's not trouble like there used to be, and a man with two pistols like yours makes people wary."

"I understand." Max nodded to him and picked his footing for the driest spots while he hurried across the street so he would not have to wait for the wagon that was approaching.

The man ran alongside him. "My name's Berry, Berry Hillman."

"Nice to meet you, Berry." Max hurried

on to the bakery door two doors down.

"What's your name, if I may ask?"

"It's Max."

When Max opened the door, Berry held it. "Well, Max, I was just wanting to talk to you, see what type of person you are. Curious if the marshal really had anything to worry about."

"He just might," Max said, looking back as he went inside. "Hi, I'd like a half loaf of bread, please."

"I'll take one of your biscuits please, Stella." Berry nodded to Max. "The biscuits are the best I've tasted."

Max nodded to him.

Stella collected the money from each of them and then gave them their orders at the same time.

Max sighed as he left, followed by Berry.

"Max, I can see you don't really feel like talking, so just answer me three questions and I'll leave you be."

Max tore off a chunk of bread and leaned back against the wall of the bakery, motioning Berry to start.

Berry leaned against the wall a couple of feet away. "You told me Yarberry may have something to worry about. Were you saying that to get rid of me, or do you mean it?"

Max looked at the man, and his searching

eyes annoyed him, but he knew they should not. Berry was sincere, it seemed, but what he wanted, Max did not know. "Both, I suppose. I've killed men. They've all been justified by the law, but I did hunt one down, and I suppose there's a little bit of me that seems to be ready for a fight all the time lately."

Berry nodded, as if he understood. "Second question. Do you have any desire to settle down, man, you know . . . wife, kids?"

Max's jaw tightened as he thought about the man's question. It took him a second to form the words. "I thought that just a couple of weeks ago I had found it, but, you see, the roughness in me . . . it's just not for settling down. It came out, on somebody who had it coming, that's for sure, but after the beating I gave the man, I was thrown in jail. And, well, the girl didn't talk to me after that happened, but her father did, saying that I wasn't really welcome around anymore, you know. I can't blame him; I guess it's better for her. I suppose I'm meant for wandering and for rougher things like hunting men, and mining." Max's voice was shaking as he finished. He felt like his eyes were about to tear up. He fought it off, and his voice came out harsh. "Why are you asking me this?"

Berry held up his hand soothingly. "That brings me to my third question, which is going to wrap all this up." He nodded to the gun belt. "It sounds like to me you chose to fight instead of love. I mean you did not stay and try to change for this girl, show her father you could be somebody other than the rough guy, as you said. Rather, you strapped on your guns ready to hunt another man? Is that really how you would want to live? Wouldn't you rather give your life to the Lord and find hope in his salvation?"

Max took a deep breath. "You don't understand. He killed my best friend, the man I hunted. And the man I beat basically spit on my friend's grave. And Ron was a good man, who gave that guy the benefit of the doubt every time he did not deserve it. He had it coming, and the man that killed him had it coming also."

"It says in Psalm 37, 'Abstain from anger and cease from fury; also do not inflame yourself to do evil. For evildoers shall be cut off; and the ones waiting on Jehovah, they shall inherit the earth.' "

Max shook his head and pushed himself away from the wall. "You've had your three questions." He walked past the preacher.

Berry reached out. "Max . . . ," but Max

pushed his hand away and strolled down the street.

The man had no idea what he was talking about. What if Berry's friend had been killed, and he had the ability to hunt him down? He'd be thinking differently then. Max had been turning something over in his mind earlier in the day, and he had made his decision. He needed some spending money and holing up in a fancy hotel in Albuquerque for a couple of days had drained him some. He went into the news- paper office.

The man behind the counter looked up. "You want some more information?"

Max smiled. "No, I'm selling some infor- mation."

"About what?"

"Juicy piece about an outlaw."

"Which outlaw? I've probably already heard it, but I'll listen, and if it's good, fresh news, I'll pay."

"No. You will claim you've already heard it. It's a good story and worth ten dollars."

"I deal fairly, my friend, which you don't. Ten dollars is way too much; go spread your rumors for free, or accept four dollars if it is worthy."

Max shook his head. "Seven."

"Five."

"Six."

"Done, if it'll sell, here and on the wire to other papers."

"It will."

The man took out a sheet of paper and grabbed his pen. "Let's hear it then."

"Dirty Dave Rudabaugh has joined up with Billy the Kid."

The newspaper man raised his head. "That is interesting, but I need more than that."

"A man saw them together like they were partners. He knew Billy from previous meeting and Rudabaugh from seeing his poster."

"Where was this he saw them?"

"He didn't want to say for fear of the gang."

"What's the man's name?"

"Didn't want that information given out either. Don't even think he'd like me giving you this information."

"But here you are?"

"Well, I was going after Rudabaugh, and now that I know he's with Bonney's gang, I'm off that trail but don't want my funds to get too low, so I can use that six dollars."

"So you think you are biting off more than you can chew to go against Billy the Kid, or both Billy the Kid and Rudabaugh?"

"Well, neither sounds very smart. But to be honest, I also have a weird kind of respect for the Kid and don't think he got a fair end in the Lincoln County war."

"You're with those that think it was the corrupt rich land owners and politicians painting a bad picture of him."

"Yeah."

"Were you there in Lincoln County?"

"No."

"Just curious, Mister . . ."

"Joe Smith."

The newspaper man chuckled. "Okay, Mr. Smith, have you ever killed a man?"

"Why does it matter?"

"Type of source."

"Four."

The man looked up, then back down at his paper, finishing writing, nodding his head. "Good." He stood up and went to the counter. "Six dollars it is." He seemed a bit nervous but came back with six dollars and dropped the coins into Max's hand.

Max shifted it to his left hand and offered his right. "Thank you, sir." They shook hands, and Max left, heading down the street toward the saloon that offered whiskey and women.

Max woke up with a dull ache in his head

from the five or six whiskies he'd had the night before. He'd bought a couple for the slender, mocha-haired saloon girl before they went to her room. The six dollars from the newspaper man was now gone. He poured water into the basin and splashed it on his face, taking away some of the grogginess. He gathered his gear and walked downstairs. The innkeeper looked at him, and then down at his ledger, frowning. Max sighed and walked past.

After buying some more bread and gathering Hardy, he was back on the trail. He did not feel as rested as he thought he would after two days.

The day was warm, and Max had taken a midday rest in a copse of trees. Two days had passed since he left Albuquerque, and Max had seen few people along the way. A freight wagon, a few single horsemen, and a hunter had all ridden past with just a cursory hello before moving on their way. A few men riding the range watching their herds had talked to Max a bit, just to make sure Max knew they were watching for rustlers. Max ate bread, jerky, and a squirrel he'd shot the previous night. Hardy was doing most of the work now, and there was plenty of bunch grass for him to eat.

Max had traveled without interruption to his own thoughts for the most part. Life had handed him some bad luck. There were men like Cal who had done all right in mining, found a good wife, and made a decent living at a stage stop. It seemed that things went right for some people, and wrong for others. Max had lost his father when he was young and left when the first job came along, so his mother did not have to worry about feeding him. Then the company he worked for went under, and his next promising opportunity ended when a good friend was killed. There had been an amazing girl interested in him, and that went all to hell also. His life was obviously not meant to be like Cal's life. He could go from mine to mine and maybe hunt men; nothing else seemed to be in his future.

The sound of running horses shook Max from his thoughts, and he looked through the trees to see three riders in the distance, pushing hard through the field. The slim one in front raised his hand holding a rope. Then Max saw the wolf come out of the dip in the slope, and the man managed to land the rope around its neck. The wolf rolled when it reached the end of the rope and bit at the rope. The man rode the other way, dragging the wolf. A stout looking rider circled and roped the wolf's hind legs. He pulled back, and they stretched the wolf out. The wolf started yelping. The third rider, tall and square-shouldered, dismounted. Grabbing a shovel from his saddle, he walked toward the wolf, raised it, and brought it down into the wolf's ribs. A louder yelp. The man raised the shovel again.

The gunshot made the tall man jump, blood drops hitting his face as the wolf went limp. He looked toward Max twenty yards away, and the thin rider twitched.

"Don't!" Max had already re-cocked and had his rifle aimed at the thin rider. "The first sudden movement from any of you and I shoot. You just keep your hands on that shovel with it resting on your shoulder. You two keep both hands on the reins held high."

"You could have shot me," the one with the shovel said.

"If I'd wanted to. Well, I did want to but decided against it. I hit what I aimed for."

"Mister . . ." The thin one started to speak.

"If you're killing it to keep your herd safe, I can't blame you. But torturing the thing for hunting food like it's made to do . . . Well, you're just a bunch of no-good bastards to me."

"You think you can kill all three of us before one of us shoots you?" the thin rider said in a cocky tone.

"Maybe. But the thing is I don't mind dying, as long as I take a couple of you with me, and you, Mister Big Talker, would be the first to go. As it is, all I want to do is leave, but seeing as your type's likely to shoot me in the back, I'll have you hold your right hand up, turn your horse, and dismount; as soon as your boots hit dirt, raise your left. If you drop your right or make any odd movements I shoot. You others don't move."

The thin man sighed but did as Max said.

"Now, keeping your hands up like your life depends on it, 'cause it does, walk over and stand three feet away from your friend, keeping your back to me." The man complied.

Max had the other rider do the same. "Tall man, lift that shovel above your head, both hands on it. Now all three keep your hands up and start walking the other way. I'm letting you keep your guns, because I understand how tough it would be to part with them with me holding my gun on you. So keep your hands up, and walk, not looking back. You lower your hands, I shoot. You look back, I shoot. You do as I say, and this is over, and no one gets hurt." They started off, and Max took a step back. "Oh, and if I hear of you torturing more animals, I will be back, with a rope and a shovel of my own." The thin one stopped when he said that. "Keep going! I'm a better shot than you, and this rifle's a lot more accurate at this range. It ends here. You come after me, then I know what I'll have to do. Hands up and don't look back." He kept his eyes on them as he backed toward the trees and Hardy. The men kept walking. Max turned and ran the last several steps, swinging into Hardy's saddle and riding full speed on the path through the trees. He came out the other side and continued at full gallop until he could ride behind the next thicket of trees three hundred yards away. He looked back, his hand on his rifle in its holder. He watched the other edge of the field for a few minutes. They had listened and believed him. He put Hardy back on the trail again at a fast trot. He would have to make good time. He did not know if they would gather more men and chase. He shook his head. Now he had to look over his shoulder. He probably should have just shot all three before they knew what was happening.

CHAPTER 13

Max pushed hard for the next couple of days, half expecting men to be chasing him down, but there was never a sign from anyone behind him. He was even nervous when going past somebody heading in the other direction. He only realized that he had entered Arizona when the only man he had seen in four hours of riding stopped to ask him how much farther it was to the New Mexico border. Max was unable to help that man, but he had told Max that he might be able to make it to St. Johns by nightfall.

The vegetation had become a little thicker, and in the very late afternoon the trail became thinner and overgrown, obviously not heavily traveled. But the sound of water let Max know the Little Colorado River was just through the brush. He urged Hardy in and forded the river. It was up due to all the rain, and he came out with water in his boots. He was looking forward to a bed and a meal.

Max pushed Hardy, and, just as full dark came on, he saw a farmhouse in the distance off the trail that widened at that point. He continued and had taken another side trail right to another farmhouse. He was riding on toward it to ask directions when he noticed another building and another house across from it. The large ranch house was just off the street. He hoped that the ranch house might board a passer-through as well. He trotted his horse up to the hitching post and looked toward the stables about thirty paces away. Two men and a boy of around ten came out of the house, each with a gun in his hand.

"I'm sorry, I was just wondering where I may rest for the night?"

"You can rest here," the soft-spoken man said. "We are just careful. Geronimo was seen not too far from here last night, according to a few army scouts that rode through this morning. William here was keeping watch when he saw you riding toward us. Son, take care of his horse for him." The boy took Hardy's reins and started for the stables.

"I appreciate it."

"You're welcome. You are just in time; we

were just starting supper. We don't have much room inside, so I hope you don't mind the loft of the barn?"

"Better than out in the elements, and I'd be glad to pay."

"If you wish to pay a dollar or two, that's fine, but you're welcome all the same. Anna, we need another plate," the man called inside.

"I'm Ammon Tenney, and this is my brother William." He and the younger man each gave Max a firm handshake as Max gave his name. "Come on in."

They prayed before they ate, and it was slightly different than what Max had heard before, but he knew that many people had different practices. The meal of roasted beef, tomatoes, and bread filled Max better than he had been since leaving Albuquerque. Max looked at Anna (apparently Ammon's wife), William, a younger woman named Eliza, and the eight children, with the boy from outside being the oldest. It was a beautiful, big family.

"When did you settle here, Ammon?"

"We moved here just about two years ago now."

"Where did you move from?"

"Aways up north," Anna answered.

"Well, it seems like this is a pretty tight-

253

knit community."

"Most of us moved here together," Ammon told him. "As a matter of fact, my brother owns the property just to the east."

"You've built it up pretty well."

"Oh, much of it was here before. We bought it out from a man named Soloman Barth. He used to make the crossing of the river here around ten years ago hauling salt from the Salt Lake in Zuni territory to Prescott. He had a big win in a poker game, and he and his brothers bought a bunch of cattle and land here and started a ranch. He wasn't the first, though. It has been settled by farmers and ranchers for over fifteen years now. He just became very prominent."

"Where are you from, Max?" William asked.

"East Texas originally." Max took a sip of water. "I've been through parts of Texas and New Mexico with a mining company, though, the last few years."

Ammon looked over at him a moment while he finished chewing some beef. "Do you know God, son?"

"I've heard about him quite a bit, but . . . I don't know about all that. There hasn't exactly been a lot of proof in some good God during my life."

"Well, we're all His if we come home to Him, and give our lives to Him. I was down in Mexico a few years back, and there were many of the natives — been there before the Spaniards — did not know Him, had no proof of Him during their lives, but they accepted Him. That's why God called me down there on a mission."

"You're a preacher then, sir?"

"I'm an Elder, but it's all of our place to do the work of the Lord, spreading the real message."

Max finished his last bite and nodded to Ammon. "I appreciate your words, sir, but I'm too tired to think about this right now."

Max excused himself and went out to the barn. He climbed into the loft and fell asleep within seconds.

Max awoke ready to start early. From what he had heard, the trail between St. Johns and Globe could be dangerous due to renegade Apache tribes.

"The White Mountain Apache have always been more peaceful, but the Apache to the south have attacked travelers," Ammon told him. "And they have even ventured into these areas lately while avoiding the soldiers."

It was not possible to make the entire trip to Globe in less than two days, and it usually took a full three, especially with a wagon. Ammon's wife made a tasty egg and biscuit breakfast, and, while eating, Ammon asked him if he wanted to wait and join him and some of the other men when they made the trip in three days. But Max was eager and did not want to wait.

Ammon told him that he would send his son to ask the other men if they would like to make the trip earlier. They often went to Globe for supplies and sold a cow or two and excess grain when they went. It would be slower traveling with a wagon, but with five men with rifles it was safer.

Max agreed to wait another day and also to help around the place for the extra day's board. He went with Ammon to patrol the edges of the pasture to be sure that the cattle were safe. Along with worrying about Apaches taking the cattle, there had been a mountain lion spotted in the area the previous week. There were plenty of deer and elk in the area, so the big cats would probably stay clear of the cattle, but there had been attacks in the past. Max grabbed his rifle and his pistols.

As he was strapping the holsters around his waist, Ammon nodded to the two guns. "You had much call to use two guns?"

"Not since I've had them, but there was a

time when a couple of highwaymen jumped me that several extra rounds would have been useful. I was fortunate then. Now I'm prepared."

Ammon led them out toward the barn. "I have to admit I was a bit hesitant last night, you with the two-gun belt. For what my advice is worth, I'd only wear the one gun, keep the extra in the saddle. It will make people think you're trouble."

Max sighed. "I'll think on it. Actually, if I can find work in the mines, I won't have much use for wearing them at all. I'll have to store them away so nobody knows I have them."

"I don't know if the mines in Globe are hiring. They had all the help they needed last I heard."

They led the horses out the back of the barn and through a gate at the end of a small fenced yard. They climbed into the saddle at that point and rode through tall grass. There were more than a dozen cattle visible right away over the rise and more than twice that many grazing, some in the flat grassland, some visible in the woods on the other side of the pasture. They rode across and into the woods looking through, and across, a steep wash.

Nothing seemed awry to Max, but Ammon seemed agitated. "Something wrong?"

"Young black, white, and chestnut cow. Haven't seen it yet."

Max looked back through the trees and did not see one that matched that description. "What now?"

"There's a shallower place in the wash to the east; we'll check there."

They rode for a few minutes along the wash until they came to the place where the embankment was not as steep. They had placed bramble brush there, but it looked trampled. Ammon climbed down and looked at the ground, walking in a circle. Max looked at the ground from his horse. He saw horse and cattle prints.

Ammon shook his head. "Cattle, horse, boot, and possibly cougar, but that one could be as old as last week."

Max pulled his rifle from its saddle holder and climbed down. "Well, let's go see."

Ammon took rope from his saddle, and Max fastened it around a thick branch of the bramble brush while Ammon tied the other end around his saddle horn. Then he urged his horse back, pulling the brush out of the way. Max looked at the narrow gorge that branched off of the wash. "I'll walk this way. You take the horses up top and look around."

"You sure?"

"Yeah, I'm gonna earn seconds on tonight's meal." With that Max started out into the gorge. He saw the cattle tracks right away, but the cow could have climbed out somewhere up ahead.

He walked on, traipsing across uneven ground, thinking that the cow surely struggled through this slot. Soon there was a place where the gorge branched off, and he took the path to the left where he thought the cow may have gone. He was not sure about the tracks, though, because the ground was rockier. Max could not see anything where the dirt and flat rock joined. The gorge narrowed, then curved, and he went around the bend. There, lying at his feet, was an Indian, unmoving, his neck bloodied. Max looked forward several feet to where a brown and white cow lay with flesh torn from its flank.

"Found it!" Ammon called in the distance.

Max turned and saw the big cat bound from behind him.

He fell backwards as he turned. The cat hit the barrel of the rifle just as he pulled the trigger, and there was a screaming whimper. Then everything went black.

"Max!"

Max opened his eyes. Ammon looked

down at him from the rim of the gorge. The big cat lay upon him dead, the gunshot going through its jaw out the top of its head. He made to push it off of him, and he elbowed the dead Indian next to him.

"You all right, Max?"

"Yeah," Max said shakily. "Got lucky with that quick shot."

Max pushed himself free of the cougar and stood, looking down at the big cat. That very well could have been how his father died, and Max had nearly suffered the same fate. He doubted he would live to an old age either, the direction his life was going. "Looks like it got your cow."

"Yeah, but not the one I had breeding plans for. Got an Apache, too."

"Yeah, he must have come upon the cougar while it was feeding."

They took the Apache's body and buried it out near the edge of Ammon's property.

"Not like them to raid alone," Ammon remarked as they traveled back with a wagon to gather the cow and the cougar.

"Yeah, he may have split off for some reason," Max offered.

"You're still a little shaky aren't you, brother?"

"I guess so."

"The Lord can comfort you in your trials."

"Ammon —" Max started, then stopped. "Ammon . . . from Utah, right? You're Mormon?"

"Yes, I belong to the Church of the Latter Day Saints."

Max was a bit shocked. It had not dawned on him, but the name was Mormon, and from up north meaning Utah, and he had the feeling that Eliza was not William's wife. Max did not say anything for a moment. Ammon had been a great host and seemed to be a good man. Why should this change his thoughts? Max sighed and helped lift the cougar and carry it up the gorge to put in the wagon.

"Max, a man must come to know his creator or —"

"Ammon, I don't mean to be rude, but I'm not up for hearing this. I almost died back there the way my father did."

"I'm sorry to hear about your father; I really am, Max. I think it's a good time to look at your life and the purpose behind it, but we don't have to talk about it now. It is a big part of who I am, though, so I may mention it without necessarily trying to preach to you."

"Fair enough."

They loaded the cow on the wagon and hauled the dead animals back to the barn, where William said he would take care of them.

They went inside and had a bit of bread, and, when Ammon looked up at Max, Max spoke first. "I think I'm going to go ahead and get a start for Globe."

"You sure you won't wait?"

"No, thank you, Ammon, but I think the earlier I check on the mining jobs the better chance I have of getting one."

"All right. The least I can do is give you some food for your work today, and I'll give you a dollar for the cougar hide. That's about what we'll get for it down in Globe. I insist," Ammon added when Max held up his hand.

"Thank you, Ammon. You're a good man."

"It's my pleasure. You're . . . just think on what I've said, Max."

CHAPTER 14

Max rode out several minutes later with a bag of dried beef and bread. He was nervous about being out on the trail alone, especially after almost being killed by a mountain lion, but he did not want to travel all the way to Globe with Ammon preaching at him.

The trail out of St. Johns was like most of western New Mexico and Arizona so far. There were small areas of trees and good grama grass; then there were large areas of dirt, and sparse grass and sage. But he could see for quite some distance when there weren't large mountains nearby, so that comforted him.

In late afternoon, the brush thickened, and there were a few trees growing. Max made camp as night fell. There was a farmhouse just visible in the distance, and at dark he saw a few more lights in the distance, probably the town of Showlow. With his supplies from Ammon, Max did not need to stop in Showlow, so the next morning he passed through the small ranch settlement quickly. The pines thickened in the area, and he was surprised to find himself in forest. He thought that Arizona was supposed to be almost one big desert. The pines gave shade until midday, when the sun was directly above. As the sun began to fall, the pines began to thin, and he was in high desert again by late afternoon.

Max found himself descending switchbacks, and the light was dimming quickly, with a lot of descent still ahead of him. Hardy was sure footed on the rocky trails, but when the trail brought them to the eastern side of the mountain, it seemed to be evening already. The trail reached a small ledge that was twenty yards across, and, although it appeared that the switchbacks ended on flat ground not much farther below, Max did not want to risk his or Hardy's ankles on the loose rock trail. He worried as he unsaddled Hardy that this was likely the only way through for any bands of Apache traveling through, or large animals for that matter. He sighed and tried to push those thoughts out of his head. He had made his decision, and full dark was coming on now.

He enjoyed the salted beef and bread

while sitting there looking at the last colors of the evening sky with its rust and dark purple. The sky and valley below soon darkened, and the moon was nowhere to be seen. Max heard coyotes yipping somewhere below. He also saw a flickering speck of light in the distant horizon, likely somebody else making camp for the night. Could be Apache; could be a traveler like him.

He curled up in his blankets, his head on a rolled-up shirt. He tried to put mountain lions and Apaches out of his mind.

Something scurried over his blanket, and he bolted upright. A ground squirrel darted into the brush nearby. Max looked around and saw the graying landscape as morning dawned. Hardy seemed a little restless, and Max looked at the edge of the bluff. He saw a large bull snake and figured it had been after the squirrel. The shiny gray reptile was almost four feet long. It slowly moved on away from where Max stood.

It did not have a rattle, so Max was not concerned, although he would have hated to have awakened to that thing curled against him. He gave Hardy some water and oats and ate some of the bread he had before saddling the horse. Then, as the landscape ahead of him brightened, he descended the rest of the switchbacks. As the morning was warming toward midday he rode across the Salt River, trying to seek out the trail on the other side. There were places where the trail was obvious; wagon ruts and hoof tracks easily marked it. In other places, there were tracks that followed the river. Max had to turn Hardy and backtrack twice before he saw the trail continue up the other side. Late that afternoon, as darkness was closing in, he camped at the top of a bluff, overlooking the canyon he had ascended a few minutes before. It had tired him and Hardy. He had swung down and walked in several places to let Hardy keep his energy for the tougher parts. He watched the sunset again, eating the last of his food. The noises of the night kept him up for a while after full dark had come, but Hardy was not acting nervous, so he convinced himself to relax and sleep.

The next morning as he saddled Hardy he saw movement in the distance through the trees. He watched until he could make out that it was a black bear on the trail, heading toward Max. He quickly tied on his bags and was off, making his way over the trail. He looked back several times that morning but saw no more of the bear. In mid-afternoon, he saw Globe in the distance. It appeared to be one of the bigger mining towns he had seen. He took his gun belt and stored it in his bags, keeping one pistol in his regular belt.

He saw the mine structures and then many houses spread out away from it. Max was surprised so much had been built up around the mine, especially with the trouble with Geronimo and the renegade Apache in the nearby hills. At that moment, he heard something in the brush to his left. He thought he made out a face with dark hair looking through the branches. He spurred Hardy to a quick trot and kept the pace until he was into the town, houses and businesses to each side of him. Some houses were built among the hills around the town. He brought Hardy to the stable near the center of the town, and a slow-moving, gray-bearded man came out and collected a buck for Hardy's stall and food. Max thought it should have been half that, but he was in no mood to argue.

He lugged his gear with him, toward the mine. There was a small wooden structure near the mine, and a few men lingered about it. "The boss around?"

A well-fed man with dark mustache looked at him and shook his head. "If it's work you're lookin' for, son, we don't have any."

"I've worked in mines for years, sir; I can

do most anything."

"Be that as it may, I've got a list of men ahead of you promised a position if we need more men."

"All right. Thanks." Max turned back around and moved toward a flop house he'd seen. Work was not going to be easy to find, and his money supply was dwindling fast.

There was an eating house a couple of houses down. The woman's husband had died in a cave-in, and to earn money for her and her young one, she cooked enough food for twenty men for supper and breakfast. Max had the feeling she made better money than her husband ever had. Maggie Lacey, a plump woman with brown and gray hair, charged a dollar for supper, and breakfast was free if you came back in the morning while there was anything left. The food this night was ham, corn, potatoes, and bread. It was good. The man next to Max told him that you got nearly twice as much as you did at the café or saloon, and the cooking was better. The lemonade washed it down nicely.

"There could be mining work at Tip Top up north of Phoenix in the Bradshaws," Maggie Lacey told Max.

"Maggie, don't be telling non-Arizonans about jobs our pals may be wantin'." The man who had been friendliest to Max turned to him and shrugged. "No offense, but we just met, and I know men around who have been lookin' for work for weeks."

"He seems like a good lad, Ken," Maggie said, pointing a serving spoon at Max. "Anyway, most of us was born outside Arizona. My father moved us to Tubac when I was fourteen, and we were some of the first ones here in truth, except for those who stayed when we took the land."

"Thank you, Miz Lacey," Max said.

The woman laughed and grabbed another basket of bread. "Just call me Maggie. This is a simple place, and everyone here is my friends."

"That's right, Mags." The miner at the end of the table held up his cup of lemonade as if toasting her.

"So, Mags," the man next to Max started, "if you were some of the first ones into Tubac, then were you around during the massacre?"

"No, I was married and living in Tucson by then. My husband had joined the Confederate army, the fool. I loved him like crazy, but we had words about that for years."

"Maggie," one of the older miners started, "he was standing up for the rights that were guaranteed us when we become a territory. That's what the dang charter —"

"Past, Ed. That was past, and right was decided on the field. There was lots of bad in the war and after, but right came out of it."

"Next you'll be sayin' that we should give the savages back their land and leave."

"No, but we could try to live in peace and stop callin' them savages!" Maggie sighed and softened her tone. "Of course, I have a soft heart for the stubborn men and their hard attitudes unchanging; reminds me of my dear old daddy." She winked at Ed and smiled, then started to take the empty plates.

Ed could not help but smile. Max had the idea that this was a common argument between the two of them.

Later, while taking off his boots, Max wondered if it was the miners that had made him feel so at home while at supper or maybe Maggie's personality. He laid his belongings against the wall behind his pallet. He sighed and lay down. He would have liked to stay in Globe, but that was not to be.

He looked over to another man across the room who was sitting on his blankets, taking his boots off. The man nodded to him and lay down. The room was a bit stuffy, considering that it was cooling outside. The windows, all on the south wall of the building, were open, but if there was a breeze it must have been blowing from the opposite direction. The floorboards and walls were well built with few cracks that would allow air to pass through.

The next morning Max woke upon hearing the movements of the other men in the bunkhouse, as the black of night turned to gray. He saw some of the younger, heartier-looking men working out the kinks in their muscles as they contemplated another day in the mines.

In the cot next to him, a thin, white-haired man's snoring abruptly stopped, and he popped up and glanced at the younger man. "It gets easier, Johnny." Then he chuckled. "Most of the time anyway." The older man stretched out his arms before sitting back down and pulling on his boots quickly and heading out the door. The younger man watched him go, then stopped rubbing on his shoulder and hurriedly made his way out with the majority of the men. A few men straggled out behind them. There were a couple of men who rolled over and stayed in their cots, either too hungover to work for the day, or travelers, but Max hoped to have some breakfast at Maggie's before he started out. The main room of the house was fairly packed when he entered, and there were only a few biscuits and a couple of slices of ham left on the table. Men were standing with tin plates, and Maggie was chatting intently with a couple of them, or Max would have said goodbye to her. Instead he put a small slice of ham in his mouth and grabbed a biscuit. Maggie glanced at him and gave him a wink, then turned back to the discussion.

Max smiled sadly, wishing he could stay. It was not just that Maggie treated the house full of men as something more than a way to make money. It was that feeling in the morning — going to the mines, seeing those men rouse themselves in varying degrees of vigor, but with the purpose that bound them as brothers of a sort. He missed that.

He stepped out, though. Lugging his bag and his rifle, he made for the stables. There were no mining jobs in Globe at the moment, and his money would soon run out. Leaving the stables with Hardy saddled he took a deep breath of the morning air and started to the west.

He rode out along a rough, rocky trail broken by short stretches of woods. After ten to fifteen miles, the trail became easier and stayed that way through the rest of the morning as they descended toward the west. By afternoon, Max was edging around a cluster of large rock formations, which must have been the Weaver mountain range that the stable man had talked about. They were tall and jagged. There had been a trail that went into the mountains, but the easier route was around them.

During the day, traffic on the trail was light. A few horsemen and a couple of wagons were all he had seen. As the sun dipped low in the sky, Max put the cluster of rocks behind him. He saw a group of mules ahead, merging on the trail from the north a bit.

Hardy's gait soon had them approaching the three mules, being led by a dusty older man. Max called out. "Hello, sir."

The bearded man looked back at Max, and his eyes narrowed, his hand hovering along his belt. "What do you want?"

Max was not sure what to say for a moment. "Just saying hello, sir. I was thinking —" Max now did not want to tell the man he was thinking of making camp soon and had been considering asking the man if he wanted company. The man's eyes stopped on Max's pistols for a couple of seconds and then scanned the area around them.

"It's kind of a lonely road; thought I would chat for a bit, but it looks like you're not in the mood for company, so I'll just move on." Max urged Hardy to a fast trot and arced around the jittery old man. He glanced back and saw the man's jaw set tight and his hand still on his belt next to his pistol.

Max did not feel comfortable until he was some distance ahead of the old man. He wondered if the man was wanted. Perhaps that was why he was jittery and scanned the area, as if there might be more men coming to capture him. Max let that idea roll around in his head a moment as he rode. Perhaps Max should have asked his name. Of course, if he was wanted, he would likely give another name. Max thought that when he made it to Phoenix he would check the posters.

Then the thought came to Max that the man might be scared of being robbed himself. That made more sense. The mules did have big loads on them. He was transporting some sort of supplies, or maybe he was a prospector bringing in samples for assaying. The man looked like a miner or prospector, maybe. Perhaps he even had a rich load of gold or silver ore that he was bringing from a mine in those mountains to Phoenix.

Max then thought about what it would be like to find a mother lode himself, as opposed to working a company mine. Striking it rich and living off it for the rest of his life. He could move back to Trinidad perhaps; he liked it there. Have a two-story house built at the edge of town, with enough land behind it for two horse stables and a yard for Hardy and maybe another horse. Then he thought perhaps he would check out Baton Rouge, Louisiana. When he was a boy there were more than a couple of stories of wealth in Baton Rouge. He could have one of those large plantation style houses built. He would, of course, have to find something to do and not just sit around all day. And he was not sure that he would feel comfortable among the wealth of Baton Rouge. He had never spent much time around anybody that wealthy. He would find a place, though, and something to put his time into that he would enjoy. And he would not have to worry about having money for his next meal. Perhaps he would travel around the entire country for a couple of years to find the best place to settle. He daydreamed about that until he looked back and could not see the old man or the mules any longer.

Of course, with dark setting in, that did not mean he was that far ahead, but, regardless, he was ready to make camp for the night. He rode Hardy off the trail a ways, then dismounted and walked him further so he could watch for holes. It had been an extremely hot day, and the cool air felt good, so he did not make a fire. But he gathered a few twigs and sticks just in case he changed his mind later.

It was nearly an hour later as he was thinking of lighting the fire that he saw movement out toward the trail, but he thought it must be closer. He stood and thought he could make out the three mules and then the old man, holding a rifle. The man saw him stand and froze for a moment. Max took a step back towards where his rifle leaned against a rock. The old man turned and led the mules off in the direction of the trail at a brisk pace. Max thought he saw the man glance back a couple of times. Max held his rifle following the man's path into the dark until he could no longer see him. Max put the saddle back on Hardy and led him back to the east for at least a half mile before nestling in among some ironwood. He then backed up to a smaller bush fifteen feet away and sat behind it peering through the branches into the night. He dozed off sitting up at some point and awoke to see nothing but his horse standing there, but he was nervous. What if he had not seen the man circling around because he was asleep? He looked around every direction, and, when something skittered through the brush, he jumped, a moment later realizing it was the same sound he had heard in the desert many nights on his travels. The night stretched long, with him drifting off to sleep a couple of times. And when the black lightened to gray, he saddled Hardy and started for Phoenix again. He was tired, but ahead he saw the fields of the farming community, and glancing back he saw a beautiful sunrise creeping over the higher peaks. Something about that made him smile.

The valley, as it was called, was lined with irrigation ditches, originating from the Salt River. Main ditches, and then side ditches branching off from those, helped bring water to the fields. For a place that was surrounded by the rocky ranges, it was prospering. There were fields of corn, hay, cotton, wheat, barley, and even potatoes. There were orchards of oranges, pecans, and olives.

Max rode into the town itself just after noon. It was like most towns he had visited in the west. Tents lined the outskirts, some next to more permanent adobe or wood structures in various stages of building. Then there were some residences and businesses, and toward the center was the pride of their town — a square with a bigger building housing local civic activities, a court, the mayor, claims office, etc. The sheriff's office was likely in there also. After a quick ride through the main streets, Max took Hardy to the stables and looked forward to a bed in a hotel room that night.

Max did not even bother eating. He checked into the hotel and went to his room and went right to sleep. It was dark when he woke up. He heard men laughing in the street and thought of going down to a supper or such, but he did not feel like being around anybody. He rolled over and lay there thinking. He did not feel like doing anything. He was tired of traveling, and he still had to travel up into the Bradshaw Mountains and see if the Tip Top mine was hiring. There might not be any jobs, and he did not know where he would go from there. There were rumors of railway work up north, but he was not sure how long his funds would hold out. He could not keep staying in hotels, that was for sure. It would be camping. And it was hot. It had been scorching when he rode into Phoenix. Traveling a long distance in the heat did not appeal to him at all.

His eyes focused on the guns lying on the small table next to his bed. He could just end it now. His life did not appear to be going anywhere. He reached over and gripped the handle of one of the guns. He looked for a reason not to do it. He had nothing to look forward to, and nobody was relying on him, or expecting anything from him right now.

Well, there was Hardy. Someone would end up with a good horse, but maybe they would not take good care of him. Max probably had not been the best at taking care of the horse, but there were men who were just mean to their horses. No, he let go of the gun, tears streaming down his face. Perhaps if somebody who seemed like he would be good to horses offered to buy Hardy, maybe then he would end it all. No, right now that would be selfish, not knowing who would care for the horse he inherited from Ricky.

Max stared at the ceiling, and, after a long while, he fell asleep. He woke as the sky was graying from black, and he grabbed his gear and made for the stables. He and Hardy had enjoyed a long rest, and he wanted to start early before it became too hot. Gillette was the town that serviced the mining camp of Tip Top, and it was a full day's ride. He saw a stage readying to leave on the street as he rode out of the stables. They started out at a near trot, which Hardy handled smoothly. Outside of the city there were more orange groves, where men were already out picking the fruit. Max rode over and offered some money for a few oranges, and the supervisor made the trade. He ate two right away, the juice giving him some energy and making his fingers sticky while he rode. It was not long before he was riding into rockier country, and Hardy picked his steps more carefully. It was still a well-worn road. Ruts where wagons and the stage ran lined the road. The heat had picked up also, and they were ascending at a slow rate, laboring Hardy. There was little water until they reached a creek or small river in the early afternoon. Max gave Hardy over to the water and filled up his own canteen before taking the horse by the reins and walking him a ways. The heat was beating down on them, and he was a bit worried about the horse. Although Hardy had never shown problems with the heat, he was lathered, and the dry air seemed to scorch Max's throat.

Just as Max rode into Gillette, the sun dropped toward the horizon, and it started to cool. It was a small town but had several saloons, a blacksmith, general store, stage stop, hotel, and stables, as well as the mill along the creek that serviced the mine.

Max rode to the mill, where a man was directing others toward a shed. "Who can I talk to about a job at the mine?"

"I'm foreman," the stout man told him. He reminded Max a little of Jim back in Raton. "Why should I hire you?" He eyed Max up and down. As a precaution, Max had packed his pistols into his bags when Gillette had come into view from the distance.

"I'm experienced, mined for the last five years, a hard worker, and get along with just about everyone."

"Well, we could use another man up there. We'll give you a try. What's your name?"

"Max Tillman." Max bent down, offering his hand.

"I'm Klein. The top man up at Tip Top is Bill Chapey. I'll send you up there at first light with the supply wagon." He paused, looking at Hardy. "That's a fine horse. He been used in any work?"

"No, sir, he hasn't."

"We could probably use him."

"I'd prefer not to, sir. I kind of promised the former owner I'd keep him just a riding horse."

The man narrowed his eyes at Max and shook his head. "Well, I suppose a man who keeps his word over making some extra money is rare, and I can respect that. There's not a lot of room for non-working animals up at the mine, so you can either sell him, or volunteer him as a messenger animal when word needs to come down from the camp. Chapey's son usually does that, and from what I've seen he takes care with the horses. I'll let you work that out with Chapey tomorrow. You better get something to eat and some rest; you'll be put to the test come morning."

CHAPTER 15

Max helped to steady the cart as they pushed it through the narrow spot between two support beams that he felt were not as steady as they should be. One bump and they could be sealed in the dark. Once they were past he went on his way back down the tunnel, a fresh lantern to use to replace the broken one. He ducked into the pocket that was his work area and began to chip away. The air was still, but it was cooler than the blazing sun outside. He chipped away at the wall with the pickaxe and placed the ore in the bucket. The mine was fairly rich, the second richest he had worked in his time as a miner. It was encouraging to actually be pulling out valuable ore. Not like the last couple of mines he had worked with Clay. He did not like the dust that got in his eyes or his mouth, but he could honestly say that he had not minded the labor in the two years since coming to Tip Top. He worked on for a while, looking up at the supports to see that they were still firmly in place above. He set a full bucket out and began to swing away. He would get lost in the rhythm of the work, and his mind would wander to the book he had read, or the saloon girl down in Gillette, or even back to his earlier days as a child. That led to him considering writing a letter to his mother. He had not written to her since he had mined outside of Trinidad. He had the money for postage, and the stage that came through Gillette carried the letters.

His thoughts went back to the petite saloon girl, Tanya. Her blonde hair shone so brightly in the sun the day he had seen her walking down the street. He had not even known her name, but Lee knew it when Max mentioned her. Lee spent most all his money in that saloon. Max had been in a few times and had been struck by how Tanya's brown eyes contrasted with her blonde hair. Her voice did not sound like it came from such a small girl either. Many small women had mousy voices, but hers was deeper than most women's. There was just something about her that intrigued Max, and he told Lee the same.

Lee looked at him and smiled. "Same things that intrigues us all, my friend. But you won't go spend no time or money there, so I'll find out the mysteries for ya."

Max got along well with the man from California. Lee would say that mining was in his blood, being born to a forty-niner who had just enough success to feed the family of six. Lee had worked mines through California, but he thought that Arizona held more opportunity now. He said the California mines had all been claimed, and that when he saved enough money he was going to go find his own claim. Max was not sure how he would ever save money, going to Gillette every day off. Lee would drink, whore, and gamble. He did come back once with three hundred dollars winnings from a card game. But he thought he could double it the next time he went to Gillette and instead came back broke.

Max would shake his head while listening to Lee's stories. Max had saved nearly half of what he earned from the mining company, although he had followed Lee's example the last time he'd gone to Gillette, except for the gambling. A man had his needs, Lee would say.

The food cooked in camp was cheap and not that good. Usually beans and dried pork, or some sort of stew for supper. Breakfast was simply bread; occasionally there was honey to spread on it. Max was content with that. Some men would buy food at Joe Mayer's little place at Tip Top or down in the town and bring back supplies and cook over their own fire. Max was happy to not have to go to the trouble after a full day's work.

Max would visit Hardy each evening after supper. Hardy was well taken care of by the foreman's son, Blaine. Hardy and Chapey's horse were kept under a tarp for shade, given plenty of water and oats, and Hardy only had to travel back and forth to Gillette a couple of times a day. The lanky fourteen-year-old boy was a skilled rider and treated his mounts well. Max had been uncomfortable with the arrangement at first, but it worked well, and Blaine was fond of Hardy. If Max was going to stay and work the crew, he really did not need a horse, and maybe he could sell Hardy to Chapey.

He was conflicted on that though. He loved working with the men, Chapey was a fair supervisor, and he was happier than he had been traveling around. But, there were times when he thought about going in with Lee, making the other man stick to his plan of saving money, and the two of them setting out to stake their own claim. He would be fine most of the time, but there was a restlessness that would come on an hour at a time, and the feeling was becoming more frequent. He did not plan on chasing any more bounties but perhaps a different sort of endeavor, and not alone this time. While Max did like his time to himself, it seemed his travels on his own had been too lonely. He had been near the bottom when he had ridden into Gillette a couple years back. The fact that he did not feel down nearly as often now made him wonder why he would be so restless to leave in those moments.

Lee and Max shared their tent with Joe from Georgia, Gavin (born in Tucson seventeen years before), and Ian, an Irish immigrant who had been working his way west since he landed in Virginia fourteen years earlier. He claimed that once he got to the California coast he might as well get work on a boat and continue west, thinking he would make it back to Ireland from around the world by the time he was ready to be buried. Of course, Ian claimed many things, and nobody was even sure if he was thirty-one years old as he claimed or possibly in his mid-forties. Of the men whom Max shared his tent with, Ian was the only man he did not really like.

It was an oddity that the man seemed the friendliest with the other two men in camp that Max was apt to avoid. It seemed certain types drew towards each other, and the loud Irishman associated the most with Willie and Dick. Willie was as loud as Ian but lacked the wit that Ian had, while Dick was less talkative, but with a mean spirit. Dick had first become friends with Willie and Ian after the two had been mouthing off and annoyed him one night. He walked over and just started swinging. He was tough, and he fought the two for several minutes until they all stood across from each other bruised and panting. Then Ian looked at the other two men and asked if they wanted to get some whiskey. Dick looked at him as if he were crazy, but Ian just shrugged and said that fighting made him thirsty, and plus it would help the pain in his jaw. After drinking for most of the night, the three made it a frequent habit. A couple of men had accused the three of taking half of their bottles and replacing the missing spirits with water. The three had jumped on one man after his accusation, but Chapey shot his gun into the air and told them that if they were trouble again he would send them packing.

Aside from them, the men were all right. Sure, they were rough and coarse mannered, but Max was used to that. He felt nearly as comfortable in the Tip Top camp as he had with the Newton mining crew. That was why it was so puzzling to him that the camp could feel like home in one moment, and yet these urges to leave would come on in the next. When he began thinking about those conflicting feelings, he would shake his head and try to turn his thoughts down a different path, like Tanya, the brown-eyed saloon girl.

His next day off, Max rode down to Gillette to bring the reports to Klein. He planned on meeting Lee afterwards. Lee had come down the night before and said that he would likely be in the saloon at the end of the street, winning some money gambling.

When Max walked into the office, Klein was talking to Mitch Reese, the sheriff of Gillette. "This is the third time! You tell them that. Boss says they will cover it; that's why we hire them."

Max stopped and held up the reports. "From Chapey."

Klein waved him over and took the reports.

Max turned to leave, then looked back. "Another stage robbed, Boss?"

"Yes, but it is going to end soon. We'll not put up with it being a regular thing and neither will Wells Fargo. They killed the men this time."

"They're gonna hang for sure," Reese added. "I imagine the Pinkertons will be hired now."

Klein looked down at blank paper on his desk then back up. "Unless you can help us catch them, Max, go on. I've got to write a couple of letters."

Max walked down the street and into the saloon. He did not spot Lee, but Tanya was sitting at a table talking to a couple of miners.

Max went to the bar and ordered whiskey. He looked over at Tanya, who glanced up and gave him a brazen smile and wink. Not knowing what else to do, Max smiled back and turned back to the bar. She was very cute and had a playful sparkle to her eyes. He was trying to think of what he should do next. He was not sure if she was just a saloon girl, or if she was a "sporting girl," as Lee called them. Max was not even sure which he wanted her to be. Part of him did not want her to be a sporting girl, but part of him did. He sensed someone next to him and looked over to see Tanya standing there, the smile still on her face.

"Want to buy me a drink?"

"Sure."

Tanya nodded to the bartender, and he

filled two of the whiskey glasses. "So, where are you from, mister?"

"Up at the Tip Top mining camp." Max smiled at his own joke.

Tanya rolled her eyes but smiled flirtatiously. "They need to learn better jokes up at that mining camp. What's your name, Joker?"

"Sure, that will work, or you could call me Max."

"No, I think I'll stick with Joker." She grinned teasingly. "I'm Tanya."

Max smiled. "A pleasure."

Tanya turned and looked at him sideways. "I'm not sure how to take that, Mr. Joker."

"It's a pleasure to speak to you."

She smiled again. "I am a pleasure, aren't I?"

Someone put their hand on Max's other shoulder. Max's head swung around to see Lee standing there.

"Hello, buddy, and a very special hello to you, Miss Tanya."

"Lee, don't go interrupting us. This here young man has me intrigued."

Lee laughed. "That's what he said about you when he spotted you. I was just going to fill my friend in on the latest on the stage robberies."

"I heard," Max told him. "Third one, the

men were shot."

"News does travel fast. I heard that mining company and Wells will be calling in Pinkertons."

"Heard that also. Heard that Tip Top's gonna make Wells reimburse for all the losses."

"Did you hear they expect the losses to be around eighty thousand dollars?"

Max turned and looked at Lee in surprise.

Tanya whistled. "That's more money than most men can imagine having. You would think the man would just run off and retire."

Lee shrugged. "Well, I can imagine it and more. Anyway, there's three of them to split it, and they think that they know who two of them are."

"They do?"

"Yep. Pat and Tom Lewis."

"Who are they?"

"Local boys, lived around Bumble Bee for a while, prospecting. Ruffians, accused horse thieves, and reported to have spent a lot of money in Prescott last month after one rode in on a tall, white horse like the one reported in the last two robberies."

Max shrugged. "Sounds like they won't need the Pinkertons."

"They will likely need them to find the third one. Plus, the Lewis boys may not be easy to catch. Pat's been known to win money challenging men at shooting contests. He's got a Sharps fifty caliber that he uses, and he can hit a target well over a hundred yards away. Looks like it was the fifty that was used on the men on the stage according to the undertaker. He's a talker. I bet Pat Lewis saw that there was a third armed man and thought it was better to just shoot them before they could do anything."

"If those are the same Lewis boys I'm thinking of," Tanya said, "they are a rough bunch. I think they were at Stu's saloon down the street a year ago when I worked there. They beat the heck out of some old drunk who asked them to scoot over a little and make room for him."

"Well, they're gonna have to be mean to last," Lee said. "Undertaker said that he overheard them say that, in addition to Pinkertons, they were going to put out a general reward for the bandits: a thousand each, with an extra thousand if one's brought in alive and tells them where any money's hidden."

Max looked at Lee. "That would be plenty to give us the time to find a good claim."

"Only, neither of us are bounty hunters. These men are killers. I ain't ever killed nobody, have you?"

Max looked down at the bar and exhaled.

"Really, Max, you —" The sound of multiple gunshots outside interrupted Lee.

A man stood from the table and walked toward the open door but then abruptly stopped, grunted, and fell sideways.

Max pushed Tanya back toward the back wall and down to the floor, and men were ducking under the tables. More shots sounded; then they heard the sound of a galloping horse.

Max looked over to Lee, who had followed him to the back wall and ducked down. After several seconds of silence, staying low, Max made his way toward the door, Lee following.

One of the other men crawled over to the fallen man. "Ed's dead."

Max looked back at Ed and the blood on the floor, and then outside. There in the street men were starting to approach a body lying still. Max walked out. Looking at the trail out of town, he saw that a man was already over a quarter mile away, still riding full out, too far away to see what he looked like.

Lee ran toward the fallen man, Tanya following. "It's Sheriff Reese," Lee called out. "Who shot him?"

"Jeff Wright," Klein, the mill foreman, said

looking up from where he knelt by the body. Lee looked down the street. "The blacksmith?"

"That's right," Tanya said. "He used to drink with the Lewis brothers."

Klein looked at her and nodded. "Reese remembered that when he saw Wright saddling his horse."

"Wright must have heard the news on the Lewis boys and thought he would be connected," Lee said, turning to Max.

Max nodded, thinking. "That and the news of the Pinkertons."

A woman's scream made everyone jump. A red-haired woman was bawling as she ran toward the body, two children running behind her. She fell upon the body. "No, Mitch, no!"

"I'm sorry, Evelyn." Klein knelt down and put his hand on her shoulder, but she flung it off, smacking him in the face in the process. He lost his balance and fell onto his backside in shock.

Everyone watched, not knowing what to do. Klein stood up and looked at the woman and the children that had joined her on the ground, now screaming nearly as loud as their mother. Then he looked at Lee and Max, motioning them to follow him away from the family. A little distance down the street he stopped and looked at the men, blood beginning to trickle from his nose. "When she's calm, help her with the body down to the undertaker."

Max nodded. While Klein walked back toward his office, he and Lee stood against the blacksmith's building, waiting for a sign that they could help. Max did not want to approach the woman, and Lee did not appear to want to either. Max had no idea what he could say, and he knew it wasn't his place. The red-haired daughter stopped wailing after a couple of minutes and just lay there on top of her father. Both the mother and the son cried so hard they had trouble getting their breath and sat back gasping. There were a few of the town's women nearby who seemed to want to go to them to try to comfort them, but they were apprehensive. They had seen the backhand that had bloodied Klein's nose.

After several minutes, Evelyn Reese stood up and started grabbing at her husband's arms. Lee jumped forward. "Can we help you, ma'am?"

She gave him a level look. "If you can bring the man who did this back here to hang, that would be helpful."

Lee stopped. "I'm no lawman, ma'am."

"No." Evelyn looked at Lee. "I suppose

you ain't. I didn't want my Mitch to stay a lawman, but now he's dead. He would say somebody had to do it. He did it, despite having us waiting at home for him. You don't have anybody waiting at home for you, though, do you?" Lee just stood there silent, unable to say anything. "But now a man with a family is gone, but you I will imagine will drink, whore, and gamble away into the night, despite the fact that a good man died today, and his killer will ride away uncaught." The woman walked toward Lee, who backed away. "Ain't you great to offer help, though!"

Max stepped forward. "Ma'am," his voiced cracked. "Mitch Reese was a fine, brave man. Let us help you move him off the street. Then we'll go after Jeff Wright."

Evelyn looked at Max a moment as if about to cut into him also, but then tears started running down her face again, and she just nodded her head. Max tapped Lee on the shoulder as he walked by, and Evelyn gathered her two young ones so they could lift Mitch and carry him down the street. Mitch was hit once in the stomach and once in the throat. Max looked at the wounds as they carried him. Lee glanced at them and then looked away. The sheriff's wife and children followed, now joined by a couple of the other women. It was odd carrying a body. Max just wanted it to be over with and was glad when they reached the undertaker, who had readied a table. Max and Lee hoisted the body onto the table and turned to leave. Lee stopped and dropped his head to the widow Reese but could not find any words. She looked at him and then to Max before going to the undertaker. As she began to talk she started bawling again, and, upon hearing their mother, the kids started crying again as well.

Max and Lee left and started back down the street. Three men were carrying Ed across the street to the undertaker. "That's terrible," Lee said. "One minute you are gambling and having a good time, or married with two cute children, then a couple of shots and it's done."

"It's the way of things in the territories, I suppose. I've had my share of seeing this," Max said.

"You aren't really going to go after Wright, are you?" Lee looked over at Max.

Max walked on a ways, quiet a moment. "Can you shoot, Lee?"

"I've hunted some." Lee looked down at the ground and followed a moment. "I'm not really a great shot, though."

"So, it may be better if you don't come

with me then."

Lee fell quiet a moment. "I think you're right. I'm not cut out for it." Lee stopped following. Max went to the stables and saddled Hardy before making his way up the trail to Tip Top.

On the ride up the trail Max started to have doubts. He had basically given the widow his promise that he was going to chase her husband's killer. It was foolish of course. Wright had a lead on him, and, if he met up with the Lewis brothers, then Max would be outnumbered and killed. But even as he had told the widow that he would chase her husband's killer, he knew that a big part of it was the reward that was going to be offered. Part of it was that somebody should be chasing Wright, but Max did not think he would be going if it were not for the reward.

But, now thinking of leaving the mining company, Lee, Chapey, and Blaine to chase a man who had just killed two men before riding out of town, he really did not want to go. Likely he would either not find them, and his job at the mine would be taken by another man, or he would find them and get shot. Maybe they would gather a posse before he returned to Gillette, and he could ride with them and share any reward.

CHAPTER 16

Max rode into the camp, and Blaine was sitting by the horse corral. "Blaine, where's your pa?"

"In the mines."

Max nodded and started toward the mines. It could be hard to track Chapey down. He would walk through all the shafts, sometimes helping, sometimes just prodding the men to work. Max considered just waiting for him, but he did not have the patience. Fortunately, Chapey emerged from one of the openings as Max approached.

"Aren't you off today?"

"Yes, I was."

"Was? Well, if you want to go back to work I won't stop ya; get to it."

"That's not why I'm here. Sheriff Reese was shot."

"Oh, hell. What happened?"

"Jeff Wright, the blacksmith, shot him.

Turns out Wright was one of the stage robbers."

"Oh, hell. Now we don't have a blacksmith to mend our tools, either."

"No, he made it out of town." Chapey started walking toward his small building, and Max followed. "Chapey, I need the gear you're holding for me."

"Oh, hell!" Chapey cursed the loudest yet. "You're going to become the sheriff of Gillette?"

"No, but I am leaving."

"Chasing Wright?"

"Yes, sir."

"Reward?"

"Yes."

"Are you any good with that gear?"

"I've been either good or lucky."

"Luck will run out some day, son, and good only gets you so far in something like that."

"I know, but I'm going anyway."

"Well, come on."

Chapey unlocked the cabin and led Max inside. Pulling out another key, he knelt down by a long chest at the far end, working the lock. It seemed like it would not work, but finally there was a click, and he lifted the lid. He lifted the holstered guns out and handed them back over his shoulder to Max. The Winchester and small bags of ammo followed.

"If you come to your senses, come back. You're a good worker."

"Thanks, Chapey."

"Good luck, Max."

They stepped out of the cabin, and Chapey locked it. Max leaned his rifle against the wall and fastened on his guns, feeling the weight of them that he had not felt in a long time.

When he went into the tent to grab his bedroll, Ian, Dick, and Willie were in there. Ian stood up from where he was rifling through Joe's bags. Dick was kneeling by Lee's, and Willie was holding Max's bedding. Upon seeing Max come in with a rifle, Willie dropped the bedding, then dove to the floor and squeezed out a gap at the bottom of the tent. Dick just paused, glancing up.

Ian sighed. "You were supposed to be gone all day."

Max stared a minute, his anger rising. "You were supposed to be working in the mine."

"We took a break," Dick told him from where he was kneeling. Then his hand flickered, and a knife flashed by Max's face. Max realized that he had almost been hit with a knife and saw Dick launch at him. Max thrust out with the rifle barrel, catching Dick in the face as they collided. Dick fell to the floor, and Max stumbled back a couple of steps. The man on the floor cried out. "You bastard!" He clutched at his eye, rolling around.

Ian made to lunge at the opening Willie had gone through. Max hopped over and stomped on his back twice and his leg three times, but Ian made it through. Max turned and saw Dick up on his knees trying to stand but then crawling toward the tent flap. Max took two steps and cracked him in the neck with the rifle. The man flopped to the floor motionless.

Max gathered his bedroll and looked at the man lying on the ground as he left the tent. He walked over to where the horses were and was glad to see Chapey there talking to Blaine.

"Ian, Willie, and Dick were looking through our stuff in the tent. Willie got out right away. Dick tried to stick me but missed. He's lying in there unconscious with an eye injury, and Ian got out, but he may be limping with some bad ribs."

Chapey stood up and exhaled. "I'm surprised you didn't shoot any of them."

"Didn't load my guns yet." He put the

bedroll on the saddle and commenced to load his weapons.

Chapey shook his head. "You're a colder customer with those guns on, Max." He started toward the tents. "Blaine, bring your gun and some rope." Chapey pulled a short-nosed revolver out of his pocket.

Max trotted Hardy down the trail. The trail was thin in places, and it was not long before he was stuck behind the wagon bringing the ore down to the mill. The tight switchbacks down the trail gave him no room to pass for several turns until it widened out at one spot. Quinn called out as Max passed at the turn. "What's with the guns?"

Max just waved and rode down the switchbacks as quickly as Hardy could safely handle. Once into Gillette, Max tied Hardy at the mill office and went inside. He was surprised to see Tanya sitting behind Klein's desk. Klein and Lee were standing against the wall.

Klein looked up, and his eyes ran over Max's guns. "So, you have the gear, but you really think you have a chance?"

Max shrugged. "As good as anybody else I guess." Max looked back at Tanya, who had a pencil to paper.

Lee smiled. "Tanya can draw a little, so

she's drawing Jeff Wright." He walked over and glanced at the paper.

Tanya looked up. "I told you I can't draw with you peeking over my shoulder. Now go over there." As Lee retreated she went back to drawing.

"We're going to have her draw a few and send one to Prescott for printing." Klein turned around and pulled two posters off the shelf next to him and held them out to Max. "We had these printed in Prescott a couple of days ago . . . arrived this morning — the Lewis brothers."

"They are a fair likeness," Tanya said, not looking up.

Max took the posters and glanced over them. One picture was of a man with a chubby face, dark hair, and mustache. *Tom Lewis. Short to average height, brown hair. Wanted along with brother, Pat Lewis. $1,000 each. An extra $1,000 if one brought in alive and can tell us location of third stage robber and stolen property.*

Max pulled the next poster out. This man was leaner, with a face that was angular. He had a meaner look to him, and his hair seemed to be shaded lighter. *Pat Lewis. Average height, dark-blond hair. Wanted along with brother, Tom Lewis. $1,000 each. An extra $1,000 if one brought in alive and* *can tell us location of third stage robber and stolen property.*

"Copies of those went out from Prescott to other towns as well," Klein told him. "There may have even been copies on the stage that was robbed, so they may have known before Wright shot Mitch. You go ahead and take those. Make sure you know who you are looking for. A couple of men rode in from Bumble Bee a while back. They said a man fitting Wright's description was heading the other way, so he's going north. That's all we know."

"Nobody else wants to get up a posse?"

Klein shook his head side to side. "Seeing two men dead is not a thing that lifts men's courage."

Lee had been looking at Max's holsters and his guns. "So, you really going?"

"Yes."

Max set the posters down and stepped outside to Hardy. He pulled a small bundle out of his bags and his rifle out of his scabbard before coming back inside. He sat down in a chair across from Tanya, who glanced up but, seeing that he was paying her drawing no mind, went back to drawing her second copy. Max pulled his Colt from his right holster, unloaded it, and then set to cleaning and oiling it. He reloaded and holstered it then went through the same process with his other Colt, then the Winchester. Klein and Lee watched for a while. Klein then decided to clean his own sidearm and the rifle he kept in the office and sat down in the chair next to Max. Lee left while they were cleaning their guns. As Max finished reloading the Winchester, Tanya placed four copies of the picture of Wright on the edge of the desk.

Klein stopped cleaning the rifle a moment and leaned forward. Max looked at the pictures and nodded. "Good likeness, Tanya."

Klein agreed and paid Tanya three dollars for the drawings, and she left immediately. Klein looked at Max as he stood up. "Are you leaving now or waiting for morning?"

"I'm going now. There's still a couple of hours of light. I can make it to Bumble Bee." Max took the posters and shook Klein's hand before walking out and mounting Hardy.

The afternoon ride was odd. It brought back memories of all those days spent on trails before he had found a home at Tip Top. In Bumble Bee, Max boarded Hardy and rubbed him down. It was a warm journey with the sun heating up the March day. Hardy had stayed in fair shape climbing to Tip Top from Gillette, but the afternoon sun had beat down on them both during the demanding ride. He went to the saloon and, after ordering a drink, struck up a conversation with the bartender, asking him if he'd heard the news from Gillette yet.

"Shooting? Yeah, said it was the blacksmith?"

"They think he was working with the Lewis brothers, who used to live around here."

A man next to the bar nodded. "I'm not surprised. The blacksmith was in here with them a couple of times a year ago. That man's big and looked like he could turn mean."

"There's already been a bounty hunter in here asking about them earlier today," the bartender said. "You a bounty hunter?"

"Not exactly. I was working the mine in Gillette. Seen what he did to a couple of men, one with a good family, plus he's slowed our payroll a time or two with the robberies, so I thought I'd just go take a look around."

"I imagine the bounty hunter will have him soon," the other man said. "It was Jack Sutter. He rode out a couple of hours ago."

"Why do you think he'll find them soon?"

Max's stomach sank. Why did Jack Sutter always end up in the same region as him?

"One of the men who drank with the Lewis boys a couple of weeks ago said that they mentioned staying at Canyon Diablo in the past. If they know they're wanted that's probably the only place they'll show up."

The bartender shook his head. "I know Sutter's supposed to be good, but Canyon Diablo is an iffy place to go without a small army for anybody on the side of the law."

Max looked at him. "Really?"

"Yeah. They hired their first sheriff last month who started his job at 3:00 in the afternoon. They were burying him that evening."

The man finished the last of the whiskey in his small glass.

Max motioned to the man's glass, and the bartender poured. "This Canyon Diablo's along the railroad, isn't it?"

"Thank you," the man said, holding up his glass. "I worked there for a couple of days, until they found out they had the wrong size pieces to build the bridge across the canyon. The whole thing's been put on hold temporarily."

"Where's it at?"

"You aren't really going, are you?" the

man asked. He just shrugged when Max didn't say anything. "It's east of Flagstaff. They started a stage to it from there, so there's a decent trail."

"And Flagstaff is up northeast of Fort Verde, right?"

"Yes. You really don't know the territory very well, do ya?"

"Not that part. Came in from New Mexico through Globe and Phoenix, then stayed at Tip Top for some time."

"Well, I worked the rail for a while until I understood that it would be a while until the thing was finished. I left a couple of weeks after work stopped. It started getting rougher than most rail towns by then, and after landing here it wasn't long before men I'd worked with started passing by, heading south and saying that it was getting even rougher."

Max motioned for the bartender to fill both of their glasses again and thanked him.

The man nodded to him. "You know the canyon was named by Lieutenant Whipple. Think it's the same man Fort Whipple was named for, outside Prescott. Back around the time the southern part of the state was bought, in the 50s, he was surveying the territory, and the canyon caused them to go a long way around. He named it Devil's

Canyon, Canyon Diablo. Turns out it gave the railroad trouble, too. And the town that's sprung up there fits the name even better."

"Well, from what I hear, the name's damn appropriate for the town," the bartender agreed.

Max took a deep breath and sighed. "Well, I've seen Jack Sutter up close myself, and he'll probably do all right." Max paid the bartender and wandered out of the bar feeling the whiskey he had just drunk. He went to the boarding house down the street and felt fortunate that they had a room.

He lay there that night trying to decide if he should go on. His last run-in with Jack Sutter had gone very badly, and he did not know what Sutter might do if he found him after the same bounty again. He might seriously hurt Max, or even kill him if nobody else was around when they crossed paths.

Also, Canyon Diablo sounded bad. Max was really a miner, not a man hunter. He had hunted down a man in Santa Fe. That had been different though. Max rolled over, tired. He could decide in the morning whether to go on or go back to Tip Top and hope to get his job back.

The next morning, he woke as the first rays

of sunlight filtered through his window. He put his arms behind his head and looked out at the light. He felt refreshed. He had the urge to go on. He really did not want to go back. Who knew how long Tip Top would produce? And he wanted a challenge. He wanted to see Flagstaff, and he even was curious about Canyon Diablo. Plus, he was considering paying back Sutter for jumping him in Cimarron. Max had proven himself competent, and he wanted the reward. The money would go a long way toward setting him up for the future. At the moment, he wanted to get the taste of last night's whiskey out of his mouth. He sprang out of bed, gathered his things, and went downstairs for the breakfast that he smelled cooking.

Mrs. Wilson, the landlady of the boarding house, was crossing at the bottom of the stairs as Max was coming down. She stopped, staring at him, her graying black hair up tight in a bun swaying a little as she shook her head at him. "No, sir. No firearms in the room at breakfast. Go store them back in your room while you eat."

Max stopped short, annoyance flaring in him, but he sighed and turned around. People had their rules, and he was likely safe in the boarding house. His gear was safe, too. There was no way out besides down the stairs in sight from the dining table.

When he returned to the table there was an empty seat, which Mr. Wilson motioned to with his hand. There was a man who wore the ragged, plain clothes of a miner, and also a man who wore the white shirt and coat of a merchant, seated between two younger ladies. Upon second glance, Max thought one was old enough to be the other's mother. The plate in front of each person held eggs, a small steak, and two biscuits. Max was glad that he had taken his gear back upstairs. This was a feast. He sat down and picked up his fork, but Mrs. Wilson cleared her throat. Max looked up to see that the others were waiting for something. Mrs. Wilson lowered her head and shut her eyes, as did the others.

"Lord, we thank you for the provision in front of us," Mr. Wilson began. "Please see us through this day and bring us to know your ways, O God. Amen."

The others echoed the amen; then everyone picked up their forks. Max cut his steak and then rotated between bites of egg, steak, and biscuit. He paused eating for a moment and looked at the woman who had cooked the food. "This is a fine meal, ma'am."

"Thank you." She beamed as she poured coffee into her husband's cup after he had downed his first in one tip.

Max sipped some from his cup, and the rich taste along with the breakfast made it seem worth the ride itself. The camp coffee was terrible really, but it was all there had been, and Max had forgotten what good coffee was like. The food was much better here, and Max momentarily wished he could just stay another day, but he had a distance to go, especially before it became too hot.

After finishing his food, the first to do so at any at the tables, Max inclined his head toward the lady of the house. "Excuse me ma'am, but I have to move along with these short days. Thank you again."

"If you must. Be careful."

Max looked back as he went to the stairs, then hurried up and gathered his things. He made his way out the door a moment later and walked swiftly toward the stables. The cool morning was just warming, warning that it could be hot later.

That day Max rode in the rising heat until stopping at Fort Verde well before the sun was at its peak to water and rest Hardy. The horse was beginning to lather. Max drank several cups of water himself. He sat against the wall of the building with Hardy in front of him, the sun blocked by the height of the building. Although the heat was nothing like the summer in the Bradshaws, it was a hot spring day. When it approached midday and the sun cleared the top of the building, they hit the trail again. Max felt a little weary from the heat and from squinting his eyes.

A few miles up the road Max saw a man coming out of the bushes out of the corner of his eye, and he jerked upright in the saddle, nearly grabbing for his gun. Then he realized the man looked groggy and had apparently been napping in the trees. The man had been startled by Max's hand jerking toward his holster. Max tipped his hat toward the man and rode on past. It did make him think, though. There was no guaranteeing that the men he was seeking would be in Canyon Diablo. Perhaps they were somewhere just off the road, waiting to rob riders.

Max became more alert, despite the effects of the sun. Near mid-afternoon he dismounted and walked Hardy. He felt like he was baking and knew the heat was doing the same to Hardy. He walked for a couple of hours until the sun began to dip. Then he rode on for another hour until darkness threatened. Max would have traveled on in the dark because it was much cooler, but for concern for Hardy's footing. He camped and was surprised that in the middle of the night he pulled his blanket around him.

The first morning light woke him, along with the sound of a bird chirping nearby. There was a good chill, but he welcomed it. He saddled Hardy and moved on, continuing to gradually climb. He began to note pine trees here and there, and eventually they were all around. He felt like he was back in the forests around Santa Fe. It was late morning when he saw the buildings of Flagstaff in the distance through the trees. At the same time, he heard the thwack of axes and saw to his right that there was a crew of nearly a dozen lumbermen working on felling trees.

Max stopped and watched them for a moment, imagining what it might be like to work on their crews. He did not think it was harder work than mining, and, although the mines shielded him from the sun, it was cooler here.

He stopped in the town of Flagstaff, where buildings were being erected at the edges of town and in spaces left when the earliest were built. A train station had been built, because they expected the train to be making its way through regularly, but it looked like there had been a small settlement here even before the train came through. There was a new hotel and an older one, a saloon and eatery, a doctor, and a livery. Max stopped at the trough and let Hardy drink before walking into the local sheriff's office and asking about the men on the posters. The sheriff had not seen the men and told Max to be careful not to let loose a stray shot if he came across the men in his town.

Max asked directions to Canyon Diablo. The sheriff smirked but did not say anything except for giving him the directions. Max hurried out and started east down a trail. He was anxious to get to his destination and wanted to make it before dark.

Max passed a stage coming from the opposite direction just before the trail descended into a gorge and came back out the other side. On the other side, the trail forked off north, and that was the way he went. The gorge grew deeper as Max rode a distance from it, and the canyon went on for several miles before the town became visible in the distance. Max sat and considered the poor planning of the railroad. True, a bridge would have to be built across the gorge he crossed anyway, but it would have been a much easier task than bridging the canyon he stared at now. Perhaps it was not as straight a shot, or they did not want to run right along the old existing trail, but it seemed like it had cost them more than it was worth. As he urged Hardy forward, he realized there were probably many factors of which he was ignorant.

CHAPTER 17

Max rode into the town, which was a mix of storefronts backed by tents. There were also several permanent buildings, one being the livery at the edge of town, with a nice house built behind it.

Max rode to the livery just before dark.

A tall man with a full head of thick, brown hair walked out of the house to greet him at the barn. The man's weathered face put him in his fifties. He extended his hand as Max swung down. "Henry Lawrence, sir."

Max took his hand. "Max Tillman."

"Good to meet ya, Max. What's your business here?" Henry's eyes had dropped to Max's guns.

Max pulled out the posters, although they were difficult to see with the darkening sky.

The man looked at them and sighed. "Max, let's get your horse taken care of; then we'll go inside and eat, and I'll tell you about these men."

"Why not now?" Max asked as politely as he could. There was something about Henry that he liked, but the man was definitely holding something back.

"It's just better to talk inside. Plus, it's almost dark, and morning would be a better time to venture down the street anyway. We have a couple of rooms we rent out to some guests, and one is available."

"All right." Max and Henry worked together by the light of two lanterns taking care of Hardy and were soon done. Max guided Hardy through the tight space between the stalls and a wagon parked in the middle of the barn. There were twelve stalls, and Hardy made eleven occupied. Henry put a chain through the barn doors and a lock through the links before they walked to the house.

As he entered there was a hall directly in front of him with four doors. To his left the room opened up into the kitchen, and to his right there was a sitting area, nicely decorated. The graying woman in the kitchen turned from where she was putting plates on the table and smiled.

"My wife, Patricia."

"Hello, ma'am."

"Max Tillman, Patricia."

"Nice to meet you, Max." She motioned

with her head. "The first room on right will be yours. You can stow your things and wash up. I put a basin of water in there."

"Thank you." Max glanced into the sitting room as he started down the hall. There was a slight, fair-skinned man with mixed gray and blond hair sitting with a young, fair-featured woman. Max made hurriedly to wash up, taking in the smell of beef cooking along with other smells, from which he could pick out the carrots and bread.

After washing up he went back to the kitchen and saw everyone sitting at the square table. The other guests were sitting on one side, the Lawrences were across from them, and there was a plate set for Max at the end between the two men. As Max sat down, he noticed that the other guest had a white collar around his neck.

Henry introduced Max first. "Max, this is Todd Porter and his daughter, Michelle."

"Nice to meet you." Max nodded to them and saw that they shared the same blue eyes. Michelle smiled and told Max it was a pleasure, and her father reached over and shook his hand.

"Will you pray, Pastor?" Henry asked.

Porter nodded and bowed his head, and the rest followed his lead. "Father, we thank you for the safety of those at this table. We are grateful for our kind hosts, for the plenty of the food in front of us, and we ask you to bless it. Most of all we pray that all will know you. Amen."

"Amen," everybody echoed. The bread was passed around, the roast sliced, the carrots and greens scooped. Everybody began eating, and Michelle complimented Patricia on the food right away. Todd echoed, and Max did also.

"How did you come to live here?" the pastor asked.

Henry and Patricia looked at each other as if wondering the same thing. Henry finished chewing. "We heard that the train was coming through and thought if we could build a livery at the edge of this spot, with the bridge that had to be built and the canyon separation, this might be a good place to build up some capital."

Patricia patted her husband's hand. "Henry worked with the horses at Fort Whipple nearly from the time it was built eighteen years ago. I cooked and did laundry."

"I finally left soldiering. I'd seen some terrible things with the Indian wars on both sides but realized I'd missed out on opportunities in places like Phoenix and Globe — to get in at the start of the boom — and thought this was my chance. The general at Whipple had some pull and got me this spot and the lumber to build at a huge discount. We got set up with the help of a few soldiers just as the rail people began arriving."

"It seems that there is an opportunity here," Porter said.

"Yes," Henry nodded. "We've done all right, especially handling the stage's change horses right now. But there is an element here. That is why I beg both of you gentlemen to reconsider your plans in this town."

"Mr. Lawrence," Porter said in his deep voice, "from what you tell me, this is a place that needs God's word heard more than any other."

"There are some that would benefit," Patricia interjected. "There are people here who are decent, and others who are lost but could be guided, but there are a few who are beyond reaching, and they are very dangerous."

"Nobody is beyond reaching," Porter said. He looked sideways at Max.

Henry sighed.

Max looked at Henry. "The men I am looking for?"

"The most dangerous. There was another bounty hunter here yesterday."

"Jack Sutter?"

323

"You know about it."

"I heard he was coming."

"He's hanging by a rope over the edge of the canyon. Wright recognized him and waylaid him as he entered their hangout, Wolf's. They beat him and then hung him."

Michelle gasped.

"Henry!" Patricia said. "Sorry, Miss Porter."

"It's all right. I just have trouble thinking of how people could do such things."

Max looked at the two other guests. "Where are you from, Pastor?"

"Pennsylvania originally, Pittsburgh. We lived in Missouri for a while, spent a couple of weeks in Prescott, and then headed here."

"Prescott would have been a better place to stay," Henry told them.

"Perhaps, but I heard that this place was a den of godlessness, named for the devil himself, and decided that I should come."

Patricia looked at Michelle, then at Mr. Porter. She moved her mouth, then pursed her lips before looking at the food people had stopped eating. "Let's talk about something more cheerful."

Michelle nodded. "Where are you from, Max?"

"East Texas, originally. Spent a little bit of time in Colorado and New Mexico, but the last couple of years I've been in the Bradshaw Mountains down south."

"We crossed through New Mexico. Did you see the old pueblo buildings?"

"Yes, from a distance. I was in a bit of a hurry and didn't look at them closely."

"Although we are not Catholic" — she looked at her father — "you must admire their commitment to bring God to the Indians, building a mission among their village."

"Yes," Max nodded. "Of course, it all looked empty when I saw it."

She nodded back. "But at some point, the priests were there among them, teaching, living side by side."

"It is interesting," Henry said before taking a bite.

"How different is it back East?" Patricia asked. "We both grew up in Missouri."

"The city is different," Porter said. "Big buildings with steel frames; smoke rises up out of the steel mill constantly. There are areas in the city that may be as dangerous as this camp, I think. But there is a police force. There is not as much open space, that's for sure. Things seem to move at a busier pace, and you probably don't know what's happening on the other side of the city unless it's put in the paper."

"And it's not as hot," Michelle added, smiling.

Max noticed at that moment how striking her blue eyes were, and an interest surged up that he did not have when he first saw her. "It's hard for me to imagine places like that."

"Perhaps one day you will go to the eastern cities," Michelle offered.

"Or San Francisco," Henry said. "I was stationed near there before Arizona. It is quite a bit like that. You should see the size of some of the ships that come into harbor."

Max sat thoughtfully. "Perhaps one day." He ate the last bite on his plate.

The next several minutes were passed as Henry told them about the growth of Prescott from its early mining days in 1864 when he arrived and helped build Fort Whipple until now, with its courthouse, three-story hotels, large stores, and bank.

Max helped carry the dishes in and offered to help, but Patricia said there was only room for her and Michelle to do the dishes. So Max headed toward his room.

Henry stopped him at the hallway. "Max, you seem like a good young man, going after —"

"Henry, I'll think on it, all right? I'm not wanting to die, and it sounds like it could be more dangerous than I thought."

Henry nodded. "Good night."

Max lay in bed for a couple of hours, his mind working. Jack Sutter's body was hanging off the cliff, not far away. The man was a famous bounty hunter, and Max was really a miner. What chance did he have of taking the three men?

Shots down the street grew his fear. It reminded him of the night he spent in Cimarron and saw a man gunned down as he watched from his window. He had only practiced his shooting one morning since he had collected his guns from Chapey, and had shown his rust. This was a stupid idea.

But he was here. He had left his job, traveled all the way to this lawless town, knowing it was dangerous. Now that he was here, and the men were near, was he going to be a coward? What if he did die? Hardy was the only living thing counting on him, and he could leave the horse to the Lawrences. They would take good care of him. He would prefer to leave him to Blaine, but it was too far to Tip Top for it to be a reasonable request to deliver the horse.

Max sighed. That was it. He was going in the morning, and whatever happened would happen. Oddly enough, committing to that decision helped him to relax, and he fell asleep.

He woke just a few hours later, light beginning to show through the window. He rolled out of bed and filled the wash basin, splashing water on his face. He deliberately dressed quickly to avoid thinking anymore about the day's task. He walked down the hall and out the door, not slowing in front of the kitchen, where he heard pans being moved.

The air outside was chilly, but he welcomed it. It felt good at the moment. He walked to the stables, and the door was open. Henry was putting hay in the stalls of some of the horses toward the back.

Max grabbed a handful of oats from a sack on a shelf and walked over to his Choctaw horse. The horse ate from his hand, and Max stroked his neck. Hardy nuzzled up against Max's shoulder for a moment. Max fought back a tear and turned to see Henry standing there. The older man stood looking at him, then shrugged his shoulders.

Max nodded. "If I don't come walking back down the street, the horse is yours. Keep him or sell him. Just please make sure he'll be treated well."

Henry's jaw tightened, and he nodded agreement. Nothing else was said, and Max turned and went out of the stables.

He almost ran into Michelle outside the door. She smiled. "You're up early."

"Yeah, seeing to my horse."

"Me, too. I've grown to enjoy taking care of the animals on our trip."

Max stepped to go around her. "Tell your father good luck on his . . . mission."

"It won't be luck, Max."

He stopped and looked at her. She was waiting for him to get into a conversation. "Goodbye, Michelle. I'm glad I got to meet you and your father." He turned before she could say anything and started striding quickly down the street.

The street was fairly dead. There were a few men leaving one of the saloons, stumbling toward a group of tents off the main street. Max saw a couple of men asleep between buildings, rolled up against the wood or canvas.

Max saw a sign indicating Wolf's across one of the few wooden buildings, this one with a smaller second story. He felt his stomach sink. He did not want to go in there, but he kept walking and pushed through the door.

He was relieved to see it nearly empty, and those that were there paid him little attention as he entered. There was an

L-shaped stairway to his left as he entered, and the rough-hewn bar ran under where the stairs turned on the second ascent. The bartender with long, graying hair raised his head from where it had lain on his arms on the bar and looked at Max before grabbing a bottle and pouring. There was a slight man on the floor to Max's right among some scattered chairs, snoring. The only man who had been awake when Max entered was a large man with a long, thick, unclean yellow beard in the corner.

"Half dollar," the bartender told Max, who wanted to argue but put the money down.

Max smelled the whiskey and took a sip. It was rot gut. He took it, went to a table near the far corner, and sat down. The man with the dirty yellow beard was eyeing him. Max nodded to him and leaned back, resting his right hand on his thigh just above his holster, his left hand holding the whiskey and touching it to his lips.

He sighed and let his shoulders relax. He had chosen to come here, first the town, then to this saloon.

"You want to try your hand at cards, son?" the big man at the other table asked.

"No, thanks."

"You sippin' that whiskey like it's tea time

someplace fancy."

"Not that great a glass of whiskey. No offense." He lifted his glass to the bartender. The man chuckled, but the bartender shook his head side to side. "Well, if you're going to keep sitting there you'll have to keep drinking."

"I usually speed up as I go, so take it easy. It's not like I'm keeping your other customers from a chair."

The bartender looked over and glared, and Max met his eyes but stayed aware of the yellow-bearded man, who looked over at the bartender smiling. "He makes a good point, Wolf. Anyway, take it easy with him. He seems a bit jumpy." Then the yellow-haired man chuckled and went back to shuffling the cards, and the bartender started wiping at the stains on the bottoms of the glasses.

Max looked at the glass in his hand. Henry's words came to his mind from the previous night. This was a rough way to choose to live. He had no idea what might happen between Yellow Beard and him this morning, so he had to keep his hand near his gun. He realized that someone had either pissed in the corner, or the man sleeping a few feet away had pissed himself. He was sipping rot gut, just to stay in this hellhole, and he was afraid to ask questions because he did not want to end up like Jack Sutter. He would drink a bit more of this nasty crap so as not to upset anyone, and then he would leave.

"Where you from, son?"

Max looked over at the man holding the cards in his left hand. "Texas, originally."

"Me, too . . . Galveston area, and you?"

"East Texas, near the Louisiana border."

"Come out here seeking your fortune, eh?" He laughed. "Ain't gonna find it I don't think."

Max smirked. He was nervous. The man was trying to lull him, but he also was right.

"Now, I came out here twelve years ago —"

Movement at the door stopped the man talking. Max looked over and saw Michelle. She was being hauled along by a short, chubby man, and the look of terror on her face made Max's stomach sink. Her lip was swollen and bleeding. There was a thin young man with them carrying a rifle, and he snorted as he laughed.

Max wanted to do something, but there were two, possibly three or four, men with the bartender and Yellow Beard that he may have to face. Plus, Michelle was in between him and the man holding her.

The bartender looked at them with indifference. "What's going on, Tom?"

"Got me a preacher's daughter. I never had me a preacher's daughter." Tom looked around, and Max saw that it was Tom Lewis. Lewis saw the man on the floor rousing. "Mase, go see if my brother's back in town. Tell him we got us a preacher's daughter."

Mase started to get up, stumbling toward the door, and Tom began hauling Michelle up the stairs with the other man following. Max looked out the corner of his eye toward Yellow Beard, who was keeping an eye on Max more than he was the stairs. Max let out a quiet breath. Michelle's eyes locked onto Max at that moment, and she stumbled, falling down onto the next step. Max stood, sliding his pistol out of its holster and cocking it as he aimed at Lewis's head.

Lewis's eyes grew large, and he let go of Michelle and grabbed for the pistol at his belt. Max's shot went high, but he had recocked and aimed at the man leveling the rifle at him. The shots happened within a quarter second of each other, but the rifle shot went wide as the man was hit and fell backwards.

Max fell back into the chair, his side searing. He nearly dropped his gun, but instead he raised it. Cock and shoot, cock and shoot, cock and shoot, cock and shoot, click. Empty. Lewis's other two shots had missed him. It was hard to see through all the smoke, but the big shape that should be Lewis appeared to collapse, and there was a sound of something rolling down the stairs. Max pushed himself up and grabbed at his side. He had been sliced by a grazing shot.

"Max!" Michelle's scream made him look up just in time to see movement by the door. Mase, a pistol in his shaky hand, shot at him, and Max felt the breeze of the shot. He dropped the empty pistol and reached across his body, screaming as his wound flared, but he pulled the other Colt and took deliberate aim, while Mase was fumbling to cock and aim. Mase's head snapped back, and he fell. Max looked about.

Yellow Beard looked on, his hands tense on the table. The bartender had ducked behind the bar. Yellow Beard nodded to Max. "Nicely done, son. You got no worries from me; I'm staying out of it."

Max nodded. "Bartender. Stand with your arms up, and we have no problem, but I want to see you!"

The man slowly did what Max said. Max took his left hand off his wound and picked up his other pistol off the table where he had dropped it and put it in the holster. Grabbing his side again he grimaced and coughed but walked toward the stairs. The rifleman was lying at the bottom of the stairs reaching for the rifle beyond his grasp. Max shot him in the head, then looked at Lewis, unmoving on the third step.

"Michelle?" he looked to the blonde girl crying on the stairs. "Michelle, we need to go." She pushed herself up, still crying, and slowly walked down the stairs. "It's okay," Max said.

"No, they killed Daddy."

Max exhaled and nearly started crying himself. "I'm sorry. Let's get you out of here, all right?"

She started for the door and jumped as Tom Lewis moaned and gasped. Max saw the wound on the far right side of his chest. He wouldn't be going anywhere, at least not without help. Max looked back at Yellow Beard and the bartender, both passively watching, and then holstered his gun. He reached down and pulled Lewis off the steps to his feet. "Walk!" He pushed him toward the door, half holding him up. Lewis fell against the door frame and started to slide down, passed out. Max caught him and turned him, hoisting him over his right shoulder while stifling a scream and grabbing at his left side, but he went out the door with his heavy load. "Come on!" he called back when Michelle just stood there staring at him with the man slung over his shoulder. She followed but at a distance as he stepped onto the street and made toward the southern edge of town.

Men were out watching. The shots had drawn all their focus to the saloon, and people were emerging into the street to see what was going on. Max forced himself to walk without looking too hurt. He carried the man the distance of the street, ready to drop him and grab his gun if there were any shots. If Pat Lewis or Jeff Wright were in town and saw him carrying Tom, he probably would not make it. His side and hip were moistening with his own blood, and his back with Tom Lewis's blood. There was a gasp from the man over his shoulder just as they reached the end of the street.

They made it to the Lawrences', and Henry ran out to grab Michelle and hurry her inside. Max carried Tom into the barn and dropped him on the Porters' wagon. Then he turned and walked back to the house. He was breathing heavily and sweating even more heavily. Patricia took him at the door and helped him onto a stool. She took his shirt off of him and ripped at it, tying half around his torso with a wad of the rest against his side to provide pressure where he was bleeding.

"You'll live if you don't move."

"He's got to move!" Henry growled. "He carried one of those men's bodies down here."

"Injured as you are?" Patricia's eyes were confused. "Why'd you do that?"

"No reason not to, since I had him right there. It's why I came."

"To kill a man for money."

"He saved me!" Michelle's voice brought Max to look into the other room. Lying on the couch next to where she was sitting was her father, Pastor Todd, his head bandaged, and his eye swollen.

"He's alive?" Max almost smiled.

"Yes, but he's only been conscious for a moment, called out for Michelle, then tried to get up to find her." Patricia's voice was a growl.

Max sighed, grabbing at his side. "We need to get them out of here."

"He shouldn't be moved," Patricia said.

"It's for their safety and yours," Max said, pushing himself up.

"He's right," Henry said.

Patricia looked at them both a moment and nodded.

"Will you get my things from my room?"
Patricia made for the hall.

"I'll hitch the horses to the wagon," Henry said.

Max nodded. "Thanks."

He walked into the other room. "I'll do my best to see you safe to Flagstaff."

Michelle did not look up. She kept looking at her father.

Max walked back to the hall and was reloading his pistols when Patricia came back from his room. He finished and pulled a shirt out of his bags, and Patricia helped him put it on. Henry and Patricia practically carried Todd out to the wagon and lay him on soft bags by the front. Tom Lewis's body lay at the back of the wagon, and Max took some rope and lashed it around him quickly. After tying Hardy's reins to the back post of the wagon he started out on the road driving the wagon out of town, men watching them go. He tried to move the horses fast. He was worried about looking over his shoulder and seeing Pat Lewis and Jeff Wright riding up on him. Every bump set his side on fire, but the makeshift bandage seemed to be holding in most of his blood. The shot could have been much worse. He was fairly sure he'd live. They rode in silence for some time. Max was not sure what else to say to the girl. He felt bad that her lip was swollen, but there was nothing he could do about it. Perhaps if they crossed a cold stream, they could stop, and she could wet a cloth to soothe it.

"Thank you, Max, for saving me, whether it was to take this man or not, it still —"

"I'm glad I was able to stop them," he said quickly so she would not have to find the words to use. There was a long pause. Max's gut was bothering him, and not just from the crease in his side. "I would have done it no matter what man it was, you know."

Michelle nodded. "I know. I shouldn't have said otherwise."

She looked back into the wagon at her father, his head resting on a soft sack of clothes. "We went out early just a couple minutes after you left, and Father went to a spot near one of the flop houses. He started preaching, gathering a small crowd, telling them how God loved them and would forgive them for anything they had done, if they would just come home to Him. That's when that one came and smacked my father across his face and said, 'Will I be forgiven for that, preacher man?' "

Her eyes were tearing up again as she continued. "Father told him yes, God holds no grudges, and neither would he, and he held out his hand to shake it. The man laughed and took it saying that was right kind. Then he looked at me and said, 'I think I'll take your daughter and get to know if she's as sweet as you are.' Father stepped in between us and asked the man to please be decent. That's when he punched Father. Then with him down he and his friend kicked him several times. I tried to stop them, and they slapped me. I nearly lost consciousness." She was talking through sobs for the last few words.

"I'm sorry this happened to you and your father." Max wished he had better words to stop the sobs, but that was all he could offer.

She stopped crying after a moment and looked at Max. "I suppose that God uses all sorts of men, whether they are His or not. You were there not for God's purpose, but I believe He used you to help us."

"We have a ways to Flagstaff yet, so I wouldn't count your blessings so quick."

She glanced back behind them, looking for horses. Then down at Tom Lewis. "How much money will you get?"

"A thousand."

"That's quite a bit of money."

"He and his friends have stolen nearly a hundred times that from the stage and other

340

shipments."

A while later they had to move to the side of the road as they passed the stage going the other way. That encouraged Max. He figured they were likely halfway to Flagstaff. His side was still bothering him, and he felt like he was getting a fever, but they were getting close. The road was smoother, but the jostling still aggravated his side. He was starting to feel like his stomach might empty out, and his head began to pound from the inside. Michelle looked back frequently, which Max was glad for, because it was all he could do to keep his attention on the road.

He felt the blood running down his hip again and began to feel woozy, but, at the sight of the town, his spirits picked up. Although they stretched out, the last few minutes were filled more with anticipation than anything else. As they entered town the blood on Max's shirt and pants got the attention of some men, but the dead man tied to the wagon received more. When he pulled rein on the horses in front of the constable's office, two men were hurrying inside. As he was getting out of the wagon a stout, bearded man with a badge came out followed by the two men. "What's going on here?" the peace officer demanded.

"I got Tom Lewis here, sir," Max said, nodding to the back of the wagon with his head. He was gripping his side with one hand and steadying himself on the wagon with the other. "He's the stagecoach robber, one of them."

"Oh, ya, from Bumble Bee area down south."

"Yes, sir, and he beat this preacher and attempted to take his daughter. They need the doctor."

"You don't look too good yourself, mister," a man dressed like a merchant said from behind the constable.

"No, he's shot and bleeding," Michelle told them. "I'll be all right, but please help me get my father and Mr. Tillman to the doctor. He saved us."

The constable nodded to the other two men, and they helped get Todd Porter out of the wagon. Mr. Porter regained consciousness to a certain extent, and between Michelle and the two men they were able to walk him down the street to a house with a doctor sign outside it. The constable walked alongside Max and after several steps grabbed his arm and helped him.

The doctor was looking at Todd's head when Max came stumbling through the open door with the constable. The short, balding man took one look at Max's bloody side and motioned to the men that had stayed standing in the corner. "Lay this one down in my bed for now. That side looks like it's more pressing."

The doctor sighed when he looked at Max's wound. "It's inflamed," he said as he cleaned it, first with water, then with something that caused Max to jerk and yelp at the burn. "You should not have traveled with it, but you'll recover." He gave Max a spoon of powder of some sort and a cup of water to wash it down. Then he began sewing on his side. It hurt, but Max was glad the bleeding would be stopped. "Lie here and rest," the man told Max. "You were very lucky."

The slender doctor looked at Michelle then and said, "Let's go see about your father's head." Max did doze off. He thought it must have been something the doctor had given him, but actually the blood loss had drained him.

CHAPTER 18

Max woke in a haze and started to sit upright. The shooting pain in his side brought him to full alertness, and he realized he was still at the doctor's. The light coming in through the window was dim. It was evening. Max brought himself to a sitting position with a grunt.

The doctor came around the corner. "Here, drink this." He handed Max a cup of water, and Max gladly drank it. The doctor used a pitcher to refill the cup and handed it back to him again. Max drank that cup, too.

The doctor gave a satisfied nod. Then he handed Max a hunk of corn bread nearly the size of Max's fist. "You need something in your system with all the blood you lost."

Max took a large bite and chewed it while the doctor busied himself by his stove in the corner, sterilizing some of his instruments.

"How's the pastor and his daughter?" he asked.

"He started to get his strength about an hour ago. He looks to recover. The town minister heard of the attack on him and offered them a place to stay. They left just a few minutes ago."

Max swallowed another bite. "Good. Thank you, doctor. What do I owe you?"

"Six dollars."

Max looked up at him a moment and then nodded and gently pushed himself up to dig in his saddlebags in the chair next to the bed. "You probably saved my life. I'm grateful." Max handed the doctor eight dollars. He had plenty more coming to him.

The doctor took it and smiled. "Sure, son, I'm just glad you were there. Miss Porter told me about it."

Max nodded. "Me, too, despite the pain in the side."

"Come on. I'll help you over to the hotel." He grabbed Max and his saddlebags and stayed close to Max as they left the house and made their way down the street.

Max concentrated on steadying himself, and he was on the porch of the hotel when a man walked up to him. "You were the man at Canyon Diablo today, weren't you?"

Max looked at the man's hands and waist

and realized he did not have guns on his hips. The man looked somewhat familiar, but Max could not tie him to anything. "Why do you ask?"

"I drove the stage there today." The man shook his head, and Max realized that was where he had seen him. "Heard you put down three men who attacked a preacher and his daughter." He looked around the street and lowered his voice. "Good for you. Seems like almost anything can happen in that town."

Max nodded. "Yes."

The stage driver looked around again. "Be careful. The man's brother and the big man came back into town just before me. The brother was pi-issed. He put several bullets into the stableman's house on the way out of town."

"The Lawrences?"

"They're all right. Just glass broken."

"Thanks for the warning."

"Nah, I'm glad to do it." The man nodded to Max's companion. "Doc." Then, he turned and walked back down the street.

Max breathed heavily, wincing at the pain in his side. "My horse is safe in the stables, right?"

The doctor motioned toward the door. "Actually, it's at the minister's house with the Porters, but you won't be riding for a few days."

Max turned, and the doctor helped him get checked in and struggle up the stairs to his room. He nearly collapsed into the bed. The doctor left him, and Max felt weak and helpless. He did not want to sleep until he thought things through, but sleep was coming whether he wanted it or not.

Max's eyes suddenly opened into the dimness of the room. There was a creak outside the door. For some reason, Max did not think it was another patron of the hotel. Whatever it was just didn't sound right. He reached for the guns he'd put next to himself before plummeting into sleep. His room door flew open as it was kicked in. Two men with pistols shot into his bed from across the room, recocked, and shot again and again.

The smell of gunpowder and the smoke from the shots filled the moments after Pat Lewis and Jeff Wright erupted into Max's room with vengeance and murder on their minds.

Max's first shot made them both stumble as it passed through Pat Lewis and into Jeff Wright. They appeared to struggle through the pain and shock to try and find their assailant. Max struggled through his own pain as he pushed himself up a bit more from his unrolled trail bedding, which he had laid down on the floor in a dark corner of the room. He sent his second shot into Jeff Wright's chest just as Pat Lewis fell to his knees. Lewis reached for the gun he had dropped, but the third shot from Max hit Lewis square in the head, and all movement stopped.

Painfully, Max pushed himself to standing. He stumbled a little doing it, but he retrained his gun in the direction of the door in case they had brought more men with them. When he saw no one else, he turned the gun back to Jeff Wright, who was gasping. Max shook his head and kicked the gun a little further from Wright's reach. Then he went into the hall and sat down against the wall.

A couple of minutes later the constable and another man with a gun came cautiously around the corner of the stairs holding their guns, trying to make out Max's shape. Max had left his gun sitting on the floor next to him.

"The other Lewis brother and Wright are inside dead." Wright had stopped gasping after several seconds.

The constable walked around him and looked in the room. "Yep, looks that way.

They came after you, huh?"

"Yep."

"You hit again?"

"Nope."

The other man spoke. "They kicked in the door and opened fire, and you put them both down without getting hit?"

"I had a funny feeling they might come, so I bedded down in the corner of the room, leaving my bags and hat under the covers."

The sheriff came out. "Looks like you have more coming to you."

"I guess."

"You sure you're all right?"

The doctor peeked around the corner of the stairs and after his eyes adjusted asked what happened.

"He killed all the stage robbers and managed to not get shot again," the constable told him.

"Good. They whacked Sol around bad downstairs. You sure you're all right, Max?"

"I'm not hit, but I don't think I'm going to get much rest."

"I'll have an extra bed as long as Sol is the only other patient. Come sleep there, you need it."

"Thanks, Doc."

Max woke the next morning, barely remembering the walk to the doctor's. His guns lay beside him. He moved and remembered the wound in his side, but it did not feel as bad as the previous day. He felt a little stiff and tired, but he pushed himself up as gently as he could and dressed. The doctor greeted him and told him the hotel manager had given him another room. With that the doctor said it had been a long night, and he wanted to go back to sleep. Max thanked him again and walked back down the street carrying his gear.

He checked in and handled the stairs easier. He came back down, went to the café next door, and ate a large breakfast. He had eggs, ham, biscuits, and milk and paid to have a second plate. The merchant who had helped bring Todd Porter to the doctor's the day before came in and waved to him.

Max was wishing he had not ordered a second plate when the man came over.

"Mind if I sit?"

Max motioned to the chair.

"You didn't get much rest last night, did you?" He looked around. "You did earn some more money from what I understand."

Max just stared at the merchant. He did not really want to talk, especially about the shooting or the reward.

"After you heal up, I suppose you will be looking for another bounty?"

"I don't really know."

"Well, most bounty hunters are pure ruffians, but you I think are different."

Max sighed and looked at the man again, feeling his anger rise.

"I'm sorry, what did I say?"

Max remembered that the man across from him had helped get Todd to the doctors. He started to say something, but the man excused himself and left.

Max ate his second plate, and occasionally someone would wave to him, or tell him good work, or congratulations. He tried to figure out why he was angry. Sure, he was shot, and perhaps that was it. He had accomplished what he set out to do though. He had a lot of money coming to him. He should be happy.

He left the café, and, as tired as he felt, he wanted to go back to his room and sleep. He needed to check on the reward though, so he made the walk across the street to the constable's office. The door was locked, but the constable's voice brought him around.

"You're looking better."

"Feeling a little better."

"Well, we found their horses tied at the edge of town. No money in their bags, of course. They probably stashed it somewhere. There was about two hundred between them on your hotel floor. Unless I can track their trail somewhere, we won't know. But they won't be robbing any more."

"No." Max looked away.

"I sent the telegram just a minute ago; let them know to send your reward."

"Thanks."

"I asked them if I could get a piece if I found the money. You follow tracks?"

"Not very well at all."

"All right . . . well, I'll let you know when I hear from them. Won't be until I get back later. You probably need rest anyway."

Max nodded his head. He started back to the hotel, waved to the clerk, made his way to his room, and was asleep in minutes. He woke up feeling half himself again physically. His side itched, and he was stiff, but the pain was not as bad.

He was ready to walk some. He looked at his holstered guns with the belt laying on the stand next to the bed. He stood there for nearly a minute. He needed to clean them sometime. He probably should buy ammunition. The guns had earned him money. They had saved his life, and saved Michelle. He slowly stepped over and strapped the belt around his waist.

Downstairs the clerk greeted him. It was a young man who was eager to talk. "Mr.

Tillman?"

"Yes."

"You did well with those men who beat my father."

"How is your father?"

"He'll be all right. He's resting right now." The teenager's look became worried. "You don't think any other men will come looking for you, do you?"

"I don't think so." Max thought of what to say. "It was just because of his brother."

The boy nodded, but then Max started to think. What about the other men Max had shot? They may have brothers. There was Wright, the man that was with Tom Lewis, and Mase, the man who killed Ron that he had hunted down. There were those two men who tried to jump him, but how would any relatives know who he was? There was Carl Bradshaw. There were also men who were alive who might happen across his path, like Jim, the bully he beat in Willow Springs, and the ropers he had held at gunpoint in southern New Mexico.

"Did you say something?" the young man asked.

"Uh, no, but could you tell me where the minister's house is?"

"Follow the next street," the boy pointed, "up the hill. It's next to the church."

"Thanks."

Max went out the door and started that direction. He was feeling a bit tired but had decided he wanted to see how Pastor Porter was doing. The hill was a bit of a struggle. His side bothered him some but not really that much. He felt like he had when he was younger and was recovering from pneumonia. He would start to feel normal, and then as soon as he moved for a little while he seemed exhausted to the point he needed to take a nap. He saw the white building that he assumed was the church right at the top of the hill but then spotted Michelle sitting on the small porch at the modest house he was approaching.

She looked up and smiled. "Max, you are doing well, or at least moving around on your own."

"I'm all right. What are you reading?" Max was curious but realized as soon as he asked what the small book was.

"Psalms. I like to read through them occasionally when I'm struggling with what's happening around me, or in this case to me." She looked back down and started reading. " 'Rest in the Lord and wait patiently for Him; inflame not yourself with him who prospers in his way, with the man practicing evil wiles. Abstain from anger and cease with fury, also do not inflame yourself to do evil. For the evil doers shall be cut off and the ones waiting on the Lord, they shall inherit the earth.' "

Max swayed and put his hand out to hold on to the chair across from Michelle. A look of concern formed in her blue eyes. Max felt worried also but at the same time felt drawn to those eyes.

"What is it, Max? Sit." She stood.

It took Max a moment to reply. "I'm all right. At least it's not the gun . . . the wound. The preacher at Ron's funeral, my friend in Northern New Mexico, the preacher said something similar."

She looked at him, and a smile started to form on her face. Max felt himself getting angry. Why would she smile at that? She seemed to realize that she was smiling. "I'm sorry, Max, about your friend. But I think God's trying to talk to you."

"What . . . I . . ." He sighed. "How's your father doing?"

"Much better. He's moving around all right. He is taking a nap right now. As a matter of fact, the minister here thinks he knows of a town where we could start a church."

"That's . . . that's good." He did not understand why he was having trouble talking. "I have to go. I think I may need more rest myself."

"I'll walk you."

"No! No, please stay here; I'll be fine."

She gave him an odd look as he turned and started back onto the road. "Tomorrow's Sunday. Will you come to church with us?"

Max turned and caught himself from stumbling, hoping she did not notice, or she might decide to walk with him after all. "No, I don't think so. Thank you, though." He turned back and walked hurriedly down the hill. Downhill was much easier.

He felt better by the time that he reached the bottom of the hill. He was hungry again, but he wanted to avoid the café and people. As it was, he hurried past a couple of men who seemed like they wanted to talk to him. He went into the general store and purchased some dried meat. The merchant he had talked to at breakfast was behind the counter but said nothing except "Twenty cents, please," and "Thank you."

After hurrying past the desk clerk, he went up to his room and ate all of the meat while he stared out his window and watched people walk past. While drinking the last of the water that was in his canteen, he realized he had not checked on Hardy when he was at the minister's house. Michelle had . . . he was not sure what she had done. There had been a small fenced yard in the back with plenty of grass growing. He would check on Hardy tomorrow while everyone was in church.

Max sighed and realized he still had his guns on. He stripped them off and tossed them on the floor. Then he looked at them and sighed. He picked them up, pulled the one chair in the room up to the small stand next to the bed and reached into his bag. After cleaning his guns, he felt exhausted, crawled into bed, and went to sleep.

He woke during the early evening and used the chamber pot before going back to sleep. It was becoming light when his eyes opened again. He felt rested and more solid than he had the previous day. He rolled out of bed with less pain than before and rubbed his side lightly when he really wanted to scratch at it.

He dressed and went down the stairs.

"Mr. Tillman. You look like you are feeling better."

"I am," he told the clerk with the bruised face. "You look like you're on the mend as well."

"Yes." The man glanced at Max's guns, then nodded to him.

Max walked to the café next door, which was serving breakfast before church. There were a few men there dressed in nice clothes and one woman eating with another man as well. The constable was actually one of the men and waved Max over to the table where he was sitting with the storekeeper. "Got the wire. We can go to the bank tomorrow when it opens and take care of it."

"Thanks. Thank you."

"Would you like to join us?"

Max looked at the merchant, who looked suddenly sullen. "Thank you, but I'm actually not feeling that well, and I don't know that I would be very good company."

The constable looked at him a moment and nodded. "All right then. You should probably check in with the doctor after church."

"Not a bad idea."

Max went and sat at a table toward the back and faced away from the front in hopes that nobody would talk to him.

He ate eggs and a biscuit and drank several cups of water, declining coffee. He stood, thinking that he would walk around town a bit until everyone was in church. Then he would go check on Hardy. Maybe he would take the horse to the stables.

CHAPTER 19

Max started down the street. There was a fair-haired man sitting out on the porch of the closed saloon, strumming his guitar and singing. Max stopped and listened.

I'm running through the same trouble,
Keeps making my life into rubble.
I need to ride down a different trail
Cause this one's like a living hell.
If I'm honest, I'm empty deep inside
But all I do is find a way to hide
For all I've done I don't want to face,
But I must lean on His loving grace.
From these bonds, He'll set me free
Reach down, embrace and comfort me
Travel from this darkness into His light.
Shed my ways, surrender to His might.

Tears were rolling down Max's face. He hurried around the building and leaned against it, then went to his knees. "Yes,

God," he whispered. "I need you."

Suddenly he felt a comfort come over him like he was being embraced. He knew it came from God. This was something that he had never experienced, and it was without a doubt God. "Thank you," he whispered. He just stayed there on his knees experiencing the Glory.

When he opened his eyes and looked up, the couple from the café were looking at him worriedly. The man who had been playing the guitar stood behind them smiling.

Max smiled also, then laughed a little and pushed himself up. "Thank you." He looked back at the couple. "I'm all right."

"Do you want to walk up to church with me, brother?" the singer asked.

Max nodded. "Sure."

They walked ahead of the couple, and the singer patted Max on the back. "Did I just see you pray to God for the first time?"

"I think the first real time, the first time I really felt it."

The singer nodded and offered his hand. "Sean Donald."

He shook it. "Max Tillman."

"Do you live here, Max?"

"No."

"Where are you from?"

"I've been around, most recently Gillette

down south, before that New Mexico, Colorado."

"You're the bounty hunter."

"No." Max had not really thought of himself as that ever, but then he realized that's what he had done more than once in the last two years. "Well, I have done that, but I don't think I will anymore."

Sean nodded.

"Where are you from, Sean?"

"I live down south, east of Prescott a ways." He smiled at Max. "But I'm looking to leave. I don't really want to take over my father's land, but we haven't found a buyer."

"Where will you go?"

"I think California. I'm not sure, but I feel a nudging to go."

Max looked ahead and saw Todd walk out the door of the small house. He started toward him, looking back. "I have to talk to somebody. I'll see you after church." Max hurried, realizing how little the slight pain in his side was bothering him, and how he no longer felt so tired.

Todd looked back and saw Max coming at a fast walk toward him, and he stopped. "Max! I need to thank you for what you did. You don't understand how grateful I am."

"Sir, pray with me." Max knelt in front of Todd. Tears started rolling down his face, and he closed his eyes. "I don't understand it all, but I know there's a God and I need Him, and I'm sure of the rest, but I don't understand it."

Max felt the older man grab him by the shoulders, and he must have knelt with Max. "Understanding will come with time, but not all of it, not this side of heaven." Max opened his eyes and saw Todd smiling. The older man nodded and closed his eyes, and Max closed his again as Todd began to pray. "Lord, forgive me of my sins." There was a pause, and Todd gently tapped Max on the shoulder with one of his fingers. Max repeated what Todd had said. Todd continued. "I know I need you, I accept you, Jesus, as my savior and Lord. I thank you for lifting my sins from me, for forgiving me. I will follow you, Lord." Max repeated Todd's words, and after opening his eyes he stood and helped Todd up.

Todd gave him a warm handshake, and they turned toward the church. There halfway between them and the church was Michelle. She had tears in those stunning blue eyes as well, but she was smiling. Max felt a warm feeling inside as they all quietly walked into the church.

The service was of the fire and brimstone variety, but Max did enjoy singing the hymns, something he never really felt before.

After, Max agreed to dinner at the minister's house. They were walking out of the church when he saw Sean up ahead. Excusing himself, he caught up with Sean.

"Sean, how long will you be in town?"

"Just tonight. Heading back down to Big Bug area tomorrow morning early."

"Thanks for . . . well, thanks."

"Sure, Max. It doesn't end here, my friend." Sean smiled and kept walking.

Max turned back to join Todd and Michelle as they were going into the minister's house. Max took off his guns and laid them along the wall by the door. He felt a big relief. Michelle went to the stove, where the smell of food cooking came from a large pot. Max guessed that there was a roast simmering.

Max sat at the table across from Todd and sighed.

"I heard you may be starting a church."

Todd nodded and looked at Michelle. "I think we will put down roots, at least for a little while. It's a small farming and ranching and mining community east of Prescott."

Max was shocked for a moment, and both Michelle and her father saw his reaction. Slowly a big grin started to form on his face.

"What is that smile about?" Michelle asked, starting to smile herself. Her father turned and looked at her.

Max winked at her. "God's trying to tell me something."

Todd, a puzzled look on his face, looked back at Max, who was laughing. Michelle winked back at Max.

CHAPTER 20

Four years later–southeast of Prescott, Arizona

Max glanced at the darkening sky. The sun was setting, and he had just groomed the mustang stallion after working him the majority of the afternoon. The nearly three-year-old horse was an unbelievably strong horse already. Sam Donald, the old horse breeder who'd been working for Max ever since he took over Sean's father's ranch three years earlier, would go back and forth on whether the age they'd been given was correct. At around sixteen hands with a profile of sleek power, this horse looked to be a sure breeder. But after biting his original owner a couple of times, the horse had kicked the Chino rancher's oldest son square in the chest, nearly killing him. The rancher almost shot the horse. After calming down he decided to geld him instead.

Max and Todd had made the journey by

wagon to Chino just before winter. They had stopped in Prescott the previous day for the few supplies not offered closer to home before traveling on to Chino for extra hay for the winter. Four of the hands were gathering to geld the horse and told Max about it. At the sight of the beautiful horse, Max offered a hundred dollars even. Thompson sold, telling Max he was buying more trouble than he could handle, but after making the agreement, Max saw the man's tightened jaw as he stopped and looked over the stallion in the corral.

Max struggled leading the horse to the first night's camp. It was pulling so hard at the lead on the back of the wagon he worried about it hurting itself. Max worked with the horse, feeding it and trying to groom it that night. He nearly was bit twice, giving it a small rap on the nose for the second attempt. After a minute, he lightly patted the horse's neck and gave it a little more hay. The next day the horse fought the lead by the wagon again.

They stopped after a couple of miles and rested, and Max gave a little more hay to the animal. When they started out again Max walked the horse, leading it. Max was patient but firm, and the horse allowed him to lead it. Max was proud of that first step, leading the horse, walking for several miles before resting in the early afternoon. The stallion allowed the wagon to lead that afternoon. Max finished the journey having walked about half of it.

That had been five months ago. Today he had worked with a longeing line in the smaller corral he had built the prior year. The horse actually did well changing directions only by Max's signal and voice. Max kept that work short to make sure the young horse's legs stayed solid. Then when the horse tired he ground drove, getting it used to having reins directing it without anyone being mounted on its back or close enough to be kicked. He also tied a little bit of weight to the saddle he had the horse wear. That went as well as he could have hoped for the second time. After the stallion followed direction well, Max always gave it kind encouragement. When the horse appeared to be nearing a fatigue level where frustration was beginning, Max ended the session and gave the horse some oats for the work. Sam said it was either this way or hire a bronc rider, since neither of them were up to that task.

It was satisfying to see the training paying off. Max knew nothing about it until he started the ranch. Sean's father had instructed him, although he had only trained one horse and one mule under Sam's instruction. As part of the deal they struck, Sam agreed to stay on for a year and a half to give him guidance. Now, the older man and his wife, Martha, had a small house, really a shack, at the back end of the orchard, near the Agua Fria River bed, where he spent most of his time walking the maturing orchards near the river and watching the sunset. Occasionally, Sam would mount old King and ride to Cordes, Big Bug, or Spaulding to talk to men who had been in the area longer than him.

Max had grown fond of sunsets also, taking a moment on the porch of his house to look to the west at the purple, orange, and gold in the sky. His house was just west of the center of the ranch on a small rise. Off the back porch, they could see a glimpse of the Agua Fria during the wet season. They had around half a mile of river bordering their land — great for the dozen head of cattle they had, as well as for the orchard. There were two operational wells, one by the barn and one inside the house. Max felt very fortunate to have this land. The wide-open beauty of it made him smile.

If the rise to the southwest was not blocking the view, he would have been able to see the lights of Curtiss and the vague outlines of the buildings. It was the closest town. There was a general store there, a rough, drunkard-filled saloon, an eating house that doubled as a second saloon, a blacksmith, an assayer, and a couple of other small businesses. Curtiss, near Big Bug Creek, existed because there was a smelter there to process the ore from nearby mines, the closest being Hackberry and Boggs mines. Otherwise, there were other settlements in the Big Bug area if Curtiss did not provide what was needed, such as Mayer, which was also south a few more miles along the meandering Big Bug Creek. Almost directly to the northwest several miles, Max would enter Agua Fria Station land owned by the Spaulding family. There were plenty of stores and even eateries in the region without having to go all the way to Prescott, although Prescott had much more than these smaller locations.

The house door opened, and Ronnie ran out before Michelle could grab the toddler. Max scooped up his son, and Ronnie touched his nose. "Horse."

Max nodded to the blond-haired child. "Yes, I smell like a horse."

"Well, wash up." Michelle leaned in for a kiss. "Supper's ready."

"All right, baby." He put Ronnie down and went to the wash basin Michelle had put out on the porch for him. He stripped off his shirt and hung it on a peg on the corner of the porch to air out, then washed his hands with soap and water. As soon as he splashed water on his face a breeze kicked up, and he shivered. It got cold suddenly in the Big Bug region in springtime as the sun dropped behind the mountains.. Max quickly splashed his body and dried before stepping in and grabbing his other shirt from the inside peg.

The main room of their house was fairly large. The stove was at one end next to the pump, while the table sat in the middle with six chairs crowded around it. The fireplace was in the far corner with a door to a room branching off either side. Beds could be kept close to the doors of the rooms to get the heat coming in from the fireplace. The house had been well designed.

Max buttoned up his shirt and quickly stepped to the table just in time to pull out Michelle's chair for her. She leaned over and kissed him before sitting down, her pregnant belly not allowing the chair to be pushed in completely. Ronnie was already sitting down.

Max sat down, looking at the plate in front

of him: beans, tomatoes, bread, and lamb. This was the last of the lamb they had purchased from their neighbor to the northeast across the river. If he did not find game, they would have to kill a steer soon. He did not want to have to kill too many of the chickens either. He reminded himself that they were in good shape, though; he had nothing to worry about.

Max closed his eyes and prayed for gratitude for the food, for the health of his family, and for the friends they had.

Max took a bite of the lamb and nodded. "Good. You know I think it's better than beef; just doesn't sell as well."

Michelle smiled. "I don't know . . . it's different, but both are good."

"Does Todd need help in the morning?"

"No. He thought he had some volunteers."

"It would be nice for him to have a church building."

"Perhaps in Mayer."

"Maybe, but Curtiss is a good location, kind of central to a lot of places."

"That's what Dad says. Says the miners need someone there."

Max nodded his head in agreement, bringing Michelle to smile. He had told her how many of the prospectors' and miners' main object of worship was gold. "Although he'd love to live and work around Joe Mayer. He really likes him."

"I like him, too. I still can't get over it after four years. We move down here and start ranching, then hear that somebody bought Big Bug Station and was building new, bigger buildings. Ride in to take a look and see if they need any stock, and what do you know but it's Joe Mayer, man who ran the small store and eatery in the camp at Tip Top."

Ronnie grabbed some beans and pushed them into his mouth. Max smiled, watching his son and thinking about the new baby on the way. His life had certainly changed since he had hunted down Wright and the Lewis brothers. Michelle and he spent most of two days together in Flagstaff while Todd was fully recovering. They walked the streets that first Monday. Then, the next day they went to the edge of town in a clearing by the woods and had a picnic. They talked, and laughed, and had their first kiss.

Max had offered his hand to help Michelle up, and she thrust herself into his arms and kissed him. He had never kissed any woman that he had already built up feelings for, and it had shaken him on the inside quite a bit.

They traveled south together, Max plan-

ning to look into the ranch and Todd looking to build a church. The three of them
grew closer on that trip, having already
experienced a bond through the events at
Canyon Diablo, and Max's new faith being
nurtured by the two of them. By the time
they reached the Big Bug region, Max knew.
He was helping Todd hitch the wagon from
camp that morning.

"Sir, I'd like to ask your blessing to marry
Michelle."

"Max, you have it." Todd clapped him on
the shoulder. "After the last several days, I
know you two are right for each other. I
never would have thought it when we first
met, but you are a good man to be her
husband, if she says yes."

Max instantly turned and walked over,
gently taking the coffee pot from Michelle's
hand and setting it on the ground as he
went to one knee. "Michelle, will you marry
me?"

When he had dropped to one knee her
eyes had gotten large. After he popped the
question, a large smile shone, and she nodded, giggling. "Yes!"

Max stood and grabbed her in a hug and
kissed her.

They arrived at the home of Sam, Martha, and Sean Donald late that morning and

agreed on the purchase within an hour after Sean showed them around. Max thought that Sam and Martha were pleased to be selling to a young couple just starting out, and Todd being a pastor may have pleased them as well. That afternoon they all bathed, and, as the sun set, Todd performed the ceremony of marrying Michelle and Max at the edge of the orchard.

Now, there was a second child on the way. They had people they cared about in their lives, and Max could look out over the land — his land — and see himself staying here all his life. Sure, he was curious about cities like San Francisco and New York, the lands up in Montana and Canada, places he would like to one day see if they had the chance. But it did not matter if it did not happen.

Max enjoyed his work. He enjoyed checking on the cattle, seeing the calves grow. He had been hesitant at first working with the horses, and the mules that were not fully tame, but now he was gaining confidence and found the process rewarding. He liked harvest time at the orchard, and gathering the hay in the field that was not grazed. He just loved working outside, on his own property. He loved the feeling in the summer when the sun would hit his back while he was repairing some fence. Max never wanted to go into a mine again. There were several men around who had their hand in ranching and mining. Max really was not interested. Of course, if he thought he could pull some gold out of the water without too much work, then he might do it. Really, if he could build good herds of horses and mules, then supplying the miners, the stages, and the citizenry would be very profitable.

After supper and washing the dishes, Max lit the wood in the fireplace, and they sat talking. Ronnie had a carved bear that he had been given and was walking around with it, making the growling noises that Sam had made with it.

They had heard many of each other's stories before, but there were still new ones that came out. Michelle told Max about the city of Pittsburgh back East, the hustle and bustle and the size of the steel mill. Max told her about east Texas, the river near the town where he grew up.

Ronnie began to tire, so Max put him into bed, covering him with a heavy blanket. Then he and Michelle snuggled up in their bed and fell asleep in each other's arms.

Max's eyes opened, and he saw through the slit in the curtains that the sky was lightening. He leaned over and kissed Michelle on the cheek, then rolled off the bed onto his knees and prayed. He prayed for all to go well, for health of his family, including the Donalds, for Sean (who was in California), for the livestock, and most of all for people to come to God on this day.

Standing, he threw on his clothes and walked through the main room, grabbing his coat and stepping out into the chilly morning. After gathering the eggs, he carried them to the house, where Michelle met him at the door to take them. He turned back and fed the horses and the milk cow, milking the cow while she ate.

"Morning, Max," Sam said from the barn door. The old man had trimmed the white hair of his mustache and beard, as well as his head. Usually he had a stray hair this way and that way.

Max looked back. "Morning. Martha inside?"

"Yes, she's got a cold, and this chill is not settling well with it."

"I could have hitched the wagon to come get you."

"Nonsense. It's not even a full mile to our cabin."

Max smiled, standing with the pail. "All right. Let's go get some hot breakfast then."

Max enjoyed the coffee and hot breakfast more on account of the cold. After, they took the wagon on the trail southwest. Max looked back at his ranch with the barn to the east of the house with three divided corrals. There was another wood fence running the distance off the back of the barn all the way to the bluff that was too steep nearly everywhere for the cattle to climb. Hardy was in the largest corral with three mares and a gelding. In the next to largest corral, the stallion and his best mare were loose. Max thought it was time to let Rowdy breed. Max had decided the name for the stallion when he was more dangerous. Now things had progressed. There were still times like this morning when he made to lead the stallion to the corral that the horse stamped its front hoof a couple of times. Max held up his hand like he had all along to calm the horse, and said, "Don't get rowdy." Of course, when he first started he gave an extra bunch of oats or an apple when the horse calmed down. When the horse calmed now he just patted it on the upper shoulder.

Max not only felt proud looking back. He was nervous leaving Rowdy out with the mare with nobody around, although Rowdy had never shown aggression toward female horses. Also, he almost never left the horses out when he was gone away from the ranch. Of course, it would be just as easy or even easier for a thief to grab one from the barn.

The four mules pulling the wagon now were the only four he had. Mules were most miners' choice for beast of burden. Max may have been wiser to concentrate on that area of business, but he liked the horses more.

They had actually walked into Curtiss several times before he got the wagon and mules, but it was a long walk for Sam and Martha. Max had to admit that he wanted anybody considering buying a mule to see them, although he would not actually negotiate a price on the mules on a Sunday. He would tell men he would get together and bargain first thing Monday.

They crested a small rise, and Curtiss was visible just to the north across Black Canyon Road. The smoke of the smelter was the first thing that could be seen. Max spotted a man walking from the south on the road. Max stopped along the road just as the man was walking past and did not recognize him. The lanky man, maybe a few years older than Max, was carrying an old single-shot rifle, and his clothes were tattered. His face was scratched along one cheek.

"Hello, mister." Max waved his hand.

The man nodded and walked past the team of mules, continuing down the road. Max started the mules along next to him and looked again at the red-haired man.

"You all right?"

The man looked at him. "Yes, sir."

The man had no bag slung over his shoulder, or Max would have guessed him to be a traveler. Some men with no means to purchase a horse would walk a great distance. "You can hop on if you like, but we're only going to that town right there." Max pointed to the group of buildings.

"Thank you, but I'll just walk."

"All right." Max got the mules going and moved up the road. When they reached Curtiss, Max looked back and saw the man still walking steadily toward them.

Sam leaned toward Max from the back of the wagon, as if the red-haired man might have overheard from a couple hundred yards back. "Looks like that man got into it with a wildcat."

Max shrugged. "He's a quiet one." Max saw the chairs and benches set up on the open land between two-story buildings. One had a large white sign on the front reading *General Merchandise.* The other was the mill office. Max passed the buildings and parked the wagon on the other side of the general store. He hopped down and helped Michelle down from the back. Sam, moving more spryly than Max expected, hopped out of the back and helped Martha down from the bench where she had ridden next to Max. Ronnie was down and running around the store to his grandfather.

Max and Michelle were following when a tall, wiry man with a dark-gray beard stepped off the porch of the general store. "Max, Michelle." The man smiled warmly and shook hands with Max.

"Einar, good to see you." Einar Morand helped run the smelter. His main job was providing security for the ore, and that had spilled over to keeping things from getting too rough in town also. Max and Einar got along well. Einar had started at the smelter when it was first built. The general store and saloons were being built when Max had first bought his ranch.

Einar looked at Michelle. "That father of yours has captivated quite a few of my men."

"That's good," she said, smiling.

"Oh, I agree." Einar looked behind him. "Makes them think twice before pocketing any ore, and I'd rather them be here on Sunday than off drinking all day." Einar looked at the team of mules, then to Max. "Old Luke Kelly came into town this morning. Think he's looking for a second mule."

"Maybe I can sell him one tomorrow."

Einar shook his head. "Might be gone tomorrow. You won't get struck by lightning, you know."

"I know. It's not from fear, Einar." Max clapped the man on the shoulder and started toward the small gathering.

Einar smiled, giving his head a small shake, and followed them to the other side of the store.

Todd was standing in the middle of the benches talking to Jenny Mallory, the widow of Bill Mallory, who had died when a small portion of a local mine collapsed. They bowed their heads together, Todd speaking quietly. Her young daughter and son, both a year or two older than Ronnie, sat on the bench behind them and watched. The brown-headed boy eventually bowed his head as well.

Max leaned into Michelle. "I think Dad's actually looking younger."

She glanced over and smiled that smile that meant she liked something he said. "I think we have a good life, and 'Dad' is happy."

"Yeah, well we all are." Max reached over and tickled her, receiving an elbow in the ribs for it.

Todd and Jenny finished praying, and she gave him a hug. When Todd moved, Max and Michelle saw Ronnie was standing behind him holding the Bible. Todd took the good book from Ronnie and leaned down to whisper something in his ear. Ronnie ran back to Max, and Todd walked to the front of the group.

"It is good to see you all here. Let us open in prayer."

After service, three miners came up to see Todd. Todd looked back to Max, and Max knew Todd wanted him to come pray with them as he had last time. Max strode up and knelt with the other three men while Todd led them all in a prayer similar to the one Max had prayed in Flagstaff a few years back.

The burly miner that Max had knelt beside put his hand on his shoulder, stood, and looked at Max and then back to Todd. "Thank you. You know I always . . ." The man's voice began to crack, and his eyes were moistening. "Thank you!"

Max nodded. "It's an overwhelming feeling, I know."

"Yes," the man said strongly. He started looking away like he was not sure what to do now.

"Is it Hal?" The man looked at him and

nodded. Max extended his hand. "I'm Max, Pastor Porter's son-in-law. We'd love for you to join us for a small meal. We have some stew in the wagon, and we'll be heating it up in a few minutes."

A smile formed in the middle of his thick beard. "That sounds right nice."

Hal helped carry the big pot from the wagon to the fire.

Luke Kelly pulled Max aside after he had started the fire. "Max, them look like all right mules. Are they for sale?"

"Every one of them."

"Well, I only need one. How about . . ."

"Can we talk about it tomorrow morning, Luke? It's Sunday, and I don't do business on the Lord's day."

"I will be heading over to Mayer's later today."

"Will you be there tomorrow?"

"I will be heading back to my claim first thing in the morning."

"Well, I can come out early. You just tell me which one or two you're considering."

"The tall, lighter one and that stockier one."

"You got a good eye."

"Now as long as you aren't lookin' to charge —"

Max held up his hand. "We'll get to it

383

tomorrow."

Luke shrugged. "You know Joe may have some stock there himself."

"Maybe, but I'll take my chances." Max motioned to the pot. "You joining us for some stew?"

"You think I'm turning down food I don't have to cook myself?"

Max started toward the pot. "You get much game around your camp?"

"No, occasionally I get a rabbit but mostly eat what passes for cornbread in my camp and a little bit of dried jerky. But you know I did get some other game a few days ago. Cooked me up a couple of scorpions."

"You run out of cornbread?"

"No, but one of the little bas—" the miner looked to Todd — "um, suckers, it stung me. Hurt so bad I cut off its stinger and decided to eat the thing to see if my red friend was right about them. Then saw another and added it to the first."

"How was it?"

"Well, I've been on really hard times in my life, and I could appreciate it on account of that, but I'm not going to go hunting them unless those hard times come back."

Hal laughed hard at Luke's joke, and a chuckle went around the group.

Max nodded. They sat down on one of

the benches, and another of the miners who had knelt with them looked over at Max. His eyes grew a little wider.

Max recognized the man also, the Irishman from Tip Top. "Ian."

"Hello, Max."

Todd walked over, seeing how Max's face had changed.

"I don't want any trouble, Max," Ian told him.

Max looked up at Todd and sighed, then looked back to Ian. "We all have the opportunity to change." He extended his hand. "Sorry things went the way they did last time we met."

Ian took his hand. "I had it coming." He shook his head. "I had a heck of a time hobbling away from Chapey, though. I was wheezing from the kicks to my back, and my knee was messed up, but I knew we'd gone too far."

"The past is the past. It doesn't have to dictate who we are now."

Ian looked at him as if thinking about what he said, then nodded.

"You work at the smelter?"

"Sometimes. Sometimes at the Hackberry. Actually, hobbled down to Big Bug after Tip Top. Mr. Boggs, he hired me, had me work in a couple of his other mines before this one."

" 'Twas Boggs that set him straight." Einar had walked up behind them.

Ian looked up, at first with a flash of anger, but then it softened. "I suppose he did to a certain extent."

Max smiled at the way Ian talked now. "I've actually never met him but heard good things."

Einar laughed. "You keep to yourself too much on that ranch of yours. Of course" — he motioned towards Michelle and little Ronnie — "you've got it nice out there. Fine looking start of a family."

"Thank you."

"I always thought I'd have a good family, but now I'm more than twice your age, and it's not happened."

"It's never too late." Ian nodded back toward the creek. "I know a man out there nearly twenty years older than you just married him a woman. They're having their first child."

"You mean Ted and his squaw." Einar chuckled. "He's not twenty years older than me; plus it's not the same as what Max has."

"He seems happy," Ian said with a smile.

"I'm sure he is." Max stood up and clapped Ian on the shoulder before going to pass out bowls.

Chapter 21

The next morning Max was up at first light and riding the tall mule, Bodie, with Bonnet in tow. Sam had volunteered to do the morning chores for him when he heard he was making an early trip to Mayer.

"I kind of enjoy the chores when I only do them six times a year," he had joked.

Max spotted the town as the sun was nearing mid-morning point.

Joe Mayer had gone to work building up the stage stop after he purchased it from William Muncey in 1882. The stage station now had a decent size barn and corral, a family home with guest rooms divided by a large hallway, and a store with an attached eatery and saloon. These three buildings were the originals. Recently a separate blacksmith shop had been built. Mayer's extended family on Sadie's side had a house in town with an extensive garden that many considered a small farm. There were a couple of other houses that had been built recently, and a couple of tents were set up nearby, right next to the creek.

Max led the mules down to the station. As Max approached a man rode toward him, a broad-shouldered man, with a very neatly groomed dark mustache and a nice coat to match. The man rode a well-built chestnut stallion that pulled toward the mules. The man countered with the reins, and the horse obeyed. He nodded toward Max, but his blue eyes seemed wary. Max nodded back and rode to the hitching post.

Max walked into the small café attached to the store. Luke was sitting there with the proprietor drinking coffee. Joe Mayer's bushy mustache and worn, light-colored coat were a stark contrast to the man who had just ridden past, but Joe was not just a merchant behind a counter; he performed all types of work around the small town. A smile crossed his face. "Want some coffee?"

"I'd love some." Max put down a nickel as Joe got up.

"Anyway," Joe continued, looking back at Luke, "give me the summers here anytime over the winters in New York or Nebraska. I didn't care for those. Breakfast, Max?"

"No, thanks."

Luke pointed off. "I traveled up around

Flagstaff area prospecting once. It gets pretty cold there. Arizona territories got all kinds of weather."

"Nothing like New York."

"How long since you been in New York?" Max asked.

"Around twenty years ago." Joe said, his French accent coming out more as he thought back to his youth. He was around his mid-thirties, so he had to have been a teenage boy then.

The door to the restaurant burst open, and Mamie and Martie came running into the diner. Joe's young daughters had the lighter, curly hair of their mother. The older one, about seven, called out. "Mom says that she needs a spool of white thread."

Joe handed Max his coffee. "I'll be back." He walked into the store with his daughters behind him.

"Oh . . ." Max dug into his pocket and pulled out a letter. Sadie Mayer was post-mistress, and Sam had given Max a letter to be sent to Sean in California. He put down a quarter on top of it.

Luke looked at Max. "Which of them mules rides better?"

"For me the taller one, but Sam favors the other. Give each of them a short ride if you want." Max took a quick sip of the cof-

389

fee and got up to go out with Luke. The coffee was just about scalding.

"I figured you were going to use the mule more for hauling."

"I have Rachel for that. I've rarely rode her, so she's more used to hauling. My legs just get tired faster than they used to."

"You named your mule Rachel?"

"Yes, sir, after a girl that broke my heart long ago."

"I see."

"It was a mistake, though. This Rachel's a lot more reliable." Luke chuckled at his own joke.

Luke ended up liking the stout, shorter mule. It showed an affinity to him and took his directions. "I'll give you thirty."

"Thirty? It's a good mule, you can see that."

"That's why I said thirty."

Max shook his head. Some guys just had to play the haggling game. "You're offering less than half what it's worth. Sixty-five."

"That's more than double. I thought you said you weren't over pricing."

"I figured I had to start pretty high since you're trying to steal her."

"Steal her? Well, I . . . what do you say is a fair price?"

"A real fair price?"

Luke nodded in response.

"All right, a real price. Fifty."

Luke sighed. "That's a bit high."

"It's fair."

"It's fair if I'd not just shelled out a small fortune to pay off Joe for backing me. What about forty?"

Max shook his head while looking at the mule. "I'll tell you what, Luke. I'll meet you at forty-five even though I think it's low, if you'll promise to come to me next time you're gonna buy."

Luke reached up and lifted his hat with one hand and scratched his head with the other. He looked over at the mule, then nodded. "That's fair, I suppose."

"You want to talk about the price of the saddle?" Max asked.

"The saddle? You mean that's not in the price you just give me?"

Max opened his mouth but had trouble finding words.

Luke's face changed to a big grin, and he started laughing. "I'm messing with you. I already have a good saddle. That's the reason I started thinking of getting a mule to ride."

Max smiled, relaxing and offering his hand. "All right then. It's a deal?"

Luke shook it. "Deal." He pulled out the

money and gave it to Max. Max was glad it was not gold dust they would have to go ask Joe to weigh.

Max tried to sell Joe Mayer the saddle, but Joe said he had enough of them to sell, so, after riding a short distance holding it awkwardly in front of him, Max dismounted and walked alongside the mule. The sky was clear, and the sun was warming. Max put his coat over the saddles and walked along the trail, moving over and waving to Bob the stage coach driver as the team of horses kicked up dust going past. It was midday as Max walked around the rise and into view of the ranch.

Something did not feel right. The horses were not in the corrals. They should have been there all day. Max quickened his pace, looking to his Winchester in the saddle sheath. Sam stepped off the porch waving, but he held his shotgun. Max trotted the rest of the way to the house.

"What's happening?"

"Nothing here, Max."

"Where's the horses?"

"In the barn. That Rowdy's a tough one, but he's better than he used to be."

The door opened, and Ronnie ran out to the edge of the porch. "Hi, Daddy!" Michelle, Todd, and Martha came out behind him.

The tension released a bit from Max's shoulders, and he smiled. "Hi there, Ronnie!" Ronnie jumped down and ran to where Max was and turned around to look at everyone else, a son standing with his father. "So, anyone want to tell me what's going on?"

"The Clarks." Sam motioned back with his head. "They were found dead, killed."

Max felt his stomach clench. He looked northeast. He could not see their place, but they were on the other side of the Agua Fria. You could look down the river a few hundred yards and see where their land met the river.

Todd stepped forward and laid his hand on Max's shoulder. "Morgan, from Cherry, was going to see them to buy a few head of cattle for his eatery. The coyotes were on them, out in the yard. He scared them off and saw the four bodies." Todd's voice began to quiver. He looked down at Ronnie. "Them and their two boys all shot. They had their scalps taken also."

"Scalps?" Max said, shocked.

"Scalps," Ronnie repeated.

Max put his hand on Ronnie's head.

"They think it could be Apache, Geronimo?"

Sam shook his head. "Geronimo's nowhere near here, but Einar did say he saw a couple of Indians leading horses the other night at the edge of Curtiss going north to south."

"Who else would scalp somebody?" Martha asked.

Max looked around the ranch again. "Anybody go to Prescott and get the sheriff?"

"Morgan did, after putting the bodies in the barn where the coyotes wouldn't get them further." Todd shrugged. "They've no idea. They're looking at the possibility of Indians who left the San Carlos agency heading back to the Fort Verde area. Clark's horses were all taken, one of the bulls was killed, they think another two head are missing, but there were still a dozen or so around. There was a little bit of money in the cabin, although it had been ransacked."

"Terrible!" Michelle said, tears in her eyes.

Max nodded. "Well, Sam, Martha, you're welcome to bunk in with us for a while."

"Thank you, Max, but I got this here shotgun, and Martha has one as well. We've lived in scarier situations."

"Offer's open if you change your mind."

394

Max shook his head. "Well, I'll leave half the herd down there then; they'll make noise if something's around."

"Maybe," Sam said. "Apache can be pretty quiet."

"Anybody check on the other ranches?"

"Ed Bowers over by Agua Fria Station volunteered to send out riders. That's how we found out."

"What are they going to do?"

Todd reached over and took the second saddle off the mule. "Riders said some they talked to are calling for a posse, but there's also men who don't want to leave their ranches. Sheriff has a deputy with him, and they're sniffing about. Morgan had to go back to his business in Cherry. Said his trip to Prescott cost him already."

"Come on in," Michelle told him. "I have some stew heated."

Todd took the reins to the mule. "I got this, Max."

Max stepped onto the porch, putting his arms around Michelle. She clung to him tightly and let out a sigh. "I'm glad you're back."

"Me, too, darlin'."

She released him and walked inside. Max soaked his hands in the wash basin several seconds, then wiped at them briskly with the cloth.

He came in and sat down, and Michelle put the stew and a hunk of bread in front of him.

"How'd the sale of the mule go?"

"Forty-five. It's pretty fair." Max hungrily scooped stew into his mouth.

"How are the Mayers?"

"They seem well," Max said around a bite of bread. "I only saw Joe and the girls, but everything is going well for them. The girls are getting big."

"Good. We need to bring Ronnie over next time we get a chance to see the kids. They all get along well."

"Um-hmm." It seemed to Max that Michelle was trying not to think about the news anymore, but Max couldn't help but think about it. He sighed and started considering carrying the pistol that he had stored in the upper cabinet. He had sold one of his guns and the two-holstered belt in Prescott years earlier, soon after buying the ranch. He hunted with a rifle and kept it handy to protect the stock from predators.

He had kept the one pistol in the event that this very sort of thing happened, and he needed to protect his family from another type of predator. But he really did not like the idea of putting the pistol through his belt. He just preferred to never handle it again if he could help it. He thought about Chapey's words: *You're cold with those guns strapped on.* It was true. He had been a cold man then. He had even paused in removing Michelle from the saloon to scoop up a dying man for cash. He sometimes wondered if he should have even taken the money from the bounty and used it, despite how much he loved his life on his ranch.

Todd walked in and put the rifle on the hooks above the door. Max smiled at his father-in-law and decided that the pistol could stay put away for now.

Ronnie was playing with his carved-wood horse, having it run across the bed, toss its head, and run back. Max smiled as he watched him.

Michelle was washing the dishes from earlier. He handed her his empty bowl and kissed her on the cheek. He looked back at Ronnie and grabbed his rifle on the way out the door.

He checked on all the horses, then released Rowdy out into the smaller corral. Rowdy let out his energy by running around the corral, just as Ronnie had imitated with his wooden horse. Max went in and released Hardy into the bigger corral. He saddled him, which was a simple task with the

Choctaw horse. The horse would often come to him when it saw the saddle, as it did today. Max had not been on Hardy in a few days and not giving the horse too long a break between rides would keep age from setting in too soon. Max started off trotting the horse around the corral, then sped things up and moved Hardy through some maneuvers at about three-fourths speed. After having the horse run the stretch of the fence at a decent speed, he trotted it around a bit more.

Then he brought his friend in and washed and groomed him. Max was feeling a bit tired already from the trip to and from Mayer and thought about abandoning his idea but pushed on.

He stepped into the smaller corral where Rowdy was. He approached the horse with his rope, and the horse tossed its head and ran to the other end of the corral. Max followed and resisted the urge to use oats to lure the horse.

He made the same noises he did with Hardy and called Rowdy. The horse slowed, but Max had to toss the rope and was glad he managed to lasso him the first time. Rowdy actually calmed down, which he often did of late once Max had him caught. Max came and patted the horse's shoulder.

He led the horse to where the longeing line was and put it on him. He worked the horse for nearly half an hour, and, although the horse was not near tiring, Max himself felt really tired.

Max brought the horse in, tied it off, praised it, and gave it oats. Then he put the saddle on the stallion. Rowdy fussed and threatened to kick, but Max just talked calmly to him and patted his shoulder again, and it was not a big ordeal.

Max took a deep breath as he untied the reins from the post and swung quickly into the saddle. Rowdy pulled sideways as Max seated himself, then the stallion froze, its muscles tightening up. Max reached Rowdy's shoulder patting. "Easy boy, it's al—"

The first buck was so sudden Max almost went off the saddle and over Rowdy's head. Max clung to the saddle horn and endured the next two or three bucks. Rowdy stopped for a moment, and Max got the feeling the horse was considering rolling. He used the reins, guiding as he had practiced from a distance, and Rowdy actually followed his guidance for a moment before bucking a couple more times. Max lost his grip on the saddle horn for a split second but grasped Rowdy's mane as he lunged sideways. He caught his balance long enough to grab the saddle horn again. The horse stopped bucking a moment, tossing its head. Max used the reins again. "It's all right, Rowdy. It's all right, boy." Rowdy let himself be guided around the small corral, a couple of times tensing to buck again, but Max diverted the horse's attention, having it move in a wide arching turn, keeping it from speeding up too much. Rowdy calmed, seeming to fall into the work of obeying rather than bucking. Max trotted the stallion around the corral, reaching down and patting its shoulder. "Good boy, Rowdy, good boy." He stayed on for a few more minutes, carefully guiding him.

He noticed everyone standing at the other end of the fence near the barn. Michelle was holding her gardening hoe and waved. Todd held Ronnie, who waved also. Martha stood near Michelle, her hand on her shoulder. Max could see some pride in their faces, but Sam's face was beaming. Sam had been his teacher, and, although Sam had never been thought of as a great horse trainer by himself or others, he had given Max the basics, and Max had just tamed his first stallion — one that some had said was untamable without gelding, or maybe at all. Here he was trotting it around the corral.

He rode it up to the post by the fence, and Sam took the reins and tied them. Max swung down gently, soothing the horse as it danced sideways. He patted it on the shoulder, and Sam passed him the oat bag. Max fed Rowdy, praising him. Max felt like his exhaustion was gone at the moment. He had done it. He leaned over and kissed Michelle and then ruffled Ronnie's hair. His son's play had prompted him to jump the training to riding. Rowdy fussed a little being groomed, but nothing that was dangerous like it once had been. Max stabled the horse and went and sat on the porch. He could smell food cooking, roasted chicken. Sam came out carrying a bottle and sat down beside him. To the west, the sky was dimming to a dark blue, with golden light shining between the clouds.

"Well done, Max. A little celebration nip." Sam handed him the bottle. "You've got no need for advice from me anymore."

"That's not true." Max took a small sip from the bottle and passed it back to Sam, who took a little bit bigger sip. "A man can always use some advice from those who aren't fools, and sometimes even from those who are."

Sam smiled. "Are you saying I'm a fool sometimes?"

Max laughed. "No, sorry, I didn't mean that. You've not been a fool since I've known you. There was a man I saw yesterday who used to be a fool years ago, but he seems a bit more wise now."

"Remind you of anyone?" Sam laughed now, and so did Max. Sam knew of Max's past and how he now looked back in distaste at the direction he had been heading.

"Yeah, we all have our opportunities to change." Max took another sip and handed the bottle back to Sam, who corked it and set it over to the side. They sat there watching the dark blue and gold in the sky turn to dark violet and rust.

Max reminded himself before he stood up that there is good and bad in this life. It's partly what you do and what you focus on that determines how your life goes. He said a silent prayer to God, thanking Him. Then they went in to eat.

CHAPTER 22

Max rode Rowdy first thing the next morning. After one attempt at bucking, Rowdy settled down and let Max guide him around the corral for nearly half an hour. Max rode his finest mare, Jewel, the short distance to check Sam and Martha, and Sam helped drive half the cattle up to the fence on the other side of the corrals. After Max groomed the mare, he set her loose in the corral with Rowdy.

Max was about to take another mare out to work when a familiar man rode into the yard, trailed by another. The lead man wore rancher's clothes, but they showed little wear. His horse was fine looking, a rival to Rowdy, whom the big man eyed for a moment. The man behind him was big also, but his clothes were more worn. He stayed back a bit.

"Max Tillman?"

"Yes, sir."

"You probably don't remember me; we met once in Curtiss. I have a ranch up north a ways."

"Not too far from Cherry?"

"That's right. Morgan told me what happened to the Clarks, and I thought I'd ride down to see what's being done. He and I were sort of close, helped each other out now and then."

Max nodded. "I remember him telling me that the corners of your properties were actually just about a mile away." Max remembered Walton a little better now. His place was sizable, just south of where the trees started to thicken.

"Yeah, as far apart as our houses were, the odd shape of our lands made us close neighbors." Walton shook his head. "I can't believe this. Scared me a bit, too, about what may be coming my way, if Indian wars start again."

Max looked back towards the Agua Fria. "I can't tell ya anything really. I've only heard that the sheriff is looking into it."

"Nobody else seen anything?"

"No, not really."

Walton looked at Max a moment. "I was afraid of that. Indians can be as sneaky as they are ruthless. Too bad nobody saw any of them with horses, so we'd know which ones and what direction."

Max remembered that the rider delivering news had said Einar saw what looked like Indians leading horses in the dark. It was mostly speculation, seeing as how dark it was.

"Might not even be Indians. It could just be an isolated incident."

"I hope so, but I doubt it. Have you ever been around a place where there's been Indian skirmishes?" He did not even pause for an answer before continuing. "Once they start they don't stop until they've been completely whooped. You haven't seen any hint of them, have you?"

"No, no signs of Indians. Any other news about it?"

"Not really. Oh, Morgan did say looks like it was an old rifle that was used, ball and powder job like some of the old ones some sell to the Indians cheap."

"Whoa, wait. I saw a man on Sunday, on the road, carrying a gun like that."

"Yeah?"

"Yeah, looked like he'd been through some sort of scrape, too. I thought he'd probably been attacked by an animal. I should have thought of it before, but he didn't have any horses or scalps. He was walking."

"Doesn't sound like much to do with this then."

"No, maybe not, but I should probably still report it."

"Suit yourself. Keep a watch out for Indians, though." With that Walton rode west, followed by his ranch hand.

Max took a deep breath. He wanted to stay close to home, but he felt like he should talk to somebody. He could ride into Curtiss and tell somebody and be back in time for lunch. He saddled the mare he had planned on working and rode down to Sam's cabin.

Sam was sitting down on the river bank with a fishing pole in hand, which surprised Max. There were hardly any fish in the river. Matter of fact there was hardly any river. It had rained a few days back, and there was a small flow. Sometimes a heavy rain would connect the waterways, and fish would end up in a seasonal river.

"You get any bites?"

"No, but it's relaxing. I did catch something a week or two ago — surprised the heck out of me."

"What'd you catch?"

"A turtle. There's even less of those around than fish." Sam laughed.

"I need to run into town for a while. I was

wondering if you would mind keeping an eye out."

Sam looked over. "Sure. I'll saddle old King and Queen, and we'll ride over."

"If you like, but Todd's there. I just thought maybe you could keep a listen. I don't really know. I just have the urge not to leave, but I remembered that fellow we saw along the road Sunday morning."

"What fell— Oh, him. I didn't even think about that."

"Me neither, but turns out the rifle used to kill the Clarks was an old powder job."

Sam looked at him and nodded. "Worth reporting. Don't worry, Max, we'll ride over. Of course, we'll just have to eat there, maybe sleep there tonight."

Max smiled. "Of course. I should see you for lunch." Max whirled the mare around and trotted her back toward the house to tell Michelle he would be gone for a while.

As Max was riding into Curtiss he saw Nathan Bowers walk out of the smelter office. Max waved to him as he rode to hitch his horse next to the old rancher's.

"Bowers, you didn't see a man last Sunday walking up the road with an old musket, did you?"

"No." Bowers looked up. "Oh, an old musket, like the one used at the Clarks'."

"Yes. I didn't even think about the man until Walton told me about the ball."

Bowers nodded back to the office he had exited. "Walton's in there right now with the sheriff."

"Sheriff's here?"

"He's set up here in Curtiss, since Einar claimed to see Indians passing by town with horses a few nights ago. He's got a couple of the Prescott Grays with him." Bowers smirked. "They like to think of themselves as rangers. I'm not putting them down; I just don't know how much of a help a newspaper man can be."

"Newspaper man?"

"Bucky O'Neil. I guess he's been around enough action, but never in it that I know of. I heard a rumor he's considering running for sheriff next term."

"I've not heard that."

"Yep, well it's all hearsay. You know sometimes men in stores and saloons gossip worse than a group of women."

Max shrugged. "What action's he been around?"

"Think he was in Tucson during the Earp-Clanton feud."

"Hmm."

"Yep. The only other action I heard of is at the faro table; that's why they call him

408

Bucky, 'cause he bucks the tiger." Bowers gave a wry smile. "Well, I'll see you around."

"Take care, Nathan."

"You, too, Max."

Max walked into the office. It was small, and there were already five men inside: Einar, Walton, Sheriff Mulhenon, and two men in gray uniforms. One was middle-aged, burly with a light beard, and the other was about Max's age, slim, with a neatly trimmed mustache. They all looked over at Max.

Einar looked around. "Always good to see you, Max, but we were in the middle of something."

"Sorry for barging in. I just had news I thought the sheriff should know about." Every eye focused on him, waiting. "When Mr. Walton told me about the bullet being from an older rifle it made me remember that Sunday I saw a man I'd never seen before carrying an older rifle up the road toward Prescott. Looked like he'd been in some sort of scrape."

"Was he Indian?" Einar arched his eyebrows.

"No, he was white, tall, slim, scratch across his cheek."

"What color hair did he have?" The younger Gray had spoken and then looked back at the sheriff, who sighed.

"I couldn't tell. It was short enough that his hat covered it, and I was up on the buckboard. His hat was tan, and his shirt was a bit darker. I think he was wearing denim pants. All well worn, but the shirt looked torn around the shoulder."

Mulhenon nodded. "Thanks. Max, is it?"

"Yes, sir."

"We'll consider that."

"When we talked," Walton said, "you told me he had no scalps or horses or cattle; in fact, he was walking."

Max nodded. "You're right. But, I just thought it was worth mentioning."

"We need to get after the Indians before they get rid of the horses, or do this again," Walton insisted.

Mulhenon sighed again. "It doesn't sound like he had anything to do with it. Seems like he would have been staying off the road if nothing else."

Max nodded. "Makes sense. I'll get out of your way." Max started for the door.

"Well," the younger Gray interjected, "not all men have the sense to think that far ahead, and he could have been part of it and then had a falling out with his partners. Got left without a ride."

Max looked at the man, then back at the sheriff.

Mulhenon was looking at the younger man. "That's a great story, O'Neil. I'm sure you'd like to print it, but it doesn't make it true."

"Sheriff, I was only saying that it was worth somebody asking around, see if we can find this man."

"If we don't find the horses with the Indians then we'll think about it."

"Do you need any help?" Max asked.

The sheriff looked at Max's waist, where there was no gun. The other men did the same.

"Max, you're a peaceable man with a family," Einar told him. "You don't want to go riding into a possible battle with savages. But, if you really have a suspicion about this fellow, I don't think anyone here would have a problem with you riding the road asking people if they've seen him, what direction he was heading." Einar shrugged. "Of course, I have to agree with Walton here — you'd probably be wasting your time."

"I'll think on it. Good luck, men." He nodded to O'Neil. The man held himself all right. He thought Bowers might have been wrong about him.

He stepped out of the office and was walking toward his mare when he noticed Ian over behind the general store waving his hand to him.

Max walked over and looked around. "What are you doing?"

"I saw you walk in. I need to talk to you, Max. They're going to go after Ted's two brothers-in-law."

"What?"

"The Indian woman Ted married. Her two brothers work with them at the mine. Heard Walton and his man earlier today talking about how they thought it could be them being that they'd been to Clark's place, then with Einar seeing Indians leading horses through here, in the general direction of the mine. Plus, story has one of them bringing down a mountain lion with an old cap and ball."

Max looked to the south. "Definitely sounds like it's worth checking out."

Ian shook his head. "I've spent time in their camp, Max. I can't see that happening. They were at the Clarks' because Ted was a cousin of Mrs. Clark. They aren't wanting to scalp anybody. Ted had even started reading the Bible to them on Sundays, and they . . . well, they listened and talked about it like a close family would. Ted's the one suggested I come to the

412

service on Sundays."

Max sighed and looked around the corner toward the office. "I don't know, Ian. If they ride in and don't find any evidence then it'll be fine."

"Max, you know how it is. People want quick justice, so they just may pick the most expected suspect. Plus, I just have a bad feeling about it."

"They've told me they're going to look for evidence; I believe them. As long as they don't fight when they ride in I think an arrest will be all that happens. In the meantime, I have another lead to follow up on."

"What other lead?"

"Saw a stranger walking down the road Sunday with an old rifle, like the one used."

"Well, I guess that's all we can do, that and prayer."

Max nodded. "Yes, pray. I'd better get moving." He clapped Ian on the shoulder and started off, then stopped at an urging he was feeling and turned back. "Ian, you're doing good."

Max pushed hard for home and got there just as lunch was being put on the table. He ate with the family, telling them he felt obligated to see if he could find the man. Michelle pursed her lips, not liking the idea but not saying anything. Sam offered to stay at the house. Todd patted Max on the shoulder. "You're doing good." Todd often gave Max encouragement.

CHAPTER 23

After a quick meal, Max gave Michelle and Ronnie a hug goodbye, saddled Hardy, and started off at a quick trot. He ended up riding alongside the stage to Prescott for a ways once he hit the road. He and Bob, the driver, talked about the killings for a while, but Bob had no information aside from the fact that it was the talk of the area, and at all the stations there was a building fear of Indian attacks. Half thought maybe Geronimo was around.

Max rode on to the Agua Fria station, ahead of the stage. He asked the stable hand to water Hardy and went in to talk to the keeper. Turned out the woman who worked the station on Sunday was in the separate parlor, so Max walked into the place for the first time. He had never seen anything like it, except when he had looked into some of the fancy hotels when he had passed through big towns. Still, he did not think any place he had seen had been so nice. Michelle had told him that she had come here with Todd once when he was out visiting. She said it reminded her of some of the nice houses back East, not something expected at a stage stop for sure. There were two women in there, and another serving them tea.

"Ma'am, sorry for disturbing you, but did you see a lanky, tall man come through on Sunday, on foot? Looked like he'd been in a fracas."

"No, nobody that fits that description or on foot. And Sunday turned out to be such a nice day that I spent nearly the whole afternoon on the porch."

"Thank you, ma'am."

Max abandoned the idea of going on into Prescott based on the woman saying she was on the porch all afternoon and did not see the man. Max knew he was grasping and might never find anyone who had seen the man, so he followed a different hunch.

He climbed the hills and rode into Big Bug as the sun was nearing its final descent. A tall, slender man in the distance waved him over. As Max drew near, he saw the man looked in his fifties, strong and sure.

"What are you looking for, son, work?"

"No, sir, I have a place not too far from here."

"Didn't think so, but you're looking for something, though."

"I am. My name is Max Tillman."

"Theodore Boggs."

Max swung down and offered his hand. "Pleasure to meet you, sir."

As Boggs turned to extend his hand Max saw the other side of his face was scarred and malformed. Boggs grabbed Max's hand in a solid grip. "What can we do for you in Big Bug?"

"There was a man on the road on Sunday, tall, thin." Max hesitated until Boggs nodded to him. "He had a scratch on his face and was carrying an old single-shot rifle, from before there were cartridges. Wondering if you've seen him?"

"What if I have? You wanting to pin that murder of the family on him?"

"No, sir, not if he didn't do it. Just that it was a rifle like that was used in the killings, and I'd never seen him before, and he did look like he'd been in a fight of some sort."

Boggs smiled. "He had been in a fight of some sort, I guess. You can hear the story from him. He's a former employee of mine. He was working down outside of Phoenix for a while, then in Stoddard. When things

417

went bad there, he came to see if I would give him a job. Come, let's get your horse into my stable, and then I'll introduce you to him."

With Hardy settled into a shelter alongside the barn, Max and Theodore Boggs went into his house. It was nice, and bigger than any other in Big Bug, but not as big as one would expect of a man with his success. It was the size of the typical home of a somewhat successful merchant.

Walking into the dining area, there sat the man, with dark-blond or light-brown hair, Max couldn't decide. He looked cleaner and wore fresh clothes. The scratch lines on his face had scabbed over. The wounds were not severe.

Boggs addressed the man, whom Max decided was in his early thirties. "This is Max Tillman. He saw you on the road a couple of days back, and it was around the time of that family's murder. He wants to ask you some questions."

"Hello." Max reached out his hand.

The man shook his hand, then leaned back, looking to Mr. Boggs, who nodded to him. "Hi, Mr. Tillman. I didn't have anything to do with that. I caught a ride on a wagon going from Stoddard to Phoenix, and when we hit the Black Canyon Road, I started for Big Bug. I swear."

Max sighed. "I'm not trying to pin anything on you. It's just that you weren't very talkative and looked like you'd been through something. I thought it might be an animal attack at the time."

Boggs chuckled. "I'm sorry. What happened wasn't a laughing matter, but the animal that scratched James was mighty funny." He motioned to James to continue.

The man hesitated. He looked down for a moment, took a deep breath, and then started. "I'd lost everything in a card game while I was drunk. Lost my money, my horse, my gear. Everything except for my grandfather's rifle that he used in the Mexican war.

"I had an unpaid bill for room, food, drink, and um . . . company of the landlady. When I told her I'd lost all my money and gear, she went wild on me, scratched my face, hit me with a skillet, and then grabbed a knife. Luckily another man held her back long enough for me to get out of her sight."

"See?" Boggs pointed to his own face. "This is the mark of a wild animal, a grizzly. That's the mark of a wild woman, not quite as dangerous."

Max turned his attention to Boggs. "A grizzly?"

"Yes. Most men around here know the story. I've told it so many times, I'll give you the quick version. I lived in California until I was around your age. I liked to hunt, and you know these single-shot guns mean that if you don't put the animal down the first time, you could be facing a pissed-off animal with just a club. Well, I was mauled, mainly taking this one swipe to the face. I played dead, which wasn't hard 'cause I couldn't really move much, and the thing walked off. Because of this my brother got to be the good-looking one of the family." He gave a wry chuckle at that.

Max nodded. "Thank you, Mr. Boggs. And, James, I assume all this can be verified in Stoddard."

"Yes, sir." He shook his head side to side. "You can ask Christopher Wilkins, or Janie Tyne. But, please, don't tell them where I am. I'll send her the money when I have it."

"All right. Did you see anything out of the ordinary on your journey?"

"No, sir."

"So, you don't think it was Indians," Boggs asked.

"I don't really know. All signs point to it. But that old single-shot gun made me want to check — same type of gun was used."

James sat up straight, a worried look on

his face. "I don't even have any ammo powder or rounds for that gun. Just been passed down in my family."

"I believe you, James," Max told him. "Plus, you wouldn't have been walking if you were involved. It will be easy enough to verify."

James leaned back and nodded. "Yes, sir."

"He's working at the mine here, and I have no reason to think he would do this." Boggs spoke authoritatively.

"Like I said, I was just following up. It's just that nobody with sense thinks Geronimo is in the area, and the Indians they have in mind don't really have a motive."

Boggs shrugged. "In the early days, I had my own battles with the Apache, but I was surprised to hear of this happening now. Most have accepted that they can't win back their land, but there's renegades there just like there's bandits among us whites."

Max nodded. "Well, I thank you."

"You're welcome to stay the night," Boggs told him. "There's a bit of supper left on the stove, as long as you clean the pans."

Max thought about it. He wanted to get back home, but the ride down from Big Bug was a little rough, and he did not want to risk Hardy's legs. "Deal. I appreciate it, Mr. Boggs."

Boggs was actually quiet most of the rest of the evening, reading a book. Max was tired and collapsed to sleep wrapped up in a blanket. He woke at first light and went out to feed Hardy and get him ready for the journey. When he came in, James was cooking eggs and ham.

"You're welcome to stay and eat." Boggs came in from the other room. "I've not had houseguests for a while. Once James's tent comes in, I'll be on my own again. It was a fair trade, not having to cook my own meals or go down the street to the same old food."

"Thank you, sir."

They sat down, and Max nodded to Boggs. "I appreciate all your help. I see why you're so respected."

"Am I now?"

"Your men speak highly of you, Ian and Einar."

Boggs took a sip of his coffee. "That Ian, I see as a man who just took a while to calm, like an ornery young stallion or a pup. But you know what you have with him. Whereas Einar . . ." Boggs's voice trailed off. "Oh, I'm just babbling. Like I said, I've lived alone too much."

Max was about to sip his coffee but put it down. "Sir, I know them both, and I'd say you pegged Ian pretty well. I'd be obliged to hear what you have to say about Einar, and it won't leave this table."

"It's nothing really. He's never done anything wrong that I know of, and he runs my smelter well. I'm appreciative. But, despite the fact that he's given me no reason, I have trouble really liking the man even though he seems likeable. It's really my own problem."

"Well, I really like the man." Max sipped his coffee.

"Like I said, my problem. He does well by me."

They ate, and James talked about Stoddard at night. "It's something to see. You would not believe the amount of drunkenness, gambling, and whoring that goes on."

Boggs glanced up at Max and then turned to James. "Where'd that get you, James?"

James stopped mid-chew and considered it. He nodded to Boggs.

Max nodded also. "You ever get the itch, James, there's a church service held in a space near the general store in Curtiss. You might like it."

The look that came over James's face nearly made Max laugh. He imagined he looked like that when people brought up God and church to him in the past. "Thank you, Max, but I'm not . . . I'm more likely

423

to go on into Prescott for that."

Boggs smirked as he put a fork full of eggs in his mouth.

"Sure," Max said. "Offer's always open, though."

After eating, Max helped with the dishes and then mounted Hardy for the ride back.

Max entered Curtiss late in the morning and found Einar's office empty. The smelter workers were busy, though, and the heat from the smelter could be felt all the way to the edge of Einar's office. After asking one of the workers, he found out that Einar had "went with the sheriff, the two Grays, and another couple of volunteers to the mining camp where the Indians worked who slaughtered the family."

Max sighed and mounted his horse to ride for the ranch. He had done his part. Within minutes he was coming over the rise, his home in sight. Michelle was hanging clothes on the line alongside the house, Ronnie following her. Todd and Sam were out by one of the corrals, and Martha was sitting on the porch in the shade.

Rowdy and Princess were in the other corral. Max patted Hardy's neck. As great a horse as Rowdy was becoming and as valuable as he would be breeding, Hardy was still his favorite.

He rode on down, and Martha waved to him from the porch. Michelle heard Hardy's steps and glanced up. She had hung up the last shirt and came walking quickly toward him. Due to the pregnancy, she did not run as she did at times in the past, when she would launch up into his arms, causing Hardy to dance a few steps to balance. Max dismounted this time and embraced and kissed her.

"How's things been, baby?"

"I've missed you."

"I've missed you, too."

"There's been nothing big. The corral gate you've been saying was wearing snapped. They're putting new leather strappings on it."

"I should have done that earlier."

"It's fine. Dad's glad to be working. He says you don't let him help enough. And Sam . . . well, he was bored all day yesterday sitting on the porch."

Max kissed her again and then caught Ronnie out of the air as he jumped up to hug his father.

"You find the man?"

"Yep. Don't think it was him. He just got taken in a game of cards and roughed up by someone he owed some money. Theodore Boggs all but vouched for him."

"You met Mr. Boggs?"

"I did. He's the real deal, old Hassayamper."

Michelle smiled. "You love talking to those men."

"I do. They were here when there was nothing else . . . well, but the Indians." Max felt his jaw set. He saw that subject different than he once did.

Michelle looked toward the house. "You hungry?"

Max shrugged. "Not too much."

"There are a couple of leftover biscuits from this morning. I'll get you one." She motioned to Ronnie.

Max smiled. "I'll keep him safe." He swung him onto Hardy's saddle and told him to hold onto the saddle horn tight. He kept an eye on him all the way to the barn and then set him down on the milking stool and told him to watch how he took care of the horse, and that he would need to do the same one day.

Michelle came out and fed him a few bites of the biscuit while he groomed Hardy, eating the rest herself.

By the time Max made his way to the corral, Sam and Todd were testing the repaired gate, swinging it back and forth.

"Good work. Maybe I should ride off for

another couple of days and get you to do more of my work."

"Go ahead." Sam nodded to the other corral. "The way Rowdy's progressing, you could probably stud him out, collect a decent fee."

"I think I want to keep his blood in our stock only."

"Need more mares then."

"I know."

Todd came and grasped Max. "I'm glad to help any time."

"I know. I just don't want to take you away from God's work."

Todd nodded. "Not that much to do right now." He looked to the house. "You find the man?"

"Yes, sir. Found him staying at Theodore Boggs's house in Big Bug."

Sam cackled. "I don't suppose he did it."

"No. He lost his money at cards and was . . . um, handled roughly by the mistress of the boarding house he stayed at."

Sam shook his head with a smirk on his face. "Well, you had to trail it out."

"Yes." Todd clapped Max on the shoulder. "It was the right thing to do."

Max nodded solemnly. "They weren't in Curtiss. They had already ridden for the camp with the Indians they're blaming."

"You've done what you can." Todd tried to console him. "And it just could be those Indians."

Max sighed. "You're right." He looked back and forth at the two of them. "Do you guys know Boggs's story about his face?"

"Yes," they both said simultaneously.

"Einar is right. I don't get off this ranch enough."

CHAPTER 24

Max walked over and entered the corral with Rowdy and Princess. Rowdy turned and charged. Max caught himself from jumping out the fence. He held out his hands and stepped forward.

"Easy, boy." Rowdy came to a halt a couple of feet away, baring his teeth and stomping his foot. Max held his ground. "Easy. Calm." Rowdy stopped a moment, eyes piercing. Max backed up and grabbed a feed bag hanging on the fence. "Let's go, boy."

There was a long pause, and then Rowdy marched over. Fortunately, there were a few oats left at the bottom. Max put it on him and then saddled him. Rowdy once again became the horse he had worked with the last couple of times. Max decided to move forward with his plans.

Max swung onto the saddle with the least reaction yet. He trotted Rowdy around that part of the corral a few times, keeping him from trotting over to Princess. Rowdy responded well. Max turned and nodded to Sam, and the old rancher opened the gate. Max rode out and through the other gate Todd held open leading back to the cattle.

Max rode Rowdy at a good clip toward the river and the largest portion of cattle. The horse seemed excited to run at first but slowed a bit just before coming over the rise that showed the river and the cattle grazing alongside. Max did slow him more and guided him to walk slowly down. He was glad that Rowdy was tired at the moment. He brought him near enough to each of the cattle to give them a decent inspection to make sure they did not look sick. There was a calf running alongside its mama that had been born just three weeks back.

After that, Max turned and trotted Rowdy at a good clip back toward where other cattle had stayed grazing closer to the house. There were five of them spread out. Two of them darted when Rowdy got close, but Max decided their movements showed they were healthy.

Max had to restrain himself from putting Rowdy through more training. The horse was doing so well. He could take the horse across the river, drive some of the cattle back toward the front, and climb the big hill to the northwest, which kept the cattle penned. Of all the animals, only Hardy had conquered that hill. But Rowdy needed more time to build trust and obedience, and Max did not want to push the horse and possibly cause a setback.

He rode Rowdy back, climbed down, guided the horse through the gate, and then climbed back on for the short ride to the stalls. Afterwards he gave Rowdy a good grooming. Max was exhausted and decided to call it an early day. He spent the next half hour soaping up and filling the buckets to rinse himself off, shaving, and finding his comb. When he turned away from the mirror along the back wall of the house Michelle was bringing him a fresh set of clothes.

"You do clean up nice, mister."

"Thank you, missy. I got to work to keep up with the looks of my wife." He grabbed her and kissed her as she went to hand him his clothes.

She rubbed his smooth face. "We'll kiss more later. I've just started supper and need to cut up some potatoes." She pushed the clothes into his hands but gave him one more good kiss before heading back inside.

Max dressed and then went inside to see

Ronnie darting through the house pretending he was riding a horse. Max held out his hands, and Ronnie ran into them. Max scooped him up and spun around several times. Todd looked up from where he was taking notes out of Scripture and smiled.

Max looked around. Martha was in helping Michelle with supper but no Sam. "Where's Sam?"

Todd nodded toward the other room. "He's using your room for a nap. After coming in, he and Ronnie rode the room rounding up cattle."

Max nodded and went into the kitchen, giving Martha a pat on the back and then kissing Michelle on the cheek. Then he spun out of the cooking area into the main room with Ronnie before putting him down. He pretended to be dizzy, wobbled, and fell on the floor himself. Ronnie fell on top of him laughing.

Max held Michelle, her head on his chest. Everyone had turned in early, tired. Supper was delicious, and the time spent at home with his family had been relaxing. The day's work and play had tired out Sam. He and Martha left to walk back to their cabin while there was still light. Todd turned in tired as well, and Ronnie had finally worn himself out and had to be carried to bed while asleep.

Max was still tired from his journey, and Michelle tired more quickly while carrying their daughter. They had decided this would be a daughter. But despite their tiredness they did spend some time kissing.

It had not even been dark an hour, though, and everything was quiet in the house and around the ranch. They had all earned their rest for the night. He drifted off to sleep.

The bellow of a bull woke Max up. He pushed out of bed and grabbed the rifle on his way out of the bedroom. Maybe it was a mountain lion or a bear. He unbolted the front door and swung it open. Walking onto the porch his eyes adjusted.

The cattle were quiet, and nothing seemed unusual. Max sighed, looking around in the dark. His stomach clenched. He had never thought the darkness of his ranch was spooky before, but right now he just wanted to go inside and lock the door. He gazed in all directions again, then walked inside, locking the door behind him.

Todd was sitting up in his bed. "What is it?"

"Heard a bull; just thought I should check."

Todd nodded. "It feels odd now, doesn't it?"

"What?"

"Thinking of facing men with a gun."

Max looked at him. "It always was odd."

"Was it?" Todd waved his hand. "I don't mean the action itself — I imagine the closer it came to actually facing the men, the more odd it felt — but the thought of it, what led you out chasing them."

Max sat down at the table, thinking about what Todd said. It was a minute before he answered. "I suppose you're right. The thought was not as strange until it came up on the moment. But now . . ."

"You're not the same man, Max." Todd smiled. "You'll do what's right to protect your family, but you don't seek it out."

"Yes." Max stood back up. "I think I'm going to try to get back to sleep."

The distant sound of a shot froze him on his first step to the bedroom. Then there was a second. Max looked to Todd. "Sam's place."

Max took a step towards the door and stopped. He didn't want to leave Todd, Michelle, and Ronnie. If it was an attack like at the Clarks', then he needed to stay and protect the house. He could not leave them. He looked back at Todd. The man was a good man but not good with a rifle.

Todd looked at Max, then got up and grabbed the other rifle they had for when Max was gone.

Max leaned against the front door, his insides twisting. Sam and Martha were alone down there, but, if he left, his family here would be alone. Michelle and Ronnie were his first priority. Sam and Martha were actually pretty tough; they could take care of themselves. It still tore him up to not be able to go see to them. He knelt down by the window and looked that way.

"Someone or something did spook the cows a few minutes ago. Then down at Sam's. That may have been his shotgun."

After a couple moments of silence Todd spoke. "Max, if you want to go down there, I'll do my best here."

Max exhaled, then looked toward the rooms. "Let's make sure those windows are shuttered and get them out here."

Just then Michelle walked out. "The windows are locked in our room." She went into Ronnie's room. Max walked in quickly and looked through the door as she checked the windows in there and woke Ronnie. Max walked into their room and grabbed his boots, pushing them on quickly.

He turned, and Todd was looking out the

window. Max knelt down beside him. "I'm going to go out and look around. If I don't see or hear anything I'll saddle a horse and ride for Sam's. I'll check on them and get back here as quick as possible. Keep the doors locked and keep them clear of the windows. You be careful also. Fire a shot if you think you're in danger. I'll turn and get back as fast as I can."

Max looked back at Michelle and Ronnie coming out of the room. His eyes met Michelle's. She looked afraid. Max took a deep breath and opened the door. He stuck his head out, looking around before stepping out and off the porch. He heard the door lock slide into place behind him.

Max walked to the corner of the house and peered around the other side, looking as far as the moonlight would allow. His finger twitched just above the trigger. He looked behind him, then circled around to look at the other side of the house.

Movement made him jump, but in the same moment he knew it was just a tiny ground squirrel running into its hole.

Max sighed and trotted toward the barn. He opened the door and went to Rowdy's stall first. It was the fastest horse. The horse stomped its foot and showed its teeth. Max turned back to Hardy's stall. Rowdy sensed his anxiety and was still not trained enough.

He quickly saddled Hardy and led the horse out, closing the barn behind him. He flung up into the saddle and rode the short distance to the gate. He dismounted and opened the gate, pushing away the cow just on the other side, pulled Hardy through, and then closed the gate. He remounted and was off at a very fast trot. Max reached down to make sure the rifle in the scabbard was not too tight to pull quickly and scanned the hills and depressions, trying to spot any dangers. He heard the call of a wildcat somewhere in the distance.

As he came over the rise to look down upon Sam's place, two riders were coming up the hill toward him. He pulled his rifle before he realized it was Sam and Martha. "You all right?"

"Yeah, we're all right. What about back at the house?"

"Everything was fine when I left. Was that your shotgun?"

"Yep. Heard the cattle out here and came out and saw three riders. Indians, I'd say. They lit out as soon as they spotted me. I shot and think I may have peppered one with my first shot, but they were a good forty yards away. Fired a second time just to keep them riding. They went down into the Agua Fria and across."

"I'm glad you're all right."

"You should have stayed back at the house. You know I can take care of myself."

"I know. You coming to stay for the night?"

"Yeah, I suppose what's left of it."

They fell in side by side. Max noticed that both of them had shotguns across their saddles. "You think it was the same Indians?"

"I don't know why any would be riding around here this time of the night."

"Yeah, they must have snuck through the gate up there. The bull started bellowing and woke me up."

"Well, at least they were sneaking through the gate and not up on the house," Martha said.

Max looked over at Martha. She was right. They could have just as easily been up at the windows of the house, and Max would not have had any warning.

When they rode up to the barn and opened the doors to put their horses in, Max saw a light flicker on inside. Todd had seen that he and the Donalds were all right. They got the horses unsaddled and into stalls. As they approached the house, Max glanced around into the night. It seemed the spookiness had eased up.

The door opened, and the smell of coffee brewing drifted out. Michelle and Todd greeted them all with hugs, and Ronnie did the same, imitating them. Max was glad to get the hugs. It was a different type of fear than he had years back, this fear for his loved ones. It ran deeper than any fear he ever had for himself.

They all walked toward the table. Sam took everyone's guns and leaned them against the wall in the corner. Ronnie was looking at them.

"Ronnie," Max called to him. "Stay away from those." They never kept guns at a level the young boy could reach. Michelle was pouring the coffee. Max went and opened up the cabinet in the corner. He reached onto the top shelf in back and pulled out the bundle of cloth, then a pouch. He unwrapped the cloth to show his old Colt 44 caliber. He opened the pouch, took out the ammunition, and loaded the pistol. He put it on top of the cabinet along with the pouch of bullets.

When he walked back to the table Todd reached out and patted him on the arm. He had seen. He knew Max did not want to take the gun out.

Max took a cup of coffee from Michelle. Sam was finishing telling the story of what happened. "I guess in the morning we go into Curtiss and report it."

"They'll want to know," Max agreed. "Everyone needs to keep more alert. Look around before you first go out. Keep a lookout in the distance. Listen for unusual sounds."

Sam nodded. "That's right."

"Also, Sam, Martha, I don't like you down there by yourselves."

"It's awfully crowded in here though, Max."

"We'll make do."

Martha reached over and put her hand on Sam's arm, and the argument faded from his face. "All right."

Nobody felt as if they could sleep. They made some bacon and biscuits and ate breakfast, finishing just as the light was seeping through the windows. The sound of horses approaching sent Sam to the corner, grabbing guns to hand out. Max walked over and peeked out the window.

"It's all right. It's Mulhenon and some men." He walked out onto the porch to see Joe Mayer with the other men. The others were Einar, the two Grays, Walton, his man, and two others.

"Hi, Sheriff, Joe."

"Tillman." The sheriff looked angry. "You

hear anything last night?"

"Actually, we did. Sam Donald was going to ride into Curtiss this morning and report it. He shot at some men who crossed through here last night, thought they were Indians. He's inside. Want some coffee?"

"We should give the horses a few minutes," O'Neil said.

The sheriff puffed angrily but climbed down.

"Could you brew some more coffee for these men?" Max called inside.

Einar stepped up next to Max. "Was Sam here or down at his cottage?"

"Down by the cottage. He'll tell you. I'll get your horses some water." Max grabbed the reins of a couple of the horses and led them toward a trough at the other end of the yard. "Surprised to see you here, Joe."

"They stole three of my horses."

"Plus, they killed old Ted," Einar said. Max stopped and looked back. "Savages," Einar sneered before walking inside.

Max let the horses drink for a couple of minutes before pulling them away from the trough. He grabbed another two and brought them to the trough. He wanted to be in there to hear about what happened, but Todd and Sam would be able to give him the details. He went to get another pair of horses. Einar came out and set his coffee cup on the porch bench, grabbed the last pair, and followed Max to the trough.

"So, what did you find at the camp?"

Einar circled around to the other side of the trough with his pair. "Ted was lying there dead. Looked like he'd been shot once with the old powder rifle, then again with his own repeater. They left theirs and took his I guess. Poor old man. He was happy to just dig in that dirt all day and pull out barely enough to live on."

"What about his wife?"

"She must have been in on it, 'cause she was nowhere to be found. Must have went with them. I never thought that was right, him hitching up with her. Now look what happened to him." Einar leaned his lanky frame on one of the horses while it drank. "Ted must have hit one of them; there was some blood trailing away." He spat. "Found one of the small scalps there, too. Damn savages!"

"Well, it was them. Think they're heading for the woods up north?"

"Yeah, it was them. They had the horses hidden less than a mile from their camp, and we found a butchered steer." Einar grabbed the reins of his pair and herded them back toward the porch. "You're lucky they just passed through your property. They've gone completely renegade."

Max nodded. "Did you men sleep last night?"

"We dozed a little while along Big Bug Creek. We were tracking them, but it got hard in the dark. There wasn't much moonlight last night."

"I noticed."

"We woke before morning and decided to cross and take the road into Mayer. To be honest, I think we were afraid they were going to sneak up on us. Well, we got there, and Joe told us that they'd stolen his horses." Einar walked up to the porch and picked up his tin cup, taking a sip. "That's how we ended up here, following their trail . . . well, what we hoped was their trail. Moe, he's pretty good at reading trails."

"Which one's Moe?"

"Shorter one, looks sour all the time." The men came out, calling thanks back inside for the coffee. Einar handed his cup to Max. "You could saddle up and ride with us."

"I'd prefer to stay around here. It's a ways away from town."

"Don't blame you." Einar swung into the saddle. "You keep watch, Max. If you see one put them down."

"If you can," Moe added.

Einar looked at him. "I've heard Max here's a decent hunter. Sam says you pegged a deer top of that rise." He jerked his thumb toward the hill the direction of town.

Max started walking toward the gate to let them through and keep the cattle from getting loose. "No, it was much closer than that."

"Oh," Einar started chuckling. "Sam doesn't only exaggerate about his fishing, but about your hunting."

Max laughed. Sam did catch that big fish in the creek, but it got bigger every time the subject came up. He opened the gate, watching the cattle to make sure they stayed back, and waved the men through.

O'Neil waved going past. "Thanks, Tillman." Some others gave their thanks, too, as they passed. Max watched them ride through. He looked around over the hills. Time to get to work.

"Well, the good thing," Sam called as he headed over to meet Max by the barn, "is that it looks like it's only three of them, not a whole war band like Geronimo's."

"Yes, but they don't seem to be shy about killing." Max grabbed the door and looked back at the riders. "Was surprised to see Joe Mayer with the posse."

Sam looked back at the fading riders.

"Well, his horses were a sight better than the mules that were left."

Max looked at him. "Mules?"

"They left the mules they rode tied a bit away from Mayer, snuck in and stole the horses."

"I thought they had good horses stolen from the Clarks."

"Yeah, that didn't make much sense, but I guess they had their reasons." Sam paused, thinking. "Maybe they were keeping them at a distance, hidden, but the posse back there was spotted, and they could not make it around."

Max tumbled that through his head. "But I got the impression that Ted was lying out in the open." Sam nodded agreement. "Then why would they keep the horses hidden?"

"Maybe they hadn't gotten around to getting them."

"How long do you think Ted had been dead?"

"Don't know."

"I mean did they give you the impression it just happened?"

"No, no, I got the impression they thought he'd been killed the day after the Clarks. What about you?" Sam looked to Todd, who had walked up behind them during the conversation.

"That's what I thought they were saying, but we could be wrong, and they may not know."

"Yeah," Max sighed. "Sure seems like they would try to find a way to get to them horses. But then again there could be all kinds of reasons we didn't think of." He shrugged and opened the doors to the barn.

The afternoon workout with Rowdy went well. Max tied him to the hitching post instead of stalling him.

Sam had been helping Max with the horses. "You didn't work him very long."

"No, I didn't. I'm going to ride him into town, see how he does."

"All right. Should be interesting to see how he acts with horses he hasn't been around. Want any company?"

"Nah, but thanks. I think I'll just make it a quick trip."

Max walked into the house and went to the small table on the other side of the room. Michelle was at the table sewing, using cloth they had bought a month earlier. "I'm riding Rowdy into Curtiss, thought I'd pick up a couple small things at the store. You need anything?" Max opened the drawer on the small table and reached into the back of it, pulling a few dollars from a small roll.

"I could use some things, but you told me we'd make a trip into Prescott sometime this month. They have a better selection."

"Yeah, you're right, I did. I don't want to leave the place unattended with what's going on, and it's not fair to ask Sam and Martha to keep watch."

"Oh, I don't mind at all, Max," Martha said coming from Ronnie's room. "I've seen Prescott plenty enough times, and Sam will be glad to be useful. Just bring him to Curtiss or Mayer next time you go. He likes talking to Joe and Milton. I was half afraid he was going to ride off with that posse so he could catch up with Joe."

Max sighed as he thought about Sam and Martha all alone, but it would just be during daylight, and he had promised Michelle. He walked over to the door and opened it, yelling toward the barn. "Sam, saddle up, if you want to come along to Curtiss."

"Thanks, Martha," Michelle smiled. "I was hoping to pick out some lace for the neck of this dress."

"Oh, you two are silly. Do you know how much time we spent out here on our own when Sean started traveling around?"

Max went over and gave Michelle a kiss.

"I'll tell Dad."

"Good. He will like a chance to chat with Reverend Larkin."

Max went out and around the house to where Todd was weeding the garden. "Todd, Sam and I are riding into Curtiss briefly." Max looked over to where the second rifle was leaning up against the house. "We will be back before dusk." Todd nodded. "Also, we're going into Prescott tomorrow; I figured you'd want to come along."

"Yes, I would at that."

"All right."

Max turned to go, but Todd spoke up. "Max, why are you going into Curtiss if we're going to Prescott tomorrow?"

"Taking Rowdy in to see how he does."

Todd read him. "And?"

"I'll talk to you about it when I get back. I want to be back by dusk."

Todd nodded.

Max went around and grabbed his own rifle from the porch, putting it in the scabbard on Rowdy's saddle.

Sam rode King up next to Max. "Noticed you'd put your main saddle, scabbard and all, on Rowdy earlier. Wasn't sure of the reason until now."

"Yep," Max said swinging on and starting Rowdy off at a trot. Rowdy looked sideways a moment at King. He had not spent much time around the older horse, and Max took it as a good sign when the stallion just glanced but did nothing else.

Max felt the power in the stallion's trot. But Rowdy followed the lead of the reins. As they reached the road and he caught a whiff of the smelter, Rowdy did balk and want to go the other direction. There were a few seconds of Rowdy battling the reins, and Max thought for a moment he would buck, but Rowdy gave in and followed King. Then he trotted past King, wanting to be in front. Max looked ahead and saw the six-mule team hauling a wagon of raw ore from the other direction into town. He considered waiting back at a distance, but Rowdy needed to get used to these things.

Max halted the stallion a few feet away from where the roads met to let the wagon pass. Rowdy's eyes rolled, but, other than a tension Max felt through his flanks and the reins, the horse did nothing else. The odor from the smelter did not help to calm the horse either. Max almost did not notice it anymore. It was part of Curtiss. They rode up to the store, and Max tied off Rowdy. Looking around, he worried someone might come too close and get kicked.

"Sam," Max pulled out four dollars,

"would you mind buying thirty rounds of the 44-40 caliber and another thirty of the 45?"

Sam took the money. "You staying with Rowdy?"

"No, I'm going to go see an old friend at the smelter." Max handed Sam another dollar. "Buy yourself some more shotgun shells also." He turned and walked toward the men who were now unloading the ore. He waved to Ian, who was walking out to help. Just then he heard a whinny and looked back to see a man leaping back as Rowdy turned and kicked backwards. Max ran back. The horse was trying to buck, and the hitching post was shaking. Max reached for Rowdy's reins and was nearly bitten.

"Easy, boy." He grabbed the reins, and his eyes met Rowdy's. "It's all right." Rowdy stopped pulling but showed his teeth again. "Come on now."

"I was just walking up to take a look at him," the man said. "He's a fine looking horse."

"He is, thanks. I've just got him to the point of riding a few days back."

"Doesn't look like he's tamed yet."

"Oh, you should have seen him before." Max stepped around and patted the stallion's neck. "Sorry about that. I'm glad you're OK."

"How's he ride?"

"Like he wants to race all the time."

"You gonna race him?"

"Nah, I'm breeding him, with a strong mare I have."

"I'd be interested in looking at that foal."

"Well, let me know where to write you, and I'll send you a letter when it's born, if we don't decide to keep the first."

"Spencer Cole, in Skull Valley."

Max looked at him a moment. "All right, Mr. Cole. Thank you." He stepped over and shook hands.

After Cole walked away, Ian came over. Half the wagon of ore was unloaded already, as they pushed it off into rail carts. "Max, good to see you." He looked past Max at the stallion.

"You, too, Ian." Max sighed. "Guess you heard."

"Yes." Ian looked toward the mountains where Ted's camp was.

"Sorry about Ted."

Ian shook his head. "I guess I was wrong. Sorry for getting you to ride all over. They just seemed so close when I was there. Didn't think they'd kill anyone, much less Ted. But I guess it's hard to judge men on just a couple of visits, especially Indians."

"Yeah, anybody, really. Sorry about it. It's a tough thing when people aren't what you thought. Actually, they came through my land early this morning. I guess riding through on the way to the area around old Fort Verde."

Ian stared at Max as if he were crazy, then shook his head side to side. "Max, they aren't stupid. They would know they would be found there."

Max looked at Ian flatly. "I don't know, Ian. They must be going someplace else, then. My part in it is done."

Ian nodded. "I appreciate what you did do."

"Would you be able to do something for me?"

"What's that?"

"Is there any way you could spend the day at my ranch while I'm in Prescott? With all this, I just don't feel right leaving the Donalds out there alone."

"I have to work." Ian paused and looked up. "If you think Ted's wife and her brothers did it and are on the run up north, then why worry?"

"Because there is enough odd that it makes me doubt . . . and I'm not going to guess the actions of anyone. North one day, double back the next, who knows?"

"Well, I'll see what I can do, but I make no promises." Ian looked back toward the smelter. "I better get back." He started to walk off.

"Ian, if you do come, plan on staying for supper."

"If, if."

Max patted Rowdy on the side of the neck and went into the store. Sam was leaned up against the counter smiling, as was Milton. "Milton." Max tipped his hat.

"Max, heard you had visitors last night."

"Yes, stole our sleep was all they did, though."

"Oh, then they stole your valuables."

"Bah," Sam shook his head. "Sleep is overrated; all you do is miss out on a few hours of life."

Milton looked at Max and winked. "Are you telling me that you don't sleep, Sam?"

"Oh, of course I sleep, but I don't go calling it valuables."

"If it isn't so valuable why'd you shoot at the Indians for stealing it?"

"That's the only thing that kept them from stealing some cattle I bet."

"They were gonna bring cattle with them on the run."

"No, they'd store them away somewhere else and come back and get them. Don't you know anything about Indian rustlers?"

"Apparently not. I didn't know they'd rustle your sleep."

"You're the one that . . . oh, never mind." He held up the bag. "See you next time, Milton."

When Max swung into the saddle Rowdy started off at a trot before he was completely settled, and he had to grab hold of the saddle horn with his other hand.

Sam clucked as he got into his saddle. "That horse loves to go."

Max kept Rowdy still until Sam had started out and then fell in beside him. "Ian who works at the mill may stop by tomorrow while I'm gone."

"Max, I told you we'd be fine."

"I know, but an extra man around will just make me feel better. Anyway, he may like to see what ranch life is like. Man's spent nearly all his years in a mine or a smelter since arriving from Ireland."

"You trust him?"

"I do." Max thought about the Ian he knew years ago. "Surprisingly, I really do."

Max reined in Rowdy, but the stallion kept King going at a good trot all the way back to the ranch.

CHAPTER 25

Max's eyes popped open in the dark. He listened. Was that the sound of a horse outside? He rolled gently out of bed, grabbing the rifle leaning against the wall. He stood and saw Michelle's eyes open.

"What is it?" she whispered.

"I think I may have heard something," he whispered back. "Probably just my imagination."

Max stayed out of the view of the window until he reached it. Then he peered out the corner over the yard, moving until he had the full view. He saw and heard nothing. "Think it's just over an hour or so to first light?"

"Maybe; you're better at knowing that than me."

Max came back and leaned the rifle back against the wall before leaning over the bed and giving Michelle a kiss. "I love you."

"I love you, too."

Max put a hand over Michelle's belly. "You sure you're up for the road?"

"It's probably the last time I'll take it until after." She grabbed his arm and kissed him again. "I think I'll go crazy if I don't get somewhere besides Curtiss for another two or three months."

Max nodded. "I'll go feed the animals, milk the cow, and hitch the mares."

"Perhaps one of these days we should get some more horses to pull the wagon."

"I've been thinking about that. I think we'll be able to get one to team with the gelding this summer."

Max dressed and put on his boots. He went into the main room as quietly as possible. He went to the back window next to Todd's bed, looking out to scan the distance. Then he went to the front of the house and looked out, doing the same thing. Finally, he pulled the locking block and went outside, stopping on the porch to listen. The cattle were up on the lower slopes of the hill, quiet; a couple of them looked to be grazing. Max felt satisfied and relaxed a bit, stepping down and going to the barn.

By lantern light, he milked the cow first and gathered eggs and brought them in for Michelle, who was making her way to the kitchen just as he carried the bucket and basket inside. They kissed, and then he was back out the door. After Max fed the horses and mules and hitched the two mares that were equal in strength, he went inside into the lantern light.

Todd handed him a cup of coffee. The smell of the biscuits rising made his stomach growl. Michelle was just starting the eggs. Max took a sip of coffee and set the cup down on the table. He walked to Ronnie's room.

"Ronnie." The boy's eyes opened, and he struggled to tilt his head toward the door. "Time to wake up and get dressed. We'll be eating soon."

"Then travel to the city," the boy said groggily, sitting up.

"Yes, son." Max wondered what Ronnie would think in a real city. Prescott was decent sized, but Santa Fe had been bigger, and Max knew there were places much larger. He'd seen pictures of the buildings in the East, San Francisco in the West. Michelle and Todd had talked about Pittsburgh enough for him to feel like he could find his way around if he visited.

After eating, Max glanced out to see light was just bordering the top of the hill to the east. "We'll leave in a few minutes." Todd was helping Michelle do the dishes. Max went on out to see if he could get the mares to drink a little more water before they started off. Chloe drank a little, but Paw didn't drink much, as usual. Paw was named so because of the paw shaped marking on her right hip. Paw had been raised down in the lower desert according to her seller. Chloe had been raised on this land by Sam.

Michelle, sitting next to Max on the buckboard, looked over at him and smiled as they passed out of Curtiss. At that point, Ronnie stood up in back and looked around. He had not been past Curtiss but two or three times since he was old enough to really gain an interest. Around mid-morning and in view of Agua Fria Station, they had to move to the side of the trail when the stage left the station, pulled by six horses as it moved quickly up the road. It must have been a full stage because a man and boy rode on the roof. They waved, smiling as they went past.

Ronnie pointed at them and then waved as they squeezed past. Dust was up, and Michelle covered her face with her handkerchief. Ronnie turned and watched them, pointing again. "I wanna."

"One day, son," Max said, getting the

horses going down the main road again.

When they veered off into the station, Captain Calderwood motioned them right up to the trough. "Stretch your legs for a couple of minutes, folks. I'll see to the horses. There is coffee and lemonade inside."

"Thanks." Max hopped down and helped Michelle down. Todd was next to him hoisting Ronnie down. Michelle walked over to peek inside the separate house that held the parlor. She had mentioned how one day it would be nice for her and Max to come alone and actually sit and have tea and biscuits.

When they first married, Max had worried that his wife wanted a different life than he could provide, but then he realized Michelle just wanted the occasional moment of something different. She liked their life together, and so did he, but he knew that back in Pittsburgh she had enjoyed some exposure to a more affluent lifestyle.

Max smiled. He was already planning for their fifth wedding anniversary next year. He would surprise Michelle by having Todd watch Ronnie and the baby, and they would leave later in the morning and get to the parlor just in time for lunch. Then they'd ride on to Prescott for an evening of supper, maybe even dancing and a night at the new hotel that was being built. Perhaps in the future, if the ranch did well enough, they could plan on a trip to the coast.

With the temperature rising, Max actually drank lemonade instead of coffee. After resting for a few minutes, they went outside to see the team waiting by the door. "Thank you, Captain."

"Sure, Max, Mrs. Tillman, Pastor." He looked at Ronnie. "You come back some time, young Mr. Tillman." Ronnie reached out his hand, and Calderwood shook it. Michelle looked at Max with the biggest smile on her face, and Max had trouble not kissing her right there in front of everyone.

The ride out and along Lonesome Valley brought them through rolling hills, with an occasional farmhouse visible in the distance from the road. The ride was tiring, but, as the trees began to thicken, Max knew they were getting close to their destination. The trees thinned out where farmhouses had been built, and, as they circled a hill, downtown Prescott rose up in the distance. Thumb Butte was further off in the background. In the center of town stood the courthouse, rising in the middle of the wooden and brick businesses around it. Houses dotted the area, spreading out from the plaza in the center.

They reached the Plaza Stable, an enormous, multi-stalled establishment just off the main square of Prescott. Max hopped down and gave the reins to one of the older boys working there. He reached up to help Michelle down. "Could you feed and water them and stall them for about an hour and a half for rest? We'll be leaving in a couple of hours, and we have a long trip home."

"Sure. We'll see to them and then have them ready in two hours."

"Thanks." Max handed them a dollar.

There was an eatery near the store. The family entered a nearly full café. There was a group standing to leave, so they made their way to the table. Max nodded to the gentlemen who were leaving.

The room had several tables with men in suits, some eating with other townsmen, a couple with women. There was a table with a lone miner sitting in a corner. A few men looked like they might be ranchers, or laborers of some sort.

"It's a shame, too," one of the four men at the table behind them said. "This just whips up people's hatred of the Indians."

"Well," a deeper voice began, "it's not as if it's unfounded. Geronimo's off raiding. We'd be better off wiping them all out."

461

"Two or three Indians do something wrong, and they're all bad. By that logic all us whites are bad, because nearly every week somewhere in the West, a white man kills and robs somebody."

"It's not the same. You weren't here ten years ago when there was more of this, like the —" The man just stopped talking. Max almost turned to see what had stopped him cold, then the other man spoke.

"The Wickenburg stage coach. We've talked about this."

"That's why I stopped. I don't want to talk about it again."

"Yes, please," one of the other men at the table chimed in. Another chuckled.

Michelle kicked Max under the table. Max realized he was probably being obvious in listening. He smiled, and she smiled back. Max was surprised how quick news spread. Of course, there was a newspaper man riding with the posse, and he could send letters via the stagecoach. Max wondered what the newspaper had said.

A young man came and cleared their table.

A woman with a touch of gray going through her dark hair came and stood at their table. "We have steak, with stewed tomatoes and string beans. Also, chicken, potatoes, and string beans."

They ordered, and Max leaned back, reached over, and grabbed Michelle's hand. "You're beautiful."

She smiled. "Thank you. You're not bad looking yourself, Mr. Tillman."

Ronnie looked back and forth at them, then to Todd, who was smiling. Todd just patted Ronnie's head. Max many times did not even eat lunch, at least not sitting down. He'd eat breakfast, then grab a chunk of bread, dried beef, an apple, whatever was handy to eat quick while he worked. Sundays were usually the exception.

"Prescott's grown since we've been here," Todd said.

Max nodded. "The whole area has. Remember when Joe only had his three buildings there?"

Todd nodded. "New towns popping up everywhere."

"It's a good place we've settled," Michelle said, looking at Max, then Todd. "Despite what's happened recently, it's a good place." She looked back at Max. "There's no place that doesn't have its troubles, as you always say."

"The lady speaks wisdom." Max chuckled.

Ronnie was twisting around looking at the people in the café. Max almost told him not to squirm and sit straight but then shrugged.

He was a kid, in new surroundings. He should be curious. "I suppose next year we should think about getting him a pony to start learning to ride."

Michelle opened her mouth for a moment, not saying anything at first. "Oh, I think it's a little early yet."

"Well, not a wild pony to match Rowdy, a calmer pony." Max smirked, and Michelle realized he was joking.

A couple of seconds later Ronnie's head whipped back around. "Me? A pony?"

Michelle arched her eyebrows. "Max, now you've done it."

Max looked at Ronnie. "Well, son, it's a year or two away, but we'll work up to it."

Ronnie smiled big, then looked up and waved to the miner who was leaving. The miner waved back.

The food came, and it was good. The chicken had been flavored with rosemary, potatoes with pepper. Max sat back feeling full after the meal. Michelle, now eating for two, finished and ordered the apple pie, although she shared it with Ronnie.

"We'd best be about it, if we want to make it back before full dark."

Todd headed toward Reverend Larkin's place. Max assumed they talked about minister things. He really did not know. He escorted Michelle and Ronnie down to Goldwater & Son's department store. She went one direction to fit Ronnie with a pair of shoes, and the next size up also, since he was growing so quick. Max turned to the hardware section. He needed to do some repairs to the chicken coop, and he was also getting low on nails. He left his items with the clerks to hold with Michelle's purchases and went down the street to the leather shop, needing more straps in case the ones on the gates gave again.

He reached for the door to the leather shop, and it opened. A burly man who looked like a miner came out. Max and he both did a double take at each other. "You're Hal?"

"Yes, sir. You're Pastor Porter's son."

"Son-in-law, yes. How have you been?"

"I'm all right, all things considered." He grimaced. "Just heard about Ted today in town."

"Yes, it's terrible. You knew him well?"

"As well as I knew anybody. He's the one suggested I go to that church service." Hal shook his head. "Hard to believe. I assume the Indians took the gold, although seems hard to figure what they'd do with it, wanted as they are now. Seems like it would slow them down also."

Max tilted his head. "From what I heard, Ted's mine wasn't that rich."

Hal shrugged. "Don't think he was telling people . . . heck, he only hinted around it with me, but we'd worked a mine together once. I got to know his meanings. I guess there's no harm in telling you now that he's gone. He told me that he'd been doubting that thirty years of mining was worth it until a month ago. I took it as meaning he'd hit a vein. I tried to ask him how rich, but he changed the subject." Hal sighed and leaned against the building. "Everything was going so well for him. He loved his wife, even liked those brethren of hers, kid on the way, and then they turn on him. If . . ." Hal shook his head.

"What?"

"Nothing. Just letting my imagination go crazy." Hal extended his hand.

Max took it. "See you this Sunday?"

"Nah, maybe next month. Take care, and tell Pastor Porter I said hello."

"You can tell him yourself. He's just down the street."

"Nah, I better head out."

"God bless you."

After gathering the leather straps from the shop, Max went back to Goldwater's. He looked around for Michelle through half the store until the man behind the counter noticed him. "Mr. Tillman, your wife said she was going down the street for a few minutes and would be back shortly."

Max nodded. "Thanks."

"She did add her items to yours, if you are ready."

"Sure."

"Would you like to pay or put it on credit?"

"I'll pay now. I'm not big on credit if I can help it."

"A wise decision," the man who was now at the other end of the counter said. He had a vest and tie on, and his hair and thick mustache were dark. "Credit is needed at times by most of us, but too many can fall into the habit of forgetting they have the debts."

Max nodded to the man. "Well said."

"Milton Goldwater." The man extended his hand. He was perhaps a little older than Max, but Max was not sure.

Max took his hand. "Max Tillman."

Goldwater looked at the assortment stacked next to the corner of the counter: a roll of chicken wire, and three different colors of folded cloth, some fringe, two pair of children's shoes, and some seed packets.

"Where abouts is your place?"

"Off the Black Canyon Road, about two miles northeast of Curtiss."

Goldwater nodded and then looked up quickly. "Near the Clark massacre?"

"Yes, just across the Agua Fria."

Goldwater shook his head. "My uncle got injured in an Apache skirmish near Granite Mountain years ago. I thought that was all over, but maybe they are starting to follow Geronimo's example."

"I don't know. From everything I hear this doesn't make sense, but, you know, the world doesn't always make sense."

"I hear you there." Goldwater looked around Max at a customer in a worn suit wandering through the men's clothing. "Look forward to seeing you again, Max." Goldwater was off to assist the new customer.

Max paid for the items and left them there while he made his way down the street to find Michelle. Two steps out the door he saw his smiling wife coming across the street with Ronnie in tow. She had a bolt of cloth and a heavy looking pail. Max grabbed the pail and looked at it.

"Oh, I forgot we were starting to get low on salt."

Michelle smirked. "Me, too, but they just got a delivery, and it reminded me."

"Where to next?"

"I'm done."

"Well, you stay here, and I'll go get the wagon."

Max carried the pail of salt with him down toward the Plaza Stables. The teen that had helped him that morning was sitting against the wall laughing with another boy. When he glanced up and saw Max coming toward them, he hopped up and pulled the other boy with him back into the stables.

Max glanced in to see them putting leads on his mares in the stall. Max sat down where they had been sitting in the shade and waited. It was only a few minutes before they brought the wagon around to where he sat. Max stood up and tossed them a coin. He put the salt in the corner of the back and started down the street.

After gathering the purchases and his family, and giving a brief hello to Reverend and Mrs. Larkin, Max started back toward home. This was good work for the mares, and they would be able to rest all day tomorrow. There was a little bit of traffic on the road. They passed another wagon in a wide spot on the trail, then several riders rode past them. The stage from Phoenix was at Agua Fria, almost ready to leave for the last leg. Max let the horses drink heartily,

469

then they were off. The sun was setting as they approached Curtiss. Max looked back, admiring the view. Total darkness had settled in just before they crested the hill that overlooked their spread. Max brought the horses down the familiar hill and felt the relief from being back home.

The Donalds and Ian came out as they approached. Ian and Sam came to grab items out of the back of the wagon.

Max helped Michelle down, and Todd helped Ronnie out of the back. "How was the trip?" Ian asked.

"Good!" Todd answered, looking from Ian to Max smiling.

Max knew he must be smiling because of Max's initial reaction when he saw Ian in Curtiss. "Got what we needed, I think. What's it been like out here?"

"Quiet," Ian said. "I've not spent such a quiet day."

"He's a worker," Sam said, "but doesn't know too much about cattle or horses. Or, for that matter, cards."

"Come on now," Ian clamored. "If we'd played a bit longer, my Irish luck would have kicked in."

Sam chuckled. "We'd played a bit longer your Irish butt would've been broke."

Ian laughed. "All right. My luck was not

on today, and I don't know that much about cattle or horses, but I do know how to ride them."

"Well, at least you know not to ride the cattle. Heard that some fools are doing it for sport."

"I didn't —" Max started, then looked back at Sam.

"Milton in Curtiss told me it's becoming part of the rodeo."

Max shook his head. "I didn't know that much about cattle or horses either until Sam here taught me. He's a good man."

"I see that." Ian lugged the salt inside, while Max and Sam guided the team into the barn.

"What's the talk in Prescott?"

"The Clarks for one thing."

Sam nodded. "Figures."

"That Goldwater store's doing a fine business."

"Yes. I'm not surprised. They set it up right from the start with one buying in California and shipping the items here."

They unloaded the other items in the barn and stored them in the corner on a few shelves. They took good care of the mares, giving them plenty of water and extra food.

The air was beginning to really cool, and Max actually felt a chill as they walked back to the house. The smell of beef stew and bread whiffed out the front door when they stepped onto the porch.

Laughter erupted from inside, and Max peeked through the door. In the room, Ronnie was on top of Ian, who was down on his hands and knees pretending to buck. Todd was balancing Ronnie so he didn't fall off. Michelle and Martha were watching, laughing. Then Max heard Ronnie saying, "Easy boy, you're all right." Max would tell Rowdy the same thing when the stallion got feisty.

Max smiled and went to the basin to wash up. It was a crowded table, and they had to pull a trunk over for someone to sit on. Ian jumped on it before anyone else could. Ronnie sat on Max's lap, and Max fed him out of his bowl.

"Ian, do you know Hal who's got a claim out there somewhere?"

"I've talked to him a couple of times."

"What do you think of him? Think he's a man of good judgment?"

"I suppose. Seems all right, but I don't really know. Why do you ask?" Before Max could answer, Ian arched his eyebrow. "He was a friend of Ted's."

Max nodded. "Ran into him in town. He had the same opinion of Ted and his little family as you did."

Michelle sighed.

Max glanced at her, as did Todd. Ian and the Donalds concentrated on their stew.

"Well, it's surprising to anyone who knew them," Ian said after a moment.

"Did you eat at Abigail's Café?" Martha asked.

"We did," Michelle said. "She has the best apple pie. It's the cinnamon, I think."

"I've not had it." Martha looked at Sam. "I think we've eaten there about half a dozen times. The best thing was her roasted lamb. I asked, and she said that they slow cooked it for a full twenty-four hours."

Ian smiled. "I imagine that the smell has people thinking of coming in there all day."

"Exactly," Sam exclaimed. "That's how we ended up in there."

"When I was a young boy," Ian started, "my mother used to make the best thick stew you have ever had."

The rest of supper was spent talking about childhoods, and differences in upbringing in different lands.

After supper Ian went to the sink and began to wash his own dish. Martha came and took it from him. "You enjoy having somebody do this for you for a change."

"Thank you, ma'am. Thank you, Max and

Michelle. I should be getting back to Curtiss. I'll see you Sam, Todd." He waved to Ronnie. "You be good for your folks."

"Hold on," Max called. "We can saddle a couple of horses, and I'll bring one back."

"No, Max, I don't mind the walk."

"I can loan you a mule."

"I don't . . . well, can you spare it?"

"Actually, you'd be doing me a favor, giving it a little exercise."

"All right then."

Max went with him out the door, toward the barn. "I'll come get it tomorrow. I don't think Einar will mind you pinning it in one of the stalls."

"I suppose not. He's not there anyway. I'll take good care of it."

"I know you will. Now it's dark, but the mule will probably know the way anyhow. I sometimes bring him rather than the wagon, when I come to get a few supplies."

In the barn, Max handed Ian the saddle. "I appreciate you coming out here."

"Sure, Max. It's nice. Makes me think maybe I'd like a place like this rather than traipsing the rest of the way 'round the world back to Ireland."

"Yeah." Max leaned against the stall door.

Ian saddled the mule, then looked back at Max. "What you thinking about?"

474

"Aw, nothing."

"About Ted and the Clarks, isn't it?"

"It's just every time I think I can put it to rest in my head, something else comes up."

"I know what you mean. What can we do, though? We have no way of knowing for sure what happened."

Max nodded his head in agreement. "Nothing to do about it."

Max watched Ian ride out of the yard and up the hill fading into the dark as he passed over. He went inside, and everyone was settling down to sleep. Martha and Sam were in Ronnie's bed, and Ronnie squeezed in with Todd. Max went into his room to find Michelle settling into bed.

"Is everything all right, darling?" Max asked.

"Yes, why?"

"At supper . . ." Max had trouble figuring out the right way to word it, wanting to avoid any argument.

"I just don't know what business it is of yours. Ours. Those men came through, they're hunting them, they're lawmen. You are starting to get this look, and I'm . . . I'm worried."

"Worried about what?"

"That you're going to get hurt. You went off looking for that man from the road when it was none of your concern and proved it wasn't that stranger, but what if it had been? I just think you may be getting restless again, and now you have me and the kids." She put her hand on her stomach.

Max leaned into the bed and put his hand over hers. "I promise, I'm not getting restless, not like I used to. I suppose it's just too much happening too close to us; makes me feel like we're on the fringe of involvement in it."

She looked at him for a long moment. "I see. It still worries me, though, but the whole thing worries me."

Max kissed her belly. "Me, too, a little, but we'll be all right." He kicked off his boots and pulled off his clothes. He turned off the light, and they cuddled in bed as they fell asleep.

CHAPTER 26

The next afternoon Max was repairing the chicken coop in the rising heat when he saw a rider coming from the direction of the Agua Fria. Sam and Martha had gone home that morning, so he imagined they'd seen the man. When he recognized that it was Joe Mayer, Max figured that he had stopped by and said hello to the Donalds. Joe waved and dismounted at the gate and led his horse through, shutting it quickly before one of the calves could get loose.

"You catch 'em?"

Joe shook his head. "We lost their trail but went on to Fort Verde. They said they would keep an eye and an ear out. They're sending word to General Crook to see if he wants to send some troops out looking."

"The others still looking?"

"No. Mulhenon and the Grays were heading back to Prescott, and Walton back to his ranch."

"What about Einar?"

"He said he was going to Prescott with Mulhenon, see if there was any news on other family members of the Clarks."

"I suppose somebody needs to look after their remaining cattle."

"Einar said he would see to that. It reminds me, though. I think I saw a couple with your brand over there."

Max nodded. "They do that except the few times when the water's running heavy. We haven't had that much rain this year."

"Not yet, but it will come. I told Sam about the cattle also. He said he'd go get them."

Max looked to the northeast, toward the river. "You don't think they doubled back on you, do ya, hanging around here?"

"I wouldn't think so," Joe told him. "But I never hunted men either."

Max looked up at Joe.

"Don't act so surprised, Max. Most people didn't hold onto your name or know much about you, and what they did know, they forgot. I'd thought you may have been the young man they'd wrote about some in New Mexico when you showed up at Tip Top. Then your buddy Lee told me about you chasing after them. I was sure you wouldn't find them or, worse, end up dead from them or someone else. Then I saw your name in the paper from taking them down in Canyon Diablo and Flagstaff.

"I think it went over most people's heads, though, especially when you show up married to a minister's daughter, not wearing a pistol, and having such a gentle spirit."

"I imagine you didn't mention it to many others, 'cause this is the first I've heard of it."

"No, not my place to go spreading things. Of course, you know someone else probably knew."

"Maybe, but thanks for not telling it anyway."

Mayer shrugged. "I should get home."

"If you hold on a minute, I'll ride as far as Curtiss with you. I let somebody borrow my mule."

"Sure." Mayer swung down and led his horse to the water trough. He wet his handkerchief and wiped the sweat from his face.

Max strode to the barn, deciding to ride Hardy. He did not want to try to guide the mule back riding Rowdy. After saddling the Choctaw horse, he let Michelle know he was going to get the mule. He collected Joe from around the house where he was speaking with Todd while he gardened.

"First posse you've been on?" Max asked.

"No, I rode with another in the past. Just about as successful. The first one was a stage robbery years ago. This one for my own horses."

"Think they'll find them?"

"Don't know. These are young men, were just children in the time before most all the tribes were reined into the reservations, then moved to San Carlos, but they may remember or have been shown the old rancherias, hidden lands atop some of these mountains. Some have caves, others some grass. They may be in one of these spots."

"So they can stay hidden for a while."

"Maybe not. The military discovered a lot of these. Crook will probably send an officer who hunted the Indians back then to help find these three."

"You sound a little sad about it."

"I know. I'm sad for what it may cause. A few have drifted back, and I've come to know a couple. The Yavapai were here before us, and the ones I see just across the creek don't bother me none. There's good and bad men, Indians and whites."

Max nodded, and they rode on to Curtiss in silence. Joe bid Max goodbye and headed back toward his station. Max went on to where he usually hitched in front of the general store. There was a fine looking horse that looked familiar by the smelter office. When Max went to poke his head in he saw Theodore Boggs sitting at the desk, Ian with him.

"Max?" Boggs called out. "Come on in."

"Sir, good to see you."

"You, too, I think. I believe you absconded with my employee yesterday."

"Yes, sir. He was kind enough to come help at my place while I was gone."

"That's what we were just talking about. I don't think I'll be sharing my workers with you in the future, Mr. Tillman."

"Yes, sir."

"But, these are extenuating circumstances with murderers roaming the countryside, so I understand."

"Thank you, sir," Ian told him. "May I fetch the mule for Mr. Tillman?"

"Sure."

Ian stood up, and Max made to go with him.

"Max," Boggs said, "I have something to discuss with you."

"I'll hitch the mule by the store."

"Thanks, Ian."

After Ian left, Boggs motioned to the empty chair, and Max sat.

"So, you are not still looking for other killers, are you?"

"No, hard to say it's not them after what's happened."

Boggs nodded. "I agree. I did have an odd piece of information if you were still involved."

"I'm not. It's really not my business, and I think it may be best for me to keep out of it."

Boggs leaned back and nodded, then looked out the small window. "All right then."

Max sat there a moment, then sighed. "What was it?"

"You said better to stay out of it."

"Yes, but I'm curious."

"Uh-huh." They stared at each other a moment, then Boggs straightened up. "Yesterday, just after I rode in, I saw a man ride through that looked familiar to me, from several years ago. I couldn't place him right away, and I'm not one hundred percent certain still, but I think he was a man who used to ride with Francisco Vega."

"The bandit of Weaverville?"

"Yeah. I had business there years ago just before Vega completely took over the town. We ended up staring off for just a few seconds. If I hadn't had several men with me, I'm not sure what would have happened. Well, this man I believe was standing with Vega that day."

"Really, and you saw him here yesterday."

"I think so. He was riding by and I standing just off the street, but I'd bet a bar of gold it was him."

"Do you know his name?"

"No, only knew a couple of the names in that gang aside from Vega. He's a shorter man though, looks half Mexican, half white. Has one eye that seems to droop a bit. That's what reminded me."

"So, you think he's involved?"

"Don't see how, but you looking for suspicious characters the other day just made me think."

"Yeah."

"Anyway, just good to keep a lookout. I'm not sure what he's up to these days, but that was a bad bunch."

"That's what I hear."

"Well," Boggs stood, putting a pistol through his belt, "with Einar gone I need to go do a walk through and make sure nobody is tempted to pocket anything." Boggs held out his hand, and Max shook it.

Max went out and gathered his mule from the hitching post by the store. He waved to Milton, who had come out to post a sign on the outside of his store. The short ride was filled with thoughts about this new man. Max had hoped that trouble would stay clear of this area. First murders by Indians, now men from one of the worst gangs in Arizona. From what Max had heard, lawmen had avoided Weaverville. They had not wanted to go into town looking for the gang. That and there were a few Indians a year seeping back into the area, usually under employ of someone gaining them a pass. But now look at what happened. For the first time since he had purchased it, he was considering leaving his land. Only he did not know where to go that was guaranteed safe. He could go back East but was not sure about purchasing land there.

He got back to the house and unsaddled the horse and the mule. He looked at the stalls, the corrals, the house, and the hills surrounding the place and felt a little sick at his stomach thinking about leaving, but he also felt sick about staying someplace that might not be safe for his family. He could not stand the possibility of harm coming to Michelle or the kids, or Todd. He sighed and went back to work on the chicken coop.

The chickens for the most part kept their distance as he put on the new boards and nailed the new wire into place. Max then spent the better part of the hour leading up to twilight chasing down three of the chickens that had escaped, two before the repairs and one during.

He walked into the house and gave Michelle a kiss. Ronnie came running, and Max scooped him up and gave him a kiss on the head before putting him right back down. Michelle looked like she was almost finished with the meat and potatoes. Max reached into the cabinet and took out the bottle that sat in the corner. He poured just enough to cover the bottom of the cup in his hand. She looked at him, concerned. Max saw out of the corner of his eye Todd glancing up from where he sat reading what he had written earlier for a sermon.

"I need just a couple of minutes, okay?"

She stared at him a moment, then nodded.

Max walked back out to the porch but did not sit in the chair or on the steps. He stood looking at the hills surrounding them for a moment and then walked out and around the house. A few minutes later he realized he was sitting on the fence to the corral with an empty cup in his hand, Michelle walking toward him from the house.

"Is everything all right, Max?"

"Yes . . ." he paused, but he was lying. "No, I really don't know."

"What is it?"

"I'm worried."

"About the Indians?"

"Not just them. This area's still plenty dangerous with bandits, robbers, and the like."

"No more so then when we moved here." She was right, of course. They got to know each other with both their lives in danger. "What are you thinking?" she asked after a long stretch of silence.

"I don't know." He hopped down and turned, looking out over the land in the distance, then turned and looked into the dark behind Michelle. He stopped scanning the dark and looked at her and her belly with their second child inside. "I guess I somehow feel like I have more to lose. It doesn't make that much sense to me, though."

She nodded after a moment and stepped up to him, putting her hand on his chest. "It does. You've experienced peace, a life with loved ones you care for and that you take care of."

Max looked at her and smiled, then pulled her to him and held her. "You're right." She was right. Not only did he know what he had to lose now, but he was responsible for more. He had taken that on, and now with danger hitting so close it was weighing on him. "You're a smart woman."

"I know." She pulled back and looked at him. "Are we all right?"

"Probably. I just heard that there may be another bad man in the area, and it got to me."

She looked around herself. "You always say worrying does no good."

"I know. I was just wondering if we should think about moving back East."

"What?"

"It's more settled."

"I . . . maybe, but what about this?" She looked from the corral to the barn. "I've never seen you prouder than when you rode Rowdy."

"We can continue what we're doing there."

Her face changed. "You really think it's getting that bad?" She looked around again. "What exactly did you hear?"

"I'm sorry. I didn't mean to frighten you."

"Max, what did you hear?"

"Boggs was in Curtiss. He said he thought he saw a member of the gang from Weaverville pass through Curtiss yesterday."

"Weaverville?"

"Down toward Wickenburg, by Rich Hill."

Michelle's eyes widened. She had read the stories about the gang in the local papers, as had everyone over the years.

"It was one member, and he may not even be part of the gang, or a criminal anymore."

She sighed. "Come on in, Max."

He nodded and put his arm around her and let her guide him toward the house. The table was set, and Ronnie and Todd were already sitting. Max washed his hands and came to the table.

Todd looked over at him and gave him a reassuring nod. "Would you like to pray?"

Max sighed. "Sure." He closed his eyes and bowed his head, not really being in the mood, but he started anyway. "Lord, we thank you for this food, ask you to bless it. We thank you for all you provide for this wonderful family, this land, for our good friends. We ask that you watch over us, guide us, protect us. In Jesus' name. Amen."

He kept his head bowed a moment longer; peace was washing over him. When he looked up everyone began eating. He did also, a smile forming around his mouth as he chewed his food. He looked at Todd, who noticed, and, as their eyes caught, Max nodded to him, a thank-you. He had needed to actively pray.

Todd smiled and nodded back, then went back to cutting his food. "Anything interesting going on in town or around?" He paused. "That you want to talk about?"

"No, maybe later; right now everything is pretty good."

The food did taste good, and Max watched Ronnie eat the potatoes. He ate a little of the beef now and then, but the potatoes were what he liked the most. Max looked up and saw that Michelle was watching him watch Ronnie. They smiled at each other. Max finished what was on his plate but passed on seconds.

"Ronnie, want me to read to you before you go to bed?"

Ronnie nodded. Max went to the bookshelf and pulled out the Bible. He flipped to the section about David and Goliath and started just before David joined up with his brothers and Saul the King.

Ronnie listened intently once Max reached the part about the giant mocking. After the battle Ronnie asked, "He beat the giant?"

Max nodded. "Because David relied on God's strength, and God was with him."

Ronnie smiled and started poking at the pages of the Bible.

"I'll read more to you tomorrow night, all right?"

Ronnie nodded his head. "I want read."

"You will, but give it about a year. Go get ready for bed."

Michelle came and followed Ronnie into his room.

Todd came and sat across from Max. "It's good that you're starting to read the Bible to him."

Max shook his head. "There's rumors of another bad man riding into the area. That kinda shook me up after the Clarks and Ted. Was actually considering moving us."

Todd nodded. "You've got a peace about it now."

"I suppose. It's still a possibility it may come to leaving, but not without more thought, discussion with Michelle and you, and a lot of praying."

"Like I said, you've got a peace about it. Life's not always gonna have a nice, easy-to-spot path carved out for us."

Max nodded. "I should know that by now. Look at what I was about when you met me."

"Sure, but look at where you ended up." Todd motioned to Ronnie's room and then the house. "God knows our lives better than we do, and he'll use all things for the good of those who love Him."

"Well, that's definitely been the case since I've come to know Him. Right now, I'm thinking I just need to try to listen, and go about life."

Todd stood and clapped him on the shoulder. "It's been a lot for you over the last ten days. You should get some rest."

Max stood. "You could be right. Thanks again, Dad." Max gave him a hug and went in and said good night to Ronnie before he and Michelle went to bed.

Sleep came to him fairly quickly, and he did sleep solid. He awoke and the slit along the curtains showed a sky mostly lit already. He rolled out of bed onto his knees and prayed. Then he dressed. When he went into the other room, the kitchen was lit from a lamp, and Todd was starting to heat up the stove. Ronnie was standing and watching.

Todd turned. "You can go lay back down for a while if you want. We already milked the cow, fed the animals, and gathered the eggs. Tell Michelle she can keep resting."

"I will," Michelle's voice called from the other room.

"We'll call when breakfast is ready."

Max stood there a moment, then took his boots off. "Thanks, Todd, thanks, Ronnie."

He went back into their room and lay back down. He kissed Michelle when she looked over at him.

She cuddled up to him and laid her head on his chest. "I love my Dad."

"Me, too."

Max dozed just a bit until he heard Ronnie's footsteps. "We're letting you two sleep a little while longer, even though the food's ready. It won't get that cold."

Max started to laugh and felt Michelle laughing also. She raised up and rolled onto her feet. Max stood. Ronnie had already run back to the kitchen. They walked in, and Todd was pouring coffee, with Ronnie standing by the table smiling.

"Thank you so much." Michelle looked at the kitchen before sitting down, not used to coming straight to the table. Todd put the coffee cups on the table and put the eggs, bacon, and rolls on the plates. He sat down and bowed his head, saying a quick prayer.

Still smiling, Ronnie said, "Eat the breakfast we made."

They dug in, enjoying the warm food.

After a couple of bites, Todd motioned to Ronnie. "He really deserves the credit. He woke me up before it was even light. I figured why not do something? So we went out and got to work. He even handed me the eggs as I cracked them into the pan."

"Thank you, Ronnie." Max smiled and winked at Michelle. "Maybe it won't be but a few years before Ronnie takes over all the work around here and takes care of us."

Ronnie looked at him a moment and then

laughed.

"Or maybe not."

After eating, Max put his boots back on and went out to see to the horses. He had just let them out to run in the corral when Sam and Martha came striding up.

Sam pointed toward the west. "Rain's comin'."

Max studied the dark clouds in the distance and the wavy shadows beneath them. "Got about an hour or so."

"About that," Sam said. "If the water gets to running maybe it will keep those cows on this side for a while. Joe told me he'd seen one or two of ours over there." Sam motioned toward the river. "I crossed and found them on the hillside. Nearly got shot for it, too."

"What?"

"Apparently, Einar has taken it upon himself to hire a man to watch the Clarks' ranch."

"Oh, yeah, Joe told me that was going on."

"Well, this short fella came riding down on me like he was riding down on a rustler. I managed to explain that I was your man and that the cattle sometimes cross. He'd had his pistol out the other side of his horse all concealed. Didn't know it until he holstered it."

"Then everything was all right?"

"I suppose so." Sam shrugged. "He told me he'd been hired temporarily by a man named Einar and helped me get the cows across the river, then gave a quick wave and was riding back."

"I wonder why Einar's taken that up."

"Perhaps he's thinking of trying to buy the place and leave the smelter."

"I guess. Was it one of his workers from the smelter?"

"I don't know. Never seen him before, but I usually only go to the store. He was a shorter man, was part Mexican or maybe Indian and had an eye that didn't work all the way . . . Max, are you all right? Max?"

"I don't know."

"Do you know the man?"

Max shook his head side to side. "Boggs told me about a man like that, ex-criminal from Weaverville."

A moment stretched out, and Sam blew air through his whiskers. "Vega's gang?"

Max nodded. "I said ex-criminal, but I'm not sure about the ex."

"We can hope," Sam said, "and pray."

"Yep."

Max walked them to the porch, and Martha went inside to borrow some flour and salt from Michelle. Max sat down on the

494

porch, and Sam sat next to him. "What should we do?"

"I don't know, Sam. I got myself worked up last night over Boggs saying he'd seen this man. Then I got to thinking this morning that Boggs is not that young anymore, though, and may not see as well. Or maybe this man is just looking for an honest job. We all have the right to change."

"I suppose you're right."

Max sighed. "I guess we just keep an eye out, and I'll talk to Einar sometime soon. He may know this man, and it's nothing to worry about."

Sam stared at Max like he had when he taught him about caring for horses. He was waiting for Max to get something.

Max stood up and leaned on the porch railing, looking out over the land. "I have trouble imagining Einar planning this. We've both known him for years."

"I know. I'm not accusing him. I'm just saying if he's going to try to get the land, maybe at a good price, it's something to consider, especially him being one of the witnesses."

They just stood there on the porch. Martha came out, and they both looked to the west. The rain was getting closer. "We're going to try to make it back dry."

"Keep an eye out."

"We will."

They started back. Max walked back toward the corral to stable the horses. Thunder sounded in the distance, and Max saw a couple of lightning bolts far off in the sky.

Rowdy eyed the lightning, and Max thought he spotted that old wildness in the horse again, but he had no problem getting him into the stable. The gelding seemed a little more skittish. But, as the first drops were falling Max got the last mare in the barn and stalled her. He walked up to the porch and sat down, watching the rain fall. The air cooled, and Max watched as the rain fell heavier and heavier.

Michelle came out and sat next to him. "Ronnie's out. He woke up too early I guess."

"How about Dad?"

"He's working on his sermon, but if it keeps raining I don't think he'll get the crowd from the camps."

"No, I suppose not."

"It's cool."

"Feels good."

Lightning struck nearby, making Max see spots, and the sound rattled the windows. "I think I'll go in now," Michelle said.

"Me, too."

The rain let up in the afternoon, then started again after dark. Max had gone to sleep to the sound of the rain on the roof. When he woke, it was quiet. He lay there thinking that men in the camps would probably not come to town for Todd's message. They wouldn't want to make the trip in the slop.

Max himself worried about getting the wagon stuck in the mud. Also, he did not really want to leave the ranch unattended, but he wanted to go into town and was not going to ask Sam and Martha to miss the service or stay behind. He went out and did the chores.

Sam and Martha rode King and Queen into the barn as he was hitching the team. "We didn't want to make the walk in the wet."

"Don't blame ya."

They were down and unsaddling the horses. "The river's up, flowing really good."

"Guess the cattle will stay this side for the day anyway."

"Yep."

They walked in for breakfast, and when they were done all six loaded into the wagon.

There were a couple of places where the

water had accumulated that Max thought they were going to get stuck, but luckily the horses pulled them out of it. The hills were hard on the horses in a couple of spots where the mud turned all loose and gave little traction. Max was relieved when they were on the rutted road into Curtiss. The sun was coming out, and he did not expect it to take more than a couple of days to dry the ground.

The town was fairly quiet. The lot they used for the service had a few puddles standing, and the chairs would sink into the ground a bit when men sat in them, if any did. Max helped Todd and Sam set up, and, as they finished, he walked over to the office.

Einar sat at his desk with a glass in his hand. Max could smell the whiskey from the doorway.

"Ah, Max. Is Todd still setting up out there?"

"Yes, sir."

"I don't know that he'll get a turnout today."

"Probably not." Max motioned to the glass. "You're drinking early, especially for a Sunday."

"It's the rain. Makes me a bit melancholy."

"You thinking of becoming a rancher?"

Einar looked at him, questioning.

"Heard you are having a man watch the Clarks' place."

Einar looked at him flat for a moment, then smiled. "What, you don't want me as a neighbor, Max?"

"I didn't say I have any problem with it."

Einar shrugged and set his glass down. "I've checked, and there's nobody else with a claim to the place. I figured I'd give it a run. I know it's quick after their death, but if I don't move someone else might." Einar took the bottle from the shelf and poured a little more in his glass. He pulled another glass from the shelf and lifted it towards Max.

"No, thanks."

Einar set the bottle back on the shelf. "Remember when we were talking and I said you had it good? I thought I'd try to get something similar."

"OK. I get that. Do you know anything about the man you hired to keep an eye on the ranch?"

"What about him?"

"Word is he may have been with the Vega gang ten years ago."

Einar's eyes narrowed. "I don't know. When he came through a few days ago looking for a job, we had all the men we needed.

Then I saw him on the trail on the way to Prescott so I hired him. Seems a good enough man. Who told you he was with Vega's gang?"

"Boggs."

Max had never seen Einar tense as he did now. "When did you talk to Mr. Boggs?"

"Couple of days ago when he was here. He mentioned seeing a man whom he matched to the Weaverville man, the same description Sam gave me. Just thought you ought to know."

Einar licked his lips. "I'll talk to him, feel him out. Don't worry; if I think he's dangerous, I'll see him off."

"Thanks." Max stood up. "You coming to join the service?"

"No, not today."

"Take care, Einar. Good luck with the venture."

"Thanks, Max."

CHAPTER 27

Six people showed up for Todd's message, all from the service two weeks prior. Three were smelter workers including Ian. Milton and his wife, Gladys, were another two. The only one who came in from the hills was Luke Kelly.

Max had trouble listening to Todd. His mind was turning. Max was surprised when the men were standing, and Todd was down talking to everyone. Luke came over to Max. "That's a fine mule you sold me."

"Glad you like her. How's things around your area?"

"Good. Not affected at all by the trouble others have had."

Ian came up behind him. "You are lucky then."

Max shook hands with Ian, then looked to Luke. "How long have you been in the area?"

"Oh, I've been in the territory since

seventy-one," Luke said. "Was transferred out here with my regiment during the Indian trouble. Then when my enlistment was up in seventy-four I started prospecting."

"Were you part of tracking down the rancherias?"

"No, I wasn't. I was stationed at Whipple and hardly left."

"Do you remember hearing about them?"

"Yes. You thinking of chasing them? Has some reward been issued?"

"I'm not interested in any reward!" Luke's eyes narrowed at Max growling at him. Max took a deep breath and spoke in a soft voice. "I'm just wanting to put it to rest. It happened just across the river from my land, and they rode through my land a few days ago."

Luke was quiet, studying the ground for a moment. "With all the prospectors climbing through the hills, taking up mining near some of the rancherias, I'm not sure there would be a place for them to go. My first thought is Turret Butte, but there's no telling about that. There's also plenty of ravines that they could have been hiding in with the horses, but the rains would've driven them out temporarily. If I was them, I'm not sure

I wouldn't be looking to join Geronimo's band."

Ian had been quiet, looking at Max thoughtfully. Max gave him a quick glance and then looked back at Luke. "I was really just curious, but I'll probably just stay out of it."

"That's not a bad idea," Luke said firmly. "First, if you did find them, they may just pick you off, or they may have joined another small group that's drifted off the reservation, and they'll all have reason to make sure you don't make it back to spread the news. Second, the most likely thing is you'll waste your time. There's easily a hundred different places for them to possibly hide, and they may be continuously moving."

"You're right, Luke. Thank you."

"Sure. You just stay around and keep an eye on your family."

"Good idea."

Luke turned and followed Milton into the store, and Max turned and walked a distance away from everyone with Ian following him.

"You've latched onto something, haven't you?" Ian asked him.

Max nodded. "You mentioned visiting Ted's camp a few times."

"I did."

"You were known as a friend to Ted's wife and her brothers."

"Maybe. They knew Ted and I got along."

"Would you come with me on a ride?"

"How far?"

"Turret Butte."

"Max, I don't know how far that is, but I don't think we'd be back tonight."

"No, maybe by tomorrow night."

"I don't think Einar will let me off."

"No, probably not."

"Anyway, Luke's right. There's no way of knowing they're there, and, if they are, we might be walking into something we don't want."

"I'm not sure I'm going yet. I need to talk it over with Michelle, and Todd, and pray. But something just sounded right when he said Turret Butte. I think it's just off Bishop Creek."

"I don't know, Max."

"I'll bet Hal does."

Ian arched his eyebrows at Max and just stared at him a moment. "I suppose he does. He also knew Ted and his family at least as well as me."

"Do you know where his camp is?"

Ian turned to the southeast and nodded. "About six miles that way. There's a strange tree atop a hill with nearly all its branches growing to the west. You circle that hill west, and you'll see his camp."

Max clapped Ian on the shoulder. "One other favor, if you don't mind."

"What, Max?"

Max stayed close and kept his voice low. "Keep your ears open, listen for anything that will be threatening for my family."

Ian answered just as low. "Sure, Max."

"Thank you, Ian." Max grabbed his hand. "You're a great friend."

"If I was a better friend, I'd be going with you."

"No, it works out better this way. You need to work, you'll be closer to my family, and Hal'll be less of a threat to them, I think, if we find them."

Ian nodded, and Max turned to walk back to his family.

"Max, what if they aren't there?"

Max turned back. "I'll know to mind my own business and get my butt back to my ranch."

"And if they are?"

"I'll find out if they're peaceful or hostile." Max turned back and walked to his family, glancing toward the smelter office in the distance. He thought he saw the curtains move. He took a deep breath.

They had just turned off Black Canyon Road on the trail to the house. Todd was telling Sam and Martha in back about Luke telling him he had no idea why he felt the need to come to town this morning when Max spoke. "I think I need to go look for Ted's wife and brothers-in-law."

"No!" Michelle spit out immediately. "Why?"

He looked over, and her blue eyes flashed anger. "Luke, Ian, Hal, Einar. They all gave me hints that I'm supposed to look. If I'm wrong, I'm done with it."

"I remember you said that when you went after that raggedy man with the rifle."

Max sighed. "Yes, you're right. But I can't explain it. Something just feels wrong."

Michelle bit into him. "You're confused, that's what's wrong. Two nights ago, you wanted to move because of the trouble, and now you want to go looking for that same trouble. Do you want to leave me a widow and Ronnie an orphan? And the new baby without a father?" Michelle touched her swollen stomach.

Max started to tear up. "No, I don't."

There was a large stretch of quiet all the way to the house. Michelle took Ronnie and went into the house with Martha following.

Max and Sam saw to the wagon and the team.

Todd followed them. "Max, do you think the Lord was guiding you this morning?" Todd sometimes talked about such things so matter of fact that it shook Max.

"Yes, I think so, but I can't be sure." He pulled one of the mares into the stall. "Luke mentioned Turret Butte, and I just felt like that was where I needed to look."

"And why," Sam asked, "did you feel like you needed to look?"

"Einar." Max shook his head side to side. "He acted odd when I asked about his intentions about the Clarks' place. It just didn't feel right."

"Like you'd caught him in something?" Todd quietly asked.

"Yes."

"I've seen it in men I've ministered. The feel of guilt changes some as the men get older, but it's the same sense."

"I'm not going, though, if Michelle's not backing it. We're one flesh, and if she's not in agreement, then I'm not doing it."

Todd sat down on a bale of hay. "You'll do what you need to, and Michelle will see the reason of it at some point, regardless of the outcome."

Max walked past Martha when he was

walking toward the house. Martha stopped him and gave him a hug, then continued on to the barn.

Max walked inside. Michelle was speaking softly to Ronnie, then gave him a push on the bottom to start him toward the door. Max reached to rub the top of his head, but he passed by quickly.

"I'm sorry, Max, I know you wouldn't do this if you didn't think you were being led. It's old fears coming up. You were different when I first met you, and, despite the fact I fell in love with you, I was scared you were going to live that same life."

"Michelle, I —"

"Let me finish!" she said. She looked like she had not meant to be so loud. "I know you are not the same man, and you've proven it time and time again."

"Thank you for that," Max said to her.

"So, tell me." That was all she got out.

"I think it's possible something was pinned on those Indians. I think a great injustice has been done, and it's going to continue to promulgate hatred toward all Indians as well as get Ted's family killed. I can't turn away from it; I just can't."

Michelle nodded. "It's right. It's just, if it's true. I just don't know why it has to be you."

"There's nobody else."

She stood up and came to him. He put his arms around her and felt her body against his, her hair against his neck. They held each other for several minutes. Then she pushed away. "Go. Don't let me hold you back."

Max sighed. "I love you."

"I love you, too."

He turned and walked out the door. Sam saw him and pulled Hardy out of the stall and began saddling him. Max pulled his rifle out of the wagon and put it through the saddle scabbard. He checked the saddle-bag, and the extra ammunition he had put in there days ago was still there.

"Sam, you and Martha will stay at the house."

"Yes, sir."

"Thank you." He gathered Ronnie up and gave the boy a big hug. "I'll see you in a couple of days, all right?"

"All right, Daddy."

Max extended his hand and then hugged Todd.

He swung into the saddle and was riding through the yard when Michelle came out with two bundles in her hands. "Max."

He rode over and took the bundles she held up. "See you soon." At that she turned and hurried back into the house.

Max checked the bundles. In one was bread and dried beef. In the other was his pistol and about thirty bullets. Max sighed and checked the gun to see it was loaded. He put the pistol through his belt across his side and stowed the rest in his saddlebags. He remembered how awkward the weight of a pistol felt when he had first put one on a half dozen years ago. Now it felt even more awkward.

Hardy kept a good trot all the way back to the hills, the other side of Big Bug Creek, despite the afternoon heat. The horse may have lost a step in pure speed, not that he was ever that fast in the short distance anyway, but he seemed to be just as strong or stronger than he ever was in the longer distances.

Max now rode a bit slower, surveying the hills. He knew that further to the east he would be nearing Black Canyon Road and Cordes Station, so he moved west over a rough, rocky rise that Hardy handled well, picking the good footing spots and muscling up the final part.

At the top of the rise, the footing was better, and Max surveyed the surrounding land. Half a mile to the south he spotted the strange-looking tree Ian had mentioned on a rocky hill, all the longer branches pointing in the direction the sun was descending. Max urged Hardy down a spot where there was a gradual slope, and soon they were circling the bottom of the hill.

They picked their way through the loose rocks and sand at the foot of the hill before he spotted the cabin near a spot where the hill and a nearby rocky rise formed a crevice. The cabin blended into the background, made of stacked rocks with a roof of tangled mesquite branches that looked like a push might cave it in. As Max approached, he noticed a mixture of dirt and brush had been used to hold the rocks in place as well as to try and seal the roof. The door frame was the only solid wooden part of the cabin. The door itself was canvas stretched over more mesquite branches.

Max called out. "Hal, it's Max Tillman." He circled around the hut and saw that there was a lean-to with tools and a post with a mule hitched. Past that was a small cave. Just as he noticed the cave, he saw a man squeeze out, shotgun in hand. It was Hal.

"Hal, it's Max Tillman."

"My eyes work."

Max smiled. "Yes, I came to ask a huge favor."

"What's that?"

"Come with me to Turret Butte, where I think Ted's wife and her brothers may be."

Hal's eyes narrowed. "Why?"

"Well, I think the whole thing may have been a setup, to get the ranch and the mine."

"Maybe," Hal said that without hesitating. "But what does that have to do with me?"

"You know them; perhaps they will talk if you come along with me. Plus, I don't really know where Turret Butte's at."

Hal smiled and relaxed a bit. "That's a good thing you're trying to do, but it's best just to leave it alone."

"I can't. I won't."

"What if they're guilty? You know Ted was a good man, but he had a little bit of a temper. He may have gotten into a fight with them and set them off."

"You don't really believe that, do you?"

Hal shrugged.

"Well, let me ask you this: you seen a shorter man with a lazy eye around here recently?"

Hal's expression became a little more intense. "Did on my way into Curtiss that Sunday we met."

Max nodded. "Just before the killings."

"He said he rode off the road following a deer he'd seen. Then was trying to find his way 'cross to Prescott."

"He's now watching the ranch for someone."

Hal studied the ground a moment. "Perhaps he was looking for work and found it."

"Used to run with the Vega gang in Weaverville."

Hal snorted. "All right, sounds suspicious. But, either way, those Injuns, whether innocent or guilty, are gonna be scared and likely will kill someone they see tracking them, even if it's me."

Max sighed. "That's why I said the favor is huge."

Hal chuckled. "Well, why do you think they're at Turret Butte?"

"Basically a hunch."

"Oh, a hunch. Well, I s'pose I'm not likely to die then, so yes, sir, we'll ride over to Turret Butte."

Hal was saddled in a few minutes, and they started off. Hal took the lead, and Max gladly followed. The mule picked familiar spots for the best footing as Hal urged him along. They rode quietly. Hal seemed to be lost in thought, and Max certainly was. He was wrestling with the doubts of his quest, and of pulling another soul into it as well. The shade of the slopes behind them had offered relief from the heat when Hal pulled up. "Sun's starting to set, and over the next couple of slopes is the road. I suggest we camp here for the night, but it's your call."

"I'm fine with that." Max swung down from Hardy. "So, we'll reach the butte tomorrow morning?"

Hal was unsaddling the mule. He wrinkled up his nose and looked east. "We'll be at its base around noon I s'pose."

They made camp, and Max handed out half of the food to Hal. "How long you been in Arizona?"

"Sixty-six. Came out here a year after the war ended. Started prospectin', then tried some other jobs but kept getting the fever. So, I just said I'd might as well give in to it and stick with it boom or bust."

"How've you done?"

Hal chuckled. "More bust than boom." He tore off a piece of jerky and chewed thoughtfully. "Best strike I had was when I was partnered with Ted. He had a knack for finding them, at least ones that paid out some."

"Really?"

"Yeah, that one was not big, but we each got nearly two thousand out of it before it was done. Not bad for seven months digging."

"No, not bad."

"Of course, last year I think I got eight hundred out of this one. Just scraping by after expenses, but I work for myself."

Max nodded. "So, you think there's a vein somewhere deeper in your shaft."

Hal looked at him flatly. "No. But I'm hoping I'm wrong."

"I hope you're wrong, too. I used to think about finding my own bonanza when I worked Tip Top."

"You worked Tip Top?"

"Yes, sir."

"You know I passed by that mountain in sixty-seven, thought about checking it out, then moved on because I didn't like the idea of being out there by myself with Indians around." He shook his head. "I coulda been rich."

"Or scalped."

"That could still happen if your hunch plays out."

"If my hunch plays out completely, we'll be all right."

"Don't know what I'm doing coming out here to satisfy your hunches."

"Yes, you do." Max leaned back on his saddle. "You were Ted's friend."

Hal stared at him. "All right, so I do know."

■ ■ ■ ■

The next morning, they were saddled and back on their way at first light. Hal was right about where they were. Two rises and they were crossing Black Canyon Road.

Hal pointed in the distance to the peak. "That's it."

"Which one?"

"The one shaped like a turret."

"All right. I think I know what a turret's shaped like, but I'm not sure that helps."

"We're at the wrong angle; you'll see."

After some time in the saddle they reached a decent sized stream. Hal called it Bishop Creek, and they crossed the small flow of water. Hal said that it ran more just after it rained, and there was more water underneath. That Max did not doubt considering the sycamores, junipers, and a few ponderosa pines that grew along the creek bank. After a couple of miles of following the creek, Hal turned up a wash. Max followed and could clearly see the turret peak up ahead. He followed Hal up the dry wash a ways, toward the base of their destination ahead.

Something fell out of the sky and hit Hal in the shoulder from behind. Both of them swiveled in their saddles, and there was a Yavapai, holding a Spencer rifle in his hand, aimed in their direction. Another holding a lance stood a few feet to his left. The one holding the Spencer rifle was tall for a Yavapai, about the same height as Max.

Max had almost reached for his own rifle but steadied his hand. Hal had seen the slight movement. "Easy, Max. Remember, you wanted to find them. Now we have." Hal's voice was strained. "Mat, Ahakhela, I am a friend."

The one with the lance shook his head side to side. He had a wrap around his shoulder. The big one with the rifle looked around as if looking for other people. Max saw a small scattering of holes in his shirt with red around them. He had been hit with buckshot. Perhaps Sam's.

"We came to hear your side of the story," Max said as evenly as possible.

"What our side?" came a woman's voice. She stepped out from behind a tree in the distance, her belly swollen, but not as much as Michelle's. "We have no side, now that my white husband is dead, and his family is gone."

"Sunflower," Hal said. "You know me to be Ted's friend. I do not believe you or your brothers killed him. If you did, then kill me, too; otherwise let me continue to be your friend."

She stepped closer. "And this man?"

"He is good man, wants what's right by Ted."

"Right?" Mat sounded doubtful, still holding the gun pointing at Max.

"Men came into our camp acting friendly," Sunflower started, "then one pulled his rifle and shot Ted up close. Ted still struggled with the man, and Ahakhela struggled with the other and pulled the rifle out of his hands but was shot by his pistol as they traded shots. We managed to get to the mules and ride off.

"We spent a couple of days hiding and decided to go to Ted's family, but they weren't there. On the way, a man shot at us and hit Mat but not badly. We knew people would be looking for us; we'd seen men riding, trailing us."

"Sunflower," Hal said, "I share your sorrow over Ted. I also must tell you that his brother and family were killed. They were scalped, and it's being blamed on the three of you."

"We believe you, though," Max added. "What did the men who attacked your camp look like?"

"One was shorter and had eyes that did

not act the same. The other was light haired, on face also." She held her hand up to just about average height. "And the light-haired one was young."

Max sighed. "I've seen the shorter man. I will do my best to see that it is known that it was him, not you. I promise."

Ahakhela shook his head. "Promises."

Sunflower looked at her brother. "Ted was a man who kept his promises. This man may also be."

"He will," Hal told her. He moved his hand to his own belly. "How is the baby?"

"He moves well. He will be a strong man."

Hal smiled.

Max smiled as well. "My wife will have our second child soon."

"May they see each other," she said.

Max nodded. "Sunflower, these men may have had a reason. Had Ted found a lot of gold?"

Her jaw tightened. "Yes. He was very excited. But he tried to keep it hidden. He had kept the ore hidden. All but what he used to pay the debt."

"What debt?"

"He had borrowed from his brother to buy digging tools. He paid him back, plus more, to help pay his brother's debts also."

Max looked at Hal. "They didn't say

anything about finding ore."

"Those bastards must have taken it."

"So, did anyone but his brother know?"

"He brought it to be . . . measured?"

"Assayed?"

"Yes, assayed, in the town with the smelting."

Max almost felt sick. "Einar." Max's vision narrowed. And he wrestled to keep from turning and galloping the other way. He had not felt this sort of fury in years. He took a deep breath, calling to God in his mind to calm his rage.

When he was able to focus on other things again he saw Ahakhela nodding to him approvingly. The man could see his anger at what had been done. He did not know that Max had considered the man behind it his friend.

"We have to go see to this," Max told them. "Stay hidden. I will come back in a few days to this spot." He took out what he had left in rations and handed it to them.

"We will trust you," Sunflower said.

Max met her eyes, worry coming over him. "If it is not me or Hal, do not meet them. Go somewhere else if you must. But in two to four days, we should be back."

She met his eyes, and then he turned and rode back the way he had come.

Hal caught up to him. "Einar did it."

"Yes. He's laid claim to the ranch and the mine, has the man with the lazy eye out there watching the ranch, was the one claimed he witnessed Indians leading a string of horses past the edge of town." Max growled. "Should have known that was a lie. They would have more sense than to get anywhere near town!"

"Max, you aren't alone. We all liked Einar . . . thought he was a good guy."

"Yeah, he speaks with a forked tongue like a snake, making you his friend while he plots."

"What are you going to do?"

"I'm gonna —" Max stopped himself. He was not that man anymore. He was not going to ride into Curtiss and raise his pistol to Einar's head. "I'm going to think on it."

They rode in silence for some time. The Black Canyon Road was in view when Hal spoke up. "Max, I've done what I said I would. I'm done, though. To be honest, my eyesight's bad; I wasn't sure it was you outside my mine. I was not even sure about Mat and Ahakhela. I hope everything turns out well, but I'm going back to my camp."

Max stopped and looked at the man. At first, he was about to cut into him. His friend had been killed and his friend's family hunted, but then realization set in. "You have helped a lot, Hal, and I'm grateful."

"Thank you, Max."

"Keep watch. I don't know how many are involved or how they could peg you as helping, but just keep watch."

"I will."

Max trotted Hardy up the road. The sky was dimming as he rode through Mayer. It was dark when he spotted the lights of Curtiss. He sat there a moment, looking toward the town. He did not need to ride in tonight.

He realized he did not need to ride in at all. He remembered the psalm about not taking up arms in vengeance that he heard in Willow Springs all those years ago. He should have listened to it then. *Rest in Jehovah and wait patiently for Him; inflame not yourself with him who prospers in his way, with the man practicing evil wiles. Abstain from anger and cease from fury; also do not inflame yourself to do evil.* He could go to Prescott the next day, get the sheriff, and have it all sorted out. He urged Hardy up the road toward home. He looked forward to holding Michelle, to holding Ronnie.

CHAPTER 28

Hardy was tired from the two long days of travel, and Max fully mirrored the tiredness. And he was emotionally exhausted as well.

He topped the rise where the house came into view, and something just did not feel right. Hardy sensed his tension and seemed to tense as well. He loosened his rifle in the sheath in the saddle and then felt where the Colt was in his belt. Scanning the corrals, the hills, the buildings, as he rode into the yard, he saw nothing, but that feeling was there. Then he faintly heard voices in the house, and the sound was frantic.

Max bolted Hardy forward to the post in front of the house and bounded off the horse, throwing the reins around the post. He pulled his gun and pushed the door open. They were gathered directly across the room, and they all swung around, Todd with a shotgun in hand.

"Whoa," Max said, still trying to figure out what was happening. He looked around. Ronnie stood in the doorway to his room, eyes wet with tears. Martha and Michelle had been crying as well. That was Sam in Todd's bed. Max looked around again, then shut the door and put the pistol back through his belt, over the sickening burning in his gut.

"What . . ." He couldn't speak.

"His leg's broke," Todd said. "King was shot out from underneath him."

"I'll kill the son of a bitch!" Sam yelled out in anger and pain.

Max brought his hand up and ran it from his forehead back, knocking his hat off. "No. I'm sorry, Sam!"

"Not you," was all Sam said. The women turned back, putting a makeshift splint on his leg.

Max looked at Todd. "When?"

"An hour ago. Martha heard the shot and knew Sam was out riding along the river. She saw them down and brought Queen to get him."

"King?"

"I put him down." Martha's voice quivered.

The tunnel vision came back as fury overcame Max again. He turned and kicked the chair against the wall with such force that some wooden piece came back and hit him in the chest. He went out the door, pulling it shut behind him. Hardy stood there still. Max yanked the rifle from his saddle, staring out into the night.

Max wanted to see someone out there. He wanted somebody to take a shot at him. He wanted to have somebody to shoot. There was nobody, though. Nobody but the cattle on the other side of the gate, at least that he could see. There was nowhere for his anger to go. He could ride out. He knew who was likely to blame.

Instead he put his face into Hardy's neck. "Why? Why did I get involved?"

"Because you want what's right and true and just." Todd had come out quietly onto the porch.

"But look what it's brought! That man in there has been nothing but good to me, to us. And I brought this on him."

"Doing right comes at a price sometimes, not only to you but to those around you. I know this; I've experienced it." Todd sighed and stepped off the porch. "Fortunately, God sets things right. Not always the way we would have done it, but His way is best. We came together as a family like that."

"What should I do?"

"What's right."

Max nodded. "Thank you, Father. I love you."

"I love you too, son."

Max grabbed Hardy's reins and led him to the barn.

The night passed with Sam and Martha sleeping in Max and Michelle's bed. Michelle slept with Ronnie. Max sat there in the dark looking out the window, rifle in hand, until sometime in the night when Todd got up and insisted that he watch for a while. Max went and lay in Todd's bed while Todd sat up. Max was surprised he felt sleep coming over him. It had been a long couple of days of travel, but he was worried that the shot at Sam was just the beginning.

He woke at the sound of pots clanking. Michelle was in the kitchen, Todd still sitting by the window. The sky was just showing signs of lightening. Max swung his feet to the floor and stood, walking to where Michelle was working.

"I need eggs and milk."

"I'll get them." He stood there a moment. "I'm sorry. I didn't know this would happen."

"I know."

"After breakfast, we're gathering the

horses, and we're all going to Mayer."

She looked at him. "What?"

"We'll be safer there, until we can get word to the sheriff in Prescott."

"Plus, Mrs. Mayer can look at Sam's leg," Todd added. "She's the best thing aside from a doctor there is."

"Why not just go to Prescott?"

"Long trip for Sam with his leg. Plus, I'm worried about being out on the road that long."

Michelle just nodded and turned back to what she was doing. Max wanted to sit and talk to her. Tell her everything inside him right now. But he needed to go outside and get the milk and eggs, and they needed to get moving.

Max put the pistol through his belt and went out into the dim yard to the chicken coop and barn, looking nervously into every dark space. He quickly pitched hay for the horses and milk cow to eat before he returned with the milk and eggs. Nothing had happened.

When Max came in, he heard Ronnie talking to Martha but could not make out what they were saying. Michelle took the eggs and milk and gave Max a reassuring smile. "Max, I don't blame you for this. I just don't know how to handle it right now.

Pregnancy moods are tough enough."

"Thank you." Max gave her a kiss. "I love you."

"I love you, too."

Max went back out and saddled Rowdy. He hitched the other horses to the wagon. He came in, and everyone was sitting around the table. Sam's leg was out straight and was still quite swollen.

Sam looked up. "I understand we're going to Joe's."

"Yes, sir."

"Why not Curtiss? It's closer; we'll be safe sooner."

"This is all because of Einar."

"What?" Sam started to sit up and winced.

"Einar found out Ted had a rich strike. He apparently hired this man staying at the Clarks' and some other man to kill the Clarks and Ted. Pin it on Ted's wife and family."

"Are you sure?"

"I talked to Sunflower and her brothers. I believe them." Max sighed. "It turns my stomach to think of my supposed friend doing this, but he's capable. He doesn't like natives. He was the only witness to see *Indians* guiding horses past town. Why would they pass close to town? He's going to get Ted's mine and the ranch. He's been acting very odd. It's all there, although I didn't want to see it at first."

Michelle put the breakfast on the table just then and sat down. They all stared at the food for a moment. Finally, Martha spoke up. "We may not feel like eating, but we need to keep our strength. We got a journey ahead of us."

"You're right." Todd held out his hands, and they all clasped hands together and bowed their heads. "God, we thank you for this food in front of us. We ask you to bless it. We thank you that Sam was not hurt worse. We pray for your protection upon this family, upon this land. We ask your guidance and strength as we proceed, Lord. Amen."

"Amen," the rest said. They did eat, and before long all the food was gone.

Max helped Martha wash the dishes quickly. He insisted that Michelle rest. He didn't like taking her on the rough road at this point in her pregnancy, but it was not that far. After he finished, he grabbed the rest of the ammunition out of the closet and put it in a satchel.

He let Todd keep the rifle while he went out and brought the team around to the front door. He was tense the whole time, scanning the distance, nearly expecting a gun shot. The clouds rolling in added to his tension, but he neither saw nor heard anybody.

Sam hopped out with Martha supporting him on one side and Todd on the other, but he still grunted in pain, especially when he was hoisted into the back of the wagon. Martha went back in and brought out their two shotguns. Todd climbed onto the driver's seat, and Michelle sat next to him with Ronnie nestled in between them.

When they rode out of the ranch, Max rode some distance ahead on Rowdy, scanning the road for possible trouble. Hardy, unused to the harness, did not follow the lead of the reins at first, but he had been used on the wagon a couple of times before and settled into the task along with the gelding and the mares. The mules and Queen were all three lashed to the back of the wagon and allowed themselves to be led. Max waited at the top of the rise and fell in beside the wagon as it started down.

"What do we do once we get there?" Michelle asked.

"I don't know," Max lied and knew he needed to find a way to gently put it. "Todd, if you don't mind, I'd like you to take the stage to Prescott when it comes through. Tell the sheriff, the newspaper man — actu-

ally anyone that will listen and spread it —
that the Indians didn't do it."

"Sure, Max, I'd be glad to pass the message for you."

"I told you what I know. I'd leave Hal's name and the meeting place of us and Ted's widow out of it until the men are in custody."

"And the rest of us will wait it out at Mayer's," Michelle said.

Max took a deep breath. "I'll be heading into Curtiss." Michelle's face stiffened and turned red, but Max kept going. "I pulled Ian into this, Hal also. They are in danger."

"You are not the law."

"No, I'm not. Einar is the closest thing to the law from here to Prescott, and he's the criminal."

"You aren't doing this for me, Max."

Max looked over at Sam in the wagon. "I . . ." There was silence aside from the wagon wheels on the path.

"Why are you doing it, Max?" Todd asked.

"I feel like I need to. Like I said, Einar's security position has put him closest thing to the law, and it's power in the wrong place. More people could get hurt, somehow more could be covered up . . . I don't know. Really, it would be easier to sit at Joe's till tomorrow and wait it out, but the right thing isn't always the easier thing."

Todd took his eyes off the trail a moment to look intently at Max. "So, you are sure it's not vengeance?"

"I want justice for what was done to Sam, to the Clarks, Ted, and his family."

"There is a difference between justice and vengeance," Todd said. "God says, 'Rest in the Lord, and wait patiently for him; fret not thyself because of him who prospereth in his way, because of the man who bringeth wicked devices to pass. Cease from anger, and forsake wrath; fret not thyself in any wise to do evil. For thy evildoers shall be cut off; but those who wait upon the Lord, they shall inherit the earth.' "

Max stopped Rowdy. "I heard that once and did not heed it. I shouldn't go."

"Perhaps," Todd said. "Or, perhaps you should."

Michelle looked at her father with a mix of anger and confusion.

Todd held up a hand to her. "It depends on where your heart is when you go after them. Is it for vengeance or justice? In that same psalm, it goes on to say that 'the meek will inherit the earth, and they delight themselves in abundant peace.' That's what I believe you truly want, Max; you aren't going into this craving violence, at least not except as an initial instinctive reaction of protection. It also says in that verse, 'The wicked plots against the righteous and gnashes upon him with his teeth. The Lord shall laugh at him; for he seeth that his day is coming. The wicked have drawn out the sword and have bent their bow, to cast down the poor and needy, and to slay such as be of upright conversation. Their sword shall enter their own hearth, and their bows shall be broken.' Also, God calls on us to watch over the widows. He is a God of Justice. And if, like you believe, false witness has been given, and they lied about what the Yavapai have done, God speaks on that and murder of your neighbor: 'Then you should do to him as he thought to do to his brother, so shall you put the evil away from among you. And those which remain shall hear, and fear, and shall henceforth commit no such evil among you.' I always believed that was more for the officials of the law than for any offended, and I believe you are acting in their stead until the law arrives."

Max looked over at Todd. "So, you are saying that the Word authorizes dealing harshly with those who first shed blood, or did wrong. What about grace?"

"Grace. Grace is ultimately God's to give. Of course, we are to follow God's lead, but that I think is up to the law. There are many verses about the wicked turning from wickedness and living in righteousness."

Max nodded. "If he repents?"

"Yes," Todd told him.

Max continued to scan the horizon ahead of them and turned to look behind them. A couple of riders approaching after they had turned on the road to Mayer made him tense up, but he saw as they approached that they were hands at the Cordes ranch. Max greeted them as they rode past, and they were on the road by themselves again.

Max jumped at the loud crack, and Rowdy danced. It was thunder. The dark sky was gaining on them from the northwest, with the sun fading behind darker clouds.

They traveled relatively quietly, with each person seeming lost in their own thoughts, and Max trying to stay focused on watching the road. Relief swept over him when Mayer appeared in view in the distance, especially since, right then, large, cool drops of water began to hit him on the neck.

The few drops soon became a torrent, and as they pulled up in front of the station, water was running off of Max's hat, his clothes weighed down. Michelle's dress clung to her form. Ronnie kept wiping his head like he was going to dry himself.

Joe and his brother-in-law came trotting out of the house across the road, Joe's brother-in-law got just as soaked as the arriving travelers, but Joe was wearing a slicker and a hat that appeared to keep him dry. "Max, I thought that looked like you, and . . . is Sam all right? What happened?"

"No, Sam needs Sadie to take a look at him. His leg's broke. Someone shot his horse out from under him."

Joe looked through the torrent of rain back down the road. "The Indians?"

"No, we'll talk about that once we're settled, if you don't mind our patronage for a while."

Joe shook his head. "All right." He looked at his brother-in-law. "Will you help get their animals settled? I think we got just enough room. Todd, help me get Sam inside the house. The rest of you go get settled in the station; get the fire stoked so you can dry and warm up."

The rest consisted of Michelle and Ronnie, as Martha followed Sam, who was being nearly carried by Joe and Todd.

Max and Hiram quickly got the animals situated. There were not enough stalls, as some were in use, but there were places spaced far enough apart in the barn to tie the other horses. Max got Rowdy settled in a stall but left him saddled. After the other horses were taken care of, he hurried to the station to make sure a fire was going strong to warm Michelle and Ronnie.

Of course, Michelle already had a fire at full blaze and was putting coffee on to brew.

Todd walked in right behind Max. "Sadie's set it, and says she thinks he'll be all right. He's drinking some wine to help him sleep."

"Wine?"

"He said he preferred whiskey, but she told him that wine would be better for sleeping, and rest was what he needed. With Martha and Sadie standing over him, he didn't argue."

Max half chuckled but then looked at Michelle. "You need to change into something dry."

"Right here?"

Max looked around. "I'll go out and make sure nobody comes inside until you've changed." He stepped out quickly to make sure there was no discussion. Just as he stepped out Joe and Hiram stepped onto the porch.

"Mind waiting a minute while Michelle changes?"

"Of course not." Joe leaned his back against the wall to stay clear of the downpour, looking at Max expectantly.

"Joe, sorry to just barge in like this, but I wasn't sure we were safe out there. I've come to find out that Einar was behind the Clarks, and Ted."

"What?"

Max told him about the man out at the Clarks' ranch, about Hal, talking to Sunflower and her brothers, about Einar acting different.

Joe sighed. "I don't want to believe it, but something did seem odd when I was riding with them. Einar seemed to be trying to rile us up some more, I suppose so we would just shoot at first sight. It's still not going to be easy to convince some people of his guilt. Einar's fairly popular."

"Yes, I know. But he must have the gold from Ted's mine."

Joe nodded. "What's your plan?"

"Todd's going to ride the stage in to Prescott when it comes through, let the sheriff know, and spread the word that it appears the Indians weren't guilty."

Joe tilted his head.

"I know," Max said. "But maybe if it spreads, at least it will ease the chance of someone hunting them down."

"You're welcome to stay. There's a couple of small rooms out back."

"Thanks, Joe. I'll be riding on to Curtiss. I think this can't wait, and maybe I can get Einar to tell me something."

Joe blew out air through his mustache. "It'd be better to wait for the law."

"I wish I could, but who knows what they may do in the meantime? I can't just sit and wait."

Joe met his eyes and was about to say something when the door opened, and Todd motioned them inside. Both Michelle and Ronnie were in dry clothes. Todd had several cups of coffee lined up, and Max gratefully took one. The air outside was cold, and he was soaked through.

"That Sam's a tough old man," Hiram said.

"Yeah," Max said, thinking about him up there with a broken leg, about the man's old horse that he had loved. His gut twisted. Maybe he did want revenge for Sam. For himself also, for what this had put him and his family through the last couple of weeks. That was stupid, though. Nobody had asked him to get involved. Maybe his family would have been all right if he had kept to his own business. But, was that right to not help, to not get involved in the process of justice when you see it going awry? Max drank the hot coffee, ignoring it burning his tongue and throat. "I've got to go."

Everyone looked at him, but Todd spoke. "In this?"

"Yes." He knelt down next to Ronnie. "Son, I'm so proud of you. You're growing into such a strong boy." He reached out, and Ronnie came and hugged him. Max held him close even though he was getting the boy wet again.

Finally he stood, and he embraced Todd. "Love you, Dad."

"You, too, son. We'll see you soon."

"Yes, sir, God willing."

Max turned and offered his hand to Joe. Michelle stood off, a confused look on her face.

Joe took Max's hand. "You're going to drown before you get very far. Take my slicker."

"I couldn't, Joe."

"You're going a lot further than I am, and I insist." Joe started taking off the slicker.

Max shook Hiram's hand and then took the slicker from Joe. "Thanks, Joe."

"If you like it maybe I'll get you to buy it when you get back." He smiled at him.

Max reached his hand out to Michelle, and she came to him, but he grasped her hand and led her to the door and out, shutting the door behind him. Once they were outside, she looked up at him with those big blue eyes. Max grinned. "You are beautiful."

She grabbed the slicker. "Then don't go." She forced a knowing smile when she said it.

Max grabbed her wrists and pulled her close, keeping her arms in between them so she would not get soaked again, and gave her a long kiss that told her he did not want to leave. Then he turned and walked toward the barn. He stopped and looked toward the house where Sam and Martha were. Sighing, he kept going to the barn.

CHAPTER 29

Like most Arizona rains, this one did not last very long. The fact that it lasted a couple of hours was surprising. It had eased to a sprinkle as Max made his way from Mayer up Black Canyon Road toward Curtiss. Rowdy slid some in the mud on the slanted parts of the road when they first started out. He began to choose his footing better and also changed his step. He became more surefooted as they made their way down the muddy road.

The road felt different to Max, and it was not just the rain. He had ridden this path many times, but now there was something different at the end. It seemed foreign, a different path, and the slop just added to it.

The drizzle had subsided by the time he approached Curtiss. The sun was actually fighting through a cloud directly above him, making it look like daytime again. Max felt the gun underneath the slicker, put through his waistband on his left hip. He looked up to the sky and took a deep breath. "Lord, be with me."

He trotted Rowdy down the main street of Curtiss. He waived to Milton, who was walking back toward the general store from the saloon.

Milton waved back. "Surprised to see you out in this. It was a bad storm."

"Could get worse," Max called to him. Milton stopped and looked at the distant skies.

Max halted Rowdy at the hitching post in front of the smelting office, swinging down and tethering the stallion. "Be good, boy."

Max unbuttoned the slicker as he walked to the door and entered.

"Max, how are you doing?" Einar called from his desk. He had a pen in hand and was filling out paperwork.

Max felt the heat rise from his gut up to his cheeks, and they became red. He took a deep breath to calm himself. "Einar, I need to talk to you." Max looked at the man he had known for years, sitting there waiting to hear him out. He knew things but looked up questioning like he was clueless. Einar was good at lying.

"Einar." Max walked over to the side window that overlooked the entrance to the smelter itself. He glanced at it and then turned to the man behind the desk. "Please stop what you're doing. It's gone too far."

Einar's eyes narrowed for a moment, then he licked his lips and looked down at the desk. Finally, he leaned back. Max thought he saw that he had something in his hand. "You're right, Max. It's gone too far. I never thought it would come to this. I never thought it would affect you, or Sam. I like you both."

"Then stop, turn away from it, and go on the right path; ask forgiveness."

"Oh, the man of God speaks. Is it that easy?"

"It's not easy, but you can do it."

"Because you did. You had a life with a wife waiting when you stopped hunting men. I have jail waiting for me." Einar's eyes were moist. He tilted his head. "You didn't think I knew? I knew. I didn't spread it either, respecting your choice to leave it behind. Can I do that? Just leave it behind and use the money from it to buy a nice piece of land?"

Max sneered. "It's not the same. Those men were criminals, and I followed the law when hunting them."

"They're all under the ground, aren't they? Did they have a chance to turn away from what they'd done?"

Max leaned back against the wall. He had sat up more than a few nights in the year after he stopped hunting men just working through it. It still pained him a bit. His voice was softer when he spoke again. "Do you really see it as the same, Einar?"

Einar closed his eyes and tilted his head back. "No. No, Max, I don't. I wish I'd never gone down this road . . . that I'd never listened to him."

"Who's 'him'?"

Einar's eyes opened, and he looked at Max, even more pain on his face. "You think this is all me?"

Max thought a moment. "All the information I got points to you."

Einar looked away a moment, shaking his head. He looked back. "No, I'm not that evil. Like I said, I never wanted the Clarks dead." His voice began shaking. "Or their kids." His eyes intensified. "I didn't know they would take a shot at Sam."

"Tell me then, Einar." There was a long silence. "I was shocked when I figured out it all pointed back to you."

Einar slumped and looked away again, his face tightening. "I make one-ten a month here. It's more than the workers but never going to give me a good nest egg. I'd be doing this all my life, or until I get old and useless. Then I'd have nothing. Well, that miner brought in ore for me to look at, wanted a second opinion. Gave me a small piece to keep it quiet, too. He couldn't hold back when I told him it was high grade. I could see it on his face. His life had changed. He was going to be wealthy, and I'd still be here. And his squaw and her savage brothers would have it, too. That's just not natural!"

Max sighed, but Einar waved his hand, knowing they felt different about the natives, but he went on talking.

"I know Clyde Parker out at Walton's ranch . . . rode out to see about maybe buying a horse out there. We ended up playing poker out there, Walton, Clyde, and Roy. Well, I got drunk and brought up that it wasn't right Ted and his wife getting rich.

"Well, he told me he could arrange it where they were wanted for stealing horses. Said he had a lien on the Clarks, and part of their collateral was their lien on the mine."

"I heard there was a debt. I thought they'd borrowed from you."

"I don't have but a hundred extra dollars, plus they didn't ask. I wouldn't have loaned it to them anyway."

545

"But Walton did?" Max should have guessed Walton was in on it. He had been way too involved, and Max just did not like the man.

"Yeah. He's smart like that. Knew he could get their land if they didn't pay. I didn't think of it but probably still would not have parted with my last hundred dollars, which is what he loaned them.

"For some reason, I thought that Ted had not told his wife or brothers-in-law. He'd wanted to keep it so secret. Apparently, the same day I'd estimated the grade of the ore he went into Prescott and traded for cash and then made it out to the Clarks' the next day. They'd paid Walton an hour before I got there. He knew that they wouldn't have had a chance to tell anybody else. Of course, Walton didn't tell me he'd been paid.

"Told me the next night to be seen out and about in the street kind of late and, the next morning, tell a couple of people I'd seen some horses being led by Indians the night before. But not too much to look suspicious. Said then repeat the story when the law came to ask about the crime."

Einar paused a long moment. "Max, I had no idea. I thought they were going to steal the horses from their own herd and then go drop them off next to the mine. Then Walton would take the mine as payment for the lien, and we'd share the profits."

Einar looked up. Max stood there, turning the story over in his head. "But Ted and his family could have said they didn't steal the horses, because there was no reason for them to steal."

Einar's eyes closed, and he pursed his lips. "Family?" He weakly shook his head. "I didn't think of them that way then. I guess I always suspected something would happen to Ted. I just didn't want to hear it, or think about it."

"Einar."

"I know, I know. I'm just as guilty."

"It's never too late to do the right thing."

"I'm in deep, Max."

"The man out at the Clarks' ranch — Walton's idea?"

"Yeah, his man. He hired him a week before. Think he was scheming something before I showed up at his ranch. Of course, I heard all this after the fact from Clyde."

"But you bought the land, not Walton with his lien?"

Einar tossed up his left hand. "They never found the paid receipt he gave Clark. Was worried it would turn up. They've scoured that place for it. They're considering burning the place down if they don't find it."

"So, what are you going to do?"

Einar looked at him sharply. "I'm thinking on that."

Max met his stare, and the silence stretched until the door opened. Max looked over his shoulder to see that it was Walton's man, and one of the others that had been riding with the posse a few days back.

"Clyde, what can I do for you?" Einar asked.

Walton's man glanced at Einar a moment and then looked back to Max, but the other man spoke. "We thought since this man's been such a busybody lately, maybe he knew where those Apache are. Do you?"

Max slowly turned to face them. "What you men are doing, repent and ask forgiveness. God will forgive if you go to Him."

The other man glanced at Clyde and smirked. "I just can't do that, but we still can part amicably. You just tell us if you know where the Indians are and look to the welfare of your own family, and we can part on good terms."

"We can, but only if you'll walk away from this."

The man's face hardened, and Max saw him tense. Max had been grasping the slicker with his left hand. He pulled it back as he reached across for his gun over his left thigh.

The man's gun was clear as Max grasped his, and he threw himself backwards as he raised his gun. Gunfire sounded, multiple shots; the man lurched. Clyde had his gun out. Max shot. Smoke was filling the room. Max was sitting on the floor. Walton's other man was falling to the floor. So was Clyde, but he was also still aiming his gun. Max recocked and shot.

The gun smoke was stinging Max's eyes. He did not see any movement through the haze.

There was a thud behind him. Max turned and saw Einar lying on the floor looking at him, Einar's gun pointing toward the two slumped bodies.

"You shot him; that's why I'm not shot."

"Yeah." Einar's voice was weak.

"You're hit."

"Yeah."

Max crawled to him, spotting the wound at the top of his chest. Max grabbed a handkerchief from Einar's pocket and held it to the wound. Men came running into the office behind Max. He looked to his gun on the floor and then to the door. It was the smelter workers, Ian one of them, behind two other men in the doorway.

"What happened?" the burly man in the front said.

"I . . ." Einar had trouble talking. He tried to lift his arm, but it was weak. The men came in a little closer, stepping cautiously over Walton's men. "I'm repenting," Einar said hoarsely. He collapsed then.

"Is there a doctor?" Max called out. "Anybody?"

"No, Max," Ian told him. "Milton's wife is the best we got here, her or Lyle at the saloon."

Max checked for a pulse. Einar's heart was still beating. "Get one of them."

The other men were looking at the two dead men, guns next to their bodies, Einar's and Max's guns lying next to them.

"Let's get him to his bed," Max said to the men. He moved to grab Einar's shoulders, and two other men came to help. Max motioned one to help take his shoulders, and Max tried to keep the handkerchief pressure applied.

Einar yelled in pain as they picked him up and flailed and kicked. Max tried to calm him, but Einar did not seem to know where he was or what was happening. He blacked out, though, after several seconds.

Einar's sleeping quarters were across the street next to the flophouse where most of the workers slept. They carried him through the mud and the small pond that had formed in the street, nearly slipping and falling into the pool. The room was ten foot by ten foot, with a wall shared with another sleeping quarters next door.

They laid him on the bed, and Max continued applying pressure to the wound. He looked back just as a stout man with more brown hair on his face than the top of his head came hurrying into the room. Lyle had two things wrapped in towels as he hurried through the door. Ian trailed behind him.

"Did it go through?"

"I think so; there's a wound in his back also."

"Well, that may be good. I'll hope." He looked at one of the men. "Go get Patricia. She can sew better than me." The man ran out the door. "Tell her to bring a clean pot to boil water!" A clap of thunder sounded in the distance a second after his yell.

"You done this before?" Max asked.

"When I was just a pup, toward the end of the war, I ended up helping a field surgeon after a skirmish. I was the only one available, and he had me doing things I had no training at, just talking me through it while he was working on another soldier. That's my extent. I've used what I've

551

learned a couple of times helping men in the mines or the mill. I've sewed a couple of men up, cauterized another to keep him alive."

Max nodded. "You know more than me."

Lyle shrugged and motioned Max to move his hand. Max stepped back, and Lyle unwrapped one towel to reveal a bottle of grain alcohol. He uncorked it and poured a little over the wound. He used the towel to dab at the wound and tried to get a better look at it after clearing some of the blood. He bent down to listen to Einar's breathing.

"One of the other men's breathing!" a man yelled from the street. "He's trying to talk but can't."

Max looked at Ian, then they both walked across through the slop. Patricia was crossing in the other direction, holding her skirts up as she hurried across, pot in hand.

They reached the doorway, and Clyde was looking up at one of the smelter workers. His wound was just below and to the right of the center of his chest. He saw Max and tried to say something but just gurgled. The sound cut off, and he was still, his dead eyes looking up at them.

Max sighed and leaned against the wall.

"I never wanted to be involved in this again."

"What happened?" Ian asked the same time as the other man.

"Einar admitted to being involved in the Clarks' and Ted's killings."

"He did," Ian said.

"No!" the other man called out.

Max nodded. "I knew it already. I found out before I even came here." He looked at Ian, who knew he had been suspicious. "Of course, Einar didn't know exactly what was going to happen when the plan was hatched, and he did not pull any trigger. That was all Walton's planning. Einar played the part of pinning it on Ted's family, though. When Walton's men came in they intended to make sure we didn't talk, but Einar saved my life. He was holding that gun behind the desk."

"So that's what he meant by repenting."

Max's jaw clenched, and he took a long, deep breath. He picked up his gun and pulled bullets from his pocket and reloaded it after emptying the spent cartridges.

Ian and the other man looked at each other, and then Ian asked, "What are you doing, Max?"

"Some other men are out at the Clarks'. There's evidence there that will help prove what happened, or at least there was if they haven't found it and destroyed it yet." Max bent down and picked up the Walton man's gun and checked the chambers — not fired. Einar had hit him before he could get off a shot. It had been Clyde who hit Einar. "Also, there's a man out there who took a shot at Sam, shot King out from under him."

"Sam's all right?"

"Broke his leg, but he'll recover." Max bent down and unbuckled the man's gun belt, rolling him and pulling it free. He pulled it around his own waist and holstered the pistol. His own was in the slicker pocket. "They may go after any of my family, or some other people who know things before the law gets here."

Ian scooped up Clyde's gun. "I'll come with you."

"No. You stay here. You talk to the law when they get here. You watch Einar. Who knows who else is around?"

Ian sighed. "Aye."

Max grabbed Ian in an embrace. "Thank you, friend." He lowered his voice then. "Please make sure Todd gets through here to Prescott all right, on the stage."

He pulled back, and the Irishman had determination in his eyes. He slapped Max on the shoulder, and Max went out the door.

Rowdy was in a poor mood. He fought Max on the way out of town, and Max thought the horse would start bucking. He eased for the short distance to the trail that took them to home, but when Max urged the stallion past, a struggle of the reins occurred. Rowdy did make a short hop, but Max spoke calmly to the horse. "Easy, boy. I know, I know, but we gotta."

Rowdy finally gave in, and they made their way another couple miles until Max guided Rowdy off the road. The clouds started to roll in and darken the day again as they picked their way through the brush up through the low point between two hills. Max could see a ranch house not very far to the east. He thought about the fact that he would like to be in his house, with his family, enjoying a warm meal, dry, and peaceful. He kept riding north up the hill.

At the top, Max dismounted and looked nervously down the descent. Steep and muddy. He patted Rowdy lightly on the neck before he reached into the bags and pulled out the ammunition and put it in the slicker pocket. He pulled the rifle free from the scabbard, then turned the stallion back the way they had come. "You be careful, stay out of trouble, all right?" He slapped the horse on the rump and nearly got kicked. He fell to the side to get clear. Rowdy trotted off, though, back down toward the road.

Max picked up the rifle and started down the other side of the hill. After a few steps, he slipped and slid a few feet down. He stayed on his butt and slowly worked his way down the hill. By the time he stood up at the bottom, his pants were soaked with mud. He walked through the marsh that had formed in the small valley. A bright flash momentarily blinded him, and the loud clap of thunder followed quickly, letting him know how close the strike had been.

Max sloshed to the next rise and began to scramble up the slick hill. He reached the top out of breath, lying flat and looking down. Below, the descent dropped to where the Agua Fria, often dry, had come over the banks and widened. Looking at the rushing water, Max was now thinking his plan was stupid. He was here, though, horseless and soaked. He was not turning back. The next lightning strike brightened the sky, and in that instant he tried to scan the opposite bank. For what it was worth, he saw nobody. He did not expect to see anyone here. But that did not mean there was not a shooter waiting, neither did his quick glimpse, but that was all there was to ease his mind. He took off the slicker and wrapped it over his rifle the best he could and tied the sleeves to keep it tight. Then he slid down the hill just as he had the other one. He reached a spot just above the water. He started to lunge in, but his legs locked. His body would not act.

"Nothing to do but just go." He finally forced his body to move and slid the rest of the way down, pushing off just as he reached the water. Holding the bundled slicker above the water, he tried to swim with one hand.

The current caught him, and, if he had not been swept up against a large rock just under the surface, he would have been swept right downstream. As it was his breath was knocked out of him, and he almost lost his grip on the bundle before he pulled it into the water. He managed to kick against the rock, and he crossed as he was pulled downstream. He reached out and grabbed a branch, and it did not break. He pulled, and his feet caught in the tree. He pushed until his feet hit ground and then clawed his way up out of the water and collapsed, fighting for breath.

Finally, he was able to breathe and think and realized that drops of rain were falling again, and the downpour was getting harder and harder.

Max pulled himself up and scrambled up the hill a ways, worried that the river would suddenly rise more and wash him away. He stopped again and rested and caught his breath. He realized his hat was gone. He unbundled the slicker and found that the rifle had stayed dry. The pistol in the holster had come out in the river. Max pulled the one from the slicker pocket and placed it in the holster. He put the slicker back on, but, with him already being soaked, it did not feel as comfortable. He scrambled up the hill and at the top hurried over to a tree that sheltered him a bit from the rain. He took off the slicker and hung it over one of the lowest branches. He felt heavy enough with the soaked clothes. He dumped half the bag of ammunition into his coat pocket and stuffed the bag holding the rest into his pants pocket.

Max looked around. He guessed it was late afternoon, but with the thick cloud cover he was not sure. He was not exactly certain of his location in regards to the Clarks' house. The bend of the Agua Fria made it hard to gauge. He noticed movement on the rise to what he thought was the west. It was a couple of cows. He watched in the dim light for other movement. After a few minutes, he made his way slowly across the field and up to the rise where the cattle were, being cautious to not spook them. He kept down almost at a crouch and moved slowly.

CHAPTER 30

There were some trees between him and the house a hundred yards away. He saw the outlines of the barn and the house when lightning far behind him brightened the sky a little. Max just stood against the tree near a white and brown cow and watched. Through the rain and the trees, he thought he saw light around shutters on the windows. There was somebody in the house. He figured that the man with a lazy eye was in there. He walked slowly to trees closer to the house and stopped to again look at the situation.

His hair was soaked; his clothes were soaked. Water was in his boots. He squished inside his boots when he walked through the field of mud puddles. The sound of the falling rain covered his footsteps some. He could move with the barn between him and the house, if he just went to the left a little. His grip tightened on the rifle, and he

560

glanced around. There in the distance on the next hill over he saw the man. If he had not shifted, Max would not have seen him. He was surprised he did anyway. He did not know if lightning had flashed in the distance or not; he had become so used to it. The man was kneeling alongside a bush. Max was not sure now in the dark, but he thought that man had been looking the other way. Max let out a quiet breath. The man was waiting on a hill not far from the river crossing to Max's land. The man was waiting to ambush Max.

Just then a big gust of wind picked up, and Max had to brace his footing to keep from being pushed. Now that he was here, he was not sure that this was such a good idea. He could not tell for sure where the man on the hill was looking. He could not really see the man all that well anymore. He had no idea how many men, if any, were in the house. Max thought he still saw the dim outline of light around the shuttered windows.

He was tired, but at least the rain was easing to a sprinkle. He took a deep breath and started slowly across the grass to the back of the barn. He peeked around the corner, and at that same moment a door opened on the side of the house, spilling light out. Max pulled back, then nervously edged toward the corner of the barn again. He stopped. He was afraid of being seen. He finally lowered himself onto hands and knees and peeked around the corner at a level just above the muddy ground.

A large man holding a lantern was in view for just a moment as he walked toward the front of the barn. Max scanned the area, especially the windows and doorway of the house forty yards away. Nobody was looking.

He pushed himself up and wiped his hands on his shirt before grabbing the rifle he'd leaned against the wall. He again moved as quietly as he could through the mud around to the front of the barn. The door was open, and Max saw the man holding the lantern just above the ground walking along the backside of the barn. There were holes dug in three places along stalls and the middle of the floor. They were looking for something.

Max stepped quickly inside and toward the man. "Don't give me a reason to shoot."

The man started and almost dropped the lantern. He turned around. It was, of course, one of the men that had been riding in the posse, with Walton. "I . . ." He stopped, not knowing what to say.

"Are you looking for that payment receipt?" Max asked.

"What?"

"It's over. I know; other people know. The sheriff probably knows by now. You just hold that light steady with your right and with your left reach over and undo that belt. Let it fall to the ground."

The man did as he was told. Max moved in a circle to the side. "All right, you hang that lantern on the wall, and step up toward the front of the barn. I don't want to have to shoot you, so don't make any sudden moves. Enough people have died."

The man moved forward, and Max stepped in behind him, careful to keep a couple of feet distance between them. "How many in the house? Tell me the truth."

There was a long silence, but finally the man answered "two."

"All right. Let's march slowly to the house, and you stop when you open the door. We're going to tell them that it's over, that if they lay down their guns there won't be any shooting."

"Mister, I don't think that will work."

Max thought about it a moment. "It probably won't, but it's either that or just kill you and as many of them as I can. I'd like to try it the other way."

"All right." The man started slowly walking out the barn door that was half open, with Max keeping back a couple of steps. As they reached the door of the house he actually heard a laugh inside the house. Max still had the element of surprise.

The loud crack of the shot was only a split second before the bullet struck the ground behind Max. Max whirled and focused up at the hill in the distance. The big man lunged toward the door of the house. Seeing the flash from the hill, Max threw himself back toward the barn. He heard the splat back where he had been, and as he was going into the barn he heard the loud explosion behind him, the force helping him through the barn door, pain piercing his back, his breath knocked out. He lay there dazed and fought to regain his thoughts. The horses were whinnying and stomping in their stalls. Finally, he reached out and kicked the barn door closed.

He pushed himself up, ignoring the pain from the shotgun shrapnel. He turned and pointed the rifle at the door and backed up, stumbling over one of the holes that had been dug. He fell, and his finger pulled the trigger, sending a shot through the door. He scrambled up, his ankle hurting now, but he ignored it, re-cocking the rifle and pointing it at the door. The horses were louder. He glanced back quickly, realizing he was in the light from the wall where they would see him easily if they rushed inside. Max needed to find a place to hide and quick. He whipped his head around, seeing an empty stall in back, and one in the middle on the other side. The other four had horses.

Max had just gotten settled when the barn door swung open. He could see the top of the doors from the shadow of the back of the stall where he hid, but not the entrance. He could see the middle of the barn. The men did not come into view for a few seconds. They must have been peeking through the entrance to try to find him.

Finally, Max saw them approach the center of the barn. The big man was slightly in front carrying a pistol. Walton was just behind him carrying the shotgun, and a third man, younger looking and thin, was behind them with a rifle. Max fought the urge to just start shooting. The horses were all frightened, but the one by the back stall was the worst.

Walton's eyes widened as he saw the barrel of Max's rifle sticking through the gate of the back stall. The big man saw it at the same time, and they both raised their guns and shot at the same time. The horse screamed as the shotgun blast hit both stalls.

Max stood up from the middle stall with his pistol raised and hit Walton square in the side of the head, sending him falling back into the younger one, who stumbled back. Max missed the big man with a quick second shot. The man had spun around, missing once also. Max's next shot hit the man square in the chest, but as he was going down he got off a shot that went through the flesh of Max's upper arm. Max went down, which may have been good because the younger man's rifle shot fired, hitting the wall behind the stall. Max grabbed the dropped pistol with his left hand and awkwardly cocked it. Pushing his hand through the stall boards he fired wildly toward the front of the barn.

He glanced and, through the smoke, saw the young man running out of the barn. Max stood and pushed the stall open and hobbled to the front of the barn. The kid was not looking back, just running into the darkness of the night. Max caught the movement just to the left of the kid and dropped to the ground just as the short outlaw from the hill fired the rifle. The high caliber rifle would have ripped Max open. The man dropped the rifle and quickly pulled his pistol, running toward the barn door. Max scrambled back out of the doorway as the man fired, two quick shots where Max had been. Max's hand hit the shotgun. He grabbed it with a half-working right arm and cocked both barrels, not knowing which had been fired. A shot came through the doorway, whizzing just past Max's head. He reached the shotgun out away from his body toward the open doorway and squeezed the trigger. More pain shot through his arm as the kick jerked his arm back, sending him rolling.

He glanced up, still dazed, looking at the door, not fully knowing what to expect. Nothing happened. Max looked around and pulled Walton's pistol from his holster with his left hand. He cocked it and aimed it toward the door. He sat there like that for minutes. Using his left elbow, he pushed himself to his knees, then to his feet. He hobbled toward the door, peering around the opening. There, just out the door to the left, lay the man. Max looked around and did not see the kid, but he was nervous he was still around. Still, Max hobbled over and looked at the man with the lazy eye, still open but lifeless.

Back in the barn he heard the horse kicking and walked over and looked at it, downed from Walton's shotgun blast. If Max had not been so far away when Walton shot at him coming through the barn, he would be down as well.

Max felt sick. He had poked the horse a couple of times to rile it and make sure the men would focus on that back stall and see the rifle he had stuck there. The horse had not deserved that or to be suffering. Max took good aim with his left hand and shot the horse in the head. It stopped moving.

Max turned and saw the big man he had shot through the chest trying to move, trying to breathe. Max dropped the pistol and fell to his knees beside the man. "It didn't have to be this way," Max told him, grasping the man's hand.

The man looked at him, his eyes desperate. A couple of minutes later he stopped moving.

Max grabbed the pistol again and hobbled toward the house. He entered, gun raised, and hobbled around. Nobody was there. He grabbed a sheet from a bed, and a bottle of whiskey from the table. He did the best he could to wash and disinfect the wound on his arm, then wrapped it with strips from the sheet. He realized how hard it was to do things with one arm. He also realized his injuries might be pretty bad. His back stung, his right hand felt numb, and he was feeling weaker and weaker.

He grabbed one of the canteens and sat on the floor with his back in a corner of the room, the pistol next to him. He drank the water from the canteen until it was empty. His eyes were heavy, and he was not going to go anywhere in this storm, so he let his eyes close.

He jumped awake at the sound of the door opening and reached for the pistol. "Max, it's me." Ian stood there, soaked from the chest down. Max glanced at the open door and saw that there was light outside.

He made to get up and moved his injured arm, wincing. He switched to push off his left arm and weakly pushed up to his knees, then to his feet. His legs were wobbly, and it felt like he was too close to the fireplace. There was no fire in the hearth, though.

"Max, you look to be in bad shape. We need to get you to the doctor."

"Long way to Prescott, Ian."

"No, Max, we told Todd and the stage driver to bring one for Einar. He should be in Curtiss later."

"Einar's still alive then."

"No, but he was when they came through. Was strong for an hour or so. Told the story of how he and Walton set up the Indians.

Told it in front of Milton, Patricia, Lyle, and a couple of others."

Max walked toward the door, pain searing his shoulder and going down his back. "How'd you get here?"

"Rode Einar's horse."

"Can you saddle one of the horses in the barn for me?"

"Sure, Max." Ian darted out from in front of him and ran toward the barn sliding and squishing through the mud.

Max looked at the sky. It was a beautiful day. The sun was bright but not quite to the midmorning point, with only a couple of light clouds in view. Max took a deep breath and closed his eyes. "Lord, I'm not really ready yet. Please get me safely to Michelle and my Ronnie."

Max swayed a bit and opened his eyes. He stepped off and headed toward the barn, slogging through the mud. He stopped several feet away, looking at the man lying there. It seemed like it had been days ago since he had shot the man, not twelve hours. Max went into the barn as Ian was guiding a gelding around the holes and Walton's body.

Ian looked up, a worried look. "Looks like it was quite the fight."

"It was." Max stepped next to the horse

and, struggling, using just his left hand, pulled himself up into the saddle with Ian's help.

Ian led the horse out and then gave Max the reins and started for his own horse. "We'd better get going."

"Ian," Max called out, stopping him. "Could you shut the barn doors? Don't want coyotes and the like getting in and spooking the other horses."

"Sure, Max." While Ian closed the doors, Max started toward the trail down to the river at a walk. The horse fortunately handled the mud well. Ian caught up quickly, and they made their way down into the swamp that had formed and then back up the other rise. They stopped when they reached the spot that went down into the Agua Fria. The river was flowing less rapidly but still at a much faster pace than usual.

Max exhaled. "Nothing else but to do it." He cantered the horse down and heard Ian mutter behind him as he started after him. The horse rode in and lost its footing immediately, then swam for the open spot on the other side that was Max's property. Max gripped the saddle horn with his left hand but started to slip, so he painfully reached up and looped his right wrist around to help keep ahold. The gelding easily made it to the other side, but, as it climbed out of the water, Max slipped off and got kicked in the hip. He managed to crawl onto the bank and lie there until Ian hoisted him up by his good arm and helped him back on his horse, and they started forward again.

"He has a chance to make it," Max thought he heard Ian say.

"What, Ian?"

"Not Ian, Max. It's the doctor."

"Todd?"

"Yes, Max."

Max's eyes opened, and Todd's face was there. "You're back from Prescott already?"

"Yes, Max."

"We need to get into Curtiss. Doctor will be there to look at me."

"He's looked at you, and you're in Curtiss."

Max took in the beams above Todd's head. He was in a house of some sort. "I've been out a while."

"Yes, since midmorning according to Ian. It's been dark an hour now."

"I'm in Einar's place, ain't I?"

Todd nodded. "It's a spare bed now. Einar died last night."

"I know, Ian told me." Max's thinking was becoming a little clearer. "The sheriff . . .

did you talk to him?"

"He and O'Neil are bunking at the Clarks' tonight. They rode in and interviewed the people Einar confessed to last night. Ian told them about the scene at the Clarks', and they are going to get out there, look things over, and take care of the bodies."

"It's over then. They're safe, Ted's family?"

"They will be soon. O'Neil has a person that helps him sometimes, jotted down the story real quick before heading out, told him to get it into print and get it out. Ian's going to go see Hal in the morning and see if he'll come tell the sheriff his part, too."

"Then we can go get them."

"Whoa, Max. You're not going anywhere for a while. You need time to recover."

Max took a deep breath and realized his back stung a little worse. He moved his right arm, and there was pain, but he could flex his hand and move his arm.

"It was dislocated, your wrist and that shot-up shoulder."

Max's eyes swung to the man speaking. There was a thin man in a white shirt with a red smudge across his stomach. He wore spectacles and was around forty.

"Max, this is Dr. Terpning." Todd introduced him.

Max looked him over. "Doctor, thank you for your help."

Terpning nodded to him. "Well, I set your wrist and put your shoulder back, of course after cleaning and sewing up that wound. The gunshot to your back had started getting infected. I think I got all the shrapnel and debris out and got it cleaned. I hope. I'll check on you tomorrow morning before I head to Mayer Station to check on Mr. Donald and your pregnant wife, then I'll stop back by on my way home. By then we should know if the infection is under control. Any questions?"

"How about my ankle? I twisted that, too."

The doctor shook his head. "I saw that it was swollen." He pulled back the blanket by his feet. "I just had more pressing things to deal with. That infection had brought on quite a fever." The doctor squeezed his puffy ankle and worked it a couple of different directions, bringing a series of winces from Max. "I've seen worse sprains for sure. You're going to be off your feet for a while anyway, which will be good for it. Just try to start moving it around some when the swelling starts to go. Will keep it from getting too stiff as it heals." The doctor pulled the blanket back over his feet. "I'm tired, and you should get some rest, too, but I'm curious as to the story of how this all came about." The doctor motioned to Max's injured body. Then he turned and started for the door, calling back over his shoulder. "You can tell me when I check on you in the morning. Remember to drink lots of water and eat something."

After the doctor had left, Todd patted Max on the chest. "You gave me a scare. When we first came in, you looked awful."

"I'll be all right."

"I know. *Now* I know. I'm going to go get you some food. I'll be right back." Todd started for the door.

"Todd," Max called after him. Todd stopped and looked back. "Thanks, Dad. Thanks for backing me in what I needed to do. Thanks for taking care of me now."

"Like I've said, Max, you're a good man, and I love you, son." Todd closed the door behind him. Max was content to just lie there and wait. He was so exhausted.

CHAPTER 31

Three days later Max sat on the porch with a sweaty, worn-out Ian. Ian had been seeing to some of the work on the ranch, including taking care of Rowdy. Ian had found Rowdy in the yard as he passed through to the Clarks' to look for Max. Ian told Max that he had opened up the gate, and Rowdy trotted through. Todd had been out and checked on the place and reported that the water line had risen up to the point that a little water got into Sam and Martha's. The floor needed washing and items set out to dry in the sun. Ian had done that right after they arrived early this morning.

Max was still feeling a bit weak, especially in his right arm, but the doctor had told him he should fully recover if he rested it a couple more days and very slowly worked back into using it, resting again when it became painful.

Max looked up at the riders coming over

the rise. He reached over and swatted Ian on the shoulder, grunting at the pain of the action. "Look, it's Sunflower, Ahakhela, and Mat."

Ian smiled. "Coming to thank you, I guess."

Sheriff Mulhenon and Bucky O'Neil came over the rise just behind them, then Hal on his mule. As they rode down the hill Max saw the wagon he was waiting for come over the rise and got up and started walking out to meet them. He held up his hand and all waved back, but he was looking at Michelle in the buckboard next to Todd.

"Welcome, Sunflower, Ahakhela, Mat," he told them and then kept walking.

Todd stopped the buckboard, and Max helped Michelle down with his left hand and gave her a big hug. She was cautious with his right side but squeezed his back on the left side. The wounds were healed enough that he did not mind. They kissed, and a moment passed before Max was almost knocked over when Ronnie ran into his legs, hugging him.

Max reached down with his left arm and hoisted the boy up. Michelle shook her head but rubbed his face as she walked past toward the house. Sam clambered off the wagon using crutches and nodded to Max as he passed. Martha came and gave him a hug. Todd got the wagon moving around the people toward the barn, but Hardy moved to Max, and Max patted his muzzle quickly before sending him on with a pat on the rump.

"You did good, Max," Hal said, walking toward him, but Mat moved up and offered his arm.

"You are man of honor." Ahakhela offered his arm next and nodded to him.

Sunflower stepped up and looked at him. "You are a friend for life, Max Tillman."

Max smiled. "Thank you, Sunflower. The friendship of your family means much to me." She smiled back, and Max motioned towards his house. "Come, you are my guests."

Hal fell in beside Max as they started for the house. "You gonna be all right they say."

"I suppose. Was nice lying down for a day or so, but I'm going crazy now, ready to do something."

"It will come soon enough, son. You'll never be short of work in this life. Enjoy the rest."

"Sound advice, I'm sure." Max looked over to Sunflower and her brothers. "You met them alone?" he asked Hal.

"Yes, with the sheriff and a couple men

waiting near Black Canyon Road. I told them it was over, that you'd uncovered the real killers and put them down. They were hesitant when I told them the law wanted to apologize and escort them someplace safe. But, finally, they trusted me."

Max sat on the steps of the porch and motioned for Hal and the others to take seats. Sunflower sat on the bench against the front wall; her brothers sat and crossed their legs. Mulhenon and O'Neil stood on opposite sides of the porch.

"What happens now?" Max looked to Sunflower, then to Hal.

"We ask you now, Max Tillman. Would you be our partner?"

"What?"

"We wish you to join our businesses."

"I don't . . . I have a place to run."

"That's not what she means, Tillman," Mulhenon said.

"We will not be allowed to own the businesses."

"Well, they might," Hal told Max, "but it could get dangerous for them."

"So we will own part, and you and Hal will own part as men we trust." Sunflower looked so earnestly at Max.

"But it's not mine. It's yours."

"We would not have it if not for you. We

would still be hunted."

O'Neil interjected. "They will own forty-eight percent of the mine and ranch, you and Hal here will own twenty-six percent each." He shrugged. "That's the plan anyway. If Walton's wife and brother fight it . . . well, depending on the judge we aren't even sure what charges may go where, but there was a lien filed on Clark's full property, including his interest in the mine via a loan to Ted."

"I've met Red Walton," Mulhenon said. "He's going to fight it. Especially knowing property and gold's at stake. Likely not physically, like Edward. Red uses the courts quite a bit." He looked to the Apache on the porch. "Right or wrong, their claim won't help the case."

"It may help that you and I are part of the claim," Hal said.

"Perhaps," O'Neil offered. "Of course, the right lawyer can twist your past, Max, and make it seem you'd kill for money, including Walton and his men."

Max felt like he had been punched in the gut. He could not seem to get air to talk. He just stared at O'Neil.

"I don't think it's right. It's just how some men do things."

"You have enough character witnesses,

Max," Hal told him. "Every man I talk to, including old Boggs, holds you in high regard. It will be fine. Let's talk about the partnership. I know mining, Max. I know you do, too, but you know ranching and are right across the river here."

Max looked toward the barn and sighed. "Sunflower, a man helped me, he spoke for you when I did not know anything." He motioned to Ian when he came out of the barn. "He respected Ted. He's a hard worker and is picking up ranching pretty well. He may be convinced to work at the ranch full time. He should be your partner."

Sunflower looked at Ian. "He was Ted's friend, and a man we can trust. But you risked death for us."

Ian saw that they had been talking about him and stopped looking around. "What's going on?"

Sunflower stood and walked to him. "Max Tillman told us how you spoke for us. We thank you."

Ian shrugged. He was having trouble thinking of something to say for the first time in his life. "You're welcome. It just was not right."

Max spoke up. "Sunflower, I will be busy here but will help when I can. I will always be there as your neighbor and friend. If Ian wishes, though, make him twenty-percent partner if he will take on the work, and make me six percent."

"I don't know percentages."

Hal waved his hand. "Max is trying to give Ian most of his share since Ian will be doing most of the work. He does not understand. Max, this is part of their thanking you." Hal looked at Sunflower. "It is true that Ian helped bring you justice. We are honored you wish to honor us."

"Just split it equally, for Pete's sake!" Mulhenon said. He produced a flask from his pocket and took a sip.

Sunflower looked at him and then nodded. She pointed to Hal, Ian, then Max. "Equally."

"That's seventeen percent for each of us, then forty-nine for them." Hal threw up his hands. "From what it sounds like there's a lot in that vein, boys. If Ian takes care of the ranch, watches over Sunflower, and comes to help at the mine from time to time, I'm good with it. And you, Max, you nearly died. You're in."

"All right," Max said. "Thank you, Sunflower." She smiled at them.

"Umm, fellas," Ian said, "I missed something."

Hal laughed. "Ian, you are now seventeen-percent owner in the joint venture of the Clark-Sunflower ranch and mine."

Ian looked around and then shrugged. "I suppose it will be quite some time before I make it around the world and back home." Ian looked at Sunflower and her brothers. He nodded to them. "I am grateful, very grateful."

Mulhenon put his flask in his pocket and walked over, followed by O'Neil, and both offered their hands. "We've got to head back."

"You could stay and eat."

"No, thanks," O'Neil said. "Sheriff needs to see to other things, and I need to write the story."

"I appreciate all you men have done."

"Sure. I'm just grateful that the blame got put where it belonged, before anything happened to Ted's wife and brothers-in-law." Mulhenon waved to everyone and walked to his horse.

O'Neil opened the door and said goodbye to Sam and the ladies before waving to the others. "I hope things go your way."

Todd sat down next to Ahakhela and Mat. "I realize now that I met Ted once. I think it was my first time teaching in Curtiss, when it was just the smelter. I thought him a good man." He looked back at Sunflower.

She smiled a sad smile at Todd and touched her stomach. The child would not know his father.

The smell of food cooking from inside made Max's stomach rumble. It was moments later that Martha and Michelle brought out plates of food. Sam hobbled out behind them. Max went in with Michelle and grabbed a couple of the others. "Where did we get the bread and bacon?"

"Mrs. Mayer. She knew we probably did not have a lot ready here. We are blessed with good people in our lives."

Max looked at his beautiful pregnant wife. She was herself again. The danger had passed, and life would be good again. Max could not help but smile. He carried one plate in his left hand but realized he had to carry the other with his right hand pressed against his hip to keep it steady. He had tired it out this morning doing small tasks like gathering the eggs, which were cooked now and next to the slabs of bacon and chunks of bread on the plates.

Michelle sat next to Sunflower on the bench, and Sam and Max took the steps, followed shortly by Ronnie. Todd led the prayer. "Lord, we thank you for the safety of our family and friends here with us. We thank you for new friends, for stronger relationships with our neighbors, for the justice that has been served. Lord, we ask you to be in the relationships we are building and those we have had. We ask that you bless this food, help it to nourish us. Amen."

Everyone answered "Amen" and then started eating. It was a simple meal but for some reason tasted better than anything else Max could think of. He leaned over and nudged Ronnie. Ronnie looked up at him questioning, and Max smiled at him. "Welcome home, son." Ronnie smiled back and took a bite of his bread.

Max ate a moment and then turned to Sam. "Rowdy came home when I set him loose to slide down the ravine."

"He's tamed then," Sam said around a bite of bacon, "at least as much as you want him to be."

"I know. He's become a really good horse, thanks to your help in training." Max had to take a deep breath before he said the next words. "Hardy's yours now."

"No, Max."

"Yes, sir, you need a horse, and he's a good one."

"Max, I know how much you love that horse."

"And, I know how much you loved King. Anyway, I love you, Sam, and I know how good you will be to Hardy. He's yours."

"Thank you, Max." Sam teared up. "You know if I go before he does, he's coming back to you."

"All right. Anyway, Sam, once your leg heals you're gonna be helping teach another new rancher, and you'll need a strong horse."

Sam looked back at Ian. "I heard him from inside. He'll do all right."

Max looked back. "He better rest now, because tomorrow he should probably get busy seeing to the horses and the stock over there. Some of the cattle may have wandered away in the storm."

They spent the afternoon resting and talking. Ian then asked Max about breeding Rowdy with some of the stock across the river. Max smiled. "It's seventeen percent mine also, and we're like family now."

Mat and Ahakhela heard and wanted to look at the horses. They admired Rowdy, but also Hardy, the smaller but sturdy horse. Max could not help but feel the pride in all that he had done as they walked back to the house.

"I have another idea," Ian said to the group now sitting on the porch. "I've heard that some ranches spend money shipping in a really good breeder bull." He looked over to Hal. "Sounds like we'll have a decent amount of money so we could buy one, maybe even two between us and really build a good herd."

Sam laughed. "I think making him a partner was a good idea."

"I'll even go one better." Ian smiled. "We should consider buying Walton's place. The properties are nearly connected. It's the reason that he wanted ours."

Sam looked at Max and arched his eyebrows.

Max sighed. "Definitely something to consider, Ian. I think we should pray on it over the next day or two. We've been blessed, but we need to be careful and not get greedy. I don't want to get to the point where we're having to stretch ourselves to oversee everything." He turned to Sunflower. "Of course, it's mainly your decision."

She looked back and forth between them. "You speak wisdom, Max. You have big plans, and that is good, Ian. We should talk about it in a couple of days."

Mat stood looking at the sun. "We should cross before it starts to darken."

"You're right," Hal said standing up. He and the two brothers were going to go get them settled in before heading to the mine.

The sheriff's deputy had been sent to watch the mine for three days, with Hal's promise of a month's wages for the trouble, and to keep him honest.

They hugged and shook hands parting. Max and his extended family stood on the porch and watched them go. Ian dismounted from his horse and opened the gate for them all to go through. After closing the gate, he remounted and rode up next to Sunflower to say something to her. She looked over at him and nodded.

Michelle nestled against Max's shoulder. "I think it will not be long before those two marry."

"What?"

"I can tell Ian likes her, and she seems to respect him. If it wasn't for Ted just passing, I think she would be feeling more."

"Michelle's right, I think," Martha said.

Max looked at Sam, who shrugged at him. Todd laughed but nodded. Max looked back at the five riding off, Ian still talking away to Sunflower. Michelle was probably right, and it would work out well. Max put his left arm around his wife's shoulder and kissed her on the cheek. "Come on and sit, baby. We'll watch the sunset and then get some much-deserved sleep." He led her to the bench.

Todd scooped up Ronnie, who had fallen asleep on the porch leaning against the wall, and put him in his bed inside before coming back out. Sam and Martha sat on the porch steps, and they enjoyed the restfulness of the evening, and the look of their home as the sun lowered below the horizon. Max felt that deep satisfaction again. This was the way of life he wanted. He had no restlessness. There was only contentment, here with his family, enjoying the beauty of what God created.

The next morning, after a long night's sleep, Max helped Todd take care of the horses and some of the other chores, at least the parts he could do with one arm. Finally, Todd talked him into sitting down, which he gladly did, feeling tired already. A few more days, he told himself. He was sitting on the porch, telling Ronnie about his grandfather, the hunter, when Ian rode up with Mat and Ahakhela behind him. Ian left his horse at the cattle gate, climbed over, and started running to the porch. Max would have been worried, except as Ian came closer he saw the smile on the man's face.

"Max, we've got no worries with the Waltons anymore." He held up a folded piece of paper. "One of the horses kicked the stall door almost off, probably when you were there. Well, I was looking at it and saw he'd split one of the side boards also. The slot it had been in for the post was big and hollow and had a string sticking out a little. I pulled it out, and this, along with a ranch deed and a pouch full of money, was in there. It's the lien, noted as paid and signed by Walton the day before they were killed. It was there, but they never found it."

Max smiled. "It's over for good then. This proves he no longer had a claim but pretended he did. It's pretty much proof that he was trying to lay a false claim, and that backs up Einar's story. God is good."

Ian smiled also. "Yes, He is."

Todd had walked up behind them with Mat and Ahakhela leading the horses. He was smiling. "I'll ride into Curtiss and get word sent for the sheriff to come out. He should probably see where it was found."

"Thanks, Dad," Max said, smiling. Max just leaned back and closed his eyes, thinking about the night before, sleeping soundly with Michelle, knowing his family was safe for the first time since this had all started. Now, it was settled. He looked forward to his arm healing. He was itching to get back to work, to help Ian, Hal, and Sunflower.

He wanted to ride Rowdy again. Perhaps he would borrow Hardy from Sam later.

The door creaked, and Max looked over to see his beautiful pregnant wife come out. She looked at the men. "Is everything all right?"

Max stood up and reached his arm around her. "Everything is very right."

The baby kicked, and, with Max pressed against his wife, he felt it. Michelle smiled up at him, and he smiled back.

ABOUT THE AUTHOR

Scott Gastineau grew up in Oklahoma. As a young boy, he was enamored with the Old West, but it was not until decades later that the real details of life in the Old West reignited that early fascination. He has lived in Arizona since graduating from Oklahoma State University. He recently moved to the Prescott, Arizona, region with his wife, Kami. He loves to read, hike, and run.

The employees of Thorndike Press hope you have enjoyed this Large Print book. All our Thorndike, Wheeler, and Kennebec Large Print titles are designed for easy reading, and all our books are made to last. Other Thorndike Press Large Print books are available at your library, through selected bookstores, or directly from us.

For information about titles, please call:
(800) 223-1244

or visit our Web site at:
http://gale.cengage.com/thorndike

To share your comments, please write:
Publisher
Thorndike Press
10 Water St., Suite 310
Waterville, ME 04901